PRAISE FOR
AMANDA SCOTT'S
SCOTTISH ADVENTURES

KING O

"4 Stars! An exhilarati
story . . . Scott brings th
her previous novels tog
romance."
—*Romantic Times BOOKreviews Magazine*

"Passionate and breathtaking . . . Amanda Scott's *King of Storms* keeps the tension moving as she continues her powerful saga of the Macleod sisters."
—**NovelTalk.com**

"A terrific tale starring two interesting lead characters who fight, fuss, and fall in love . . . Rich in history and romance, fans will enjoy the search for the Templar treasure and the Stone of Scone."
—*Midwest Book Review*

"An engaging tale with well-written characters, and a wonderful plot that will keep readers turning pages . . . Fans of historical romances will be delighted with *King of Storms*."
—**TheRomanceReadersConnection.com**

"Enjoyable . . . moves at a fast pace . . . it was difficult to put the book down."
—**BookLoons.com**

more . . .

"Intrigue and danger . . . Readers will enjoy the adventures and sweet romance."
—**RomRevToday.com**

"Enchanting . . . a thrilling adventure . . . a *must* read . . . *King of Storms* is a page turner. A sensual, action-packed romance sure to satisfy every heart. Combine this with a battle of wits, a test of strength, faith, and honor, and you have one great read."
—**FreshFiction.com**

KNIGHT'S TREASURE

"An enjoyable book for a quiet evening at home. If you are a fan of historical romance with a touch of suspense, you don't want to miss this book."
—**LoveRomanceAndMore.com**

"Filled with tension, deceptions, and newly awakened passions. Scott gets better and better."
—**NovelTalk.com**

LADY'S CHOICE

"*Lady's Choice* is terrific . . . with an exhilarating climax that sets up the next [book] in this high-quality series. Scott is at the top of her game with this deep historical tale."
—**Midwest Book Review**

"Enjoyable . . . The premise of Scott's adventure romance is strong."
—**Kathe Robin, *Romantic Times* BOOKreviews Magazine**

AMANDA SCOTT

Border
Wedding

FOREVER

NEW YORK   BOSTON

The characters and events in this book are fictitious. Any similarity to real persons, living or dead, is coincidental and not intended by the author.

Book design by Giorgetta Bell McRee

Forever
Hachette Book Group USA
237 Park Avenue
New York, NY 10017
Visit our Web site at www.HachetteBookGroupUSA.com

Forever is an imprint of Grand Central Publishing.
The Forever name and logo is a trademark of Hachette Book Group USA, Inc.

Printed in the United States of America

First Edition: March 2008

10 9 8 7 6 5 4 3 2 1

Dedicated to Jim and Jen Drennan, with love
Married July 15, 2006
May you have more years of happiness together
than you can count!

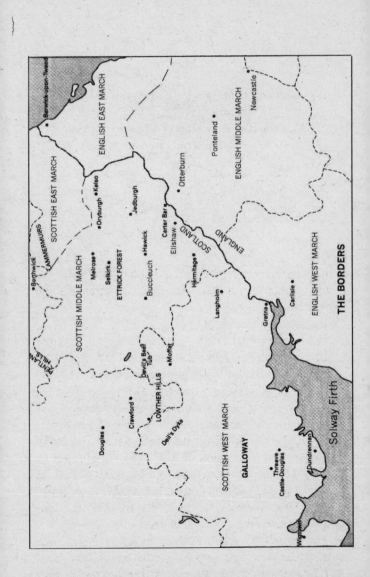

THE BORDERS

Author's Note

For those of you who appreciate some basic information straightaway, I include the following definitions and pronunciation guide:

Buccleuch = Buck LOO

Coldheugh = COLD hue

Earl = the highest rank in Scotland in 1388, other than King of Scots. England had princes and dukes. Scotland did not. The King's sons were earls.

The term "Borderers" refers in general to people who lived (or live) in the areas on either side of the border between Scotland and England, which were two separate countries until their union in 1707. The "line" refers to the actual border between those two countries, which for centuries was in constant dispute and tended to shift frequently. In present-day Scotland, "the Borders" is a specific, delineated region in and of itself.

The "marches" refers to three jurisdictions on each side of the line: east march, middle march, and west march (see map). Each of these six marches had its own warden, and in Scotland a Chief Warden of the Marches ruled over all three Scottish marches, with their individual wardens subservient to him. If England had an equivalent chief warden, it was the Earl of Northumberland because of his vast power, but his position was Warden of the East March because such appointments worked differently in England, where the King actively resisted increasing power among his nobles.

Border Law: Grievances and other matters of law, whether they occurred on the English or Scottish side of the line, were resolved at wardens' meetings that anyone could attend. The two sides would declare a truce long enough to settle their differences. Each warden would guarantee the resolutions involving his vassals and see that they abided by them (usually).

Despite such seeming civility, the region remained volatile for centuries. From the time of Edward I of England (end of the thirteenth century) through the sixteenth century, the English remained determined to annex (conquer) Scotland, and the Scots remained determined to retain their freedom.

Ugly Meg, or The Robber's Wedding

Peace to these worthy days of old,
 Cast in our modern teeth so oft,
When Man was, as befits him, bold,
And Woman, as she should be, soft.

—Lady Louisa Stuart

Chapter 1

⌒

His hands and his feet they ha' bound like a sheep . . .
And they locked him down in a dungeon so deep . . .

Scotland, near the English border, July 1388

Awakening in dense blackness to find himself bound hand and foot, lying in acute discomfort on cold, hard dirt, twenty-four-year-old Sir Walter Scott of Rankilburn became aware of a disturbing sense that all was not well.

Then memory stirred and confirmed the fact.

Lammas Gibbie's deep voice echoed through the blackness. "Tam, I'm thinking he be moving."

"Be that you, Wat, or just a few rats fussin' over summat or other?" the huge man called Jock's Wee Tammy asked.

"I'm awake," Wat said, although the raspy voice scarcely sounded like his own. His throat was parched and his head ached. "Someone must have clouted me, for my head's pounding as if the devil were inside. It's blinded me, too."

"One o' them villains clouted ye, right enough," Gib said. "Ye're no blind, though. We've nae light is all. Tam and me canna see nowt, neither."

"How many of us are in here?"

"Just us three in this cell," Tammy said. "They caught some o' the others, too, though. We canna hear them, so likely, they've stowed them elsewhere."

Wat gathered enough saliva to swallow before he said, "Sorry, lads. Seems I've well and truly landed us all in the suds this time."

"Aye, well, what comes does come," Tammy replied.

Wat grunted but saw nothing to gain by pointing out that what was likely to come was hanging for all of them.

"'Tis the Douglas's fault as much as yours," Gib muttered. "If he hadna ordered this unnatural state of idleness, we'd no be in such a fix, because Murray would more likely ha' taken English kine instead o' yours, but as it is . . ."

Silence fell. James, second Earl of Douglas, although only five years older than Wat himself, had already held his powerful title for four years, since the death of his father. William, the first earl, had been the most powerful man in Scotland—even more powerful than the King of Scots or anyone else in the royal family—and James's popularity in the Borders had increased the Douglas power even more.

Not only did James Douglas control far more land than the royal Stewarts did but he could raise an army of twelve thousand in less than a sennight, whereas the Stewarts would be lucky to raise a thousand men in twice that time. Unlike kings of England, who could simply order their nobles to provide armies for them when needed, the King of Scots had to apply to his nobles for their support. The nobility was not required to provide it, and the Stewarts, considered upstarts, were unpopular.

Among his many other titles, Douglas was also Chief Warden of the Scottish Marches—the three regions directly abutting the border with England—and as such, he had demanded peace among the unruly Scottish Borderers so that he could better expend their energies in keeping the land-greedy English in England.

For nearly a century, English kings had fought to make Scotland just another region of England, and the present king, Richard Plantagenet, was one who believed it was his God-given right to reign over both countries as one.

Douglas, on the other hand, was equally determined to prevent such a conquest. Having learned that the English were preparing to invade the country yet again and knowing that when the time came, he would have to raise his army quickly, James had forbidden the Scottish Borderers to cross the line without his permission lest the English catch and imprison or hang them. To keep peace among the Scots themselves, he had forbidden them to raid each other's herds as well.

For years, though, "reivers" on either side of the borderline had raided other men's herds as a matter of course whenever their families ran out of meat. Although it was illegal and they were subject to dire penalties if caught in the act, the Borderers looked upon reiving as nothing less than economic necessity. They were as likely to raid their own neighbors' herds as those across the line. And when need drove them, Borderers were unlikely to heed anyone else's orders, even the Douglas's.

Wat had often remarked on the futility of those orders,

but he knew he could not blame the earl for their predicament now. The responsibility for that was his alone.

His hands and feet were numb. He tried shifting position and stifled a groan when jolts of pain shot through his limbs and set nerves in his fingers and toes afire.

"How long have we been here?" he groaned.

"A good while," Tammy said.

"Ye snored," Gib added.

"Snored?" Indignation momentarily replaced suffering. "I was unconscious!"

"Nonetheless, ye snored," Gib insisted. "Likely, ye can blame them three pots of ale ye drank afore we left Raven's Law."

Wat remembered the ale. He should not have drunk so much of it. However, that was not the only error in his hastily conceived plan.

It had seemed so simple then. After spending the previous day at the horse races in Langholm, he and some friends had returned to Raven's Law, his peel tower in Ettrick Forest, to learn that in his absence, raiders had lifted his entire herd of cattle. They'd also taken a pair of valuable sleuthhounds and seven horses.

"I was right about who stole my beasts," he muttered.

"Aye, yon devil Murray had them right enough," Tam agreed. "He still has them, come to that. Mayhap we were a bit hasty, ridin' out straightaway to raid—"

"To recover what is mine," Wat interjected.

"Aye, well, that's as may be," Tammy said doubtfully. "But yon Murray will no agree that ye had the right to take his beasts home along wi' yours."

"Sir Iagan Murray has more kine than any man needs to feed one threaping wife, a pair o' dour sons, and three o' the homeliest daughters in Scotland," Gib said.

"Still, ye canna blame the man for trappin' us as he did," Tammy replied. "'Tis only natural he'd want tae keep his own beasts."

"Nearly half of the beasts he's got now are mine," Wat said grimly. "And I don't want him to keep them. As to my taking his, he can show no proof of that. He and his men rose up out of the heather before we'd touched one of them. Sakes, I should have realized it was too easy to follow those reivers. 'Tis clear enough now that he expected us to and that's why they were waiting for us."

"That was clever o' them, that heather was," Tammy said. "With all o' them wearin' white feathers in their caps as they were, and lyin' flat, they looked as much like new blooms in the moonlight as the real heather did."

"Murray kens fine that we'd ha' taken his kine, though," Gib said, ignoring the interruption. "Bless us, but anyone would."

"Even if we *had* taken them, it was Murray's fault for forcing me to come here to collect mine," Wat said.

Tammy laughed. "I'd like t' be in your pocket when ye explain that to your da' and the Douglas."

"It's what either of them would have done," Wat retorted.

"Mayhap they would," Gib said. "But that willna stop them being angry."

Wat knew Gibbie was right. James Douglas knew his power and did not let anyone forget it. Wat had known him since childhood, and facing him after creating such a predicament for himself was not something he would enjoy. Even so, the earl's anger would be as nothing compared with his own father's.

The Laird of Buccleuch was a staunch supporter of James Douglas and would not be pleased to learn that his own son had defied a Douglas order. Just thinking about Buccleuch's likely reaction made Wat wince.

Then, remembering his present plight, he said with a sigh, "I doubt I'll have to face either of them. You must know that Murray means to hang us in the morning."

"He caught us wi' the goods," Tammy said. "'Tis his right to hang us."

"It is, aye, but you'll admit that it does seem devilish hypocritical," Wat retorted. "We did nowt but try to put right the wrong he'd done to me, after all."

"We didna catch him at it, though," Tam reminded him.

In the ensuing silence, the darkness seemed to thicken and close heavily around them until Gib said abruptly, "D'ye believe in heaven, Wat?"

"Aye, and in hell," Wat replied. "Don't you?"

"I do." Gib paused. "'Tis just that . . ."

"What, Gib?"

"Sithee, me Annie's in heaven wi' our wee bairn that the English killed alongside o' her when they came three years ago. I dinna doubt that Annie's waiting for me, ye ken, but 'tis likely I'll no be joining her now, will I?"

"Why not?"

"Yon Murray's no likely to ha' a priest at hand to shrive us, is he?"

"He may have a chaplain as the Douglas does," Wat said. "But if he doesn't, you've led a good life, Gib, and I believe God counts that above all else."

"Mayhap He does, Wat, but I've broken me share o' His commandments."

"So have we all," Tammy muttered. "'Tis nae use to fret about it now."

Wat's imagination instantly presented him with a

them that, his power and connections being what they were, he would eventually do so.

That some witless wag had once labeled them three of the homeliest females in Christendom had done naught to aid their prospects. But Meg knew that when it came to marriage, beauty was not everything. Sir Iagan was a man of wealth.

He was also a man of influence. As such, she knew he believed he had no need to dower his daughters heavily. She just hoped he would provide them with enough to entice more than one potential husband. The few men she did know believed that, at eighteen, she was already long in the tooth.

Lady Murray, having told the gillie who attended her what she'd like to eat, said to her husband with her soft English lilt, "I trust you slept well, my lord."

"Indeed, my lady," he replied with a polite nod. "I slept gey fine, though I confess I did not reach my bed until after midnight."

Rosalie said with concern, "Could you not sleep before then, Father?"

"I had important duties to attend, lassie."

Meg said, "Duties in the middle of the night, sir?"

Turning to his wife, he said, "Madam, your daughters display unwarranted curiosity about their father's business. Surely, ye've explained to them that well-bred young women do not pry into the affairs of others."

"I shall explain it to them again, sir, but I own, I am as curious as they are. The only duty that might keep you so late when we have no visitors would be reivers. However, I heard none of the din that usually accompanies a raid."

He smirked, saying, "That, madam, is because my men and I were waiting for them. Having suspected the scoundrels meant to raid my herd, I'd buried two score men in the nearby heather. We captured their leader and six of his rabble. I'll wager ye canna guess who that leader is."

"Who, Father?" Amalie asked.

Sir Iagan frowned at her. "I was not speaking to you."

"No, sir, but how else can we know? Is he in the dungeon?"

Pride in his victory overcame his annoyance, for his chest swelled as he said, "I have all seven of the thieving devils locked up. And, by heaven, I mean to introduce them to my hanging tree as soon as I've broken my fast."

He may have thought the subject of the leader's identity thus closed, but Meg knew their mother was as curious as she was and looked expectantly at her.

Deftly, Lady Murray used the point of her knife to spear a slice of meat from a platter and transfer it to her trencher. As she tore the meat apart delicately with two fingers, she said, "Do you mean to make me guess the leader's name, sir?"

"Ye'd never do it, for it will astonish ye to learn that he is of gentle birth. I recognized him at once. So would ye have done, had ye seen him."

She frowned. "I doubt I could know any man who steals cattle for a living."

"Still, I must suppose ye've seen him, for he's young Wat Scott, Buccleuch's eldest son. Even if ye canna recall his face, ye'll ken his family."

"The Laird of Buccleuch? But he is a man of considerable wealth!"

"Aye, so we'll see if his young Wattie dares to identify himself. Not that I care if he does or not. We caught them all red-handed, and I mean to hang every one of them. Fetch me more ale, lad," he called to a passing gillie.

Lady Murray returned her attention to her food for some moments before she said musingly, "Does young Scott have a wife, sir?"

"None that I ken. Have ye interest in his ancestry, as well, madam?"

She persisted. "You also said that he is Buccleuch's *eldest* son, and so he must therefore be his heir."

"Aye, and what of it? Ye'll no tell me I shouldna hang the thieving rascal!"

"I hope you know well enough by now that I would not put myself forward so improperly. It does occur to me, though, that when Providence offers up a single young man who will inherit vast properties, one should not rashly destroy the gift."

"And how, prithee, is the man's trying to make off with my herd an act of Providence?" Sir Iagan demanded. "If ye're suggesting that I demand ransom—"

"Nay, for as you must have realized yourself—with Buccleuch being one of Douglas's fiercest allies and Douglas organizing raids into England to judge their readiness for another invasion of Scotland—'twould take much too long to negotiate a ransom. It would also be too dangerous. Whatever you do, you must do quickly."

He nodded, but Meg wondered if he had thought the matter through as swiftly and thoroughly as her mother had.

Lady Murray said matter-of-factly, "We have three daughters, sir. I need not remind you of your duty to find them all suitable husbands. And whilst you may easily find a husband for one, finding three will not be easy. Therefore, to hang such an excellent prospect . . ." She paused, meeting his gaze.

He glowered, saying in a near growl, "Ye believe that

scoundrel would make one o' them a suitable husband? Are ye daft, woman?"

"Nay, only practical. With two sons, as well, establishing all our offspring will require loosening your purse strings to a sad degree, I fear. But with an opportunity such as this, with care and your customary astuteness . . ."

"I've wealth enough," he muttered when she paused. But Meg saw that her mother's words had jolted him. Wealth or none, no man complained more often of penury than Sir Iagan Murray did.

"There is also the fact that England may soon reestablish control of this area as they have before," Lady Murray went on. "You have taken care over the years to create powerful ties on both sides of the line, and your English ties, along with an air of compliance, did enable us to escape harm when they came here three years ago. But we can be sure that Douglas took note of your lack of involvement then, and—"

"Sakes, madam, I could scarcely take sides without offending one or another o' those connections ye speak of."

"I understand that," she said. "But Douglas has proven himself as great a warrior for Scotland as my cousin Sir Harry Percy is for England. And Douglas is more powerful in Scotland than even the royal family is. So if he prevails in the coming conflict, our Simon's service with the Earl of Fife, albeit an excellent connection for Simon, will do less to protect us here in the Borders than would a connection to Douglas himself. And I'm thinking, sir, that this incident may allow you to establish just such a connection, for not only is Buccleuch close to Douglas, but his wife *is* a Douglas, and therefore young Sir Walter is blood kin to the earl."

"Your cousin Harry is not called Hotspur for nowt,

madam," Sir Iagan said testily. "His forces and those of the English king will prevail in the coming conflict, Douglas or no Douglas. Indeed, it surprises me that you should encourage kinship with yet another of the men you so often call 'my heathenish Scots.'"

"Young Scott may be a heathen, but he is no coward," Lady Murray said. "He has won his knighthood, I believe, and is properly Sir Walter Scott. If he is the young man I do recall, he is rather handsome, although too dark for my taste. He also has a stubborn, implacable look about him. Still, I warrant he would make a suitable enough husband for a sensible young woman like our Meg."

Startled, Meg barely managed to remain silent, but she dared not speak lest her irritated father order her from the table. She certainly could not say that she had been thinking Sir Walter Scott sounded just like Sir Iagan and her brother Simon—temperamental, stubborn, and domineering.

But then, she mused, most men were temperamental and domineering. She had not met many yet, though, so she could still hope to meet one who was not.

"What do you think of your mother's daft notion?" Sir Iagan asked her.

"I don't think I'd like to marry a thief, sir."

"There, you see, madam," Sir Iagan snapped.

"Meg is a dutiful daughter," Lady Murray said without so much as a glance at Meg. "She will do as you bid her."

"Ye're talking as if the lad would agree to the notion," he said. "More likely, he'd refuse it outright."

"Pressed to choose between a marriage and a coffin, I believe any sensible young man will choose marriage," Lady Murray said. "However, I should like to see him before you either make him the offer or hang him."

"I suppose next you will say you want your daughters to see this villain, too," he retorted. His expression said he believed nothing of the sort, but it altered ludicrously when the wife of his bosom said that she did indeed want her daughters to see the reiver.

"It will be a valuable experience for them," she said.

Meg had been as certain as her father was that her mother would decline having any such notion. Beginning to breathe normally again, she had reached for her goblet, but her ladyship's reply diverted her attention just enough to make her knock it over, spewing ale across the table and drawing a curse from Sir Iagan.

As gillies leaped to clean up the mess, he said, "You'd have me admit such a scoundrel to my daughters' presence? Faugh, I won't permit it."

"He may be a scoundrel, but he is nonetheless nobly born," Lady Murray reminded him. "I shall excuse Rosalie, but there can be naught amiss in showing Meg and Amalie what happens even to powerful men who break the law."

"Aye . . . well . . ."

"Moreover, if you should change your mind after considering my suggestion, there is surely no harm in letting them see the man one of them is to marry."

Gruffly, he said, "I'll permit it only because seeing him in his present state, if it accomplishes nowt else, should put this foolish notion of marrying him to one of them right out of your head."

"Mayhap it will," she replied equably.

With a brusque gesture to a hovering gillie, he snapped, "Have them fetch the reivers' leader here to me. Tell them to bring him just as he is."

Meg watched the gillie hurry from the hall, wishing

with half her mind that she could snatch him back. With the other half, she wished she could fly beside him, unseen, and have a look at the prisoner before they haled him in before her.

Well aware that such powers were beyond the ken of ordinary mortals and that God could read her thoughts, she surreptitiously crossed herself.

When the cell door creaked open, even the faint light from the stairwell caused a glare that made Wat wince. Believing the guards had come for them, to hang them all straightaway, he was not surprised when the two who entered each grabbed an arm and hauled him upright.

"You'll have to untie my feet, lads," he said, stifling a groan. "Even so, I doubt I can walk, for I've scarcely any feeling left in them."

The larger of the two said, "We weep for ye, reiver, but we dinna care an ye walk or no. Ye'll come with us any road."

"What of my men?"

"They're to bide here a wee while longer."

They had clearly meant to drag him. But after cursing at how heavy he was and noting irritably that the winding stone stairway was too narrow to accommodate all three of them abreast, they finally untied his feet.

"I dare ye to run," the one who had spoken before said with a grim chuckle. "'Twould please me tae clout ye again."

Wat did not reply. The circulation returning to his feet made him clench his teeth against the pain, to prevent any sound his captors might interpret as proof that he suffered. If they meant to hang him, so be it. He would not whimper.

His feet refused to cooperate with his brain, however. His ankles felt as weak as new-sprouted saplings, and he could not feel his toes. Pain from his feet and ankles radiated into his legs, and his knees felt no steadier than his ankles.

Although one guard pulled and the other pushed, it still took the combined efforts of both, and his own, to get him up the winding stone stairway and outside to the cobbled bailey. Wat turned his face to the sun, enjoying its warmth but keeping his eyes shut to let them accustom themselves to the harsh glare.

"Dinna dawdle, man," the spokesman snapped. "The master awaits ye."

"Let him wait," Wat retorted. "He cannot hang me twice."

In response, the two men hauled him forward, making him stumble along as best he could. In this fashion, they dragged him through a doorway, up another, broader stairway, and through an archway into Elishaw's great hall. He could feel his toes by then, but the fiery pain of that gift was no comfort.

They shoved him forward with his hands still bound behind him. Although he struggled to remain upright, his feet and balance betrayed him, and he fell heavily to the stone floor. Only with effort did he manage not to strike his head.

"'Tis right and proper that ye should abase yourself, ye scurrilous rascal!"

Looking up, Wat saw a thickset man in plain leather breeks and a short black cloak looking down at him with arms akimbo. Having seen Sir Iagan Murray at horse races more than once, he had no trouble recognizing the man as his host.

Forcing himself awkwardly to sit, he said, "Hello, Murray, you damnable thief. If you mean to hang me, get on with it."

"I do want to hang you," Murray said.

Feeling at a distinct disadvantage staring up at him as he was, Wat said tartly, "It was my right to regain my livestock and my dogs."

"And to whom did ye declare that right, laddie?"

Glowering, Wat kept silent. He could gain nothing by admitting to the man who had stolen his beasts that more lawful routes did exist for recovering them.

"As I thought," Murray said. "Ye and your lads are nowt but common felons, but I've the power of the pit and the gallows, just as your father does. Moreover, I've my own hanging tree outside in the bailey just waiting for ye."

As Wat digested the fact that Murray had recognized him, he heard a lilting female voice, more English than Scot, say, "Forgive me, sir, but that impudent young man should not sit in my presence—or in yours, come to that."

Murray grimaced, but the startled look he shot over his shoulder at the high table not only drew Wat's gaze in that direction but also told him that his host had forgotten about the three ladies who sat there.

To the two men who had brought him in, Murray said, "Help him stand, lads. And stay by him, for I've summat more to say. Sithee, lad, though it goes right against the grain wi' me, I have a proposition to make ye. If ye find it to your liking—which I doubt—ye might yet miss dangling from me tree."

On his feet again, flanked by the two guards, Wat eyed

Murray warily. "What is this proposition then, that you mislike it so?"

"Why, nobbut that ye'll agree to take my eldest daughter there, the lady Margaret, for your wife."

Certain that he must have misunderstood, Wat said, "Wife?"

"Aye, that's it," Murray said, nodding. "Stand up, lass," he added with an encouraging gesture. "Let Sir Walter have a look at ye."

Still stupefied, Wat gaped as one of the women got slowly to her feet.

His first impression was that her mouth was too big and her body too thin for his taste. Moreover, had he met her in the yard, he'd have taken her for a servant, because her clothing gave no indication of her father's supposed wealth or rank.

She was not near enough to discern the color of her eyes, but he thought they looked ordinary. Her pale, rather long, narrow face was red with embarrassment, and thanks to her stiff coif and veil, he could not see a single strand of her hair.

Even so, her personal appearance had little to do with his outrage.

"You must be mad," he said to Murray.

"D'ye mean to say ye've already got a wife?"

"I do not, although my father is negotiating a marriage for me with a cousin of the Earl of Douglas."

"From what I hear o' ye, they'll no be surprised an ye pick your own wife. And ye'll like my Meg better nor any Douglas wench," Murray added confidently.

The thought flashed through Wat's mind that his host could be right about the Douglas wench in question. He had known Fiona since they were children and found it impossible to imagine being married to her. But his wishes did not enter into it. Strengthening the alliance between their two families would serve both well.

Pushing these swift but irrelevant thoughts aside, he said, "I do have a habit of running contrary to plans that others make for me. But that would hardly be cause to let you choose my wife, Murray."

"Aye, well, I was hoping ye'd say that, for if ye willna agree to marry the lass, I can hang ye straightaway."

"Then do it," Wat snapped. "I'll not marry your daughter, whatever you may threaten. No Scott is afraid to die."

"Amen, then," Murray said, signing to the guards before adding, "My Meg, let me tell you, is worthy of a better man. Ye've offended her wi' your ingratitude, and by heaven, ye offend me the more. Take him to the tree, lads."

As the guards grabbed him and began to hustle him away, Wat wrenched away from them long enough to turn back and say, "Pray, mistress, forgive me. I swear, I meant no offense to you."

To his amazement, she gazed steadily back at him and replied in a calm and surprisingly low-pitched, musical voice, "I took no offense from your rudeness, reiver. I have less desire to marry you than you have to marry me."

Her words did more than prick his conscience. They stirred the swift, impulsive response to challenge that had ruled much of his behavior since birth.

It was a pity, he thought as the guards thrust him roughly from the hall, that he would die before he could teach the wench to appreciate him.

Chapter 2

"A preciouser villain my tree ne'er adorned;
Hang a rogue when he's young, he'll steal
nane when he's auld."

Determined to put all thought of the doomed young man from her mind, Meg tried to concentrate on her breakfast. But her contrary imagination presented a vision of some of her father's men dragging the reiver outside to the horrid tree while others threw a rope over a bough and prepared to hang him.

She stared unseeing at her trencher, grateful that her mother had sent Rosalie away. But she abandoned her pretended disinterest with relief when Lady Murray said, "I pray you, husband, be patient. Closer acquaintance with yon tree will persuade that young man more certainly than any words will."

"Faith, one hopes so," Amalie muttered. "He is too handsome to let our father hang him. *Say* something, Meg."

Placing a warning hand on Amalie's plump knee and shooting a quick glance at their parents, Meg saw that both were too intent on their own conversation to have heard Amalie or to scold her now. Sir Iagan had returned to his chair before Lady Murray spoke to him, and he sat glowering at her now.

Experience had taught Meg that despite her father's bluster, her mother would prevail if she believed her course was right. So she kept her hand on Amalie's knee, ready to pinch it if her impulsive sister dared to speak again. Amalie had a habit of saying whatever came into her head the minute it occurred to her.

Sir Iagan picked up his mug as if his only thought were for his ale. Quaffing deeply, he set it down with a thump and said, "Well, madam, I told you he'd refuse your daft offer. If I give him a second chance, he'll just refuse again. I am better acquainted wi' the Scotts than you are, so you would do well to heed me in this."

"Mayhap you are right," she said. "But pride carries no weight when a man faces death. Let him ponder his fate—and your tree. Then let him choose again."

"Aye, well, I dinna mind giving ye your way, if only to prove ye're as apt as anyone to be wrong. But when he refuses, I mean to make an end to it."

She nodded.

With visible satisfaction, he got to his feet, finished off the last of his ale, and said, "I'll be getting on with the business then, straightaway."

Lady Murray also stood, whereupon her daughters, perforce, did likewise. Signing to the gillie behind her that she desired him to take her stool away, Lady Murray said, "We will accompany you, my dear sir. Doubtless, you are right, and these executions will provide a salutary lesson for your daughters."

Distressed, Meg gave her a questioning look, but Lady Murray ignored it, her attention fixed on her husband.

He opened his mouth, then pressed his lips together briefly before he said, "Very well, madam. Doubtless it will prove salutary for ye, too."

"We are to see the hanging, then?" Amalie said in astonishment. "But—"

"Be silent, Amalie," her mother interjected. Letting Sir Iagan stride ahead of them, she said quietly to Meg, "I know you object, too, but do have the good sense to hold your tongue. He has taken his stand and will stick to it buckle and thong if pressed harder. However, he will give more thought to the true cost of this hanging if you and Amalie are present than if you are not. We must give him time to realize what can come of turning Buccleuch and the Douglas into our blood enemies."

Meg winced at the thought. It was bad enough, heaven knew, to live so near the border between Scotland and England on land that each country claimed as its own without purposely inciting the wrath of truly powerful entities on either side of the ever-shifting line.

"With respect, madam," she said, "why do you not just remind him of what the consequences must be?"

"Your father does not take well to such reminders. You know that as surely as I do," Lady Murray said. "If you would learn anything from me, my dear Meg, learn that men cannot be driven by women any more easily than cats can be driven by even the best sheepdogs. One does better to choose one's moments to guide than to be constantly nagging or reminding them of things they want to forget."

Meg tried unsuccessfully to imagine herself guiding her father.

Outside, the reivers' leader stood near the hanging tree with one of her father's stout men-at-arms on either side of him. The rope already dangled over a thick bough, but if the victim worried about his fate, he gave no sign of it.

Sir Iagan stopped some yards from the little scene, crossed his arms over his barrel-like chest, and spread his feet a little apart. He had not spoken to direct his men or to address the prisoner. Nor did he glance back at his wife and daughters.

Lady Murray put out a hand to stop Meg and Amalie. Then she moved to stand beside Sir Iagan.

From her position behind and to his left, Meg saw her father's jaw tighten, but he said nothing until the man adjusting the noose finished and looked his way.

"Be ye ready then?" Sir Iagan asked him.

"Aye, sir."

"Then tell your lads to bring out the others. We'll let this young chappie watch them each hang. 'Twill give him more appreciation for his own fate."

Although the reiver did not move head or limbs, Meg felt his reaction to her father's words as if his emotions had shot through her body instead. She was fifteen or more feet away, seeing only his profile, but she saw the color drain from his face.

She swallowed hard, wishing she could do something to stop it all.

"Poor laddie," Amalie murmured beside her.

Glancing at her, Meg saw that her sister had squeezed her eyes shut.

Wat stared at the dangling noose, determined not to give Murray the satisfaction of seeing him react. He was definitely having second thoughts, but he would not let his kinsmen down by showing fear or behaving badly. Many Scotts had died before their time, and most had died bravely. He'd got himself into the mess. He would not disgrace his family by weeping about it.

His peripheral vision was excellent, and he had seen the women enter the yard behind Murray. Their presence gave him even more incentive to remain stoic.

The minutes crept by. He fixed his gaze on the rope until it stopped swinging.

Thanks to the high curtain wall that protected Elishaw, no breeze touched the yard, and no person in it made a sound. For once, the sky was blue without mist or fog, and the sun shone brightly. The day a man was to die ought to look sadder.

He heard the keep's postern door open behind him, followed by sounds of shuffling feet and, moments later, by a hastily stifled feminine gasp.

Curiosity having been a besetting sin since childhood, he turned to face his men. At first, he saw only Tammy and Gib, because as tall and broad as Tam was, and as thick through the torso as Gib was, they made a human wall, concealing those who followed. Then he saw Dod Elliot behind Gib, and Snirk Rabbie of Coldheugh beside Dod, with Snirk's brother Jeb on their heels.

Another of Murray's men-at-arms followed them, and—

Wat stifled a gasp of his own, as much of anger as dismay, at the sight—now clear—of the wiry, redheaded laddie walking stiffly beside the guard. The top of the boy's head was no higher than the man's elbow.

Wee Sym Elliot had no business to be there, but Wat needed no explanation of his presence. The lad had formed the unfortunate habit of following his brother Dod and Dod's friends whenever he could get away with it. Having been sternly ordered to stay at home the previous day, and thus denied a jaunt to the Langholm races, the lad had clearly managed to follow them on the raid instead.

Hearing murmurs from the Murrays, he looked that way next.

Her ladyship was speaking to her husband, giving Wat to hope fervently that she was urging Murray to spare Sym. Surely, the man could not be so cruel as to hang a lad of no more than eleven summers in front of his daughters.

Another, bleaker thought followed. What sort of man allowed his maiden daughters to watch multiple hangings? For that matter, what sort of mother and daughters would agree to bear witness to such a grim spectacle?

Having asked himself these questions, it was with slightly less surprise than otherwise that he heard Murray say curtly, "Hang the youngest one first."

The lady Margaret cried out but clapped a hand to her mouth when her mother shot her a look of strong disapproval. The younger lass had both hands pressed to her own face, covering her eyes and her mouth.

Wat turned as the guard gripped Sym's left shoulder and shoved him toward the tree, but Sym avoided Wat's eye, looking straight ahead. His lower lip quivered, but otherwise, he gave no sign of fear. Wat knew he ought to be proud of the lad, but he wanted only to thrash him soundly and send him home to safety.

He had to say something, to try to prevent such a travesty.

To his astonishment, Murray said, "I'll give ye one last chance, reiver, and to prove what a charitable fellow I am, I'll even dower my lass. Ye can take back a half-dozen o' your beasts if ye can identify them accurately as your own. I'll even throw in a bull so ye can breed them. So now, will it be the priest or a coffin?"

Wat felt a stirring of relief but chose his words carefully, saying, "I've little stomach for it, but if I agree to your proposition, what will become of my men?"

"I'll hang them, o' course. Nae other amongst them be suitable to wed wi' a daughter o' mine, and they be proven reivers, every last one o' them."

"That lad you mean to hang first has not yet seen the eleventh anniversary of his birth," Wat said, casting a glance at Lady Murray. "Would you hang him just for following us? I give you my word as a Borderer, he had nowt to do with reiving."

"Aye, sure," Murray said scornfully. "I expect ye'll say next that none o' ye did and that ye didna even ken the lad were there."

"I did *not* know," Wat said, feeling his temper stir. He was not accustomed to having his word challenged. "Nor did my men know that he'd followed us, because they'd have sent him back with a sore backside just as I would have."

"Then, I warrant that by hanging him now, I'll save myself the trouble later. With you lot to set him an example, he'll be a true reiver in no time."

Wat looked again at Lady Murray but could read nothing in her expression. Shifting his gaze to the lady Margaret, he wondered if she might wield influence with her father. Just as he had decided that she might, a new voice spoke up.

"Aye, I *will* be a true reiver one day," Wee Sym said defiantly, glowering at Murray. "And your herds would be the first I'd take, for ye're nobbut a blackguard to be hanging men what took nowt from ye whatsoever. I saw how it was! I saw your men jump out o' the heather. And where your beasts were, that's no your land at all. 'Tis the Douglas's, and ye'll answer to him for it just as all do hereabouts."

"Enough, Sym!" Wat snapped, terrified that Murray would order the lad's hanging without further discussion. When Sym looked ready to say more, Wat added in a measured, even sterner tone, "Not one more word."

"Bless me, but I'll be ridding the world of a right scoundrel," Murray said. "Put the noose round his neck, lads, and let's get on with this."

"Wait," Wat said.

"We've nae more to say," Murray declared.

"If you release my lads—all of them—I'll do as you ask and agree to marry your daughter," Wat said, ignoring gasps from his men and Sym's goggle-eyed stare.

Behind Murray, Wat saw Lady Margaret put a hand back to her mouth. Her sister's eyes were as big as Sym's, but Lady Murray revealed no emotion.

"I'll release the boy," Murray said. "That's all."

Wat drew a deep breath and let it out. A moment before, he might have taken the deal just to spare Sym, but a glance at Gibbie staring at his own feet with visible tension in his broad shoulders told Wat what he had to do.

To Murray, he said, "Releasing one is not enough. I'll not save myself just to spare a foolish bairn who'll likely throw his life away in just such another act of defiance. You'll release the rest of my men, or we have no bargain."

"I'll do nae such thing."

"Think you that after hanging half a dozen Scott vassals you can escort your daughter to Rankilburn and return here safely with nobbut a tail of your own men to protect you? Or will you let her fate rest with no more protection than that of a man whose word you do not trust, over miles of countryside rife with armed ruffians, poachers, and lusty men-at-arms, not to mention any number of rogue English raiders? Recall that despite Douglas's orders, the area is hardly peaceful."

He saw Lady Murray touch her husband's arm.

~

Meg's fingertips pressed hard against her lips to keep the words she wanted to speak from spewing forth at her father. How could he threaten to hang a child? How could he not believe the reiver, who clearly was willing to die with his men? And what had the boy meant when he'd said the reivers had stolen nothing?

She felt relief when her mother moved, for although she had not been able to see exactly what Lady Murray did, Sir Iagan made no immediate effort to reply to the reiver's challenge. He turned to her ladyship instead.

"What is it?" he asked when Lady Murray did no more than gaze back at him. "Would you accept any terms to see your daughter wedded to this rascal?"

"It is not for me to accept or reject terms, my lord. As always, that must remain for you to decide. It does strike me, though, that Sir Walter speaks fairly. Were he to agree to marry our Meg only to save the neck of a child, one cannot imagine what use the child would be in seeing her safely to her new home."

"Bless us, I'll see her there safe enough with a large, well-armed escort."

"I am sure you will, my lord, but at what cost? 'Tis not the money concerns me, of course, but did you capture every man who rode with Sir Walter last night?"

He hesitated as Meg nervously nibbled a fingertip.

"Even if you believe you did, one can never be certain of such a thing," Lady Murray went on in her placid way. "Only consider that even Sir Walter did not know that the boy had followed them. In the uproar that usually ensues during such incidents, I should imagine that some of the raiders may easily have escaped. By now, I suspect that both Buccleuch and Douglas have heard about what happened."

"I do not fear Douglas," Murray snapped.

"No more should you, sir, for I warrant he hopes, despite your customary neutrality in such matters, to persuade you to support his forthcoming efforts against the English. But if he has already learned of *this* incident . . ."

Seeing her father stiffen, Meg knew Lady Murray's unfinished suggestion had struck home. They did not want to make an enemy of the Earl of Douglas. It would be far safer for them if he retained at least a hope of persuading Sir Iagan to support the Scottish cause. The earl was going to need all the men he could muster.

In England, she knew that whenever the King needed an army, he just forced his nobles to order out their vassals and equip them with arms. But the King of Scots was merely the chief of chiefs. If he wanted an army, he had to persuade the Scottish nobility that his cause was good. Therefore, even the Earl of Douglas, as powerful as he was, often had to do some persuading.

The earl's vast power lay in the fierce loyalty of the

enormous Douglas clan and that of other noble supporters such as the Laird of Buccleuch, who would do whatever he asked of them. But to raise the entire Scottish Borderers to aid him in discouraging yet another English invasion, he would have to persuade others like Sir Iagan, who did not leap to obey whenever the Douglas lifted a finger.

It was one thing to remain neutral. In that event, the Douglas would be displeased, but he would do them no harm. However, if aught occurred to make him believe that Sir Iagan might actively aid the English, Douglas would likely take swift, punitive action.

Indeed, in view of Lady Murray's kinship with the powerful English Percy family, which included Douglas's chief rival, Sir Harry "Hotspur" Percy, Douglas would have to be a fool to trust Sir Iagan much under any circumstance. And no one had ever called Douglas a fool.

Sir Iagan, evidently lost in thought himself, had not yet replied to his wife when that wily dame went on to say, "You will doubtless agree, sir, that Meg would be quite safe in riding to Rankilburn with Sir Walter and an escort of six men-at-arms all known to be loyal to Douglas and Buccleuch. Indeed, it might be wiser and more tactful than to escort her yourself. Moreover, you need not provision them."

Indignation rose swiftly in Meg's breast. Was her mother truly suggesting that she should ride off with the reiver and have no one she knew to protect her, not one soul whom she could trust even to talk to?

Her contrary imagination suggested that she would likewise have no one to scold her or order her about—other than this supposed husband-to-be of hers. She eyed Sir Walter speculatively, then glanced at her sister.

Amalie was watching her, probably trying to imagine

what Meg's feelings must be. Meg couldn't tell her, for she wasn't certain herself what they were.

She turned back to watch the reiver as Sir Iagan said, "Madam, we are scarcely the only people in these border-lands to have kinsmen on the other side o' the line. Fixed as we are, less than three miles from the crossing into England at Carter Bar, it would be odd if we had no such ties. Douglas certainly understands how necessary it is for me to tread carefully."

"To be sure, he must, my lord."

"I ken fine that ye believe the wisest course would be for Scotland to yield to England, so that all of us may live in peace. I've said before and I'll say again that ye may ha' the right of it, but few other Scots would agree wi' ye. Douglas would not, certainly. Nor would Buccleuch."

"You are right, as always, sir," she said. "Your detailed knowledge of such things constantly reassures me of your wisdom."

He nodded. "Then ye must see by now that if this young rascal does agree to wed our daughter and I agree to set his men free, they must all promise to protect her and to treat her with the respect her noble birth demands."

"As she will be Sir Walter's wife, we can be sure he will agree to that."

"Aye, then it's settled," Murray said. To Sir Walter, he said in a stern, clear voice, "I shall allow ye to wed my eldest daughter then, and ye'll agree to protect the lass henceforward. If I spare your men as well, they must swear to serve her loyally and protect her until death excuses them from her service."

Instead of replying at once, Sir Walter exchanged looks with each of his men in turn, including the youngster. Only after receiving a nod from each one did he say in a tone as firm and clear as Sir Iagan's, "We agree to your terms."

"'Tis wise o' ye," Sir Iagan said. "As I'm giving ye your men, though, in their stead ye'll forfeit the lass's portion as well as yon kine I offered ye earlier."

Meg saw Sir Walter's jaw tighten again, but he nodded.

"If that's settled, we've the good fortune just now to have a mendicant friar staying with us," Sir Iagan said. "I warrant he can perform the wedding as well as any priest, so we'll attend to it straightaway."

"Sakes, Murray," Sir Walter said indignantly, "I've given my word that I'll marry the lass, and whether you believe it or not, my word is good. There can be no need for such unseemly haste."

"Ye may be a man o' your word," Sir Iagan said. "But ye canna speak for your father or the Douglas, and I doubt I can trust either one o' them no to forbid this marriage if they get the chance. Ha' ye no sworn obedience to them? Will ye swear to keep your word to me if it means disobeying them?"

Without replying directly to either question, Sir Walter said, "Would you deny my mother and father a presence at their eldest son's wedding, sir? At least delay long enough to allow them to attend."

"Aye, sure, and give your father and the Douglas time to mount a raid against Elishaw," Sir Iagan said derisively. "I'm no so stupid. Ye'll marry as soon as one o' me lads can fetch the friar. I'm no the one who denied Buccleuch and his lady the chance to see ye wed, either, lad. Ye've only yourself to blame for that. I'm thinking now, though, that we'd best ha' the bedding afore ye leave, too."

Meg gasped when Amalie caught hold of her arm, squeezing it tight.

Sir Walter said, "Surely, you would not be so cruel to your daughter as to force her to lie with a man she had not even seen until today. We must both do her the courtesy of giving her time to accustom herself to me."

"My Meg will cope as well as any newly wedded lass does," Sir Iagan retorted. "Few maidens ken what to expect on their wedding night, but all o' them ken fine that they must obey their fathers and then their husbands."

"But—"

"Enough, lad! I warrant ye ken as well as I do that if ye fail to consummate your marriage, ye'd be giving Buccleuch and the Douglas good cause to demand an annulment. I won't have that. The marriage will take place here in this yard, and straightaway. Ye'll bed the lass directly afterward."

"Nay, then," Meg said, shocked into freeing her tongue at last. "I won't do it!"

Sir Iagan turned a wrathful face toward her, but she had come to realize that she wielded some power of her own in the dreadful business.

Forcing determination into her voice, she said, "I won't lie with a man who has not washed in God knows how many months, Father. Nor will I marry without having a bath myself and changing out of this old kirtle into a dress more suitable for riding. I shall also require time to pack my clothing and other things unless you mean for me to ride into my new life with only the clothes on my back."

"Dinna be impertinent," Sir Iagan growled. "Ye'll do as I bid ye." But when he glanced warily at his lady, Meg felt a surge of relief.

Lady Murray said, "To be sure, my lord, you will

agree that she must have things of her own to take with her. The servants can pack them whilst she has her bath. That young man should also bathe before he beds her, although he can do so here in the yard as well as anywhere, and someone can brush his clothes whilst he does. Meg should also enjoy a proper wedding feast," she added. "How fortunate that it is still early in the day. If I give the orders at once, we should be able to dine only an hour later than usual. That will give Meg and her new husband plenty of time to reach Rankilburn before darkness falls."

"Ye seem to have it all thought out," Sir Iagan said sourly. Fixing another glowering look on Meg, he added, "Be there aught else ye'll require?"

"Forgive me, my lord," her ladyship said. "I do think we ought to go inside if we are to discuss these matters further. You will not want to be making a gift of our further discussion to your men and these other persons."

He nodded curtly but said to Meg, "Doubtless that will give ye time to think up a long list o' your needs, lass. Just do not try me too far."

"No, sir," she said, wondering what else she might request, since he had already declared that he would give her no proper dowry, nor agree to return the kine that he had surprisingly called the reiver's own.

Once back in the now nearly deserted hall, taking her courage in hand again, she said, "I would like to take at least one maidservant with me, Father. I would feel most uncomfortable as the sole female in such a party of men. But I own, the real reason is that I'd like to have at least one familiar face with me in my new home."

"And just who d'ye think would agree to go wi' ye?" he demanded.

Feeling heat flood her cheeks, she said, "I do not know, sir. I doubt that any of our maidservants will want to go so far from home. But if you or my lady mother could induce one of them to accompany me even for a few weeks—"

"I'll go with you," Amalie said. "Faith, but I'd like to go!"

Chapter 3

"I swear, then, this hour shall my daughter
be married t' ye . . .
Or else the next minute submit to your fate."

In the courtyard, Wat stood silently as Murray's men-at-
arms untied first his hands and then those of each of his
lads.

"Begging your pardon, sir," one of Murray's gillies
said. "But if ye're wanting to bathe out here, nae doot
ye'd like us to set the tub yonder in the sunlight, where
ye'll keep warm."

"Thank you," Wat said. "Do as you think best, but I
would speak privately with my men before I bathe."

The gillie glanced around as if seeking guidance but,
finding none, turned back and said, "As ye will, sir. I'll
just speak to the lads fetching out your tub."

As soon as he had walked away, Tammy strode across
the yard to say urgently to Wat, "Ye'll never be takin'
them lassies back to Rankilburn wi' ye, Master Wat. That
one he says ye're to marry's got a face on her that—"

"Enough, Tam. That lass is soon to become my wife."

"Aye, sure, and if she does, we'll no say nowt, but be ye sure, lad? I dinna ken what your da' will say about this, nor yet the Douglas. 'Tis his own cousin ye were to marry, after all."

"That was my father's wish," Wat said wearily. "I had nowt to say to it, so I don't even know how far those negotiations have advanced. Not that it matters now, of course, not where I am concerned or where their tempers are concerned. I think I should give thanks that I've won my spurs, don't you?" he added wryly. "Otherwise, I'd not put it past my father to take a tawse to my backside for this."

"As to someone deservin' the tawse," Tammy said with a grim look at Wee Sym Elliot, "I'll wager that lad has some painful minutes comin' to him."

"That he does," Wat said, motioning to Sym.

The boy approached warily. Glancing at Wat, then Tammy, and back again, he said, "Be it true that old sneck doesna mean to hang us after all, Master Wat?"

"It's true, aye."

"Are ye going to marry his daughter, then? Which one? To my mind, they both seem devilish ill favored to suit a man o' taste like yourself."

"If you are wise, you will keep that opinion to yourself," Wat said sternly, aware that Tam had put one huge hand over his mouth, doubtless to hide a grin.

"I just wondered, is all," Sym said. "The old one be skinny and her mouth be too muckle for me. The other one's too fat, and neither o' them looks cheery. I like a cheerisome lass, m'self."

"You are too young to be thinking of lasses, cheery or not," Wat informed him. "Now, what the devil did you mean by following us here?"

"I saw ye leaving, is all, and I thought I'd see where ye'd be going, the lot o' ye. I only meant to go a short way, but ye kept on, so I got curious to see if ye'd cross over the line after the Douglas said ye were no to do it."

"Have I not told you that you must not follow us anymore?" Before the boy could reply, Wat added curtly, "Has your mother not told you the same thing, and your brother Dod as well?"

"Aye, sure, I guess near everyone I ken has told me, but when the moment comes, I forget. Am I really to serve your lady then, for the rest o' me life?"

Remembering Murray's demand, Wat nearly told Sym that he need not feel himself bound by any promise made under such duress, but the lad's grimacing annoyance gave him pause.

With the Borders as unsettled as they were, and with Douglas eager to meet England's Hotspur, thus threatening battle any day now, the likelihood was smaller than ever that anyone would keep a close eye on Sym. The much greater likelihood was that with such interesting events looming around him, the lad would be in trouble again before his mam's cat could lick an ear.

"You heard what her father said," Wat told him. "What's more, when I looked to you, you nodded your agreement. You thus gave your word to me to serve her, your word as a Borderer. You ken fine what that means, do you not?"

Sym grimaced again but nodded. "Aye, sure, a Borderer's word is aye good, or he doesna give it."

"I'm thinking you have hitherto taken good care to avoid giving your word to anyone," Wat said. "Is that so?"

The boy nodded again. "I dinna like to give it, because

a man never kens what may arise afterward that he didna expect."

"That is true," Wat said. "But a man's word is important. He should not give it lightly, but when he does, he must keep it. If he fails, he breaks the trust he has with others, and he can never replace that. He may swear he'll never break his word again, and he may keep that promise despite breaking the previous one. But the trust others place in him will never be as strong as before he broke faith with them the first time, simply because the others can no longer be sure of him. Do you understand me?"

"Aye, I think so."

"Well, ponder my words until you do understand," Wat said. "For now, I want you to promise me again, on your Borderer's word of honor, that you will serve the lady Margaret until she releases you from her service of her own will. You may not ask her to do so without breaking your word to me. Do you agree?"

He held the lad's gaze with his own.

"Aye, then, I do," Sym muttered.

"Good lad," Wat said.

"I'll just be going to see what I can do to help the others then."

"There is just one thing more," Wat said as the boy turned away.

Sym froze where he stood.

"Look at me."

Swallowing visibly, Sym obeyed.

"Do you remember what I said would happen if you followed me again?"

"I didna!" Sym exclaimed. "I followed Dod and them other lads."

Hardening his expression, Wat said, "What did I tell you?"

Reluctantly, eyes downcast, Sym said, "Ye said ye'd see me well skelped."

"Do you think I do not keep my word?"

Still looking at his feet, Sym shook his head.

"Answer me properly."

"Aye, sir," Sym said, looking up at him. "I ken fine that ye'll keep your word. Will ye do it now, or wait till we get back to Rankilburn?"

"You will go to Dod right now and tell him I said he is to give you the skelping of your young life. And, Sym?"

The boy's lower lip trembled, but he said stoutly enough, "Aye, sir?"

"Do not put me to the trouble of having such a conversation with you again."

"Nay, then, I won't."

Watching him walk away with greater reluctance than ever to join the others, Wat felt surprisingly strong empathy for him. He had no doubt that after Buccleuch had described his own lack of good sense to him in a similar chat, he would be feeling much the same remorse that Sym felt now.

"Begging your pardon, sir, but your bath be ready."

Turning with no small relief, Wat followed the gillie to the waiting tub.

⁓

In the hall, as stunned as Meg had been to hear Amalie's unexpected offer to go with her to Rankilburn, she could not think what to say to her.

Their parents appeared likewise speechless.

Lady Murray was the first to recover. "Do think of what you are saying for once, Amalie," she said. "You cannot mean such a thing."

"But I do," Amalie said, looking from one parent to the other. "I think Meggie is right. She *should* have someone she knows go with her. Sithee, I need stay only long enough to see her settled into her new home and happy there."

Sir Iagan opened his mouth, met his wife's gaze, and shut it again.

Having no doubt that he had been about to point out to Amalie that happiness was not a necessity in any marriage, let alone one resulting from such a negotiation as this one had been, Meg said hastily, "I swear I would take the greatest care of her, Father. Indeed, her company would do much to reconcile me to this dreadful change in my life. Oh, pray, sir, do say she may go."

"I do not like the notion," Sir Iagan said stiffly.

"Nay, sir, nor do I," Lady Murray said. But her thoughtful expression gave Meg cause to hope she would not forbid it outright.

Nor did she. Instead, she announced her intent to see to such changes in the midday menu as might transform it into a wedding feast. "Collops of beef and a few chickens, I think," she said. "That young man's lads must eat, too, after all."

"Meantime, I will send for that friar and try to find some maidservant or other who will agree to accompany our Meg to Rankilburn," Sir Iagan said.

"An excellent notion, sir," Lady Murray said. "If Amalie does go with Meg, it would be as well to provide a respectable serving woman to attend them both. For now, Meg, you go along up to your chamber and set your Tetsy to packing your things into a pair of sumpter baskets that the men can tie to a pony. I'll send someone up straight-away with your bath water. Amalie, you go along and help her."

"Aye, madam," Amalie said.

"Prithee, madam . . ." Meg began, only to bite off the rest of her words when Amalie pinched her arm.

"Yes, Meg, what is it?" Lady Murray asked.

Thinking quickly, Meg said, "Must I try to pack all I own in two baskets?"

"Nay, just such clothing and other items as you will need for comfort until your father can arrange to send the rest of your things to you. Two baskets should suffice, but judge for yourself. I know you will be sensible in your choosing."

"Thank you," Meg said, feeling heat in her cheeks at the unexpected compliment. Such moments were rare.

When they reached the stair hall, Amalie said, "You were about to ask her if I should pack, too, weren't you?"

"I was, aye, for it would be as well to know, don't you agree?"

"You should say no more about my going, Meg. If you don't irritate her by pressing her, she is going to let me go. One could just see that."

"I saw nothing of the sort," Meg said as she followed her up the stairs. "I will agree that she is thinking about it, but she may as easily decide *not* to let you go."

"Nay, for if she means to forbid something, she does so at once. Also, recall that when Father said he'd find a serving-woman, she said I might be going."

"She did not exactly say that you *are* going, though."

"She said enough. Sithee, it is only when she thinks she

sees merit in a plan but needs to sort details out for herself that she delays. In this instance, I warrant she will quickly see how much safer you will be if I ride with you."

"Aye, perhaps, but that respectable serving woman Father is seeking would do as much to ensure my safety without your going."

"She would not," Amalie said. "Just consider those reivers, who are nearly all of the sort our lady mother calls Scottish brutes and ruffians. Do you think they would show the same respect to a serving woman of their own class as they would to me—to the two of us?"

Meg smiled again. "Surely, you do not think them any rougher than our brothers' henchmen—Simon's in particular, of course, but even Tom's men are surly—as are most others of their ilk that we've known, English or Scot. Do you think Sir Walter cannot control his men?"

Meg had lowered her voice in hopes of keeping it from echoing up and down the stairwell to anyone within earshot. Amalie did not bother to lower hers.

"What do we know about him?" she demanded. "Why should he care what they do? Is our father not forcing him into this marriage just as he is forcing you? What if Sir Walter were to decide to abandon you, or kill you, along the way?"

"Don't be foolish," Meg said. "He may be angry, but he has no cause to take out his anger on me."

"Faugh," Amalie said, rudely echoing one of their father's favorite epithets. "Men always take out their anger on the women closest to them. One has only to think of our brothers and our father—or, indeed, of any man we have ever met."

"That may sometimes be true," Meg said. "But you

will not pretend that any of them has ever killed a woman merely because someone else has angered him."

"We cannot know all they have done," Amalie said. "We see them only when they are here. They may do all sorts of horrid things elsewhere."

Although Meg could believe the ambitious Simon capable of almost anything if he thought it would gain him what he wanted, she could not imagine merry Tom behaving as Amalie suggested. Shaking her head at her sister, she said, "You know our lady mother disapproves of exaggeration, dearling. Do contain your fancies until we are alone where no one else might hear them."

"They may be fancies," Amalie said. "But you know our mother well enough to know she harbors the same opinion of those men."

"Even so, you ought not to say such things where others may hear you."

Having reached the next landing, Amalie looked back and stuck out her tongue, but she kept silent until they were safely inside the bedchamber they shared.

Then she said, "What do you think of Sir Walter, Meg? I think he is very—"

Breaking off, she shot Meg a rueful look when the door opened to admit Tetsy, the rosy-cheeked chambermaid who served them.

Meg knew that Tetsy must have been just behind them in the stairwell, ever silent in her soft-soled slippers, and wondered how much she had overheard.

"Her ladyship sent me," Tetsy said. "She said ye're to ha' a bath and she'll be sending hot water right up. I'm to fetch out the tub and then see to packing your clothes. Och, m'lady, she said ye be going to Rankilburn!"

"Do you know Rankilburn, Tetsy?" Meg asked.

"Och, nay, but it does sound gey far away," Tetsy responded as she vigorously hauled the wooden tub from its place in a corner of the chamber. "Her ladyship did say ye be going to marry a nobleman, m'lady. But I dinna ken how that can be, when none of us ha' heard aught about any such thing afore today."

Sweetly, Amalie said, "Do you doubt my lady mother's word, Tetsy?"

Looking horrified, Tetsy disclaimed any such doubt. "'Twas only that we usually hear straightaway if someone be getting married, and her ladyship did say ye'd be marrying your man today, Lady Meg."

"Do you not think that is romantic, Tetsy?" Amalie asked.

"Don't tease her, Amalie," Meg said. "It is true, Tetsy, and it happened quickly. I am to marry Sir Walter Scott, the Laird of Buccleuch's eldest son. Have you heard that name before?"

Tetsy's eyes widened. "Aye, sure, m'lady. Me da' says Buccleuch be a gey fierce man. Be his son a fierce one, too?"

"We will hope not, as the lady Meg is to marry him," Amalie said. "Would you like to travel with her to her new home, Tetsy?"

Tetsy's eyes widened, and color drained from her cheeks. "Nay, mistress, I couldna go wi' them rough, horrid men ye was speaking about."

More sternly, Meg said, "I asked you to stop teasing her, Amalie. Prithee, do so at once. You are not usually so unkind. Tetsy, I know you do not want to go so far from home. I have already told Sir Iagan that you would prefer to stay here."

"Thank ye, m'lady. If ye truly want me to go, I expect I could do it. But I'd liefer stay here wi' me own kin."

"Then you shall," Meg said, adding with a smile, "I think I hear them coming now with my water."

"Aye, sure," Tetsy agreed, hurrying to open the chamber door. "That water be for ye, too, Lady Amalie. Your mam did say ye'd also want a bath."

"There, did I not tell you, Meggie?" Amalie crowed triumphantly.

"That you are to take a bath hardly means you will go to Rankilburn," Meg pointed out. "Our lady mother may not want to waste good water on just one bath."

"You'll see," Amalie said. "You'd best decide what you want to take. That tub will be full soon, and if I am to bathe after you do, I don't want cold water."

Meg sighed and moved to begin making her selections, wondering as she did if her sister's company at Rankilburn would prove to be a boon or a penance.

In the yard, Wat finished his bath and left the water for any of his lads who wanted to use it. As he toweled himself, feminine giggles drew his attention to the postern door of the castle keep, where two lasses had apparently been watching with interest while he bathed.

He grinned at them and finished dressing. Although someone had brushed his clothes, they still bore evidence that Elishaw's dungeon lacked regular cleaning. A brief mental vision of his mother's likely reaction were she able to see her firstborn son's wedding attire drew another smile.

Only then did it strike him that he would be taking the

lass home with him. The thought of her living with him in his rustic peel tower brought a frown, but that of presenting her to his parents as his wife made him wince.

His mother would accept his decision more easily than his father would. Buccleuch had definite notions of what sort of marriage he expected for his son. Having heard them all, Wat knew that marrying the daughter of a man his father disliked to avoid hanging would not figure among them.

There was nothing else for it, though. He would have to take the lass to Scott's Hall, his parents' primary residence, in Rankilburn Glen. Not only was his tower not presentable—not to a gently bred noblewoman, at all events—but in his absence, it would not be as safe for a woman as Scott's Hall.

And he would soon be absent, certainly. With Douglas determined to stop the English in England and the English more determined than ever to conquer Scotland, Douglas would need Wat and as many men as he could take with him.

Buccleuch would also follow where the Douglas led, making it even more important that the lady Margaret reside safely at the Hall with Lady Scott.

As these thoughts flitted through Wat's mind, he became aware that the two lassies by the postern door had disappeared. Footsteps crunched behind him, and turning, he saw Murray striding toward him, his left hand on his sword hilt.

Although tempted to ask him if he feared attack from an unarmed man in his own bailey, Wat resisted and waited politely for his host to address him.

With a jolt, he realized that the man would soon be his father-in-law.

Murray tossed him a hairbrush. "I thought ye'd want to brush some o' the tangles out o' your hair," he said.

Wat caught the brush easily, but his mind was not on his hair, because Murray held a roll of foolscap in his other hand.

The older man met his gaze. "I see ye've noted me documents, lad. Whilst ye were bathing I had yon mendicant friar draw up an agreement betwixt us two. I trow ye'll ken your letters well enough to understand it."

"Aye, I can read," Wat said. "What sort of agreement is it?"

"Och, nobbut the usual sort to say ye agree to protect our Meggie and treat her well. Ye'll likewise see she's protected financially in the event o' your death, and ye'll recognize any bairns she may produce as your own."

"Let me see it," Wat said, more to give himself time to think than because he doubted the documents were other than Murray had described.

The friar's writing was clear, and the words fairly leaped off the page.

He glanced at Murray.

The older man's eyes gleamed with expectation.

"It says here," Wat said steadily, "that I also agree and give bond and promise that I will never again take up arms against any Murray of Elishaw."

"Aye, sure. 'Tis customary in such unions, where families may end up on opposing sides of important issues. Also, I'll want your promise that ye'll ride to my aid if ever I ha' need o' you."

"I don't imagine I'd be likely to take up arms against my wife's family," Wat said. "And I'll agree to ride to your aid unless Douglas himself is attacking you or the attack is by his order. But if you can accept my word as bond and promise to do those things, why must you force us into this marriage and bedding today?"

"I told ye, because that road, I'll no ha' Buccleuch or the Douglas interfering. But if ye read on," he added with a smirk, "ye'll see that 'tis no just your word I'll have as bond for these matters o' taking up arms or riding to me aid."

"I have nowt else to offer you."

"I have those cattle, horses, and hounds that came from your pasture to my own, aye? But for insurance, ye'll see just below that line there that if ye break either promise, ye'll pay me a hundred merks as well."

Keeping his temper with difficulty, and only because he knew it would do him no good to lose it, Wat said, "I do not accept that those beasts are yours to keep, sir. But I'll give you my word on the other. Do you mean to keep my dogs and my horses—even the ones we rode here—and make us all walk back home?"

"Ye'll take the horses ye rode," he said. "The rest I'll keep to teach ye never again to try to lift my beasts."

"Do you not fear that Buccleuch or the Douglas may yet seek annulment, not only of the wedding but of this damnable agreement you want me to sign?"

"Nay, lad, for the agreement be in writing. Any council will support my position that this marriage be legal. Ye'll do your part, too, I reckon, to see that our Amalie meets someone suitable to wed whilst she's abiding wi' ye."

"Amalie?"

"Aye, sure, Meggie's younger sister. Ye must ha' seen her in the hall and yet again out here in the yard whilst we were discussing your hanging."

"I did see another young woman, aye, but what has she to do with me?"

"Only that she has offered to bear her sister company on the journey and I ha' decided to permit it. Two young ladies will be gey safer than one. I did try to find a serving woman to go and look after them, but they'd all liefer stay here."

"I see," Wat said. He would have liked to refuse to take the younger girl, for he could foresee naught but trouble to come of including her. But if Murray could not persuade a maidservant to attend his daughter, he could scarcely blame him for wanting someone to accompany her. Another thought occurred to him. "I trust your younger daughter *wants* to come."

"Aye, she offered, so she must want to," Murray said. "There's no understanding the female mind, but my lady wife says it will do the lasses good to be together. Amalie needna stay long, though. Doubtless ye'll see to her safe return when she's of a mind to come home."

"I will, aye," Wat said, wondering what on earth he had brought down upon himself merely for wanting to reclaim his cattle, horses, and two dogs.

As Meg bathed, she watched Amalie bustle about, giving orders to Tetsy and another maidservant that Amalie had coaxed into aiding with the packing. She reminded Meg of a sheepdog, nipping at ovine heels to drive its flock.

Noting that Amalie was having her own clothing packed, Meg said, "Are you sure about this, dearling? With the Borders as unsettled as they are these days, we cannot be sure how long you'll have to stay with me. It may be a long time."

"Aye, well, what comes will come," Amalie said. "I shan't mind."

She was not looking at Meg but down into the sumpter basket Tetsy was organizing, but Meg saw a muscle twitch in her jaw and recognized the sign.

Her frequently, if surprisingly, stubborn sister was determined to go with her.

"Amalie, pray hand me that towel," Meg said. "And, Tetsy, I want to take the embroidered shawl that my lady mother gave me at Candlemas. I left it in her solar yestereve. And you, Letty, stir up that fire more for the lady Amalie."

When Amalie brought the towel and held it for her, Meg stood and wrapped it around herself, saying quietly, "You will need to make haste with your bath, I fear, if we are to finish everything soon enough to suit our lord father. But first, dearling, tell me *why* you want so badly to go with me."

Amalie shrugged. "It is nothing to make a song about, Meg. I just cannot let you go off by yourself with all those men."

"Are you sure that's all?" Meg asked. "Your determination is making the very air crackle in here."

Amalie shrugged. "Mayhap it is just that if I go to Rankilburn, Sir Walter will be duty-bound to find a kinsman or friend willing to marry me. I'd prefer that to waiting years more around here for our father to find me a husband."

Meg looked narrowly at her but knew when Amalie gazed steadily back that she would learn no more until Amalie was ready to tell her.

Chapter 4

Though laird o' the best o' the Forest sae fair,
He'll marry the warst for the sake o' his neck.

Having given his lads orders to join him in the great hall and bear witness to his wedding, Wat followed his future father-in-law inside, to find a quill and an ink horn waiting on the dais table beside a jug of what looked like ale.

Murray set the rolled document down beside them.

"I expect you'll want me to sign that now," Wat said.

"In good time, lad. I've asked the friar to come and witness our signing. In the meantime, an ye're willing, we'll have a drink to celebrate our bargain."

Wat gratefully accepted a mug of ale and had quaffed nearly half of it before he recalled that he'd not had anything to eat since his supper the evening before and that ale had been partially to blame for his present predicament. Much as he would have welcomed the oblivion he could count on after a surfeit of the stuff, he told himself sternly that he would be wiser to keep a clear head.

"I reckon my ladies will be along soon," Murray said,

taking his place in a two-elbow chair at the centermost place along the dais table, facing the lower hall. "Come, take this stool beside me, lad. We're nearly kin now, so I would hear more o' ye. I'm told ye support the Douglas in all things. Be that true?"

"Aye," Wat said as he settled himself on the back-stool to the right of Murray's armchair. Deciding to follow his host's lead in speaking bluntly, he said, "*I'm* told, sir, that you do *not* support Douglas. Indeed, I've heard it said that you refuse to support either side."

"Sakes, lad, did ye no observe how I'm fixed here? Not only am I just three miles from the line, but my lady was born and raised in England and has powerful kinsmen there. 'Tis as much as a man's life and property be worth to take sides with or against anyone. Nobbut what we live in fear o' being attacked by one side or the other whenever things get truly troublesome."

"But even so, you live in Scotland and are a Scotsman born," Wat protested.

"Aye, sure," Murray said. "And for nigh onto a decade afore I was born, things were peaceful enough hereabouts. To be sure, England's third Edward had conquered nearly all of Scotland south o' the Firth then, and many hereabouts swore fealty to him in exchange for permission to keep their own property."

"So your father was one who swore then," Wat said, not at all surprised to be talking of a conquest that had taken place half a century before. Scottish memories were long. Moreover, English armies had invaded many times since then. And Murray was not the only man to have sworn fealty to a conquering king in order to be left in peace. Others, perhaps even Wat's own kinsmen, had done the same to keep their estates.

"'Twas the sensible thing to do," Murray said. "The alternative was to see one's lands confiscated and given to an English lord. Other times, the English would burn everything as they came north, or the Scots would burn their own crops and drive off their own beasts to keep the English from supplying their armies wi' them."

Wat nodded, knowing it was easy, if inconvenient, for most Scottish Borderers to abandon their homes and fields, and drive their cattle to safer places. Crops could be replanted and simple cottages rebuilt and rethatched in a day or two. Even peel towers like his own were safe to leave unattended if, like Raven's Law, they were built of solid stone.

Larger establishments risked occupation. Hermitage Castle, the nearby Liddesdale seat of the Earl of Douglas, was one such. The English had taken the fortress more than once in its hundred years of existence.

"Do you not trust the Douglas and the Earl of Fife to keep the English out of Scotland this time?" Wat asked him.

Murray shrugged. "I dinna doubt the Douglas will do all he can, but Fife will do what serves Fife. I ought no to speak against the man that my own son Simon serves, but I've nae doubt ye ken enough about Fife to understand what I say. He may be the King o' Scots' own son, but if he can gain by giving away the Scottish throne to England, I've nae doubt he'll do it."

Wat knew that almost no one trusted the Earl of Fife, although many men respected his strength and believed him better qualified to rule Scotland than either the elderly, nearly blind King or Fife's elder brother and actual heir to the throne, the weak, disinterested Earl of Carrick.

Nevertheless, Wat said, "Do you honestly think Fife would agree to let an Englishman take the Scottish crown?"

"'Tis surely possible, for even a King o' Scots has tried it ere now," Murray said. "Ye willna recall it yourself because ye hadna been born yet, but surely ye've heard that when David Bruce were our king, he agreed to leave the Scottish succession to England's Black Prince. Our own Parliament put a stop to that, but not afore me da' decided it would be wise for me to take an English wife. I railed against it at the time, mind ye, but Annabel's been a good wife to me, and for a man like me to have allies on both sides o' the line be nobbut plain good sense."

Wat understood, but he could not agree with the neutral posture Murray had taken. Giving him a straight look, he said, "I hope you don't expect me to refuse to take sides, as you have, when I marry your daughter."

"Nay then, lad, for I ken fine what a hothead ye be. To my mind, ye're no better than the Douglas, ever ready to spill lives in combat over this daft notion o' Scottish freedom. And what comes of it, eh? Ha' ye seen the devastation left behind whenever a clash arises? Or are ye so safe in yon Buck's Cleuch o' yours that ye think neither the English nor the Scots will trouble ye?"

"Scottish freedom is no daft notion," Wat said, reminding himself to tread lightly. He would only anger the man if he lectured him about the sacrifices of great men like Wallace and the Bruce to win Scottish freedom from English oppressors. Instead, he said, "I doubt that you disdain the notion of freedom any more than other men do, sir. I'd wager 'tis only the never-ending attempts by England to conquer Scotland, the fighting necessary to protect our freedom, and the continuing threat to Elishaw that lead you to say such a thing."

When Murray did not challenge that assessment, Wat added, "Scott lands do lie at a safer distance from the line. But the English have never been interested in peace except at their own price, which amounts to England swallowing Scotland whole. That is certainly what their present king, Richard Plantagenet, wants."

"Aye, 'tis true," Murray agreed. "The lad's young yet and already a devil."

"He is, and he is utterly determined to conquer Scotland, if only to prove to those who oppose him that he's won the right to rule England."

"I expect, like most, ye've got it all worked out to suit your own notions o' how things should be," Murray said, clearly in better humor now.

"I know what I believe, sir, just as you do."

"In troth, lad, I care nowt what ye believe or what ye do as long as ye'll come to my aid when I need ye, and ye keep me daughters safe." With a hopeful look, he added, "I've one more, ye ken—young Rosalie—but as she's nobbut entering her eleventh year, I warrant ye'll no want to take her along, too."

Wat was just swallowing more ale and nearly choked.

As he sputtered, Murray clapped him on the back hard enough to knock the wind out of him. When he had recovered, he pushed his stool back as he stood and said dryly, "I thank you, sir, both for aiding my recovery and for your generous offer of a third daughter to take home with me. I trust you'll take no offense if I say I'd liefer not be saddled with another female, let alone with one so young."

"Aye, sure, and I doubt her lady mother would allow it," Murray said without rancor. "As it is, she'll likely fall into a gloom over losing both Meg and Amalie. So I expect our Rosalie had better stay here."

Relieved at having won a point that, under the circumstances, he had feared he might not win, Wat drew a welcome breath, sipped more ale, and waited to see if Murray would try to stir more debate. He did not, and their conversation continued desultorily until the friar hurried in.

The skirts of his dark, hooded gown fluttered behind him, revealing the white cassock beneath as he crossed the hall to the dais. He had the tanned, lean look of most mendicant friars. His face was clean-shaven, his tonsured dark hair speckled with gray. His blue eyes revealed both intelligence and shrewdness.

"Forgive me, my lord," he said to Murray as he approached. "I took time for my prayers, but we should talk about this wedding before it takes place."

"I've nae more to say about it," Murray said. "But ye're in good time to witness us signing yon wedding settlements. This be Wat Scott, eldest son o' the Laird o' Buccleuch. Ye've heard o' the laird, aye?"

"I have, indeed," the friar said, looking narrowly at Wat. "You are *Sir* Walter, are you not? I ask because I inscribed you so in that bond you are to sign."

"I am," Wat said.

"Take up that quill, lad, and put your name where ye must," Murray said.

"One moment, Sir Iagan, if you will permit me one more question," the friar said. "I must be easier in my mind about this." To Wat, he said, "One trusts you are doing this of your own free will, Sir Walter. Will you tell me if that is so?"

Exchanging a look with Murray, and feeling trapped by his own integrity, Wat said curtly, "That is so."

"Take a mug of ale, brother, and rest yourself whilst ye may," Murray said cheerfully. "My lady wife and daughters will join us soon. As ye see, the servants have already begun setting up trestles for our midday meal."

"The wedding feast, aye," the friar said, nodding with a friendly smile to the gillie offering to fill a mug with ale for him.

"A fine feast indeed," Murray said with a mocking look at Wat.

Silence fell then, broken moments later when Wat's men entered the hall.

"Where do you want them to sit, sir?" he asked Murray.

"My lads will show them," his host said. "Ye'll sit here by me when the time comes. But first, we must get you safely wedded and bedded, must we no?"

The friar looked about to speak again, perhaps to protest the haste of the ceremony, Wat thought hopefully. His hopes were not high, however, because marriages performed by traveling clergy were often hasty.

True priests were hard to find at any distance from their religious houses. Even with abbeys, priories, and friaries in the region, priests were rarely handy without notice. Friars, being travelers by duty, and rarely residing in their religious houses, often filled the priestly void in outlying areas. That Murray had one staying at Elishaw now was, in Wat's opinion, naught but curst bad luck, but Scottish law provided more than one way to bypass a proper kirk wedding, so he doubted that even the lack of a priest would have stopped the man.

Watching his men guided to a table in the lower hall, he noted that Murray men-at-arms stood by, watching them, as if fearing mischief. But there would be none.

His lads were quiet, even somber, clearly troubled by all that had passed since setting out to reclaim his beasts the evening before.

At last, the sound came for which he had only half-consciously been waiting, the hush of ladies' skirts and the soft padding of their slippers on the stone stairway. Turning toward the sound, he saw Lady Murray enter the hall first.

Every servant stopped what he or she was doing as her ladyship passed on her way to the dais. Gillies and other menservants bowed, maidservants curtsied, and the men-at-arms stood stiff and straight. For all the notice she took of them, they might all have been pieces of furniture.

Behind her, side by side, came her two elder daughters. The younger lass who followed them, he deduced, was their sister, Rosalie.

Meeting the child's impertinent gaze, he decided he was even luckier than he had thought not to have to take her back to Rankilburn with him.

His gaze shifted back to the pair preceding her, flicking over the lady Amalie to the lady Margaret. He had expected her to wear a much more elegant gown as a bride than she'd had on earlier, and to be sure, she did look less like a servant. But the flimsy blue kirtle and long gray mantle she wore now were no more suitable for riding than the earlier gown had been and no more becoming to her either.

He nearly winced at the ugly white crimped and fluted headdress concealing her hair, and as his experienced gaze took in her bodice's unfashionably tight lacing and low girdle, he tried to imagine her in finer clothing. But his mind balked at trying to imagine her as his wife. She was too thin to be a cozy armful for a man, certainly. Sakes, but she seemed to have no breasts at all.

Although he had heard men talk of her lack of beauty, and her mouth was as wide, even as large, as Sym had said it was, her walk was graceful. She carried herself well, and her lips looked as soft and—

His thoughts stopped when her mouth quirked wryly. Meeting her direct gaze, he realized belatedly that she was watching him watch her.

Meg wondered what he was thinking. She knew she was no great beauty, but beauty was rarely the first thing men looked for in a wife. Plainer women than she married every day, but although Sir Iagan was wealthy and his many alliances had kept them safe so far, Elishaw's position remained tenuous in unsettled times. Her duty, she knew, was to see that her marriage provided yet another strong alliance.

Sir Walter stood calmly beside her father, apparently no longer so violently opposed to marrying her. He looked tidier, too, and much handsomer. His cheeks had flushed when she caught his eye, and they were still pink.

"Art ready, Meg?" Lady Murray said.

Meg nodded.

About to accept a reluctant bridegroom without so much as a penny-dowry to placate him, she told herself that if she was not to be miserable for the rest of her life, she had better think how she could show him he had not made a bad bargain.

Now, however, she could not seem to think at all. She stood beside Sir Walter as the friar said a brief prayer and then asked him if he would promise to take her as his wedded wife, to have and to hold from that time forward.

Meg held her breath.

"I will," the young man beside her said firmly.

"Have you a ring to give her, sir?" the friar asked.

"Nay, for I do not wear one."

"'Tis of no consequence, as the only thing that matters is your promise before God," the friar said.

He turned then to Meg. "Lady Margaret, do you plight your troth to take Sir Walter as your wedded husband, to have him and to hold him through all the ills and pleasures that life brings you, to obey his commands, and to be bonlich and buxom in bed and at board till death parts you from him?"

"I do," Meg said, pleased that her voice sounded as firm as Sir Walter's.

With those words and another brief prayer, the ceremony was over.

Meg thought it sadly flat. A wedding, she decided, ought to have more to it.

"Well, that's done," Sir Iagan announced with satisfaction. "Next, we'll see to the bedding, and then we can eat."

The thought of what lay ahead shot a bolt of panic through Meg, but Lady Murray said calmly, "Forgive me, my lord, but mayhap I misunderstood you. Believing your intent was that our midday meal be their wedding feast, I ordered it served as close to the usual time as possible. It is ready now to serve."

"Aye, well, that's a—"

"I do hope you are not vexed," she added. "I did not expect these men to stand idly by whilst our daughter and

Sir Walter consummate their marriage. Or is it required that we ask them to bear witness to it?"

"Nay, we needna—"

"Doubtless, you are hungry yourself and just striving to do the thing properly. Still, I suspect you would prefer us all to eat first, so Sir Walter's men can load the sumpter ponies whilst he and his bride enjoy a brief respite before they must depart."

Meg glanced at the man who was now her husband but found naught to reassure her in the way his lips pressed tightly together. A muscle in his jaw twitched, just as the one in Amalie's jaw did when she was angry or frustrated but believed she would do better to hold her tongue than to speak.

~

Wat would have liked to strangle Sir Iagan Murray, because had the man plotted and schemed to destroy a marriage before ever it had begun, he could not have done better. The only thing that could make it worse would be if the old devil did insist on letting everyone watch the consummation.

He had heard of fathers who did allow it, to prevent the bridegroom from complaining later that the bride had not been a maiden. So he continued to watch Murray in trepidation, praying that he would not dig in his heels and do just that.

However, Lady Murray was giving orders to the servants, and residents of Elishaw who had not come to watch the ceremony were hurrying into the lower hall now to take their places at the trestle tables.

In what seemed to be no time at all, Wat stood beside his

father-in-law at the high table with the friar on his right. Lady Murray and her daughters lined up on Murray's left, so the bride stood in what was doubtless her usual spot, three places away from Wat, between her mother and the lady Amalie. Rosalie was at the end.

At other wedding feasts Wat had attended, the bride and groom had occupied the central seats at the high table. But evidently Murray or his lady, or both, had decided to prevent any discourse between him and his bride. Realizing he would soon find himself bedding a woman whose only words to him thus far had been her declaration that she had no more wish to marry him than he had to marry her, Wat wondered if when the time came he would be able to perform his duty.

As soon as the friar had said the grace-before-meat and they had taken their seats, Murray said heartily, "Well, now, lad, how does it feel to be a married man? I warrant ye're fair straining at the leash to have at her, are ye no?"

Meeting the older man's taunting gaze, Wat said with feigned interest, "Is that how it was with you, sir? Were you straining at the leash on your day of days?"

Hearing a hastily smothered noise beyond his host, he leaned forward and looked past him.

Lady Murray's attention was on her trencher. If she had heard the exchange—and Wat was certain she must have—she gave no sign. Beyond her, the lady Margaret held a hand over her mouth and stared intently at the table before her.

Wat heard Murray chuckle but watched Margaret until she turned her head enough for him to see her almond-shaped eyes dancing beneath lush dark lashes. He was able to discern enough of their color to guess that they were gray or a soft blue.

Before, he had always seemed to see her mouth first. Now, with it covered, her eyes commanded attention. He wished she would look right at him as she had earlier, but even as the thought stirred, she looked back down at the table.

"Bless us, lad," Sir Iagan said, startling him out of his brief reverie and still chortling as he gestured to his carver to begin carving the roast. "Ye've recalled that me own marriage were arranged for me just as I've arranged yours for you. Och, though, not precisely as I've done it," he amended with another laugh. "Still, if ye can do as well wi' your lady as I've done wi' mine, ye'll be content. Five sturdy bairns mine has given me, and four more that died young. See if ye can do as well."

"I'll do my best, sir." Nodding to the gillie offering to ladle hare soup from a basin to a wooden bowl, and to another about to fill his mug from the ale jug, he added, "I'd count myself lucky to sire such a family."

"First ye ha' to bed your bride, aye. And later, ye'll no be forgetting our Rosalie," Murray went on. "She'll need a husband one day, too, so if ye've any young noble friends as would like to try raiding my herds, ye can send them along to Elishaw when she's older."

"Perhaps you will explain something to me," Wat said amiably. "You have a fine herd of your own, so I must wonder why you raided mine. Reivers usually raid because they seek beef or milk for their families. You need nowt that I can see."

"Some seek adventure," Murray said with a twinkle.

"Do you think that's what I did? In troth, sir, I was ale-shot and angry, and came only to reclaim what was mine. My lads named you as the likely thief—forgive me if the word is harsh—but the tracks led us straight to Elishaw."

"Aye, sure," Murray said cheerfully. "I thought ye might come, for I'd seen ye at the races. I did think my lads would ha' to lie in the heather at least one night for nowt, though. Sithee, I'd seen how much ye'd been drinking and thought ye'd sleep a night first. And then mayhap . . ." He shrugged.

Wat frowned but lowered his voice as he said, "Did you mean this to happen then? To trap me into marrying the lady Margaret?"

Murray's frown matched his. "Nay, then. 'Twas later I decided to offer ye that. I'd ha' hanged ye, for ye'll no deny ye'd ha' taken my beasts along wi' yours."

"But why should I not have, if only to teach you not to take what was mine?" Wat heard his voice rising and warned himself that a battle, even of words, would gain him only more trouble. When Murray chose not to reply, he said more calmly, "I beg your pardon, sir, but surely you understand my confusion. You still have not said why you took them in the first place."

"'Tis a simple matter o' sharing the hardship," Murray said soberly. "When trouble comes, ye who live at a distance from the line ha' fair notice and can easily move your beasts and families out of harm's way. My beasts, on the other hand, nearly always serve to feed the invading army or raiders that precede it. This time, I chose to exact help from men who dinna keep a close eye on their beasts. Ye'd left yours untended in Rankilburn Glen."

"Theft is hardly a way to share trouble," Wat said indignantly.

"But 'tis only fair, ye'll agree, that the same folks shouldna ha' to feed the English army each time merely because they ha' the misfortune to lie in their path."

"If you thus provide them with more beef, I suspect

some would say you're supporting them, not just falling victim to them," Wat said, knowing Douglas would certainly say so.

"Ah, but ye see, they simply take what they want, as they will," Murray said. "This time my lads will drive my beasts north, leaving yours for the English to find so they willna go looking for mine. Ye'll just be sharing the hardship this once."

"The plain fact is that many who find themselves in Hotspur's path or that of any other English warriors do manage to move their beasts and families out of harm's way, and without stealing from their neighbors, or from folks who live nearly twenty miles away."

"Aye, well, mayhap ye can raise the matter at the next wardens' meeting," Murray said. "But for now, lad, though I've enjoyed our discussion, ye should eat your dinner. I canna doubt ye'll be needing your strength to see to your duty."

Resisting the urge to grind his teeth or growl at his host, Wat fixed his attention on his food.

⁓

Since the moment Sir Walter had leaned forward and caught her eye after his audacious retort to her father's teasing had nearly made her laugh aloud, Meg had caught no more than a glimpse of one hand or arm as he dealt with his meal. She heard his low-pitched voice and her father's, but except for a word here and there, the general din in the lower hall made it impossible to hear what they said.

Having detected what she suspected was an answering gleam of humor in his eyes, she wished she could watch as he talked with her father. However, at one point, she heard his voice rise on a note of displeasure if not outright anger, so perhaps it was as well that she could not hear them clearly.

She had little appetite, and for once her mother spoke not a word of criticism. Nor did Amalie make any effort to converse, other than making an occasional polite comment about the food. Meg had expected both of her sisters to plague her with questions, but other than to ask if Amalie would serve her another slice of lamb from the platter, even Rosalie remained silent.

Abruptly and in a tone no one could fail to hear, Sir Iagan said, "Well, lad, ye needna put it off any longer, for I warrant your lady wife is as eager as ye. So ye'd best be getting on with the bedding."

Meg's hand froze halfway to her mouth, the slice of apple between her fingers hovering unnoticed, her breathing likewise stopped, as she waited for Sir Walter's reply. Inside, organs roiled, making her wish she had eaten nothing.

"He will get on with it shortly, my lord," Lady Murray said with a smile. "First, you men must both give our Meg time to prepare herself. I shall go to her bedchamber with her myself to see that all is in readiness there." When she added as a clear afterthought, "Amalie, you may come, too," Meg realized that her mother had still not said whether Amalie was to accompany her to Rankilburn.

Exchanging a look with her sister, she arose to follow Lady Murray, pausing only long enough to give Rosalie a hug.

"May I not come with you then?" Rosalie asked. "I want to see, too."

"Dearling, there is naught to see," Meg said. "I am only

going to get ready to leave. I will see you again afterward, so you can bid me farewell."

Although Rosalie looked eager to debate the matter, a wary glance at their mother resulted in nodding obedience instead.

Lady Murray turned and strode from the dais, bringing minions in the hall hastily to their feet, to bow and curtsy as she passed.

Hurrying after her without casting even a glance in the direction of her father or her new husband, Meg caught up with her mother at the stair hall. "Prithee, madam," she said, "is Amalie to go with me then?"

"She is, aye," her mother said. "I thought your father must have told you he had decided she should go."

"No, he didn't," Meg replied, remembering something that he *had* said. "He won't set anyone to watch us whilst we bed, will he?"

"Nay," her ladyship said. "He'll be content with the evidence of the sheets."

"Evidence?" Meg said.

Chapter 5

⌒

"To fondle, or kiss her, I'll never be fain . . .
But cats they are all alike gray in the dark."

Having endured Murray's annoying comments with grim dignity, Wat approached the connubial chamber with what he hoped was similar and proper decorum. His nemesis bore him company right to the chamber door, making him wonder if the man did intend to watch.

Murray rapped three times, whereupon Lady Murray emerged.

"Is she ready?"

"She is," her ladyship replied. "I have already sent Amalie to wait in my solar. We should perhaps join her there."

"Aye, sure, unless ye think I ought to say a few words to our Meg first."

"I believe I have said all that is necessary," his lady replied. With a condescending nod to Wat, she added, "I am sure you know what to do, Sir Walter."

"I believe so, thank you," Wat said, hoping he spoke the truth and glad that his men were not there to witness the exchange. If they had been, he'd never have heard the end of it.

He wished his in-laws would go away, but both Murray and his lady lingered. At last, fearing they might decide they had better stay if he looked the least bit reluctant, Wat opened the door.

The chamber was dim despite the glow of several candles. It was chilly, too, without benefit of a fire to warm it. A dark curtain covered the lone window, but curtains framing the cupboard bed in the wall to his left stood open.

The bed looked empty, so he stepped inside. As he shut the door behind him, he shifted his gaze to his right.

She stood near a side table. She had taken off the gray mantle but she still wore the flimsy kirtle and the ugly crimped and fluted headdress. The latter looked too heavy for her slender body, as if a sapling bore a too-heavy crown.

"I thought you would be in bed," he said quietly.

She shook her head. "My lady mother thought you would prefer to . . ." She hesitated, but he waited, not moving, just watching her until at last she said, "She thought you would prefer to unwrap me yourself."

He liked the pleasantly musical sound of her voice, but her solemnity put him off. He cocked his head to one side. "Do you never smile, lass?"

"Aye, sure, I do," she replied, still somber. "But there has been naught today to make anyone smile."

"True enough," he admitted. "Although I did think at one point . . ."

She met his gaze then, and her lips twitched.

He saw the twinkle reappear and noted again the beauty of her eyes.

But she said only, "I was surprised you would speak so to my lord father."

"I think you approved, though," he said.

"I should not have done that," she said. "One should not laugh at one's father."

"Nay, but I own that I am occasionally tempted to laugh at mine."

"Are you? My mother told me Buccleuch is a fierce man."

"He is, aye. I said only that I'd been tempted to laugh. Better sense and stern childhood training always serve to prevent my actually doing it."

"Are you afraid of him, then? Should I be?"

"The answer to both questions is no," he said. "I respect him, and you will, too. I cannot deny that at times when I was younger I did fear him, but only when I knew I had angered him and deserved punishment."

"This will anger him," she said on a note of certainty.

He couldn't deny it. The thought of that anger tightened his stomach, but he could not in good conscience let her believe she should fear Buccleuch. Nor would he lie to her.

"'Tis true our marriage will displease him," he said. "But he will ken fine where to place the blame, and he will not lay an ounce of it on you."

"It may be otherwise with your lady mother," she said.

He hesitated, then said, "I did not think about that. In general, my father's state of mind concerns me more than my mother's, but you are right to consider hers. You will spend more time with her than I do, and she is aware that plans are in train for my marriage to a Douglas cousin. She approved of Fiona, because the lass is a kinswoman of hers, too, so this will not please her. She will resign herself to it, though, and she will not be inhospitable to you or to your sister."

"You know then that Amalie is to go with us."

"Aye, your father told me." With a smile, he added, "He suggested that I might also have the honor of taking your youngest sister as well."

"Mercy, I hope you refused," she said.

"I told him I'd liefer not, but I'll confess I feared he would insist. However, it occurred to him then that your mother might not like to lose you all at once."

Again, she gave that solemn nod, and he wondered if he had been mistaken in suspecting she possessed a sense of humor.

That was the least of his worries, however, because he did not feel the slightest stirring of sexual desire for her. The thought of fondling her or kissing her put him off, especially when she stood woodenly before him, gazing so steadily at him. Her eyes looked darker and larger than before, her lashes longer and thicker than any others he had seen. In truth, she did have beautiful eyes, but he would have felt more comfortable had he been trying to imagine himself hugging a post.

"What must I do?" she asked.

"Did your mother not tell you?"

"She said only that I should do whatever you say."

To his surprise, a tingling sensation stirred below at the notion of having her wholly at his command. That he could tell her to do anything he liked, that she would have to obey him . . .

He pondered a future of such total obedience. Then the image of her as she had spoken her first words to him intervened, looming large in his mind's eye.

The young woman who had said she had no wish to marry him had not struck him as subservient. That young woman had known her own mind.

Even so, if they were going to accomplish what they had to accomplish, perhaps he ought to explore the possibilities a little further.

"Did your mother say aught else?" he asked.

"Only that no one would watch us because my father would judge the results by the sheets. I do not know how that can be so, but mayhap you do."

He did, and he realized that he ought to have expected some such test. True consummation of a man with a maiden usually did provide certain expected results. Moreover, they were both young and healthy, and he was normally virile. They should be able to achieve those results without such hesitation and shuffling about.

A memory stirred then of a favorite tutor who had introduced him to some of the lesser-known works of Greek and Latin scholars, including Plutarch's *Conjugal Precepts,* in which the great moralist had written that "when the candles are out, all women are fair."

"*Do* you know what my mother meant?" Margaret asked bluntly.

"Aye, and I'm thinking we'd best get on with it," he said. "It would be as well to get into bed, perhaps."

"Will you unwrap me, then?" she asked.

Since the kirtle's bodice laced up the front, he nearly asked if she could not undress herself before it occurred to him that touching her might stimulate him. She was female, after all, and only a bit plain-looking, not hideous.

He stepped nearer, eyeing the horrible headdress. "Is that thing on your head pinned to it in any way, or does it just lift off?" he asked.

"There are two pins," she said. "But I'll pull them out for you if you like."

He nodded, watched her do so, and then lifted the headdress carefully, half-expecting it to catch in her hair. But it came off easily, and he saw that one reason for its mass was the amount of hair wrapped around her head underneath it.

As she reached to deal with the pins keeping the mass of hair in place, she said, "I'm glad to have it off. That coif is very tight."

"Then my first command as your husband is that you must never wear it again," he said.

"Pray, sir, do not be silly. I do not have so many that I can simply discard one, especially my best one. It was a dreadful price when my mother had it made, being so elaborate. 'Tis called a nebula and was so dear because of all those turned-up ruffles and the rows and rows of crimping and fluting required for its veil."

"I don't care about the price," he said, watching in fascination as she went on to remove what seemed to be dozens of pins from her hair. Clearly, it took many, many more to confine the tresses beneath the coif, than to hold the coif itself.

She stared at him in similar fascination and said, "Do you *never* count cost?"

He grinned. "Do you imagine yourself becoming a great spendthrift, my lady? I warn you, I can be as tight-fisted as any man when the occasion warrants it. Nevertheless, my wife will be dressed as befits her station. If I think you are growing too costly, I will tell you so. Until then, you must tell me what you need and I'll pay for it. But I do not want to see that headdress again."

Although her eyes widened, she said nothing. She still

held both hands close to her head, controlling the heavy coils of hair with a seemingly magical pressure of fingers and forearms as she plucked the last pins away. Her movements were deft and well practiced but nonetheless enthralling. He could not tell how she managed to pull out pins, hold them all, and yet keep the coiled tresses in place as she did.

He had never watched a woman do such a thing before. The lasses he had hitherto known in any physical sense had been willing maidservants and their ilk, with their hair simply veiled or hanging in loose plaits.

She lowered her hands at last, releasing the coils of hair, and the thick mass of it tumbled down around her in a flow of smooth, dark, shining waves that shimmered with golden highlights in the candles' glow. The long tresses cloaked her from the crown of her head to a few inches below the outward flare of her hips.

Obeying an irresistible impulse, he touched her hair, finding it silky soft and warm from its confinement. He stroked it gently, nearly pulling back his hand when he recalled that she was a lady, and then continuing, reminding himself that she was his wife to treat as he pleased.

Hoping again that lust would awaken in response to opportunity, he reached for the long, narrow band of embroidered linen that rested low on her hips and served as a girdle to belt the skirt of her kirtle where it flared out below her tight-fitting bodice. The girdle's flat knot was easily untied, as was the bow that fastened the bodice's tight laces. He began nimbly to unlace it.

She stood unmoving until he shifted the long strands of hair hanging down the front of her gown back out of his way and pulled the silk bodice-laces from the last two aglets at the top. She drew a deep breath then, and the two sides of her bodice fell open to reveal the loose kirtle top and plain linen shift underneath. Both had simple white-ribbon ties, and he dealt with the kirtle's first.

Cut lower than kirtle or bodice, the shift revealed more décolletage than he had expected. The lass had breasts!

Her tight bodice had deceived him, and he proceeded more eagerly, pushing the kirtle and sleeveless bodice off her shoulders and tugging the kirtle's tight sleeves down her arms and off over her hands until the stiff bodice and flimsy kirtle fell together in a crumpled puddle around her feet.

Returning to the ribbon that gathered the top of the shift, he untied it and spread the gathers to slip it off her, whereupon the shift followed the rest and she stood naked before him in the candlelight.

She was reed-slender, to be sure, but her soft breasts and hips rounded as they should. Her breasts sat high with impertinent tips. Their globes were large enough to fill a man's hands, and her waist was small.

Both breasts bore red marks from their tight confinement beneath unavoidable wrinkles in the kirtle, but they look softly inviting nonetheless, and the candles' glow turned her skin to pale gold.

She had not said a word, and he wanted to hear her voice.

"Do you ken what men and women do to couple?" he asked.

"Aye, in general I do, but I have never watched anyone coupling."

"Go and get into bed," he said.

She turned and walked away from him without comment, her carriage as graceful as it had been in the hall when she was fully clothed. Her hair in back was a bit longer, covering her to the tops of her thighs, and he was sorry it did. He would have liked to watch the movement of her buttocks.

Still, his body was no more than half-awake. He knew of things she could do to awaken it further, but he hesitated to give such commands to her.

As he reminded himself again that she was bound by her vows to do his bidding, it occurred to him that he did not want to command her every time the urge to couple struck him. He decided he'd do better to introduce her to sexual activities in a way that would persuade her of their pleasures, if only for his own benefit.

Accordingly, he stripped off his clothing, snuffed all but one of the candles, and strode toward the bed.

Sitting up with the covers to her waist, Meg reached back and swept her hair forward over her left shoulder so she could plait it and keep it from entangling her in bed. As she did, she watched him undress. When he snuffed the candles and moved toward her, she wondered if he could detect the tumultuous pounding of her heart or the way her nerves tingled, or when the breath stopped in her throat.

She had seen from the start, well before he had tidied himself, that he was handsome, lithely muscled, and broad shouldered. But she had not realized until he stood beside her while they recited their vows that he was a head taller than she, as if some of his forebears were Norse instead of the usual Borderer's Pictish ones.

And whether it was from Norsemen or Picts that he had inherited his temperament, she thought now that her mother had likely been right in assessing his demeanor as stubborn but wrong in calling him implacable. He had submitted to the marriage, after all, if only to protect his men and the boy.

She liked his infectious smile. His teeth were strong and white, and his body in movement had the feline grace of a man whose every sinew and muscle was ever ready for battle. He also seemed kind, though, and she had not expected kindness.

"What is it?" he asked as he reached the bed.

She shook her head, feeling heat in her cheeks and knowing she blushed because she had been evaluating him and did not want to tell him so.

"It is nothing," she said when he continued to gaze at her.

She was already coming to know that look. When he asked a question, he did not repeat it. He just waited for her to answer it.

Realizing that she was biting her lower lip, she focused on the last few twists of her hair before she said, "You are being very kind to me. I was wondering why."

He shrugged and pulled back the quilt. "This marriage is none of your doing, my lady. I'd be a brute to visit my feelings about it on you."

Remembering her conversation with Amalie, she said, "You would not be the first man to take out his anger on his wife."

"Perhaps not," he said. "But in troth, I've no wish to become such a man."

The words were reassuring, but experience with Simon and her father warned her that one ought never to trust words. She would reserve her judgment.

Then there was no more time to think, because he had climbed into the bed as stark naked as she was and with a

look of intent that told her better than words that the time
had come. She could not help seeing, even in the faint
glow of just one candle, that the part of him intended for
the task did not look like much to fear.

"Should I lie flat?" she asked.

"Stay as you are for a few moments. You have very
nice bubbies, lass."

"Do I?" She had thought them ordinary.

"Aye," he said, reaching to stroke the one nearest him.
The touch of his fingertips sent a shiver through her although she was not at all cold.

"These marks," he said, stroking one. "Do you always
get them?"

"Not always. That kirtle is loose fitting and the bodice
very tight. My mother says a tight fit is more becoming
and a lady should ignore the discomfort it creates."

"Properly fitted, though, should clothing not be
comfortable?"

She thought for a moment, then admitted, "I don't
know. My sister and I usually wear clothes that my mother's seamstress has cut from her old ones. Her knowledge
of fashion—the seamstress's—does seem limited. Then,
too, my mother travels less frequently these days than she
did in the past. In days before the last invasion she visited
her kinsmen in Northumberland whenever opportunity
arose."

"Your father told me she was English and had powerful kinsmen but not who those kinsmen are," he said, still
lightly stroking her breast.

Meg tensed. She had believed he knew, that everyone knew her mother's connections, that just mentioning
Northumberland ought to have reminded him.

She saw that his eyes had narrowed.

"What is it?" he asked her.

"I warrant you won't like it," she said with a sigh.

"Faith, don't tell me she's a Percy or a Neville, or—" He broke off, then shook his head. "You jumped half a foot then, I swear, so it must be one of those. Sakes, you said Northumberland, so it could be both, since Northumberland's earl married a Neville. Still, it must be Percy. Just tell me she is not Hotspur's sister."

Meg nearly laughed, except that it was no laughing matter. But the stiff look on his face sobered her quickly. "She is indeed kin to the Percies, but you must know she cannot be his sister," she said. "Sir Harry is much nearer your age than hers, sir, although he is already one of England's finest warriors. Sir Harry and the English king are nearly the same age and were knighted on the same day."

"Are you such an expert on England and the English then, my lady?"

His hand had stopped stroking, and the hard note in his voice caused her to say hastily, "No, sir. I do apologize if I spoke of things I ought not."

"You may speak of whatever you like to me," he said. "But I do not recommend praising the English, especially Hotspur, to just anyone."

His fingers began to move again, causing her to gasp when one drifted idly across her left nipple.

"Do you like that?" he asked, doing it again.

"I . . . I have never felt such a feeling before." As she spoke, she stiffened, but not because of anything he did. "Did you hear a noise just then?"

"Aye," he said, his tone grim. "Someone is outside the door. I'd have no fear in wagering good money that it is your father."

"I'm sure you are right," she said. "I wish you were

not, though. It makes me most uncomfortable to think he may be out there."

"Believe me, lass, it is doing nothing good for me, either," he said. He drew a deep breath. "Look here, what do you say we continue this . . . ah . . . discussion of ours when we reach Scott's Hall?"

"Scott's Hall? I don't understand. Is your home not called Rankilburn?"

"We do call that part of Ettrick Forest Rankilburn, but my home is nowt but a rough peel tower in a cleuch off Rankilburn Glen and is no place for one lady, let alone for two of you. I've no time to do much about it, either, because I'll be joining the Douglas soon to go after your cousin Hotspur before he can come after us. So meantime, I shall leave you with my lady mother at Scott's Hall in the glen."

"Just your mother?"

"Aye, plus dozens of servants and men-at-arms to look after and protect you. Sithee, my father will likewise be with the Douglas. But you'll get on well with my mother. Doubtless you'll meet my sister Jenny, too, and I know you'll like her. I hope the two of you will become good friends."

"I should like very much to be friends with your sister," she said. "But do you truly mean for us to leave here today?"

"As soon as we can get dressed and mount our horses."

"What about . . ." She hesitated, suddenly shy, then said, "What of the sheets?"

"Aye, the sheets." He had clearly forgotten, because he frowned, then said, "The evidence your father will seek is the blood from your maidenhead."

"Blood?"

"Aye, for a maiden bleeds when she is first taken, but although I am not sure I can do my part properly with your father standing impatiently outside the door, I could do much the same thing with my fingers and—I believe—at the very least, produce such evidence as he will demand."

"Then, pray do so, sir, for I can hear him pacing. Before long, he will push the door open and demand to know what we are doing."

Wat could hear the old devil pacing, too. In other circumstances he might have gone out and demanded to know what Murray meant by such behavior. As it was, he just wanted to put Elishaw Castle behind him as soon as he could.

Accordingly, he moved his hand to the juncture of her legs and, feeling her stiffen, cupped her mound gently to acquaint her with the touch of his hand.

Sir Iagan coughed just outside the door.

"I'll kill him," Wat muttered.

"I hope not," Meg whispered, clearly worried that he might. "Just do what you must, and quickly."

"If I insert my fingers too hastily, I'm likely to hurt you," he said. "They are not made as well for the purpose as . . . as other parts of a man's body. But with that part of mine as useless as it presently seems to be . . ."

"Is there naught I might do to help?"

"Aye, you could, but one does not expect maidens to know much about such things. On the contrary, one expects them to be hesitant to—"

"Pray, sir, he will be upon us at any minute," she murmured more urgently. "If there is aught I can do, tell me!"

"Touch me." Catching her hand in his, he slid up next to her on his side. "Here," he said, showing her. "Use your fingers lightly, even your lips or tongue—"

Feeling her tense and hearing her gasp, he said, "Never mind that. Just grasp me and stroke me gently until you feel me begin to swell in your hand."

As soon as her warm fingers embraced him, he felt himself stir and begin to harden. She must have felt it, too, because he heard her indrawn breath again, but she did not take her hand away.

He shut his eyes, focusing on the sensations she stirred and trying to shut out increasingly intrusive noises from the landing.

He would kill the old bastard, so help— A moan escaped him when her gentle ministrations produced an unexpected wave of pleasure.

She released him, drawing a second moan—this time of protest.

"Did I hurt you?"

"Nay, lassie, nowt of the sort. Don't stop!"

"But it's getting so swollen! I didn't know!"

He wanted to beg her again to continue. But he realized he was in a condition now that would allow him to do what needed doing—if he could just ignore the increasingly impatient noises beyond the door.

"I can do what I must, but we'll have these pillows out to make it easier for both of us," he said pulling pillows from behind her to let her lie flat.

"What must I do?"

"Just lie still. I'll try not to hurt you, but there is bound to be discomfort."

"Just do it, sir. I *don't* want him to come in."

"I don't think he will," Wat said. "More likely, he'll pound on the door first and bellow. But that would put me right off, so we'd best get on with it."

He slid into position atop her, gripping himself now to ease his way in.

In the dim light, he could barely see her expression, but she had her lips pressed tightly together, which told him she had no intention of protesting anything he did. The thought made him exert himself more to avoid hurting her.

As he pressed gently into her, the hot dampness of her passage enclosing him did more to stimulate him than her fingers had. Rigid and heavily swollen now, he pressed harder, eliciting a mew of protest.

"Sorry, lass."

She was small, and he was not, and when she squeaked again, he knew he was hurting her, but he dared not stop. He had never taken a maiden before, but he had heard other men talk of such experiences. So, when he met the expected resistance, he pushed harder. Resistance gave way, and the damp warmth increased as her passageway gripped softly, tightly around him.

He shifted his weight, letting instinct take over as he thrust firmly into her, feeling her contract tightly, the heat of her body burning his as if to challenge him to conquer her. Shifting to gain purchase on the sheets, he raised his hips and thrust again, faster, harder, gasping until release came at last and he collapsed atop her.

She made no sound, but he felt her soft breath against

his cheek, telling him he hadn't killed her. Knowing they had succeeded brought a new sense of release.

Another cough sounded from the landing.

"He ought to do something about that cough," Wat muttered.

"He does not need to cough," she said. "He suffers only from impatience."

"I'd happily put him out of his misery."

"I don't doubt it, sir, but just now, perhaps you might be so kind as to shift your weight so that I may breathe more easily."

He obliged her but felt so limp and sated that he wanted only to sleep.

"We might also think about getting up," she said a moment later. "I'm all sticky, and I'd like to clean myself. Also, if we are going to reach Rankilburn . . ."

He sighed when she paused. "I hope you are not going to be one of those wives always threaping at a man to do this and do that," he said.

"No, sir, it shall be as you please. If you prefer to stay here another night . . ."

Her ready submission irritated him, and for no reason that he could fathom. But he could hardly say so without sounding daft, so he exerted himself to get up.

"My mother put some washcloths yonder on the stand," she said. "And there is water in the ewer, although I doubt it can still be warm."

"Shall I fetch you a cloth?" he asked, uncertain what the rules were for this part of the business. "Do you need assistance?"

"No, thank you," she said. "If you will tend to your own needs and then grant me some privacy to attend to mine, I shall be most grateful."

"Aye, sure," he said, relieved. He took care of himself swiftly and competently, and when he was dressed, he went to the door and jerked it open.

Murray stood facing him expectantly. "Are ye done?" he asked cheerfully.

"Aye, we are, no thanks to you," Wat said grimly.

"Well, then, I'll just be going inside now to—"

"No, sir, you will not," Wat said, gripping him by a shoulder and pushing him toward the stairway. "The evidence is there for you to see, but you will have the goodness now to allow my wife the privacy to look after herself. Indeed, if you would be of real use, send a maid-servant up to help her dress. I want to be away from this place as soon as I can."

Murray glowered at him for a long, blessedly silent moment. But then, with a sharp nod, he headed down the winding stairs.

Satisfied, Wat glanced at the closed door to the bedchamber.

Everything had gone well enough in the end, he decided, so perhaps this unintended bride of his would not trouble him overmuch after all.

His father-in-law reinforced that belief by being so pleased with himself and the success of the forced marriage that he returned Wat's two sleuthhounds, declaring them to be his wedding present to the bride and groom.

Thus reassured, Wat spent much of the long journey to Scott's Hall imagining conversational gambits that might persuade Buccleuch that this marriage could prove useful to them.

His bride spoke little, but she sat her horse well and made no complaint. Her sister, too, was well behaved, and both seemed to take interest in the passing countryside.

They followed a track through Wauchope Forest, skirting the fells, then passed through Liddesdale north of Hermitage Castle and into Ewesdale.

The weather was fine and springlike with the sun shining so brightly that entering the deep shade of Ettrick Forest came as a relief. They still had an hour more to ride, and by the time they reached the Hall, the Forest was growing dusky.

Sym Elliot had chosen to walk or run with the dogs more than he rode, and Wat did not blame him. He doubted the lad found sitting a saddle at all comfortable.

The reality of his own situation evaded his notice right up to the moment that he and his lady and the rest of their party rode through the gates of the Hall and into the graveled courtyard.

"What a lot of horses your father keeps in his yard," Margaret said then.

There certainly were a lot of them, too many. One was a splendid bay with a lightning-shaped blaze on its face. Wat recognized it instantly, for the beast was as well known in the Borders as its master was.

The Earl of Douglas had come to Scott's Hall.

Chapter 6

$\sim$

*"To him men in arms are the same thing as thistles . . .
At Durham and Carlisle his prowess I saw . . ."*

Although they had come twenty miles since leaving
Elishaw at two o'clock, the sun had just dipped below the
horizon, because days were growing longer. So Meg had
a clear view of the three stone towers that formed three
sides of the broad courtyard at Scott's Hall. Ten-foot walls
connected the towers, but each tower had its own entry. A
strong, iron-barred gate had opened to admit them.

Meg rode beside Amalie behind Sir Walter. Having
been unnaturally aware of his lithe, muscular body just
ahead of them throughout the journey, Meg easily noted
now that something about the bustling activity in the yard
had surprised, perhaps even dismayed him.

"What is it, sir?" she asked.

"Jamie Douglas is here," he said without looking at her.

Briefly confused until she realized that only one Douglas would presently concern him, she said, "The *Earl* of Douglas?" When he nodded, still studying the courtyard scene, she followed his gaze as she added, "Does he come here often?"

"He has come many times before," he said. "But of late, he's been staying nearby at Hermitage, so he usually sends for us to meet him there."

She knew of Hermitage Castle, of course, for it was the greatest of the great Border strongholds and Elishaw was but seven or eight miles from it. Moreover, they had cut through the hills just north of it on their way to the Hall.

She glanced at Amalie, who had drawn rein beside her. But her sister's restless gaze was moving speculatively over men in the courtyard. Meg hoped she did not mean to begin a flirtation with any of the Douglas's men-at-arms or Buccleuch's.

The responsibility for Amalie seemed suddenly heavy, but Meg told herself she would feel better after a good night's rest.

She was tired, for they had stopped only once, when Amalie had insisted on answering a call of nature. Sir Walter's men had been respectful, though, and Meg felt safe with them. Young Sym Elliot had ridden beside them for a time, his curiosity about them overflowing. When he announced that he was to serve Meg until she did not want him anymore, then dared to ask her why she had married Sir Walter, he had earned himself a sharp rebuke from his master.

The lad had retired then to ride beside a large man who

was apparently his brother, and Meg had been sorry. She had enjoyed his careless chatter.

"Will you let me help you down, my lady?"

Startled, she realized Sir Walter had dismounted while she was watching the bustle around them. He stood by her mount now, ready to assist her.

"Thank you, sir," she said, turning so she could rest her hands on his shoulders as he lifted her down. His grip was firm at her waist, and he lifted her as easily as if she weighed no more than her bed pillow.

As he set her on her feet, his hands suddenly gripped harder, then relaxed as quickly. Following his gaze, she saw two men striding across the yard toward them. She had never seen either one of them before, but she had no difficulty deducing who they were and swiftly curtsied.

Beside her, Amalie did the same, and Meg realized that her sister had either dismounted by herself or had accepted help from one of the other men.

Then a voice eerily like Sir Walter's spoke curtly, saying, "What in the devil's name have you been doing, Wat?"

Meg had lowered her gaze as she made her curtsy, but she peeked up under her lashes at the speaker looming over her and saw an older version of her husband.

"My lords, may I present my wife, the lady Margaret Murray of Elishaw?" Sir Walter said as if the introduction were an ordinary one. "This is the Earl of Douglas, my lady," he added, gesturing toward the dark and frowning young man with Buccleuch. "And this is my lord father."

James Douglas was not what Meg had expected. Although she knew that men of power were not always men of great age, she had assumed he would be older. She saw now that he could not have many more than thirty summers behind him. His hair was dark and shaggy, his skin likewise dark, and as he drew nearer, she discerned authority and an intelligent mind behind his deep-set dark eyes.

His strong jaw was set hard. The Douglas, plainly, was angry.

Buccleuch, on the other hand, revealed no expression as he said politely, "I think we may allow this young lady to rise now, my lord."

"Aye, sure," Douglas said. "Forgive me, Lady Margaret. So unexpected a meeting has made me forget my manners." He held out his hand, and she placed hers in it, allowing him to assist her.

"It is an honor to meet you, my lord," she said. "And you, sir," she added, looking at Buccleuch. "May I present my sister, the lady Amalie?"

Buccleuch nodded to Amalie, then ordered gillies to see to their horses. "We'll go inside," he said. "Clearly, we have much to discuss."

Douglas nodded grimly.

Meg glanced at Sir Walter, but he had his lips pressed together. Easily deducing that he would not welcome comment, she made none.

Amalie, too, had the good sense to remain silent.

Wee Sym began to chatter to someone in the yard, excitedly bragging about his great adventure. His older brother sternly silenced him.

The bustle in the yard quieted, too, as men turned to watch curiously.

Ignoring them as the others did, Meg hurried with Sir Walter in the wake of Buccleuch and Douglas to the central tower's entrance.

Inside, as they mounted well-worn stone steps, she

judged that this tower was the keep. And when they entered the great hall at the first landing, she saw at once that, despite the Hall's stout wall and gate, it was a comfortable dwelling.

Gillies were laying out straw pallets, much as they would be doing at Elishaw at that hour, but all the bustle and noise had been left outside. Men-at-arms and servants might sleep in the hall, but they did not live there or leave their belongings lying about. The rushes on the floor seemed admirably fresh, too.

A cheerful fire burned on the hearth near the dais table. And no sooner had they entered than a plump, matronly looking noblewoman wearing a plum-colored side-surcoat over a russet gown entered through an archway at the far end.

Seeing them, she paused until her gaze met Meg's. Then it shifted swiftly to Sir Walter, and a frown creased her brow.

Buccleuch turned a sour look on his son. "You must introduce the lady Margaret to your mother and mayhap suggest that she show her to your chamber."

Turning then to Meg without awaiting a reply, he added with a charming smile, "I know you will forgive us for abandoning you so soon after your arrival, my lady, but we have important matters to discuss. Walter's duty to the Douglas requires that he take part in our discussion, but his lady mother will be pleased to show you to his chamber and help you with any arrangements you may require."

"Thank you, my lord," Meg said, making another deep curtsy but watching her husband out of the corner of her eye as she did.

He looked wary and on edge, but he waited patiently

for her to rise. Then, telling his father he would be back straightaway, he offered her an arm.

As they walked toward Lady Scott with Amalie close behind them, Meg felt him tense more with each step.

Her ladyship's eyes had narrowed.

Meg straightened her shoulders and lifted her chin. She had no idea if propriety demanded that a bride meeting her mother-in-law for the first time act in any unusual way, but she did know that she wanted to get on well with hers. Coming from a long line of proud women and having a good deal of pride herself, Meg had no trouble understanding that she stood in her mother-in-law's house.

She also knew enough not to speak until Lady Scott spoke to her.

When they reached her, Sir Walter said, "Madam, I cast myself on your mercy. I have brought the lady Margaret and her sister Amalie to stay at the Hall, where they can be safe until we have rid this area of the English threat."

Meg swept a deep curtsy at the word "madam," and was grateful that Amalie silently followed her example.

Lady Scott said, "From whence do you and your sister come, Lady Margaret?"

"They are Murray of Elishaw's daughters," Sir Walter interjected evenly, sparing Meg the need to reply. "More to the point, though," he added, "the lady Margaret is my wife."

Looking up at her involuntary hostess to see with a sinking heart that Lady Scott's stern but curious expression had changed in a blink to one of shock, Meg said as she arose slowly from her curtsy, "It is an honor to meet your ladyship."

"Your mother was Annabel Percy, was she not?" Lady Scott said.

"Aye, madam, before she married my father," Meg said.

"She is the Earl of Northumberland's kinswoman."

"Aye, they are second cousins."

Lady Scott turned to her son. "Bless us, Walter, what *have* you done?"

Unexpected anger surged through Meg. "By my troth, madam, it was not—"

"I have married, Mother; that is what I have done," he said, cutting Meg off. "I know you will treat my wife and her sister kindly, as this is none of their doing."

"Indeed," Lady Scott said acidly. "One of your men came here yestereve spinning a tale of how you rode to Elishaw to recover lost stock and fell captive to Elishaw's master. Do you mean to tell me that tale was a falsehood?"

"It is true," he said. "Whilst I was at Langholm, Murray lifted my kine, as well as several horses and two hounds. When I went to reclaim them, he captured seven of us, including Wee Sym Elliot, and threatened to hang us. He said we could live only if I'd agree to marry his daughter and do so at once."

Reading her ladyship's grim expression, Meg feared she would say she had liefer Sir Iagan had hanged him.

Instead, Lady Scott looked past Sir Walter to Buccleuch and Douglas. Then she said briskly, "If you mean to leave your young ladies here, I must see to providing them with bedchambers, so you may leave them in my charge now and rejoin your father and Douglas. They are eager to talk with you, and mayhap can provide a solution for this awkward coil of yours."

Meg felt a shiver of anxiety when Sir Walter nodded

and turned away without another word. Did he also view their marriage as just an awkward coil?

"I wager you've had naught to eat, either of you," Lady Scott said. "I'll give orders to my people to attend to that before I show you where you will sleep."

She was scarcely beyond earshot when Amalie said, "I shan't be surprised to find myself sleeping in a cellar. What a horrid woman!"

"Keep such thoughts to yourself," Meg said sternly. "She expected him to marry a cousin of the Douglas. Think how you'd feel if in the midst of arranging a great marriage for your son, he married another woman without a word to you."

Amalie shrugged. "That is no reason to be mean to us."

"If you want to go home, I will arrange it tomorrow," Meg said.

"Don't be a dafty! As if I'd leave you to face such a harridan alone!"

Stifling a sigh, Meg wondered how much comfort her younger sister would provide. By the look of things, she was likely to create even more distress.

⁓

Wat strode toward his father and Douglas, hoping he looked more confident than he felt and that his unease was not apparent to everyone in the hall. His mother thought he'd made a muck of things, but despite her displeasure, she was not unkind or unfair. She would make Margaret and her sister comfortable.

His father would not take out his anger on them either, but neither would he spare Wat. On the contrary, since manners had forced Buccleuch to keep his temper in check with the ladies present, Wat braced himself for an explosion.

The Douglas's presence did not help. Although Wat had known he'd have to face each of them on his return, he had not expected to face them both together.

Their stern, steady gazes seemed to sear him as he crossed the hall, but when he reached them, his father said only, "We'll talk upstairs in my chamber."

Wat followed the two of them into the stair hall and up to the next landing, where his father's private chamber lay. Buccleuch unlatched and pushed open the door, then stood back for Douglas to precede them.

The chamber was utilitarian, and Wat had never associated it with comfort of any sort. But with Douglas and Buccleuch dominating it and, however temporarily, restraining their tempers, the room seemed smaller than ever.

Douglas sat on the back-stool behind the table where Buccleuch usually sat to interview or berate those who came before him there. And, as Wat shut the door, Buccleuch moved to stand against the wall facing the table.

Douglas said grimly, "I have known you long enough, Wat, to doubt that you meant to insult my cousin Fiona. Still, I would hear as much from your own lips."

A shiver shot up Wat's spine. He had known Douglas well since childhood and generally thought of him as Jamie when they were together, because the two were but five years apart and their fathers had been good friends. But the black look Douglas gave him now revealed little of friendship.

He met that look and said, "I meant no insult, my lord. Murray gave me a choice, marriage or hanging. He swore to hang my lads one after the other before me, beginning with Wee Sym Elliot, who had followed us to see where we'd go."

"I trust the lad will not do that when you follow me," Douglas said.

"No, my lord," Wat said. Remembering the thrashing Dod had given Sym, he doubted the boy would try following them anywhere for a long time to come.

"I'll set aside all notion of insult then," Douglas said. "But tell me more of this incident. In particular, what were you doing at Elishaw?"

Wat began to describe the loss of his beasts and his intent to reclaim them. But he did not get far before the Douglas temper erupted.

"We have rules for sorting out such disagreements, do we not? Wardens' meetings and their ilk?"

"Aye, we do, but—"

"But me no buts, Wat! I made it clear to everyone on this side of the line that I want no conflict amongst our own whilst I organize my army and lead carefully planned forays across the line to discourage the English from returning here."

"Aye, sure, Jamie, but sithee—"

"When they do come," Douglas went on relentlessly, "I mean to show the Earl of Northumberland, his damned son Hotspur, and the English king that they challenge me at their peril. I'll need daring men and fast horses, and I've been counting on you for both. But now you've played me a trick that could endanger all."

He did not raise his voice but went on at length, his words and tone blistering. Wat stood there silently to hear it, aware that his father still leaned against the wall, arms folded across his chest, awaiting his turn.

Resentment flared when Douglas said he wondered now if he could trust him or his judgment. But as sorely as Wat yearned to defend himself, he knew better. He knew, too, despite the voice in his head urging him to fight back, that he had earned every lashing word. Had he stayed home, he would not be enduring this now. He had known from the moment Murray's men rose out of the concealing heather that he had only himself to blame. Even so, hearing Jamie Douglas say so was nearly as painful as was knowing that his own father agreed with every word.

But when Douglas said that perhaps Wat ought to stay behind when they next engaged the English, Wat said, "No, my lord. It is my duty—"

"Be silent," Douglas said, rising swiftly to put his hands on the table and lean closer. "You will hear all I have to say to you. Afterward, I *may* let you try to persuade me that you are *not* a hotheaded sapskull and can control that damned temper of yours well enough to follow my orders. If you cannot, by God, you will stay home until I give you leave to do otherwise. Do you understand me?"

"Aye, my lord," Wat said. But Jamie's usually dark complexion had paled when he had risen so quickly, and his color had not returned. Beads of sweat lined his upper lip, and despite Wat's wariness, he eyed his old friend with concern.

"Forgive me, my lord," he added then. "Are you unwell?"

Douglas shook his head, but as he did, he drew in a long breath. "In troth, I ate something that made me sick yesterday and was weak as a kitten afterward. I felt better this morning, though, and thought the sickness had passed."

"We'll have supper as soon as we've finished here,"

Buccleuch said. "I trow you'll feel better after you eat something."

"Aye, sure," Douglas said. As he took his seat again, he looked back at Wat. "I hope you won't disappoint me like this again."

"I won't," Wat promised.

"As to this curst marriage of his," Buccleuch said, "I don't doubt his account of it, Jamie, and I know you don't either. Murray forced the marriage on him and doubtless on the lass as well. I'm thinking we can lawfully demand its annulment."

The two exchanged a thoughtful look. But although Wat had briefly hoped that one or the other might demand an annulment, since Scottish law forbade any marriage performed under duress, he said, "I can't let you do that. I promised Murray I'd marry his daughter if he freed my men. He did, so I must keep my word."

"Aye, you must," Douglas agreed just as Wat recalled what else he had promised Murray. "This is no time to be making demands of the Kirk," Douglas went on. "Moreover, even the suggestion of an annulment now could stir Murray to outright betrayal. His lands are more at risk than most, and men of Elishaw have switched sides before."

"As have many others," Buccleuch said. "I hold my lands, and you hold many of yours, including Hermitage, because of just such expedient decisions."

"True," Douglas acknowledged. He turned back to Wat. "You do have every right to file a grievance against Murray for your kine. Demand that he return all of your beasts or pay for them, and demand as well that he provide his daughter with a proper dowry. But you must do it properly at the next wardens' meeting."

"I will, my lord," Wat said. Then, before he could lose

courage, he said, "I also promised that I'd not take up arms against Murray and will ride to his aid if he sends for me, as long as you or my father are not the ones attacking him."

To his surprise, Douglas nodded and said, "'Tis a common promise to exact in such a case."

Profoundly relieved, Wat added, "I'm sorry about the lady Fiona, Jamie. I'd not want to think I'd hurt her with this unfortunate business."

Douglas grimaced ruefully. "You can put that fear out of your head. She told me you were the last man on earth she wanted for a husband. Too hot at hand, she said, and would try to rule everyone in your ambit. She'd have married you, of course, because I'd ordered it. But you'd have had your hands full, my lad."

Wat sent a prayer of thanks heavenward, but his ordeal had not ended.

Buccleuch said, "I'll have someone show you to a chamber where you can rest before we sup, Jamie." When Douglas shook his head, he added, "Humor me, my lord. You outrank me, but by agreeing, you will spare me the necessity of asking you to await me in the hall. I've some few things of my own to say, and I want to say them whilst he still burns from your rebukes. He would doubtless prefer that you not bear witness to it, and although he deserves no such forbearance . . ."

"Almost do you tempt me to stay," Douglas said with a slight smile when Buccleuch paused. "In troth, though, a nap does have some appeal."

"Mayhap you should spend the night," Buccleuch said.

"Nay, though I thank you for the invitation," he said

as he got to his feet again. "I mean to ride to Teviothead tonight and on to Hermitage in the morning."

Wat noted that he stood more cautiously this time. Apparently, Buccleuch noted it, too, for he said, "I'll show you to that chamber myself, my lord. The small one just off the next landing will serve. You wait here, Wat," he added curtly.

When they had gone, Wat decided he'd be wiser not to sit while he waited. If Buccleuch were to return and find him taking his ease . . .

The vision that rose to mind was one that had repeated itself over the years, and it still had power to make him wince. He had time to remember a number of other such scenes before the click of the latch announced his father's return.

Wat faced him. They were of similar height, but Buccleuch was heavier. He still rode like the devil's own, though, and was as fierce a warrior as any Wat knew, saving Douglas and mayhap himself. A flashing memory of Douglas taking *him* to task for *his* temper nearly made him smile, but he did not let it show.

"What *were* you thinking?" Buccleuch demanded as he shut the door.

"I was not thinking at all, sir," Wat admitted. "When I learned that my herd was gone and Murray was the likely thief—" Fury stirred anew at the memory, and he added recklessly, "Faith, sir, you'd have followed them yourself in the old days."

"These are *not* the old days, and your liege lord has forbidden such behavior until we have routed the English."

Wat held his tongue then while Buccleuch gave free rein to his and proved that Douglas had not said nearly half of what there was to say about the matter.

His father's lengthy reprimand made Wat glad again that he was too old for skelping. When he finally escaped, he felt nearly as wrung out and humbled as he had in earlier days after such a session.

Under orders to make himself presentable before he joined his mother and the others for supper, he went to his bedchamber and entered without recalling the likelihood that he had acquired a roommate.

He stopped short at the sight of his wife standing near the hearth in her shift. Her arms and feet were bare. Her hair hung in thick, lustrous waves to her hips.

~

Meg heard the latch and managed not to jump at the sound. She was glad she had not, because she suspected that Avis, the young chambermaid Lady Scott had sent to assist her, would prattle of what she saw or heard to any willing audience.

Avis had been chattering since she had come in. To her credit, she had tidied the room and found places to stow Meg's things in kists and on pegs. She had also fetched hot water and, when Sir Walter walked in, she had just helped Meg take off her riding dress so she could wash away the worst of the dirt from her long ride.

Like most Border women, Meg was a good horsewoman, but it had been a long, tiring day and was not over yet. Lady Scott, having said she would send someone to tell her when supper was ready, had left her and taken Amalie to a bedchamber of her own elsewhere.

Meg had welcomed the respite between their departure and Avis's arrival, because it gave her a chance at last to think only of herself and how the day's events had affected her. To be sure, she had pondered these things during their journey, but with Sir Walter and Amalie so near, and Amalie making desultory conversation, she had done so only intermittently and with a sense of guilt.

She had expected a second respite after Avis left, but that was not to be.

A second look at her husband inspired her to say, "That will be all, Avis, thank you. I can manage on my own now."

"Aye, sure, m'lady." The girl bobbed a curtsy in Sir Walter's direction without really looking at him and hurried from the room.

"You needn't have sent her away," he said. "Douglas is resting, so I doubt they'll call us for supper straightaway."

"I thought the Douglas never slept. So the tales go, at all events."

His smile was tired, but at least he smiled. "Those tales are true. But he said he must have eaten something bad yesterday, because he has been sick ever since."

"Poor laddie," she said. "I was sick like that once. 'Tis a dreadful thing."

"Aye, well, he's not foundering yet."

She eyed him shrewdly, suspecting that what he would have liked to say was that illness had not diminished the Douglas's ability to express himself. However, she said only, "You seem a little tired yourself, sir."

He grimaced. "I don't know that I'm tired, though I should be, I expect, after all the riding I've done in the past twenty-four hours and sleeping on your father's dungeon floor. I've had a damnable headache all day, too. But if I look wretched, 'tis because I've been hearing my character shredded by two of the best."

"They are truly angry about our marriage then."

"One might put it even more strongly than that," he said. "They are not blaming you, though, lass," he added with a shrewd look at her. "They've put the blame on me, where it belongs. Is that steam I see rising from yonder basin?"

"It is. Avis brought up hot water so that we might wash before supper."

"I warrant Avis never gave a thought to me," he said. "Have you taken advantage of it? I won't use it yet if you have not."

"Don't be foolish, sir. I can attend to my needs with this damp cloth. You must use the rest as you please."

"You are kind, lass. Take care that you don't turn me into a tyrant. Some already think I seek to rule all in my ambit."

He turned away as he spoke, and she wished he had not. He truly did look wretched, and she nearly suggested that he lie down and rest as the Douglas had. She bit off the words, though, deciding that he would not appreciate any further mention of his weariness.

She suspected that his interview with the earl and Buccleuch had been more of an ordeal for him than he had admitted. But he would certainly not share his feelings about that with her. Her experience with her brothers, especially Tom, told her that young men were often more sensitive about things than they admitted.

Therefore, she said no more, performing her ablutions with quiet dispatch and donning a simple pale-green cotton kirtle with a front-laced indigo bodice and a surcoat of the bluish-gray color called perse.

There was one thing she could not do by herself, though, not if she was to appear before Lady Scott without drawing her ladyship's censure. So, after she had stepped into her soft shoes, she turned hesitantly to her husband.

He had stripped off his jack and shirt and stood barechested at the basin.

The light through the long, narrow window nearby had dimmed so that he was little more than a gray form, but the muscles of his shoulders and arms looked as hard as marble, rippling as he moved. Deciding that she did not want to disturb him just yet, she watched appreciatively as he scrubbed himself.

As if he had felt her gaze, he glanced at her a moment later. "What is it, lass? You look sore perplexed."

"'Tis my hair," she said. "I cannot put it up smoothly enough or tightly enough by myself to put on my coif, but I can ask Amalie to help me if you can tell me where to find her. Your mother took her to another chamber but did not say where it lies or even if it is in this tower."

"She'll be in this one," he said. "This is the family tower, although my younger brothers both have apartments in the one that you'll see to your left, or to the north, as you walk out the front entrance. My father's men-at-arms occupy the other one, as does the bakehouse and a few other sundry chambers."

"Do you know where I can find her then?"

"Nay, not exactly, but Avis will know. That lass knows everything. Stay, though," he said, cocking his head. "Did you bring a net with you?"

"Of course I did," she said. "But surely—"

"My sister Jenny often puts hers in a net with a plain veil over it. Supper is no formal meal here at the Hall, and won't be tonight, even with the Douglas here. He does not stand on ceremony, and nor does my father."

"But your mother—"

"Nay, lass, do not fear her. I told you, she is kind. It may take her a day or so to warm to you, because I've disappointed her. I think she must have set more store by that Douglas marriage than I knew."

"Are you sorry about that, too?" she asked before she could stop herself.

He shook his head, and even in the dimming light she saw that his eyes danced. "If there is one thing I am sure of in all of this, it is that I am well out of that. Now, if you would please your husband, do something to your hair so you can stuff it into a net, and I'll help you fasten your veil myself."

After that, with no more to say about it, Meg arranged her hair in two long plaits, twisted them round each other at her nape, and confined the result in a gold net under a white cambric veil. As she did, she encouraged her husband to talk.

The conversation continued amiably while he dressed. By asking about his horses and dogs, and then about how he had won his spurs, she led him naturally to tales he could tell about Douglas in the field.

By the time a servant arrived to tell them supper was about to be served, he had relaxed and was in a much more cheerful humor.

That her husband was well pleased with her and with himself by then gave her confidence that she was doing the right thing. The feeling lasted until she stepped onto the dais and her hostess greeted her with chilly civility.

Chapter 7

~

Now Meg was but thin, an' her nose it was lang;
And her mou' was as muckle as muckle could be . . .

Wat led Margaret to the place of honor beside his mother and noted with relief that Amalie had found her own way to the great hall. It occurred to him only when he saw her that he ought to have made an effort to find her and perhaps even to have invited her to come downstairs with him and Margaret.

Instead, he had found himself taking time with his dressing and describing for Margaret adventures that Jamie Douglas had enjoyed while following his father, the first earl, and then leading the Scots himself in the continuing struggle to keep England from conquering Scotland.

Margaret was an attentive listener, but Wat remembered as he was moving to take his place beside Jamie—now looking his usual self again—that Margaret's mother was English. She had said nothing during their talk to remind him of that.

Recalling a few of the things he had told her made him

wonder if he ought to have said so much. She was extraordinarily easy to talk to. He could not remember ever feeling quite so comfortable talking with anyone else.

His better self suggested that perhaps it was just that no one else listened to him with such fixed and total attention. His brothers and friends were more likely to interject witty, disrespectful remarks. His sister listened but had little interest in the things that interested him. And his father, with the duty of training him to take over Buccleuch, Rankilburn, and other holdings, tended to dismiss his ideas and suggestions, advising him instead to listen more and talk less.

Talking with someone who listened was a heady experience. He would take more care in future, though, to tell her nothing she should not know.

Conversation at the table drifted in the polite, desultory way of such talk. Douglas and Buccleuch spoke quietly to each other from time to time, and Wat gleaned from what he could overhear that Douglas meant to use the forthcoming meeting of Border wardens to discuss tactics and strategy for what was looking more and more like an impending confrontation with a very large English army.

"I'm told Fife means to take a hand," Douglas said at one point.

"It is most unlike him to risk his own neck," Buccleuch said.

"Aye, but now that he is ruling Scotland openly in place of his aging father and has taken to calling himself Guardian of the Realm, he cannot stomach letting anyone else command the Scottish forces," Douglas said. "Not whilst King Richard of England has taken command of his own army, at all events."

Buccleuch frowned. "If Richard manages to gather

a force like he had three years ago, we could be facing as many as seventy thousand men. If so, you won't want Fife taking command. He's a much stronger ruler for the country than his father is or his brother will be, but he's a terrible soldier and a worse tactician."

"Aye, and a physical coward withal, but I'll arrange to keep Fife and his ilk out of my hair by offering to see that Hotspur stays out of theirs. Sithee, I mean to leave Fife to command his good friend the Lord of Galloway," Douglas added, speaking of his cousin Archibald Douglas, whom many called "Archie the Grim."

As warden of the west march, Archie the Grim was a proven leader and a man wholly loyal to his chief and to Scotland. Yet Archie had somehow become friendly with Fife. Wat knew that wiser heads than his had puzzled long over Fife and his complex motives. He barely knew the man, but what little he did know of him he did not like. He would take good care not to annoy Douglas any further if only to avoid being ordered to serve under Fife and Archie the Grim.

"We'll talk no more of my plans just now," Douglas went on. "'Tis better to wait until we are all at Hermitage, where we can be private."

"I've heard that your countess has threatened to make Hermitage more homelike for you," Buccleuch said then with a chuckle.

"Aye, she threatened and more, for she has already sent me a minstrel as a gift to entertain us at mealtimes. 'Tis a foolish notion, although 'twas kind of her. The chappie sings well enough and plucks his lute strings with wondrous skill."

"Next it will be linen table coverings and maidservants," Buccleuch said.

"Nay, it will not!"

Revealing that she also could hear them, Wat's mother turned and said, "Forgive me, both of you, for pointing out that Hermitage could do with some comforts." To Douglas, she added, "I have heard much of its *dis*comforts, my lord. Surely, a bit of music and a woman's touch there would not come amiss."

"One hesitates to contradict you, my lady, but I can think of few things less comfortable than having women swarming over Hermitage, clucking about dust and trying to hang curtains. It is a stronghold, a fortress, a place for warriors. Sakes, but few of its chambers provide suitable habitation for the fair sex. Indeed, the minstrel thinks himself ill-used. The fellow is something of a prickme-dainty," he confided.

"But you must miss your wife," she said, ignoring the minstrel. "To spend as much time apart as you do must be a penance, especially as you do want an heir."

"Enough, madam," Buccleuch said with the warm smile he reserved just for her. "If you are right, you torment him. If you are wrong, he'll disappoint you. In any event, I forbid you to reveal a word of this conversation to his countess."

Wat was watching his mother when movement beyond her caught his eye.

Margaret's expression was sober as usual, but as his gaze met hers, he felt as if she knew his thoughts. Such an irreverent notion ought to have disturbed him, he knew, but although he could not have explained what he did feel, he smiled.

To his astonishment, her soft, dark-lashed eyes began to twinkle, and while he could not claim that she smiled back, her lips twitched as if she nearly had.

He found himself looking forward to talking with her more after supper. But when they had bade farewell to Douglas, his father drew him aside to say that he wanted to talk more with him before he retired.

"To discuss matters closer to home," Buccleuch said. "We'll stay here in the hall, but you should know I've had new reports of reivers or their ilk in the area."

"Mayhap 'twas more of Murray's lads," Wat said. "I'm nigh dead on my feet, sir, but if I can keep my eyes open, I am at your disposal. I do hope you don't mean to read me another lecture, though."

"Only to say that 'tis an honor and a compliment to your abilities in battle that Douglas still expects you to ride with us, so see that you deserve it. What is done is done and I'll say no more about it, so tell your lass you'll be along shortly."

Wat did tell her, and she nodded and said she would wait for him. But by the time he had heard all his father had to say and was able to retire to his bedchamber, she was sound asleep on the far side of the bed, against the wall.

He undressed quietly and got into bed without disturbing her.

When Meg awoke Saturday morning, her husband was out of bed and nearly dressed. He wore a clean white shirt, brushed leather breeks, and soft-topped rawhide boots. "You are up early, sir," she said. "What are we going to do today?"

"You may lie abed if you like," he said, slipping on a

leather jack. "I must be off within the hour for Raven's Law, and I cannot be sure when I'll return."

"Must Amalie and I stay here?" she asked. "I know you've said your tower is not suitable, but I would like to see where I am to live and take up residence as soon as we can make it more so. I feel as if we impose on your mother here, and I shall feel that all the more whilst you are away."

"You'll quickly grow accustomed to the Hall," he said. "Raven's Law would be devilish uncomfortable for you right now."

"Do you mean it is like Hermitage?"

"You *were* listening to their conversation last night then."

"It would have been hard to shut my ears to it," she said. "I was sitting next to your mother, and no one made any attempt to keep that discussion private."

"Well, Raven's Law is not at all like Hermitage, for it is just a peel tower, not a fortress. Still, the tower has housed only men for as long as I can remember, so in that respect I suppose it is the same."

"But surely, I should see it unless you mean for us always to live apart."

"I don't, but I am no housekeeper, lass, nor are my men tidy. They keep their gear in order and the night soil from burying us, but that's all I can say for them."

"I could help you put things in order," she said mildly. "I should like to do that, because then I'd not be such a stranger to the place when I do go to live there."

"When I can arrange suitable accommodations for you, you can do as you like. Until then you'll be more comfortable here. As for your fear of imposing . . . Sithee, I am my father's heir, and this will all be mine one day. So as my wife, you have as much right to live here as anyone does."

"Even so—"

"Ettrick Forest is a dangerous place these days, Margaret. The reason I came to bed late last night was that my father kept me to discuss the increasing danger. I'm not the only one who's lost beasts, or other things for that matter, odd things."

"Mercy," she said. "I know that you and my father both said that kine of yours had somehow found their way to Elishaw. But he did not explain it to me, and he does not encourage us to question him."

"My purpose in going to Elishaw was to reclaim my own beasts," he said. "Your father's men lifted them whilst I was at Langholm. They took kine, horses, and the two dogs that accompanied us home yesterday."

"But he said he caught you trying to . . . to 'lift' beasts from his herd," she said, using his term instead of any of the harsher ones her father had used.

To her surprise, he looked rueful. "I can swear we'd not touched one of his beasts before he captured us, but I'll not lie to you," he said. "Rather than waste time trying to sort them, I'd have taken any that stood with my own. But we had no chance to do other than try to defend ourselves against the score or more of his men who rose up around us out of a field of blooming heather."

"He said he'd suspected you'd be coming," she said. "I own, though, I'm surprised that so many were lying in wait. Are you sure they were not just guards?"

"Had there been guards in sight, we'd never have got close," he said. "Sakes, I had only a half-dozen men with me, and you saw the lad he wanted to hang first. Although," he added with a grimace, "young Sym was nowhere in sight when we reached Elishaw. I didn't think to ask how they caught him."

She had wondered about Sym from the beginning, shocked that her father could threaten to hang one so young and even more shocked that the reivers had brought him along. It had been the child's fierce words, though, that had made her doubt her father's account of the so-called raid on his herd.

"You believe that my father ordered the taking of your herd."

"I ken fine that he did, for not only did we follow their tracks right back to Elishaw, but your father admitted it, said he knew I would follow, so he set a trap."

"Surely you don't think he meant that trap to force you to marry me?"

"I did suspect that, but he assured me he did not. His reason, he said, was that whenever the English invade, they seize crops and cattle from those in their path. He thinks it only fair that others share his losses. Sakes, though, there will be no losses if we can just stop them before they can come at us again."

Knowing she might regret pressing the subject, she said, "You couldn't stop them last time."

"Nay, but it is different now. Three years ago, Jamie's father, the first Earl of Douglas, had just died and Jamie was new to the title. Men knew him for a fierce and skillful warrior but not for the brilliant tactician he has proven himself since. Older lairds had less confidence in him then than they'd had in his father."

"You said others had lost things," she reminded him, knowing he could talk at length about Douglas, whom he clearly much admired. "What sort of things?"

"They've felled trees, stolen chickens and other livestock, and poached game. Since they don't seem to be ordinary reivers, I'm thinking English raiders may already be seeking supplies to cache for their approaching army."

"If you suspect my father, sir, I can tell you he would not steal chickens. I cannot speak for his men, but they would not be acting on his orders to do such things. And for them to ignore his orders or act on their own would be most unusual. Indeed, your complaints sound much like those we hear from the other side of the line after Douglas has harried Redesdale or Tynedale on one of his forays and his men have herded English beasts back across the line to Scotland."

"Sakes, you don't mean to accuse him—" He broke off, shaking his head. "Nay, I can see you're not suggesting that Jamie steals chickens or poaches game. Nor does he often allow his men to slow him down by rounding up cattle to take home. But if such things are happening on both sides, mayhap someone is using the Douglas raids on the English dales to cover a similar mysterious motive there."

She nodded, relieved to discover that she had not misjudged his intelligence. That was both a relief and a warning, though. She'd have to tread carefully with him. "You mean someone may be gathering supplies on both sides," she said.

"Aye, and 'tis likely they are English because having ordered peace amongst the Scots, Jamie would not encourage his supporters to take from other Scots to supply his army. When he wants folks to provide supplies, he simply orders it. We travel with less than the English, too, with their long trains of baggage."

"If English raiders *are* scavenging in Ettrick Forest, I'd

think the more people we have living at Raven's Law, the safer it would be for all of us."

"Not until I have caught the rogues and put a stop to their raids. But that's enough about that," he added with a note of finality in his voice. "I do mean for us to live at Raven's Law, lass, but I must deal with one thing at a time. Recall that, unlike a usual bridegroom, I did not know I'd need to make such arrangements."

"Not even for Fiona Douglas?" she asked.

"Sakes, are you going to throw the lady Fiona in my face whenever I act against your wishes?" he demanded.

"No, sir," she said. "I would not do that. But you did say that your father was negotiating your marriage to her. I just wondered why you had not yet set matters in train to install her at Raven's Law."

"Because that wasn't real yet," he said. Grimacing as if he knew the words would make no sense to her, he added, "That was my father's notion, and Jamie's, to bond our families more closely. 'Tis hard to see something as real when one has nowt to do with it."

She nodded, easily able to agree with that sentiment. It was hard enough to believe she was married, let alone that she and Amalie had to live at the Hall until his return. But she'd had nothing to say about any of that business from the start, and apparently she could do nothing about his decision now.

For that matter, it sounded as if he had as little to say about things in general as she did. So it would do her no good to argue with him, not until she understood better how things customarily resolved themselves in this new home of hers.

Reminding herself that her primary intent was to be a good wife to him, she said, "I promise I won't throw the unfortunate Fiona in your face again, sir. Indeed, I did not mean it as you thought. But I would like to know what my position here is to be. Do I discuss that with your lady mother, or can you tell me?"

"Sakes, just enjoy your visit, lass," he said. "There can be nowt for you to do in a house as well run as this one. The servants look after everything, for my father trained them well, as his father did before him. My mother has only to depend on them. You'll see that for yourself."

Knowing that her own father thought much the same about the household at Elishaw, that he commanded all, she suspected the truth was that Lady Scott, like Lady Murray, controlled everything from the amount of flour in the bin to the scent of the rushes strewn each fortnight over the great-hall floor.

Even her father's men-at-arms knew better than to run counter to Lady Murray's wishes. Nevertheless, if one were to ask her ladyship who ran things at Elishaw, she would inform them that, to be sure, her lord husband commanded all.

Deciding she had no other choice but to make friends with Lady Scott, Meg sought her out as soon as Sir Walter and his men had departed for Raven's Law.

"Prithee, madam, how may Amalie and I assist you whilst we're here?"

Her hostess eyed her quizzically for a moment before she said, "Did my son suggest that I might desire your assistance?"

"No," Meg said. "Sir Walter said I'd have naught to do here except enjoy myself, because your servants look after everything and everyone. He said that his father and grandfather trained them to do so."

Lady Scott's eyes, much the same golden-hazel as her son's, began to twinkle. "Our Wat said that, did he?"

"He did, madam."

"What do you think of such an assessment, Margaret?"

"It is what my brothers and my father would say about Elishaw, my lady. So I believe it indicates an establishment run so smoothly that its menfolk need never concern themselves with how it contrives to do so."

"I see. How much did you have to do with managing Elishaw's household?"

"Very little," Meg admitted. "My mother manages it, but she believes in teaching her daughters how she does. She has taught us as her own mother taught her, by seeing that we learn to do anything we'd ask our servants to do for us."

"Anything?"

"I don't mean that we can do everything as well as they can, but we do know enough to judge if a servant is competent, and we can explain what the lack is if one is not doing a task correctly. However, every household has its way of doing things, so if it pleases you, I'd be grateful to learn anything you are willing to teach me."

"Indeed," Lady Scott said. She thought for a moment, then said, "I believe in candor, my dear, so I won't pretend I'm pleased by what your father did—or what our Wat did, come to that. But none of it is your fault. Moreover, it is your duty now, and your right, to learn about Scott's Hall. I can have no objection to showing you the place and introducing you to our people, so suppose we begin with that."

"Thank you," Meg said, much relieved. "I would like that."

"What of your sister Amalie? Will she want to learn, too?"

"Our long day yesterday tired her, so she is still asleep, but I am sure she will help in any way she can," Meg said, hoping she could persuade her unpredictable sister to behave herself. Amalie loathed everything to do with housekeeping.

⁓

Three hours later, when Lady Scott said that she was sure Meg would want to rest and refresh herself before the midday meal, Meg recognized the dismissal for what it was and did not protest.

She was not tired and would willingly have continued her explorations. But her hostess had clearly had enough of it, and Meg could scarcely blame her.

They had begun her tour in the vaulted kitchen on the lower level of the main tower, where Lady Scott introduced her to the cook and lingered to discuss the next few days' menus with him. An oven arrangement quite different from the one at Elishaw fascinated Meg, and she would have liked to ask a few questions about it, but her ladyship soon hurried her on, saying, "We must not tarry if I am to show you everything. We can discuss such things another time, as more questions occur to you."

Meg learned that the central tower boasted four stories above the kitchen, the greater part of which was below ground, with the great hall occupying most of the next level. Each floor contained one large chamber and two or three smaller ones off the main stairway. There were also service stairs in the corner opposite the main stairs. Above the great hall were three floors dedicated to family and guest chambers. The first one included a great chamber with a small inner chamber behind it where Buccleuch and his lady slept. Another small room across the landing was Buccleuch's private chamber for matters pertaining to his estates.

When Lady Scott rapped twice and opened the door to show Meg, she said, "I ken fine that he has ridden into the Forest, but it is always wise to rap first before opening this door. One enters, of course, only to see that all is tidy."

Peering inside and noting the large table with the back-stool behind it and shelves of documents and other paraphernalia, Meg easily imagined Sir Walter facing Buccleuch there and felt a stirring of sympathy.

Scolding herself for the unnecessary flight of fancy, she hurried after her hostess to the next level, where the chamber lay that she shared with Sir Walter.

"Our Jenny's chamber is there across the landing," Lady Scott said. "In the old days, Wat's present room was the nursery. Then, as our lads grew and became more boisterous, we moved them upstairs and arranged small rooms for each one. So Jenny was the only one on this level except for her nurse and my tiring woman."

"Do I call her Jenny, my lady? Or has she another name she would prefer."

"She is Lady Randolph Kerr now, but I am sure she will want you to call her Jenny. Everyone does," Lady Scott said, smiling. "Her true name is Janet, of course, after me, and I venture to guess that she will descend upon us within a day or two. It won't take longer than that for news of your marriage to reach Ferniehurst."

"I'm sure you will all be glad to see her," Meg said.

"Ferniehurst is not so far from here that we cannot see

her frequently," her ladyship said. "She is increasing now, so her husband asks that she take greater care, but Jenny is as at home on her pony as any Border lass, and impatient withal. She'll come flying to see you as soon as she hears, whether Rand forbids it or not."

Meg smiled at the thought of Sir Walter with such a headstrong sister. But she thought he was right to believe she would like Jenny.

After a brisk tour of the other two towers, laid out in a similar way but clearly the domain of servants and men-at-arms, Lady Scott gave her opinion that Meg would want to rest. Meg, perforce, returned to the main tower with her, thanked her warmly, and went to find Amalie.

At the first turn of the stairway, however, she nearly tripped over Wee Sym Elliot, who sat on the curved step with his hands clasped around his knees.

"What are you doing here?" she asked him.

"Waiting for ye, o' course. Ye've been an age and all, so Pawky and me been getting bored. What were ye traipsing all over the place wi' her ladyship for?"

"She was showing me where things are," Meg said, adding, "Not that it is any business of yours, my lad. Who is Pawky, and why are you waiting for me?"

"'Cause I promised Master Wat I'd serve ye is why. I could ha' showed ye aught ye wanted to see. Ye needna ha' troubled the mistress."

"Propriety required that I ask her," Meg said gently. "It is my duty to ask and hers to show me about. But why are you to serve me? And how will you do so?"

"As to the how, I dinna ken. That be for ye to say, I trow. But as to the why, your da' said we must, and we swore. So Master Wat said that since it be my duty to look after ye, I'd best begin straightaway. I'd liefer ha' gone wi' him, sithee, to find them what ha' been raiding the Forest and teach them a good lesson. Nobbut what I'm saying I won't do what ye ask o' me, for I will."

At a loss for how the lad could serve her, Meg said, "I'll have to think of things you can do for me, Sym. I have never had the great privilege of a personal servant before. I do think, though, that you should stand when you speak with me."

"Aye, sure, I ken that fine," he said, reddening as he got awkwardly to his feet, at the same time trying unsuccessfully to conceal the small orange and white kitten he had been holding in the space between his body and his knees. It mewed in protest until he cupped it to his thin chest. "This be Pawky, me lady. D'ye like cats?"

Smiling, Meg put out a finger to pet the kitten's soft head. "She's lovely, but she looks gey young to be taken from her mam."

"Aye, she is a bit," Sym agreed. "But the cook said the kits were getting to be a nuisance and he were going to drown the lot. But Pawky climbed up me leg, so . . ."

"So you rescued her," Meg said with another smile. "Can she lap water?"

"Aye, and she'll eat near anything I give her."

"Then I think you must be taking good care of her," Meg said. "I am going to see my sister now, but I'll talk with you more later."

"I'll just come along in case ye ha' need o' me," he said.

Realizing that Walter had probably hoped serving her would keep the boy out of more mischief, she made no objection. But when she reached the door to Amalie's room, she told him to wait for her on the landing.

To her astonishment, her sister was still sound asleep

in the small chamber she had been allotted on the floor above Meg's, but Meg did not hesitate to wake her. "What a slugabed!" she exclaimed, giving Amalie's shoulder a shake.

She woke groggily. "What time is it?"

"It will be time for the midday meal soon. Are you truly so tired?"

"We were up with the dawn yesterday and rode twenty miles after your wedding feast," Amalie said. "I slept like the dead."

"Well, it is time to get up now," Meg said. "I have been all over Scott's Hall. I must say it is a fine establishment."

"As fine as Elishaw?"

Meg smiled. "You will soon see for yourself. We are to stay here until Sir Walter's peel tower can be made more habitable for us."

"Mercy, is it not habitable?"

"It is full of men-at-arms, I think, and he was not expecting female guests. He wants to furbish it up for us, and we can scarcely blame him. Marrying me was not his idea, after all."

Amalie shrugged. "At least you are married, Meg, and if this establishment is so fine, and Sir Walter will inherit it, you have small reason to complain."

"I am not complaining," Meg said. "I am trying to roust my lazy sister out of her bed, so we can dress to dine with Lady Scott."

"Must we? I don't think she likes us much."

"Why should she? Do at least try to put yourself in her place, my dear."

"Her place seems fine to me," Amalie said. "She has a fine house, a wealthy husband who is friends with Douglas, the most powerful lord in Scotland, and she has just acquired a good-daughter who will be a great asset to their family."

Meg raised her eyebrows. "Praising me will gain you naught if you refuse to see that her ladyship has cause for disappointment. But come, get up now. I have a personal servant just outside the door that I can send to fetch Avis to help you. But I am not stirring a step until you are out of that bed."

"You have a personal servant? Shall I have one, too?"

"You would not want him, my dear," Meg said with a teasing smile. "It is Wee Sym, the lad Father wanted to hang. Sym says he swore then to serve me and means to do so. Now, up with you!"

"Oh, very well, since you won't leave me in peace. But if Sym is an example of what Scott's Hall offers us, I don't think much of the place or its mistress."

Chapter 8

Her een they war gray, and her color was wan,
But her nature was generous, gentle, and free . . .

Unfortunately, Amalie's attitude did not alter as the days passed.

Meg found her moodiness troubling but typical and thus difficult to deflect. At first, when Meg quizzed her, Amalie said only that Lady Scott did not like her, and that she could find nothing of interest to do at Scott's Hall.

"I know you enjoy learning how things go on here," she said with a grimace on their third day at Scott's Hall. "I don't care a rap about such stuff, and Lady Scott does not need my help with anything—or yours, come to that. In troth, she cares more about finding a minstrel to outsing the one the Countess of Douglas sent to amuse her lord at Hermitage than she does about paying heed to us."

Meg could not deny that their hostess showed no interest in providing for their entertainment. But neither would her ladyship expect to provide entertainment for her own offspring if they were to visit. And she had behaved kindly toward both Meg and Amalie, willingly answering any question they put to her. She simply expected them to entertain themselves.

On that thought, Meg said bracingly, "What we both want is exercise. I'd like to explore Ettrick Forest, if only to see more of it than we can see from here. Why do I not see if I can arrange an outing for us to do so?"

Although Amalie showed little interest in such an outing, Meg refused to be daunted. She went right out to the yard to see about horses and—remembering what Sir Walter had said about raiders—some sort of armed escort to accompany them.

Encountering Buccleuch as he emerged from the stable and taking courage from his cheery greeting, she said, "My sister and I would like to see more of this glen, my lord. Would it be possible for us to take ponies and . . . ?"

She paused because he was already shaking his head, albeit with a smile.

"That would not be a good idea, lass," he said. "Until we can find the men who have cut our trees and poached game from the Forest, and be certain they can pose no danger, you had better remain inside the wall."

"I had hoped that with a pair of armed men to escort us . . ."

He shook his head again. "We'll see how things are in a day or two. In the meantime, doubtless you have stitchery or some such thing to occupy your time."

Well aware of what Amalie would say to that, Meg said nonetheless politely, "We brought none with us, sir, but perhaps Lady Scott will have something of the ilk that we can do for her."

"I am sure she will," he said.

Questioned shortly thereafter, Lady Scott provided pillow covers on which she had already sketched flowery patterns, together with a collection of colorful silk threads. "I shall be very glad to have help with these," she said, explaining that she intended to replace all the worn covers on cushions there in the great chamber.

Meg and Amalie thanked her, but although Meg enjoyed embroidering, and was glad to help, she yearned for more interesting activities.

As for Amalie, for every stitch she took, she spent ten minutes staring at her work without moving. "You can do much finer work than this," Meg said when she got a chance to look at it. "I should think that you would prefer to have your best work on display here. What our mother would say—"

"I was thinking of something else," Amalie said, looking aimlessly at her stitches. "I'll fix it later, Meggie. I'm tired now. I think I'll go up and take a nap."

Meg bit back further criticism, knowing of no way to get Amalie to talk about what ailed her except by exerting patience.

Thus, two days later, on Wednesday, when Jenny, Lady Randolph Kerr, arrived in a flurry of bundles and sumpter baskets that looked as if they held enough to supply a long visit, Meg greeted her with unfeigned delight.

Amalie was polite but still seemed to be in a world of her own.

Jenny was fairer than Sir Walter but had his infectious smile and feline grace along with her father's dark-brown eyes and cheerful nature. She also had her mother's rosy complexion and the twinkle that had so startled Meg the first time she had discerned it in Lady Scott's eyes. In Jenny, the twinkle was ubiquitous.

She'd brought presents for everyone, even Amalie, because Ferniehurst had received the news of her presence at the Hall with the news of Walter's marriage.

"I'm delighted to have sisters at last," Jenny told them both with a brilliant smile. "Had it been left to Wat, I doubt he'd ever have married. He'd always have been wondering why the lass wanted him."

"But surely he was eligible enough to marry anyone," Meg said, so captured by Jenny's candor that she spoke her own thoughts for once without thinking.

"He was worthy of anyone, however highborn," Lady Scott said evenly.

"Oh, Mother," Jenny said, shaking her head. "If you think Wat was ever going to marry Fiona Douglas, you aren't being your sensible self. Fiona thinks she and her kindred are better than all the angels of God and does not mind who knows it. He'd soon have found a way to wriggle out of that match, no matter who—"

"Jenny, love, do think of what you are saying! Fiona is first cousin to the Douglas! For our Wat to have married her would have been the making of him, and you have no business to be saying—"

She broke off, apparently noting, as Meg had, her daughter's raised eyebrows. "Mercy," Janet Scott said, looking contritely at Meg. "Just listen to me scolding her for a thoughtless tongue whilst mine is far more so. I hope you can find it in your heart to forgive me, my dear. By my troth, I meant no offense to you."

So much had Jenny's warmheartedness affected Meg that she had no difficulty smiling as she said, "Only a dafty could take offense when one can easily see that you were thinking only of your son, my lady. I am sure that so grand a marriage would have benefited him far more than his marrying me ever could."

"Mayhap it would," Jenny said. "But if Jamie Douglas means to help Wat, he will do so for Wat's own sake and for no other reason."

Meg said, "Even so, my lady, we both know that important connections become even more so with time." That was, after all, a lesson she had learned many times over at Elishaw. "But I promise you, madam," she said to Lady Scott, "whatever comes, I mean to be the best wife to him that I can be."

To her surprise and infinite relief, after a steady, searching look, Janet Scott returned her smile with one warmer than she had shown before. "Do you know, my dear, I believe you mean that," she said. "Walter may be luckier than he knows."

"Of course he is," Jenny said. "He has always been the lucky one. You have only to ask Andy or John who always wins at their gaming or when they try to test his skill with a sword or other weapon. But enough about Wat," she added with a merry laugh. "You should be telling me how wondrous well I look. Rand took me to task for deciding to ride here straightaway. In fact, I'd have come sooner, only we had gone to Hawick to see his old nurse, hoping she might recommend someone for us. We only had your news yesterday when we returned home."

"You do look well, dearling," her mother said. "But you should learn to obey your husband. It is unseemly to flout his wishes so."

"I do not flout them, madam," Jenny said demurely. "I persuaded him that by enjoying such exercise I will produce a stronger son for him. I'm sure it is a son, too," she added, grinning. "I am amazingly well, and my lady good-mother tells me she also suffered little with her confinements. And she produced four stout sons. They are all left-handed, of course, as mine will also be, because all Kerr men are so. But my son will be as strong and as great a warrior as all the others, you'll see."

Lady Scott agreed with a laugh that Jenny had been the most difficult of her children right from the start, and the conversation continued in what Meg felt to be a delightfully entertaining way. Jenny made her feel more welcome at Scott's Hall than she had thought would be possible in so short a time.

Amalie remained quiet, but Meg assumed she was only tired again, or bored.

When Buccleuch joined them for supper, Jenny greeted him with the same delight she had shown everyone else, and he responded by catching her up in a hug so exuberant as to make Meg wonder if he could possibly be as fearsome as she had heard. So far, he had displayed only the polished manners of a charming courtier.

The rest of the day passed swiftly in Jenny's company, and only when Meg found herself yawning did she realize that she had not seen Amalie for some time. She had been uncharacteristically quiet the whole day, although she had responded politely to Jenny's pelter of questions and expressed sincere thanks for the bright wool shawl Jenny had brought to welcome her. But then Amalie had faded from the conversation until Meg had stopped paying her any heed.

Feeling guilty and recalling that her sister was far from her usual self, still complaining of feeling tired and wanting only to sleep, Meg excused herself to the others. Certain that Jenny's parents would welcome a chance to have her to themselves for a while, Meg went to look for Amalie.

She did not realize she had a shadow until a sound behind her made her jump.

"Sym!" she exclaimed, realizing she ought to have expected him, although he followed her so quietly that she tended to forget his presence. "What are you doing, coming up behind me like that? You frightened me witless."

"I didna mean to give ye a fright, mistress, only to keep me eye on ye. Ye slipped out once the other day, and I thought I'd lost ye till I saw ye wi' Himself. How am I to serve ye if I dinna ken where ye be? 'Tis me duty, and all."

"Not now," she said. "I want to be private with my sister, so you can await me at my chamber door. We'll see if I can think what to do with you when I return."

With a heavy sigh for one so young, he turned back down the stairs.

Reaching Amalie's door, Meg rapped softly, and when there was no answer, she gently lifted the latch. Freed, the heavy door swung open far enough to let her hear the wracking sobs within.

Entering quickly and shutting the door again, she strode to the bed to find Amalie curled on the counterpane with her face to the wall, shaking with sobs.

"Oh, my dearest one," Meg said, climbing up beside her and gripping her shoulder. "What is it? What has happened?"

Louder sobs greeted her, making her wish Amalie were the sort one could throw cold water on to shock her out of her megrims. But her sister could cry for hours if she felt wronged or hurt. Briskness or scolding would accomplish nothing, but Meg knew Amalie would usually respond to carefully measured sympathy.

"Come now," she said gently. "Sit up and tell me. I've

neglected you for hours, I know, and I owe you so much for coming here to bear me company. If you are homesick, you need only tell me and I'll arrange for you to return at once."

"Oh, no," Amalie wailed. "I don't want to go home, but I don't want to be here, either. It's horrid, Meggie. Nobody likes me, and I don't like any of them."

Abruptly then, she did sit up but only to fling herself into Meg's arms. "Oh, Meggie, I'm so dreadfully miserable!"

"But why?" Meg asked, holding her and patting her but struggling to imagine what could have brought on such a storm. "Surely, my talking with Jenny and her parents did not upset you so. You are not as self-centered as that, my dear."

"No, of course not," Amalie said, choking on another sob. "Jenny is nice, but she's . . . she's so *happy*." Another burst of tears followed, mystifying Meg.

"Why should she not be happy?" she asked reasonably. "She is expecting her first child, she loves her husband, and she is apparently able to do as she pleases."

"Exactly!" Amalie's gasping sobs nearly swallowed the single word, but Meg understood it well enough.

"See here, Amalie," she said, only to take a breath and try harder to keep her tone gentle rather than curt. "I don't understand you at all. If you are not happy here, and you do not want to go home, what *do* you want?"

"Oh, Meggie, I just want to die!"

Meg had heard her fifteen-year-old sister make many such exaggerated declarations, but her tone of voice this time sent a chill up her spine.

Drawing another steadying breath, she put both hands on Amalie's shoulders and held her far enough away to look her in the face. "You must not say that to me," she said. "It frightens me and makes me think my best course would be to ask the laird to take you back to Elishaw himself. I am sure he would, and mayhap once you can talk with our mother—"

"No!" Amalie's visible panic was painful to see. "I *can't* go home!"

"Godamercy, what have you done, then? It is no use now to say you cannot tell me, for you must. If you do not, I shall know you have become truly ill, and I will go straight to Buccleuch and ask what I should do."

"Oh, Meggie, you mustn't. Please. I . . . I just can't."

"You will," Meg said. When no further protest was forthcoming, she steadied her resolve, pushed Amalie back farther, and turned to get off the bed.

"I'll tell you!" Amalie said. "But you must promise not to despise me."

"Nothing you could do or say would make me despise you," Meg said sincerely. "You are my sister, Amalie, and I love you. Naught can change that."

Amalie drew a rasping breath, but then another period of silence ensued.

Meg said nothing.

At last, with another ragged sob, Amalie said, "I'm ruined, Meggie."

"What do you mean?"

"You must know what I mean. I'm . . . I'm no longer a maiden. I can never go home, and I'll never marry, so I'll never have a home of my own or . . . or children. That's why it hurt so much to see Jenny just bubbling over with her happiness."

Meg had been staring at her in shock, for once in her life at a loss for words.

Then anger stirred and grew to fury. Her fists clenched so hard that by the time the explanation paused, her nails were pricking her palms.

For a moment, she was afraid to speak, too well aware that Amalie would assume that Meg's anger must be aimed at her.

Only when Meg could trust herself to speak calmly did she say, "Who? Who dared to steal your maidenhood, dearest? I know you would not have given it away, so was it one of Sir Walter's men? You've only to tell me, because if it was—"

"Oh, no! Oh, please don't think that. They are the only ones here who have been kind to me. All the men here treat me just as they treat her ladyship or you. Some of them flirt a little, but that's all, I swear!"

"Then for heaven's sake, who was it?"

"I can't tell you," Amalie said, looking away. "I *won't* tell you. It doesn't make any difference now, for you must see I cannot go home. Mother would soon have the secret out of me, and she would make my life miserable. This renders me ineligible for the sort of marriage she has always planned for me. But I don't want anyone here to know either, so can't we just go somewhere else?"

Meg's wits had re-collected themselves. She said, "If it was no one here, then it must have been someone at home. But, really, Amalie, I'd have thought all the men there must be too afraid of our mother to take such base advantage of you. This is difficult for me to understand. Are you sure that is what happened?"

"Of course I'm sure. Men find ways when they want something, Meg. If you don't know that by now, you'll learn it fast enough now that you've got a husband." Bitterness coated her words. "If I cannot stay with you . . ." She spread her hands.

"Don't be absurd," Meg said. "You'll stay as long as you like. As to living elsewhere, as soon as Sir Walter makes Raven's Law habitable we can move there. Until then, though, we shall have to be patient."

Amalie did not look patient, but she allowed Meg to help her off with her clothes and put her to bed. Bidding her goodnight, Meg left. As she reached the turn of the stairs, she heard voices below and recalled that Sym awaited her.

To her surprise, the other voice was female. Even so, she did not expect to find Lady Jenny sitting beside the boy, dangling a string for Pawky, and hearing in dramatic detail about Sym's great adventure and near hanging at Elishaw.

Heat flooded Meg's cheeks until Jenny looked up at her with a grin and said, "My father rode off somewhere, and my mother needed an early night. So I came up to talk more privately with you. In your absence, Sym has been describing just how your marriage came about. What a thing that must have been!"

"Yes, wasn't it?" Meg said dryly. "Sym, where have you been sleeping?"

"Cook gave me and Pawky a pallet by the kitchen fire," the lad said.

"Then if you would please me, seek it now and get a good night's sleep. I shan't go anywhere but to my bed before morning."

"Are ye sure ye'll ha' nae need o' me?"

"I'm sure."

"That's fine then. A man can always use a good night's rest."

Jenny turned and rose in one swift movement and pushed open the door to the bedchamber, looking back only after Meg had entered behind her and shut the door. "Forgive me for rushing ahead," she said then, eyes twinkling. "But if I had not, I would have burst into laughter. How did you find such an amusing, devoted slave?"

"Your esteemed brother provided him. My father said he would free Sir Walter's men only if they would agree to serve me, so they all swore to do so, including that young scamp. Then Walter, doubtless to keep him from landing in the suds again, saddled me with him."

"Well, he may come in handy," Jenny said. "But why, if Wat takes such care to provide a bodyguard, did he leave you here instead of taking you to Raven's Law?"

When Meg did not answer at once, Jenny added, "You should know that I already asked my parents why he left you here. My father snubbed me. He said my brother's relationship with his wife is none of my affair."

"I see," Meg said, amused. "Are you always so disobedient?"

Jenny grinned. "When I want to know something, I ask. If the first person won't tell me, I ask another and another until I learn what I want to know."

"You know, I think Sym said something much the same once. The pair of you ought to get on quite well. Perhaps I should gift him to you."

Jenny laughed. "You and I are clearly destined to be friends as well as sisters. So, as we've settled that, do tell me why Wat left you with my parents."

"I am only surprised that your father did not explain it to you," Meg said. "Raiders have stolen wood and livestock from the Forest, so Walter prefers that we live safely here until he can make Raven's Law more suitable for females."

"That's a wheen o' blethers, that is—as I heard your Sym say." With a gurgle of laughter, Jenny added, "It also explains why my father did not offer that excuse to me. Sakes, Meg—I may call you Meg, may I not, as Amalie does?"

"Aye, sure," Meg said. "I'd like that."

"And you must call me Jenny, just as everyone does. But, Meg, that is all rubbish. Sithee, Raven's Law is only a mile or two from here."

"A mile!" Meg exclaimed, having envisioned many miles between them.

"Aye, for the Hall sits a half-mile from where the two burns meet. The Rankilburn is the larger and flows from Ettrick Water, seven miles west of us. The Clearburn flows from the north, beyond the Buck Cleuch. It spills over the head of the cleuch to run through it, then joins the Rankilburn southeast of here."

"The Buccleuch?"

"The *Buck* Cleuch," Jenny repeated, enunciating the separation more clearly. "'Tis how the name came to be, though. They say that in the time of the third Kenneth, a hunted buck ran into that cleuch. It is a very steep ravine, and when the buck turned at bay, a young stranger to the district scattered the dogs and seized it by the horns. Swinging it onto his back, he carried it up out of the ravine and laid it before the King. Kenneth was so delighted with the man's strength and courage that he made him Ranger of Ettrick Forest. The cleuch was named Buck Cleuch as a result, and the man's heirs have been Scotts of Buccleuch ever since."

"Is that really true?" Meg asked suspiciously.

Grinning again, Jenny shrugged. "'Tis the tale I've heard, and as one of my father's titles is Ranger of Ettrick Forest, there must be some truth to it. In any case, Raven's Law is at the head of the ravine and nearly impregnable, because one cannot sneak up on it. And, with Scott's Hall so near, help is always at hand if Wat needs it."

"But then how could my father have taken his cattle?" Meg asked.

"They generally graze in the Forest, in a clearing by the Rankilburn a mile west of the cleuch, rather than in the cleuch itself," Jenny explained.

"I see."

"Good, then as to the tower's fitness for females, Wat may be right. But who has a better right to improve it than his wife? You should put that question to him, Meg. If you don't, he will just cast orders at you and expect you to obey. No, listen to me," she added when Meg frowned. "Scott men do *not* like meek women."

"I don't want to be a bad wife," Meg said, feeling most uncomfortable at the thought of stirring conflict with her reluctant husband.

"In this family," Jenny said with a toss of her head, "a bad wife would be one who let her husband trample all over her as he went his own way with everything."

"I suspect he won't thank you for saying that to me," Meg said.

An impish smile lit Jenny's face. "He'd not thank me now. But believe me, Meg, you will both thank me one day. Sithee, I'm glad he married you. I think you will make him an excellent wife, but Wat is not easy. He can be kind, and he is fair, so he doubtless thinks of you as being as much a victim in this as he believes he is. He is not one, of course, because he brought it on himself with his stupid raid on Elishaw. But he knows that, too. And now," she added, stretching her body as a cat might, "I have dispensed all my good advice for tonight, so I am going to bed."

"You must be tired after riding to Hawick and back, and now here."

"Blethers to you again," Jenny said rudely but with another smile. "I'll admit that when I do reach the end of my string, it happens abruptly, but I'm over the constant fatigue I felt at the beginning. All I wanted to do then was sleep. I hadn't a notion what was amiss either, so I'd cry if Rand even raised his voice. But that is all in the past now. By morning I'll feel fully rested again."

She stood, opening her arms as she approached Meg.

"I'm so glad you came," Meg said, warmly welcoming the hug.

"Me, too," Jenny said as she stepped back. "I'm a meddler, though. I won't deny it, but I am going to like having a sister at last. Rand had two, but both died young and I never had one till now. So if I meddle too much, just tell me to stop."

"I will," Meg said, as she saw her to the door.

As Meg prepared for bed, she realized that, meddler or not, Jenny had given her much to think about. And as she snuffed the candles and climbed into a bed that she thought far too large for one slender woman, she found herself wondering what her husband had been doing since he had left her at Scott's Hall.

Wat was sitting before a pleasant fire in his tower's great hall, drinking ale with Tammy and Gib amid the usual clutter of men and equipment. These included weapons and assorted vestments cast aside or being polished or otherwise tended. He lent but half an ear to the jests and tall tales that the men shared as he tried to decide between riding into the Forest the next day to search for raiders—a task that had so far proven fruitless—or going to the horse races again.

Dod Elliot got up to put another log on the fire. Looking over his shoulder as he poked it into place, he said, "D'ye hear aught of our Sym, Master Wat?"

"I do not," Wat said with a chuckle. "And I see that as a good thing. He's unlikely to find mischief whilst my father is at hand. So, what do you think, lads? Do we keep after those damned elusive thieves or ride to Langholm again?"

"We didna enjoy the aftermath last time," Tammy reminded him.

Wat was about to assure him that such a disaster was unlikely to happen again when one of his lads ran into the hall, saying urgently, "Riders, sir, and a horn. And, sir, it be Himself's hornsman a-blowing it. I ken his notes fine."

"My father?" Wat leaped to his feet and cast a critical eye over the hall. "Stow those things and quickly, lads. Buccleuch is coming."

"D'ye think summat happened at the Hall?" Dod asked anxiously.

"Stop fretting about Sym and think," Wat said curtly. "If there were trouble, Buccleuch would send a messenger, not come himself. Sakes, he's scarcely set foot in this tower since I moved in. He sends for me when he wants me." The words did nothing to reassure him. "What the devil has brought him here now?"

No one heeded him, because his men were scurrying like children, scooping up their own things and anyone else's that came to hand, and disappearing up the stairs just as Wat heard quick sounds of booted feet coming upstairs from the yard.

Looking around once more and taking a breath, he went to meet his father.

Buccleuch entered, looked around, and said heartily, "You look well, lad."

"Thank you, sir. You do, too. May I offer you a mug of this ale?"

"Aye, sure," Buccleuch said, moving to hold his hands to the fire's warmth. "'Tis a brisk night. The wind was fierce round the Hall when I rode out, but in the cleuch one hears only the burn murmuring and the rush of its falls."

As Wat filled what he hoped was a clean mug with ale, he said, "It has been long since you've honored me with a visit, sir. I hope naught is amiss at home."

"What could be amiss?" Buccleuch said, using his foot to nudge a joint stool that one of the lads had abandoned closer to the fire, and sitting on it with his mug in hand. "I just thought I'd come enjoy a pleasant word with my son."

Wat's instinct for gauging his father's moods was as keen as it was for survival. Already alerted by Buccleuch's unexpected arrival, it shrieked warning now.

Turning the back-stool on which he had sat before to straddle it, he rested his forearms on the back and eyed Buccleuch warily.

Buccleuch stared into the fire.

When the silence continued until Wat could stand it no longer, he said, "Are you vexed with me, sir?"

Turning his head just enough to look at him, Buccleuch gently raised his eyebrows and said, "Vexed? Why would I be?"

"Prithee, my lord, have mercy," Wat begged. "You are asking your questions as if I ought to be able to answer them. It makes me feel as my tutors used to make me feel when I did not know my lessons."

"Then I suspect you know the answers to your own questions if you would but give your mind to them." Buccleuch turned to look around the great hall again.

As he did, Wat saw it with a more critical eye. The lads had whisked away the worst of the clutter, but compared with the well-managed Hall . . .

"What have you done to prepare this place for your wife?" Buccleuch asked.

"We've been searching for the raiders," Wat said. "There is no sense in bringing the lasses here until the Forest is safe again, after all. And, too, we may shortly be facing battle with the English."

"That would seem to leave little time for you to see to matters here."

"They'll be safer at the Hall if we have to be away."

"Perhaps, but you have been here nearly a sennight," his father pointed out. "One wonders if you've forgotten your duty to your wife and to your name."

"She is quite safe with you, is she not?"

"She is."

"Then of what duty . . . ?"

"It is the duty of every good husband to produce an heir, lad. You should be doing all you can in that regard, lest you fall in battle. If you do not mean to bring the lass here, you should spend more time at the Hall. Oh, and our

Jenny has come for a visit. You will be glad to see her, I trow."

He would, indeed, for he liked his sister very much. But as that thought crossed his mind, another jumped in.

Left to herself, Jenny would soon be meddling.

Chapter 9

—

Her shape it was slender, her arms they were fine,
Her shoulders were clad wi' her lang dusky hair . . .

Meg dreamed pleasantly that she was wearing new earrings that Amalie had given her. Her sister had been smiling and laughing when she presented them, but then, oddly, she had vanished. When Meg reached to touch the new earrings, one of them had disappeared, too.

Both ears began to hurt, and as she touched the one that still bore an earring, she heard rushing water. The sound grew louder, filling the woods— No, now she was in a dark chamber. When had she come hither, and why?

Golden light flickered, steadied, and grew brighter. She heard a thump.

She stirred, half-awake, uncomfortably aware that one entire bared leg had grown icy cold. As she drew it back and reached to pull her coverlet higher, she realized the light was not glowing only in her dream.

Opening her eyes, she saw her husband standing near the hearth, wearing breeks, boots, and a dark, thigh-length, heavy cloak. He held a lighted candle in one hand. Another, also alight, stood on the nearby candlestand.

She blinked hard, twice, but Walter and the candles were still there.

Pushing hair off her face, she knew that her plaits had come undone and she must look dreadfully untidy. Aware, too, that although the hour was late, it was not nearly morning yet, she propped herself on an elbow and said, "What's amiss?"

"Nowt," he said, the abrupt sound low in his throat. That sound and the fact that he looked at her with an intensity she had not seen before made her feel oddly vulnerable. He cleared his throat and said, "The fire was nobbut dying embers. So I lit a candle and put on some logs. This room was gey cold."

Reacting to surging guilt similar to that which overcame her whenever her mother or father noted a fault, she said, "I'd have put more wood on, but it seemed wasteful just for me. I did not know that you would come."

"Sakes, lass, you've no need to freeze in here," he said.

"But I don't! In the mornings, Avis comes and lights a fire before I waken. Indeed, I'm surprised I didn't think you were she and go right back to sleep."

But she had not thought he was Avis. And the way he was watching her was sending waves of heat through her that she could not define.

He did not comment on the unlikelihood that she could mistake him for Avis. Nor did he look like a man who had come to his bedchamber to sleep. He looked like a man with a purpose. And the only purpose she could imagine that might bring him to her at such an hour and make him look at her so was . . .

Suppressing the image that leaped to her mind's eye, she said, "Are . . . are you planning to sleep here tonight then?"

"I suppose I shall, eventually," he said softly.

She swallowed hard. She could not doubt his purpose now.

Wat continued to gaze at her as she straightened more in the bed and tried to rearrange her shift, which seemed to have tangled itself up around her waist.

He had come into the room as quietly as he knew how and, after shutting the door, had stood inside to listen to the wind outside soughing across the closed shutter as if it sought entrance through some crack or other. When he and Buccleuch had emerged from the deep cleuch into Rankilburn Glen, the wind had hurled itself at them. Buccleuch, however, had assured him that it was not as strong as it had been.

It still blew in occasional fierce gusts, but they were diminishing. And when the noise eased for a moment, he heard her soft breathing. When he opened the door, he had caught a brief glimpse of her shape in the bed. But with only the faint light from a low-burning cresset across the landing, he had noticed nothing more.

His attention had shifted instead to the hearth, where the last embers were vanishing fast. So he'd taken twigs from the basket, placed them strategically amid the brightest of the still-glowing coals, and stirred the fire to life by the simple expedient of blowing on it. When he had flames, he added more twigs and sticks, then lit the candle on the candlestand with a flaming twig. He took time to coax larger pieces of wood to burn before lighting a second candle for himself.

Turning with candle in hand, he saw that one bare, very shapely golden-skinned leg had escaped the covers, from its dainty arched foot to its hip.

He held the candle higher to get a better look.

As he did, she murmured in her sleep and the leg slid back under the covers.

He was stepping nearer when one of the larger pieces of wood shifted with a loud thud, stopping him in his tracks.

She opened her eyes.

Then she shut them and looked again, twice.

In the candlelight, with her long, dark hair tousled round her face and draped like a dark sheet over her shoulders—and her eyes looking like large, dark-lashed golden pools as their gray depths reflected tiny twin images of his candle's flame—he wondered how anyone had thought her homely.

She looked like a fascinating creature from another world.

He had meant to come to her, do his duty, and sleep. But the thought of stroking that shapely golden leg stirred his cock quickly to life. As he stepped closer to the bed, equal measures of lust and the anticipation of fulfilling it surged through him. He wanted to touch her skin, to taste its golden smoothness.

Those amazing, beautiful, long-lashed eyes widened. Her full, soft-looking lips parted invitingly.

"I hope you don't mind that I woke you," he said.

"Oh, no, for I was having the strangest dream," she said matter-of-factly.

This time, *he* shut his eyes.

Meg did not know what demon had made her mention her dream. When she saw his intent, her body had begun tingling from its center outward with unfamiliar, radiating heat. But when he moved nearer, asking in that low, sensuous voice if she minded, she had felt panic and sputtered the first words that came to her.

Now, as he stood gazing down at her, still holding the candle high, she nervously dampened her lips with her tongue, then clamped her teeth on her lower lip when he smiled. She wondered what he expected her to do or say.

When he licked his lips, too, she felt a new jolt of the tingling heat, lower down, as if her body knew what he meant to do and was eager for it.

His gaze had locked on hers. She doubted she could evade it if she tried.

She could not think of one word to say.

He turned to set the candle in a small bowl provided for the purpose, taking his time. He spilled wax into it first, then pressed the candle onto it.

Then he poured water into the bowl from the washstand ewer, so the candle would go out if it fell over. When he moved toward her again, his cloak swung wide and she saw movement of another sort at the front of his breeks.

Heat flooding her cheeks, she looked up to meet his amused gaze and a teasing sort of smile. It was as if he knew what she had seen.

"Tell me about this dream of yours whilst I take off my clothes," he said.

"It was nothing," she said hastily, knowing how silly such a dream would sound to a man. "Don't you want help? I could put away your cloak for you."

"Nay then, stay under the covers until I get in with you to keep you warm," he said. "It is too cold out here for a lass still warm with sleep."

Lowering her eyes at the thought of him warming her, she saw him stir again.

She squeezed her eyes shut then until he said quietly, "A man has a right to know what his wife dreams."

She recalled Jenny saying he liked to have his own way, but unable to think of any reason not to tell him, she said, "In troth, the dream was naught to discuss, just strange. I was in a wood, and Amalie had given me earrings. I'd lost one."

"What was strange about that?"

"When I found I'd lost it, I was no longer in the woods but in a dark room with a sound like water rushing through it. Then I saw an eerie orange light."

"That was nobbut the wind outside and me lighting candles, I expect," he said. "What did Amalie have to say to you about losing the earring?"

Meg nibbled her lip, feeling as if she were nearing a precipice, although she could not imagine why. She said, "Amalie had disappeared, and my ears hurt."

"Do they hurt now?" he asked, sounding concerned.

"No, only in the dream," she said. But the thought of him being concerned for her imaginary pain made her feel warm again. She smiled at him.

⁓

He smiled back at her before it struck him that he had never seen her smile before. He had even asked her once if she ever did smile, and once he'd thought she nearly had. But he was certain this was the first smile he had received from her.

Her even white teeth glinted in the candlelight, and if her mouth was wide, so was her smile. The sight of it made him feel much as he'd feel coming upon a newborn fawn in the woods on a fine spring day. It stirred other feelings, too.

He tossed his cloak to the end of the bed and sent the leather doublet he wore to the floor by the window. Then quickly unlacing his shirt, he pulled it off and sent it after the doublet, dealing next with his boots and breeks in the same manner and with equal speed. As he jerked off his netherstocks, he glanced at her and saw that although the smile had faded, the twinkle lingered in her eyes.

As he moved toward her, she said, "Did you come all this way at such an hour just to see me?"

He nearly told her the truth, but some lingering sense of what he decided must be self-preservation stopped the words on his tongue.

Instead, he said, "I heard my sister Jenny had come. It seemed a good excuse to tear myself away from Raven's Law to visit my wife."

"Surely, you do not need an excuse to visit me," she said. With a little gasp, she shifted nearer the wall when he put his knee on the bed to get in with her.

"Surely, madam," he said, mimicking her as he leaned over to kiss her lightly, "I came because I wanted to come."

He loomed over her, and Meg's body responded to his nearness in ways she had never known it could. She imagined where he would touch her and how he would touch her, and what he would do next. She remembered the pain from the first time. But the thought that it might prove painful again did not disturb her.

She was glad he had come to her.

"I want to look at you," he said. "But tell me if you get cold."

"Aye," she said, swallowing hard again as he lifted the coverlet off her and began to deal with her shift. She helped him until he whisked it off over her head, exposing her body as he cast the shift after his own tumbled clothing.

He smelled pleasantly of leather and horses, and his hot breath when he kissed her smelled slightly of ale.

He leaned closer, propped up on one elbow, and she trembled. When he cupped her left breast with his free hand, her breath caught somewhere between her lungs and throat. But when he brushed his thumb across her nipple, she gasped and a moan escaped. When it did, his mouth came down on hers, hard.

While he held her lips hostage, his body shifted over hers. The hand that had been idle before found her hair, and the other toyed with her breasts. It stroked one moment, teased a nipple the next. As the thought flitted through her mind that he had been the first man to touch her hair, let alone to tangle his fingers in it, the hand that teased her breast slid lower. It caressed her midriff, then her abdomen, then toyed with the curls at the juncture of her legs.

When she stiffened, his tongue thrust itself between her lips.

She was so soft, her skin velvety one moment and smooth as silk the next. He wanted to taste it, to run his tongue from her breasts right down to what his fingers explored now. But the last thing he wanted to do was frighten her.

She seemed willing, even seemed to enjoy his touch. Since a willing wife could only be an asset to a man, he marveled that he had once believed he'd never want to fondle or kiss her, let alone to lie naked with her.

Yet here he was, so eager to couple with her that it was all he could do not to bury his quhilly-lillie up to its cods in her tirly-whirlie, as common folk might say.

He strove to prepare her, using his fingers to part her nether lips and stimulate her juices. But when she stirred against him, her body eager, her moans increasing in length and volume, he could contain himself no longer.

He moved atop her and entered her eagerly. When her body clamped around him as if it would suck him straight into her fiery core, he forgot about being delicate or taking things slowly and let instinct take over.

Soon he was pounding into her, driven to frenzy by the soft sounds she made as she arced toward him. She seemed determined and eager to meet every thrust.

His climax came quickly. When he collapsed atop her, she was breathing as heavily as he was.

After several moments, he realized he was probably crushing her. She was a foot shorter and at least five stone lighter than he was. He eased himself off onto his side, propping himself on an elbow again to look down into her face.

She looked content, although he doubted she had

reached her peak. He smiled then, remembering the first time he had realized women even attained peaks. That had been with a most willing chambermaid years older than himself.

He had been seventeen. He thought her name was Sal.

"Why do you smile?" she asked.

"Am I smiling?" he replied, knowing better than to tell her why. He could not remember what Sal looked like, or if Sal had even been her name.

"You are." Her eyes gleamed in the candlelight. "I did not know that this could feel the way it does," she said. "No one ever told me."

"Did you like it?"

"The feelings are . . . They are indescribable," she said after a moment's thought. "Is there aught I can do to pleasure *you* so?"

"What we just did pleasured me," he said, but he was looking at her mouth as he spoke. Just looking at her full, soft lips and wide, "muckle" mouth, he felt his cock stir again, suggestively. He stifled the thought.

He had not bathed since Elishaw, and she was too new to pleasuring to take his cock's enticing suggestion as aught but perversion. He would wait and see how matters progressed. It occurred to him that he could simply command her, that husbands did so all the time. Some even bragged of it.

But that notion sat ill with him, and he realized he had developed respect, even liking, for this wife of his. He would do better to show her that he had other delights in store for her before he indulged himself.

On that thought, he lay back against the pillows and drew her close. With her head resting in the hollow of his shoulder, he realized how comfortable he felt and decided that some aspects of his unlooked-for marriage were very pleasant.

He was ready neither to sleep yet nor to exert himself more, and as she lay silently beside him, he recalled her odd dream and gave it some thought.

A few moments later, he said, "Tell me more about that dream you had."

"I've told you all I can remember of it," she murmured.

"But the lady Amalie was there and then not there?"

"Aye, and the earring likewise."

He did not care about the earring. It was neither real nor truly lost. Amalie, on the other hand, was both real and living right there at the Hall.

"It seems a strange dream to have about your sister, as full of darkness and pain as it was," he said. "What has she done to stir such feelings in you?"

"Why, what *could* she have done?"

He waited.

At last, with a sigh, she said, "I should not tell you all she said to me."

He rose onto his side again, shifting so he could look at her. He eased her head to the pillow as he did, but kept his forearm under her shoulders. "On the contrary," he said, looking into her eyes. "You will tell me, because I am your husband. When I ask you a question, I expect an answer—a truthful answer."

"But surely—"

"You need not worry that I may betray your confidence, because I won't. Recall, too, that before Holy Kirk, we are one now, and that one is the husband."

She gazed at him for a long moment before she said, "She is unhappy because she does not feel comfortable here. I have assured her that I welcome her company, but she . . . she feels as if I am the only one here at Scott's Hall who does."

"Aye, well, now that Jenny is here, I expect that will change."

Her expression remained sober, and he felt her stiffen. "What?" he demanded. "Don't tell me that you do not like Jenny, for I shan't believe it."

Her incredible smile appeared then, not as wide as before but still startling in the way it altered her features in the flickering candle glow.

"I'll not tell you any such thing," she said. "You were right about Jenny. I feel sure we will become fast friends."

Satisfaction filled him, stronger than he might have expected. He savored it for a time before he realized she still had not answered his question satisfactorily.

"I'm glad you like her," he said. "Is it Amalie who does not? Because if that is the case, the best way to deal with her is to send her back to Elishaw where she can be happy again. I'm not sure why she wanted to come here with us at all."

"She came to bear me company, so I'd not have to travel alone with so many men. It was kind of her, and thoughtful. I don't want her to leave until she wants to go. And at present, she does not." Taking a deep breath, she added, "What she does want is to leave Scott's Hall. So I was wondering how much progress you've made at Raven's Law. When can we move there?"

Knowing he had done almost nothing to prepare for that move, he felt a stab of guilt and a stronger one of annoyance with himself. Sex with her had proven so welcome a duty that he was already looking forward to the next time. If he got her properly settled at Raven's Law, he could enjoy her every night if he willed it so.

As it was, he said, "Not yet, lass. I have much yet to do there. And with things still as unsettled in the Forest as they are, and Douglas likely gathering his army soon, it is far safer for you and Amalie to stay here for now."

He saw her jaw set, and he did not want to fratch with her over a decision he had no intention of changing. Before she could fling another argument his way, he said gently but firmly, "You have not told me everything yet, have you?"

When she grimaced, he added, "It does not make sense that your sister would feel unhappy here and would not feel so at Raven's Law, which will never be as comfortable as it is here or at Elishaw. So tell me the rest."

"I can't," she said. "I know you and the Kirk think I must, but I just can't."

"You can, Margaret. I know you can keep your own counsel. God knows you have with me. You've not even blamed me for this marriage of ours, although I'm sure you have much you'd like to say to me. But if you are going to keep secrets, we will soon be at outs. For a wife to keep secrets from her husband is a sin."

"What about a husband keeping secrets from his wife?" she murmured, gazing at him, not as if she challenged him but as if she expected . . . what?

It occurred to him that Murray probably kept any number of secrets from his wife and daughters, especially if Lady Murray was the threaping sort Gib had named her. He said, "There are things you've no need to know, that have nowt to do with you or with Raven's Law, but I'll not keep things from you that you ought to know."

"But you will decide what I should know and what I should not. And you likewise want to decide how much *you* should know about me and Amalie."

"Aye, sure I do. I am responsible for you both. I am also involved in matters that concern many others, not just my own family. Other men's confidences are not things I mean to share with my wife—or with anyone else, come to that."

"I understand that," she said. "I shan't ask you about such things."

"Good, then we understand each other," he said. "So, tell me."

Meg was not sure they did understand each other, but she was coming to know him and doubted she could resist him long. If he knew what his touch did to her, she'd have no chance now. He had only to ask her while his fingers and lips teased her to distraction, and she would tell him anything he wanted to know.

She tried to think of an answer that would make him drop the subject. She knew he meant to keep his word, but she did not know if he could resist offering advice to Amalie or otherwise revealing his awareness of her unhappiness to her.

Meg could not imagine how he had deduced that there was more. She was unaccustomed to anyone caring enough about her thoughts to try to read them, but reflection reminded her that he was a warrior, used to reading opponents in battle.

Doubtless, then, his skill in judging another's thoughts had developed much as her own had. Hers had done so while seeking peaceful coexistence with her family. Did such a goal not match that of any warrior fighting to survive battle?

She lay close enough to feel the warmth of his body and feel his gaze boring into her even when she managed to look away. If he moved closer or touched her . . .

He stirred. His left hand moved to her right arm, stroking it gently first, then grasping it firmly and jarring her a little as he said, "Tell me, lass. Now. It will be easier than you think, I promise. What's amiss with Amalie?"

Again he loomed over her, determined and intense.

She remembered her marital promises to be meek and obedient and her private determination to please him. But this was something so personal to Amalie that she felt as if she would be betraying her.

"You have no reason yet to believe me when I say you can trust me," he said. "But I swear you can, and if there is a way I can help, I will. You have my word."

She could not see how he could help, but he meant to have an answer. That left the choice either to anger him by defying his command or to obey it and pray she could trust him. And she, too, had given her word, not just to him but to God.

"Someone has taken advantage of her," she said at last.

"Who?"

"She will not tell me. But when I asked if it was someone here, she said no."

He frowned, and she waited for him to say that he'd get the truth out of her in a trice, but he shook his head, saying, "It would not have been anyone here. Our lads may not be angels, but they have healthy concern for their skin, and my father would take a man's off him for such as this. Did the devil get her with child?"

Meg nearly denied it out of shock that he would ask the question and impulse to defend Amalie. But then, remembering, she said, "I don't know. I don't think she knows. But she has complained of being tired ever since we arrived. And Jenny said— She doesn't know about Amalie, but she said she was so exhausted at first, herself, that she just wanted to sleep all the time. So it is with Amalie."

She expected anger then, but he said only, "We'll know soon enough, I warrant. Are you sure she would not prefer to be at Elishaw with your mother?"

"Nay, she is terrified of being found out. She says no one will want to marry her when the truth comes out."

"If she were well enough dowered, such a truth would not matter."

Meg grimaced. "As you know yourself, sir, my father is not fond of dowries for his daughters. And my mother will be just as furious as Amalie fears she will."

"Then we must persuade them to be practical," he said, smiling.

The tension Meg had felt since Amalie's disclosure began to ease. She smiled softly at him. "I thought you would be angry," she said.

"Why? It was none of your doing—or hers, I'll wager."

"If we do find out who it was and my parents learn of it, they will want to force the man to marry her," Meg said.

"If the lass would agree, that *would* be the best solution."

"I'd think it would be a reward to him for his villainy," she said grimly.

"We'll think of something." He bent and kissed her, lightly at first, then more deeply, clearly savoring the taste of her, because he moaned deep in his throat.

His hand moved to her breast, and all thoughts of Amalie disappeared as he showed her that he could make her feel more than she had imagined.

When Wat awoke, the room was silent but light enough to let him know he had slept later than usual. He had also slept more deeply than he had in a long while. Remembering why, he reached for Margaret only to find her gone.

To have slipped out of the cupboardlike bed with him sleeping on the outside, blocking her against the wall, she had to have moved like a wraith, and the thought stirred niggling annoyance. He grimaced then, wondering if he had become such a coxcomb that his wife's managing to get out of bed without his permission had somehow become an act of willfulness.

With more pleasant thoughts of the night before and how different it had been from his imaginings, he got out of bed and relieved himself in the night vessel before pouring cold water from the ewer into the basin to scrub his face.

Rubbing it dry with a towel, he wished he had brought his razor. He hadn't, though, so as soon as he had dressed, he left the room in search of food.

Downstairs in the great chamber, which his sister insisted on calling the solar, he found the women gathered around the family table, chatting.

Even Amalie was there, sitting quietly but nodding at something Jenny had said. A quick assessment as he strolled toward the dais revealed that the lass did look a bit pale but otherwise showed no hint of her distress or much else.

"Good morning," he said to everyone in general. "I heard you were here, Jenny, so I came along to keep you out of trouble."

"How thoughtful," she said, grinning as he bent to kiss her. "Rand sends his felicitations on your marriage," she added. "I think them well merited, don't you?"

Her laughing eyes teased him to deny it.

He looked at Margaret, sitting primly beside her, and recalled her delight and her consideration for him during their activities the previous night.

"I do, indeed," he said, smiling at his wife rather than at Jenny.

To his delight, Margaret smiled back. She looked different by daylight, certainly, but the plain gray kirtle she wore showed off the lines of her body better than her more fashionable attire. The simple white veil looked well on her, too, because its narrow lace trim softened and widened the lines of her face.

Her smile, as always, altered her features extraordinarily.

His mother said, "I warrant you have not yet broken your fast."

"I'm starved," he said. "Is there food here, or must I go down to the hall?"

"I told them you would be along here soon, sir," Margaret said.

"She did, indeed," his mother agreed. "And young Sym dashed off to fetch your food the minute he caught sight of you in the doorway."

He had not noticed Sym, but the lad brought his food swiftly.

Wat joined the others at the table, and as he ate, the conversation flowed merrily on. Chatting with them, hearing Jenny and Amalie call Margaret "Meg," he found himself looking frequently at his wife, trying to reconcile his lusty images from the night before with the neat young woman sitting there at the table.

He liked the name Meg. It suited the lass he had discovered in his bed.

To his astonishment and no little dismay, his cock came eagerly to life again.

Shifting forward on the bench so no one else would notice, he focused on his food, wondering why that had happened. That he was so attracted to Meg sexually astonished him. He recalled again his thoughts when he'd first had to bed her. But there she sat now, a sleek gray cat. Wondering if she had claws, he stirred again.

"Don't you agree, Wat?" Jenny asked, wrenching him from his reverie.

He looked blankly at her, having no idea what they had been discussing.

Noise of booted feet thudding up the main stairway came as a welcome diversion. He turned to see his father stride into the chamber with another man at his heels. The latter snatched off a battered cap when he saw the ladies.

"This lad has come from Elishaw," Buccleuch said to Wat, his demeanor making it clear that he was irritated. "He says he brings an urgent message for you."

The man bowed, clutching his cap to his stomach. "Beg pardon, Sir Walter," he said. "Ye'll no remember me, but Sir Iagan said I should speak only to ye, to tell ye we've been besieged and to bring as many men as ye can raise, straightaway."

Wat glanced at his father, understanding his irritation. Clearly the messenger had refused to say why he had come. Buccleuch had honored the man's insistence that he speak only to Wat, but doing so had *not* pleased him.

Chapter 10

*"Oh, Master! Ye ken how the Murrays have grund you . . .
Rough Iagan o' Eli's grown doited and silly . . ."*

Who is besieging Elishaw?" Buccleuch demanded.

The man bowed low before he replied, "I dinna ken, me lord. All I ken o' the matter is me captain rousted me out o' me bed and told me to come here straightaway. When I said I didna ken just what I should say, he told me the master said that if Sir Walter be a man o' his word, I need tell ye nobbut that he needs aid. He said I could remind Sir Walter o' his bond and promise but I shouldna ha' to."

Wat was on his feet. "I won't have as many men as usual with me if I have to go at once. I should have eight days to gather my men, should I not?"

He glanced at Buccleuch, who nodded, but the messenger said anxiously, "'Tis haste that's required, sir. Me captain said even thirty men riding under the Scott banner would show them besiegers that other lairds ken what they're about and mayhap send them off to threaten someone else."

"Right, then," Wat said, mentally listing the men he could gather quickly. "I can be ready to ride in two hours. Wait for me in the great hall and have something to eat if you like. I'll find you when I'm ready."

He turned away, thinking only of how he might most quickly gather his men.

Someone cleared her throat noisily, and he turned to see his sister gazing at him with eyebrows raised. She gave a slight nod toward Meg.

Recalled to domestic duty, Wat said, "Forgive me, lass, but I must hurry. I'll be back as soon as I can. Jenny, how long do you mean to stay?"

"Just another few days," she said. "Rand grows impatient when I am away."

"I'd like to have talked with you more, but if you must go, you must," he said. "Mayhap you can come again soon."

He strode from the great chamber, deciding which men to send where, and what to say to encourage them to gather as many others as they could. Some would ride with him, and others could follow. As he left the room, he heard his sister say, "Is it not just like a man to assume that one must come to him to be seen?"

Behind him, Buccleuch said, "I'll ride with you if you want me."

"Thank you, sir, but if it is all the same to you I'll do this myself. I can always send one of my lads back for reinforcements if I need them. I'm guessing it may be nobbut a band of Hotspur's ruffians letting Murray know they want him to side with England when the conflict comes."

"Likely you're right," Buccleuch said. "But I'll let our lads know to spread the word that you may need more men at a moment's notice. They're eager to ride with

Douglas, but they do expect to get their eight days before they need join him."

~

Meg watched her husband's departure with mixed feelings. That his thoughts had turned so swiftly to the duty he owed her father did not surprise her. Men, in her experience, always believed their duty to other men came first. Duty to their families came second. That was just the nature of men.

Even so, a twinge of disappointment, even annoyance, had stirred when he moved so quickly toward the door without a word to his mother or to her. However, she had read nothing in Lady Scott's expression except interest in the conversation.

She had been glad when Jenny had stopped him by clearing her throat. She was likewise aware, due to the excellence of her peripheral vision and Walter's reaction, that it was Jenny who had drawn his attention to her. Meg wondered now if he would have stopped if she had been the one who cleared her throat so noisily.

His comments, however, had irked her so much that anyone might have seen it in her face, just as she had noted Buccleuch's irritation with the messenger.

When Jenny said that men always expected others to come to them, Meg said, "That is not really true, you know. Men and women both tend to visit their parents more often than their siblings, I think. My brothers visit Elishaw two or three times a year, and I'll wager that your brothers all come here, just as you do."

"Aye, sure, but my parents also come to visit me at Ferniehurst. The only time Wat comes is if he has business with Rand, and neither John nor Andrew has ever visited me there. They just expect me to come here to the Hall when they do."

Hearing it put that way, Meg realized that while Tom might come to visit her, Simon would not. But Simon would certainly expect to see her at Elishaw when he visited their parents. He would pretend to take offense if she were not there. She did not think he cared a whit about her, though, or about anyone except himself.

Tom was different. He would visit her, and Amalie, too. If he did not come as soon as he learned where they were, then he would do so as soon as he could.

"What are you going to do now?" Jenny asked Meg.

She spoke with such an innocent air that Meg hesitated before she said, "Do? What do you mean?"

"Only that I think you should decide whether you want to be at Wat's beck and bay all your life or be able to exert yourself occasionally to do as *you* please."

"Jenny, mind your tongue," Janet Scott said. But her tone was one of amusement rather than warning.

Leaning forward enough to look past Jenny, Meg met Janet's twinkling gaze.

"Do not let her lead you into mischief, my dear," she said. "That is, not into any mischief you find objectionable or that may lead to fearsome consequences."

Jenny's eyes danced. "You know what you want to do, Meg. Do it."

Meg grimaced, glad that Buccleuch had gone with his son and the Elishaw messenger, and hoping servants still there would not prate of what they heard.

"What are you talking about?" Amalie asked, entering the conversation for the first time that morning. "What does Meg want to do, my lady?"

"Faith, Amalie, do call me Jenny," Jenny pleaded with a laugh. "By continuing to address me so formally, you make me feel like a dowager."

"Very well, but what *are* you suggesting?"

"Meg knows," Jenny said. "Moreover, it is her choice to make. So although I may be urging her to make it, you should not."

"But how could I if I don't even know what you mean?"

"You take my meaning now well enough," Jenny said, giving her a look.

"Jenny, heed your own advice," Janet Scott said, the warning note clear now.

But Jenny turned with her bright smile and said, "Mother, you know I am right. If a female does not stand up for herself in this family, she might as well go out in the yard and lie down so the menfolk can walk all over her. You *know* it!"

"That is a great exaggeration, but even if it were true, you must not interfere between your brother and his wife," Janet said mildly. "It is unfair, for one thing, because whilst you will have wreaked the mischief, Margaret will have to pay the price for your . . . your—"

"Say it," Jenny urged. "Wat calls it my meddling, Meg, just as I told you last night. But if one does not meddle, other people wait too long to do as they know they must. Then the problem grows worse." She chuckled. "Why, I'll wager Father told him I was here when he rode to Raven's Law last night, and Wat came here today just so that he could intervene if I did meddle."

"He arrived last night," Meg said. "I remember you telling me that your father had ridden somewhere. But you did not say he'd gone to Raven's Law."

"I didn't know," Jenny said. "But Wat must have ridden back with him then, and that is a very good sign, I think."

Meg did not agree. She had a sinking feeling that Buccleuch had ordered Walter to come. If so, it had not been his idea to see Jenny or to see her. Jenny was right about something else, though, and that was Meg's right to be at Raven's Law.

"I'll go," Meg said. "That is, I will if I can make arrangements to do so."

Looking pleased, Jenny turned to her mother. "You do agree with me, do you not? If Meg waits for Wat to arrange Raven's Law exactly as he wants it before he lets her move there, she will live here at Scott's Hall until she is in her dotage."

To Meg's astonishment, Janet said, "She is right, my dear. I dared not say it for fear you would think you are not welcome here. I promise you, you are both very welcome and have every right to stay as long as you like. Buccleuch might say something to Walter in time, but it will be much better if you manage the matter yourselves, between you. I must warn you, though, that Walter will not be pleased if you take the bit between your teeth. You must prepare yourself to deal with that."

"Pish tush," Jenny said. "I have meddled, just as you say, so if anyone should have to face Wat's temper, I should. Therefore, I'll go with her. In any event, he is most unlikely to beat me whilst I carry Rand's son and heir."

"Sakes, would he beat you?" Meg exclaimed, wondering if she ought to expect similar treatment.

Jenny laughed. "Bless you, he's threatened to do so often, but he never has yet. He did smack me pretty hard on the backside once when he was twelve. Sithee, I was seven and I'd dared to sass him. But he has never done more than that."

"Nevertheless," Janet said more sternly than Meg had yet heard her speak. "You will not interfere further if Meg decides to move to Raven's Law."

"Is that what you want to do?" Amalie exclaimed. "Oh, Meggie!"

"I'm going with her," Jenny said firmly. "Nay, madam, do not fret. Recall that Elishaw is besieged, so Wat will be gone for days if not weeks, and I won't stay there above a night or two. I'm perfectly fit, and as I am the one who suggested it, I mean to help Meg settle in. It will do her no good to be wallowing in filth there, feeling miserable, when Wat returns. She must look efficient and in command of the place. I can help with that, and I mean to do so."

Meg held her breath and watched her mother-in-law. She knew she could manage a household, for she had learned from one of the best. But she had never tried to run one full of men, or to turn such a household into a home fit for a family. Nor did she think she could do so now without more help than Amalie's.

She need not have worried, for Jenny won the day without a tussle. Janet just said mildly that they'd need the help of a number of menservants and housemaids.

"Take those you need from here," she said to Jenny. Then, to Meg, she said, "Many of ours live nearby and have younger siblings who will want positions, my dear, so you will easily find some who can come to you daily. You won't want a lot of new servants who would need to sleep there, for the tower won't accommodate them. And heaven knows if any of the outbuildings can do so."

After that, things progressed swiftly.

Announcing that Scott's Hall servants could pack Meg's baggage and Amalie's and deliver it to the tower, Jenny ordered horses for them and for the servants who would accompany them. An hour later, they were ready to depart.

Sym rode near Meg, and they had not gone far before she noticed that he had attached a pouch of sorts to the rope he used to hold up his baggy breeks.

When the pouch moved, she said, "What have you got in there, Sym?"

"Just Pawky," the boy said as the kitten's head popped through the pouch opening. "She's gey content in her sack, and I couldna leave her."

He stroked the kitten's head gently with two fingers. A few moments later, it disappeared back into the pouch, and the pouch was soon still again.

Amalie expressed both pleasure and excitement as they forded the tree-shaded Rankilburn and followed a track through the forest, into the Buck Cleuch. The foliage was denser in the cleuch, the track narrower and visibly less traveled.

Although little sunlight pierced the dense canopy, birds sang merrily in the trees. The smaller burn babbled as it flung itself over cascades in its downhill haste to join the Rankilburn. The air was still and rich with moisture and woodland scents.

Meg began to relax. Buck Cleuch was a peaceful place, a place she could love.

Her sister's chatter continued until they reached the peel tower. But as they turned uphill toward its barmkin gate, Amalie fell silent.

The square, five-story, gray-stone tower sat on a rise

above the burn, near the head of the cleuch. The steep ravine walls were nearly a hundred feet high there, and they could hear the rushing of a waterfall in the distance.

"Godamercy," Amalie said. "Is this it?"

"Aye," Jenny said cheerfully. "What do you think, Meg?"

"I can't see enough of it yet to tell you," Meg said. She saw only that the tower was thirty or forty feet on a side and looked strong. Its wall was of stone, though, not timber, and she knew that was good.

"Those walls are nine feet thick," Jenny said. "So it is not as large as it might appear. It was a family residence once, though, so it should not be too difficult to turn it into one again. That was Wat's intention when he came here, but without a family, and living only with men . . ." She shrugged. "But here we are, and they're opening the gate. With his stock gone, I did fear he might have locked everything up and taken all his men with him. Then we'd have been at a standstill."

They dismounted in the yard, and Jenny led them into the tower through a short tunnel and a vaulted chamber that looked like a stable or byre, which Jenny called the pend. A heavy wooden door in one of its corners, protected by a heavy framework of iron, led to a spiral staircase.

The first landing opened into a chamber with a huge fireplace occupying most of one wall and surmounted by an equally vast chimney tapering to the ceiling. Windows on either side bowed out to accommodate stone window seats.

"The kitchen and a small dining hall lie yonder," Jenny said, pointing to the opposite side of the hall. "But come; I'll show you the bedchambers upstairs."

At the next landing, she unlatched and opened the door on her left. "You might like this one, Amalie."

"There is no fireplace there."

"Do you have fireplaces in every bedchamber at Elishaw?" Jenny asked.

"Of course not," Amalie said. "But I wish we did."

"Well, there are no fireplaces above the main hall here. The master's chamber does share a wall with the hall chimney and is usually warm, Wat says. A chamber on the next floor also shares that wall, if you don't mind more stairs."

"I don't mind at all," Amalie said. "I'd rather have warmth."

Smiling at Meg, Jenny went on. "Wat's room also has the best window. 'Tis a shot window, like the two by the fireplace. All three overlook the yard and have stout shutters and yetts, so you can secure them well if the place ever comes under siege. It never has," she added. "It is so well hidden here, I suppose, that only folks in the area know it well."

"My father knew enough to come a-reiving here," Meg said.

"Aye, but only in the glen, well away from Scott's Hall, and not here at the tower," Jenny reminded her. Opening the door on the other side of the landing, she added, "This is Wat's room. Since it will also be yours, you'll want to take a look."

It was anything but tidy, and Meg remembered how he had cast his clothes off when he had wakened her at the Hall. Clearly, it had not been lust alone that had caused that, for none of his clothes seemed to be put away. They carpeted the floor.

"He is not very orderly," Jenny observed. "The hall was a mess, too."

"Aye." Meg had noted that detail for herself.

"Do you want to see the rest?"

"I think we'd better call the others in and get right to work," Meg said. "There is enough in what we've already seen to keep us busy for a sennight."

"Aye," Jenny agreed. "'Tis good that Wat will be away for a while."

~

The journey to Elishaw took the rest of the day, because it had taken more time than expected to rally Wat's forces. He had fifty men, though, without robbing the Hall or Raven's Law of needed protection, and he had reason to believe they would be enough to send the besiegers running, or at least persuade them to talk.

If he needed help, his father could raise a thousand men quickly by lighting the great emergency signal fires. Men throughout the Borders knew that as well as he did, so he doubted it would take more than a look at the Scott pennon to deter such rabble as he expected to find at Elishaw.

They arrived as the sun dipped below the western horizon.

Tammy, riding beside him, said, "It looks gey peaceful, Master Wat."

"Aye," Gibbie agreed. "I dinna see signs o' a siege, or any activity, come to that. D'ye think the villains set a watch for us and fled when they saw us a-coming?"

"That is possible," Wat said, but his jaw set grimly.

He did not mention his suspicion to his comrades. But

when he saw the gates of Elishaw Castle standing open, he could have growled in vexation.

Wondering if there was reason to keep silent any longer, he glanced at Tam, who also looked grim.

"Are you thinking what I'm thinking?" Wat asked him.

"If ye're thinkin' that devil's spawn Murray ha' brought us here for nowt, then aye, that be what I'm thinkin'."

"Hoots now, the pair o' ye," Gibbie said. "The man may ha' persuaded the raiders to leave him be. Mayhap he warned 'em that he'd sent for us, so they knew we were a-coming. They'd ken fine that ye'd no fail him."

Wat did not answer. Briefly, he wondered if he might be riding into a trap, but he dismissed that notion as quickly as it occurred. Murray had sent for him and must realize that Buccleuch would know that he had. And what Buccleuch knew, Douglas would know if it became important or even useful that he should.

All men of the Borders knew Murray was one to avoid confrontation. He would not stir Buccleuch or Douglas to war. His lady wife might, Wat mused sardonically, recalling what Gib and others had said of her. But Murray would not.

As they rode into the courtyard, Wat glanced at the hanging tree. But before he could sort out his feelings about being there again, he saw his father-in-law descending the main steps and drew rein. He did not dismount.

"Welcome to ye, lad," Murray said heartily. "'Tis glad I am to see ye."

"Where are your so-fearsome attackers?"

"Aye, well, I can see ye've guessed the truth," Murray said in the same hearty tone. "'Twas nobbut a wee test, sithee, to see if ye'd keep your word. But ye have, and all, and I'm proud to ha' ye for me good-son, so come in now, all o' ye. Ye'll stay the night with us, and we'll enjoy a fine supper to celebrate our kinship."

"I'd rather have my cattle and the rest of my horses back," Wat said.

"Aye, well, we can talk about that, too, if ye like," Murray said handsomely. "But come inside now, and bring your lads. We've plenty for all."

Wondering if the crafty old devil had roasted Scott beef for the occasion, Wat followed him inside. He knew that his men would appreciate a good meal, a sound sleep, and the knowledge that they could soon go home again.

~

Having begun at once, with the help of an army of maid-servants and gillies from cottages in the cleuch and Rankilburn Glen, Meg and her able assistants amazed even themselves with the progress they made by nightfall.

The few guardsmen Walter had left to keep an eye on his remaining stock and the tower itself had been reluctant at first to help with the cleaning. But a few blunt words from Jenny had set them to work with a will, tidying up the main hall.

"Where do you want them to put all that gear?" Jenny asked Meg.

"Faith, I don't have a notion," Meg said. A mental vision of Walter's men returning and flying into fury when they found none of their belongings where they had left them was daunting. But memory of a kinsman's castle she had once visited with her parents soon provided a partial solution.

"Gather up all the weapons, targes, and their ilk, and

pile them together near the dais," she said. "Then bring in ladders, as many as you can find."

While some men went rushing for ladders, others bundled the clothing they found into a pile and stowed it in the guardroom at the foot of the main stairs.

"If they could find their own gear in that mess in the hall, they can sort it out here just as easily," Jenny said, surveying the resulting pile of clothing.

As ladders came in, gillies raked up the rushes on the hall's timber floor, carried them out to dry in the sun for burning, and brought in fresh ones from cottars who had cut them from bogs in the glen and dried them in their rafters.

With ladders in place, Meg explained her idea, and men began hanging the weaponry, driving pegs into the masonry between the ashlar stones of the walls and the great chimney.

Lady Scott had sent pillows, coverlets, and other household comforts, employing Jenny's sumpter ponies to transport them. She had also sent Avis to act as Meg and Amalie's maidservant until they could find and hire others for themselves.

It had taken no more than the placement of a few pillows to transform the stone benches under the hall's shot windows into inviting, comfortable seats.

Sym seemed to be everywhere, repeating Meg's orders to anyone who seemed the least bit confused, while pitching in to help anyone who needed help. Meg was amused to note that the kitten stayed with him, content in its pouch.

Two men had mucked out the pend, while others raked and tidied the yard. Guardsmen had transformed themselves into commanders, and any gillies not raking or hanging weaponry were soon drafted into their bustling army.

The midday meal had been paltry by Meg's standards but enough to feed her troops. Supper was another matter, requiring thought. But by then she had learned that the tower had plentiful stores, a good cook named Jed Crosier, and flocks of chickens. Also, Janet Scott had had the forethought to send two kitchen maids.

As they sat round the high table that evening, with their exhausted helpers at two long trestles set perpendicularly to the dais, Jenny raised her goblet.

"A toast, my sisters," she said. "To Raven's Law. Long may it prosper."

Meg smiled wearily. "There is still so much to be done. We've barely swept the surface. The barmkin needs mending, and a number of other big projects remain to do. I doubt that these lads are up to all of them. We need to find skilled workmen to do a number of things."

"Wat can attend to all that," Jenny said. "This sort of thing is infectious, you know. Once one thing looks better, everything around it cries out for attention. That's exactly how I get Rand to notice things that I want him to do."

Meg nodded. Her mother had used similar tactics with her father. "We still have nearly the whole of the upper floors to see to. I have not even seen the top floor or the battlements yet."

"All the floors are swept," Amalie said. "The parts that show, anyway. And your bedchamber and the ones Jenny and I will use tonight are both tidy enough, thanks to the sheets and coverlets her ladyship sent to us."

Meg nodded, pleased to see how much more cheerful her sister was after a day and a half away from Scott's Hall. Even the work they'd done had seemed to help cheer her, but only time would tell how long her good mood would last. In the meantime, Meg focused on what she wanted to accomplish before Walter returned.

She wanted with all her heart to please him. But she could not pretend that her decision to defy him and refurbish Raven's Law was going to please him at all.

A shiver of anticipation stirred. She looked forward to his return.

By the next day, Wat's fury with his father-in-law had faded to irritation at the time and energy wasted on a fruitless mission. He was more irked at his inability to persuade Murray even to discuss the return of his kine and horses.

"We had a bargain, lad. Now that ye've kept your part, I'll keep mine," he said, chortling at his own joke.

That memory and his annoyance lingered all the way back to Scott's Hall. But as he rode into the courtyard that evening, his thoughts shifted to Meg, and he decided to spend the night with her.

His father was right. He had a duty to produce an heir. In times of such uncertainty, whole families of men had fallen in one great battle. Thus had they left their hard-won estates and other chattel, including wives and children, to fall under the control of other powerful men. He had two well-trusted brothers who could assume his position, but no one could guarantee that they would outlive him.

Even one son was not enough. He should sire a dozen.

With this noble thought in mind, he strode into the hall to find only his mother and father at the high table. They had finished their supper and were lingering there, enjoying each other's company.

"You're back much sooner than I'd expected," Buccleuch said.

"The old devil was just testing me," Wat said. "Seemed mighty pleased with himself, too. He refused even to discuss returning my beasts."

"But you stayed the night?"

"Aye, he would have it that we should. In troth, the lads were grateful for a hot meal and pallets by the hall fire to sleep on."

"We had visitors today," Buccleuch said, frowning thoughtfully.

Wat bent to kiss his mother's cheek but looked narrowly at his father as he did. "Visitors? More raiders?"

"Aye, I caught them on our land in the Forest, skinning a roe. Their leader is a glib fellow. He insisted that they hunted with the Douglas's permission and asked me with amiable politeness what right I had to interfere. I did not recognize any of them, but they were helping themselves to wood as well as to deer."

"Jamie Douglas would not send them without telling you," Wat protested.

"I know, but I had only twenty men with me. They had a few more than that, and whilst I'd back mine against any others, I did recall that Jamie wants no fratching. So I explained that they were trespassing and that even the Douglas's permission to hunt did not permit them to take wood as well. I also said that, as Ranger of Ettrick Forest, without his having warned me they would be there, I could not let them take the deer. They left peaceably, but I sensed trouble nonetheless."

"Doubtless you were right," Wat said. "'Tis as well

that I came back when I did. But one does wonder now if Murray had aught to do with your visitors. His demand that I go to him certainly proved helpful to them, so mayhap we should put the possibility to Jamie at the wardens' meeting next week."

"I'll tell him about this little confrontation in any event," Buccleuch said.

"Where are the lasses?" Wat asked as he took a place beside his mother.

She touched his cheek but said nothing, so he turned to his father.

"Not here, I'm afraid," Buccleuch replied.

"What do you mean, not here? I thought Jenny meant to stay a few days."

"Aye, well, she is helping Margaret," Buccleuch said.

"Helping?" A frisson of unease shot through him. "Is aught amiss?"

"Oh, no. Jenny just thought she might help her set Raven's Law in order."

"What!"

Buccleuch nodded. "I thought you'd be pleased. The task will take less time if you all put your minds to it. I should not waste much time either, lad. God only knows how long you'll have before Douglas sends for you."

"I'll have time enough," Wat growled, getting to his feet again.

"Time enough for what?" his mother asked.

"To teach Margaret to obey her husband and to throttle Jenny," he snapped. "And *don't* tell me this is none of Jenny's meddling, because I won't believe you."

Neither of his parents said a word as he strode angrily to the door.

Chapter 11

He threw off his jacket, wi' harness well lined;
He threw off his bonnet well belted wi' steel . . .

Wat hurried to the yard, where he shouted for a fresh horse. Leaving orders for his men to follow when they finished supper, he set off at once for Raven's Law.

Dusk was closing in on Buck Cleuch by the time he rode through the gates of the barmkin, which swung open as soon as the guards recognized him.

His temper had not eased one whit. He would be master of his own household if he had to throttle every woman in it.

As he thought about throttling Meg and visualized touching her, instead of hands around her scheming neck, he remembered only how soft and silky her skin felt to his fingertips and palms. Telling himself that such thinking would not do, especially as the memory stirred sensations in more places than his hands, he reminded himself that there was more than one way to master a woman.

Men came running to take his horse, but none dared to

ask why he was in such a hurry. No one asked any questions at all, nor did he speak to them.

He strode through the pend and upstairs to the main hall.

As he crossed its threshold, he saw the three of them sitting at the dais table at the end near the hearth, where a fire crackled. Just then, Jenny said something and Margaret burst into laughter, stopping him in his tracks.

She threw back her head, revealing her smooth, milky white throat, and her laughter was as musical as her speaking voice. Laughing so, she looked like a different woman from the prim, plain one he had married. Before his eyes, she became Meg again, the warm and generous woman he had found in his bed.

He glanced at Amalie, and saw that she, too, was smiling, albeit not laughing with such abandon as Meg. He caught Meg's eye next, stopping her laughter as abruptly as if he had clapped a hand to her mouth.

Returning to her usual sober self, she eyed him warily but said not a word.

Sym sat not far away from her, on the dais step, likewise watching him.

Jenny turned toward him then and, never daunted, said, "Godamercy, Wat, is the Elishaw siege over so soon? We did not expect you for at least a sennight."

"I believe you," he said, grim again, his self-imposed intent recalled. "I hope you did not bring much with you, because you're going back to the Hall at once."

Margaret spoke then, saying, "Surely not at this hour, sir. There have been more raids, for one thing, and for another—"

"Madam, you would do better to hold your tongue," he

said. "Better yet, await me in my bedchamber. I am sure you know where it is."

"To be sure, she does," Jenny said lightly. "She slept there last night, just as she would be doing every night, but for—"

"That's enough," he snapped, determined to keep her from influencing his wife more than she already had. "Go upstairs, Margaret. Amalie, you may go with her. I'll acquit you of any part in this, but you'd be wise to seek your room and stay in it for now. We are not going to be very good company for you tonight."

Amalie got up at once and hurried toward the stairs. After another, rather searching look at him, Margaret followed her with Sym hurrying behind.

"Do you mean to murder me or just beat me?" his sister said, standing to face him before the others had reached the threshold. "Because, I would remind you—"

"Keep your reminders and suggestions to yourself if you want to survive this night with a whole skin," he retorted, keeping his hands clenched at his sides.

She had stirred his temper often, but he could not recall ever being as angry with her as he was now. He did not question his fury, but he did mean to control it.

"You will leave as soon as I can provide an escort to see you safely back to the Hall. But I tell you now, Jen— and I won't warn you twice—if you *ever* meddle again between my wife and me, I will tell Rand exactly what you have done."

Her mouth opened in astonishment. "You wouldn't!"

"I would, and if you think Randolph Kerr will support your meddling in another man's marriage, even mine, you had better think again."

"He loves me."

"Do you think he would side with you in this?"

"Of course he would! He is my husband!"

Wat did not reply. He just waited, giving her time for her thoughts to catch up with her hasty tongue.

At last, she shut her eyes, drew a deep breath, opened them again and said ruefully, "He would be furious with me. You know he would."

"Aye, so get your things. I'll walk out to the yard with you. You may tell anyone who asks that, as my lady no longer needs you to bear her company, you mean to continue your visit with our parents. No one will think aught of that."

"Very well." She put a hand on his arm. "Don't be too harsh with her, Wat. Meg has a right to be here. You know she does."

He did not intend to discuss his wife with her, so he said only, "Go and get whatever you need, Jenny. The light is fast fading. But if you must go upstairs for anything, do not try to talk to Margaret."

She nodded, and he knew by the haste with which she returned that she had obeyed him. He knew, too, that he had impressed her for once with his anger.

Since it was rare that he, or anyone else, could make her change her point of view, he acknowledged some small satisfaction, but only to himself and only with strong awareness that her remorse, if it was remorse, would be short-lived.

Jenny meddled as naturally as she breathed.

He saw her off, thanking her politely for assisting his lady. Then he strode back into the tower, determined to wring his lady's slender white neck.

He managed to hold that thought in his mind until he reached his bedchamber, lifted the latch, and opened the door. At that moment, however, the breath stopped in his throat for the second time in less than an hour.

Apparently, she had not heard the latch, for she stood by the washstand, using the cloth to wash her face. In the light of several candles, her hair was the rich dark brown of a pine marten's summer coat, gleaming with golden highlights. It covered her to her bottom, the cheeks of which peeped pinkly below it.

Her long, slender, shapely legs were likewise bare.

He swallowed and felt his cock grow hard. Believing he would accomplish nothing if he let lust rule his mind, he shut his eyes, pictured her father's gloating face after the success of his ruse, and thoroughly vanquished his lust. When he had control again, he focused on the top of her head and cleared his throat.

She jumped nearly out of her skin and turned around, one hand clasped over her heart. "I did not hear you come in!" she exclaimed. "Faith, but I thought it was the lads with the tub, although I did tell Sym to have them wait half an hour."

He fixed his eyes on hers. "What tub?"

"I thought you would want a bath after spending so much of these past two days in the saddle. Was there no siege at Elishaw after all?"

"No," he said shortly, determined not to lower his gaze. Even looking into her eyes did not help, though. His field of vision at that distance easily noted the soft fullness of her breasts, the smallness of her waist, and the enticing flare of her hips. "Put something on, lest those lads do come along," he said gruffly.

She nodded and picked up her shift from the bed, slipping it on over her head and putting her arms into its sleeves. The gathered, low-cut neckline gaped open, revealing almost as much breast as he'd seen before.

Leaving the ribbons untied, she picked up the robe that had lain on the bed next to the shift and put that on as well. As she did, he caught sight of her right breast again, nearly the whole of it, teasing his senses through the deep vee opening. He wanted to tell her to tie her ribbons properly, but he did not trust his voice.

He watched until she had finished tying the robe's sash around her slim waist. Then, summoning up his anger again, he said, "Perhaps you did not understand me when I said you should stay at the Hall with my parents."

"I did understand," she said, meeting his gaze too easily, as if his expression were not nearly as severe as he had hoped. "You said I should not come here, so I expect you are angry that I did."

"Angry?" Memory of his earlier fury stirred it anew. "Must I remind you yet again that I am your husband, madam? If I say you are to stay somewhere, I expect you to stay there. I do *not* expect you to defy my commands."

"I suppose it was defiance," she said thoughtfully. "It did not seem so at the time. It just seemed to be the right decision. Jenny said that you—"

"You've no need to tell me Jenny lies at the bottom of this," he said. "I know she cannot see a situation without believing she knows best what to do about it. She has a knack for meddling, does our Jenny, and she is most persuasive. Nevertheless, Margaret, I shall expect you to resist such persuasion after this."

"I am sure you are right, sir."

Deciding that he had not yet made himself clear, he said forcefully, "I know I am right. Jenny's a damned meddler, and you are *not* to allow it."

He said more in that vein and more still about her defiance of his wishes, exerting himself to speak his mind so clearly that she could not misunderstand him.

She listened respectfully, encouraging him by nodding her head as if she agreed with everything he said. But when he said, "I knew from the start whose idea it was. Do not think I did not, for I knew at once that it was all Jenny," she replied, "Oh, no, I don't think that is fair to say."

"Not fair? What do you mean, not fair?" he demanded, taking a step toward her, his hands itching to catch her by her shoulders and give her a good shake. "You admitted as much yourself not five minutes ago. First you agreed that you had defied me and then that I was right about its being Jenny's idea."

"Well, as to that—"

"There is no 'as to that.' It is plain fact. Do you mean to say now that Jenny did *not* persuade you and that you did not defy me?"

"Jenny has been most kind to me, and to Amalie," she said. "She did point out that a siege could last weeks if not longer, and I knew that you wanted to put things in order here. I mentioned that to her, but it was not all her idea to come here. I wanted to come before I met her. You know I did, because we discussed it."

"Aye, we did, and you know what I said then, too. Moreover, you will not say that Jenny did not urge you to do it despite what I'd said, whilst I was away."

"She suggested that I had a right to help you tidy up Raven's Law," she said. "We knew that even if you returned sooner than we expected, you might have to leave again straightaway. We all know that the Douglas will organize his army soon to meet the English. That could happen any day, they said."

"You mean Jenny said."

"Why, no, sir. It was your father who said that. Moreover, you had said as much, yourself. But your father saw naught amiss in our coming here, and your mother sent servants to help us. She even sent blankets, linens, and other things."

Her reasonable manner made it difficult to argue with her, although he had a sense that there was more to it than she had admitted, especially as Jenny had not denied her part in it or tried to diminish it. Still, he could not help noting that his bedchamber was tidier than it had ever been. The bed was made, the floor clear of clothing and swept, the kists all in their places, and the washstand tidy.

He'd wager a good sum of money that the ewer even held water.

Memory stirred of the scene in the main hall, and he realized it had been tidy, too. He had a notion that someone had even changed the rushes. He recalled things hanging on the chimney wall, weapons and such, laid out in patterns. Not only had it looked impressive, but the lads would easily find their belongings there.

Margaret had changed, too. She seemed confident. As that thought darted through his mind, he noticed that she had still not tied the ribbons of her shift.

His loins stirred suggestively.

⌒

Mentioning his parents had apparently silenced him. Although he had frowned, Meg saw his expression soften now and felt a measure of relief. She did not want to fight with him, but the more she had seen of Raven's Law, the stronger her need had grown to turn it into a home. If he were to send her back to the Hall now, as he had sent Jenny, the defeat would be more than she could bear.

The look in his eyes intensified, bringing certain nerve endings in her body to life. She licked suddenly dry lips.

The quick rat-a-tat on the door startled them both.

With a growl, Walter turned, snapped up the latch, and jerked the door open.

Sym stood on the landing.

From across the room, Meg saw the lad's eyes widen at seeing Walter before catching sight of her. But he squared his shoulders, touched the squirming pouch at his belt gently, and said, "Beg pardon, Master Wat—Sir Walter, I should say—but your water be hot. The men be wondering if they should bring up yon tub now."

Walter glanced back at her, deciding. So Meg smiled and said, "You will be more comfortable after you have rid yourself of your travel dirt, sir."

"I will, aye," he said. "Very well, Sym, tell them to bring it up."

As the boy turned away, Walter shut the door again and said, "I liked the way you arranged my men's weapons, targes, and such on the wall of the hall. What did you do with all the other trappings they left in there?"

"We stowed them in that wee chamber at the bottom of the stairs."

"The guards' room?"

"I expect that is it," she said. "It is quite small. I hope it was not wrong to put everything there. We just thought— That is, I thought it would be easier for them to find their belongings if we put everything in one place. All their clothes and such were scattered about, and we had no way to know what belonged to whom, so—"

She stopped because he was shaking his head, but with a twinkle in his eyes. "I see changes coming," he said. "Doubtless, we'll all have to mend our ways."

"I hope—"

"Don't say it, lass. You are right to try to impose order here. It has been missing far too long. I own, I did not care about keeping everything tidy, but I should have, because it makes for better discipline. It looked much more welcoming when I came in tonight. You have done well. Now, come here."

She hesitated. "They are bringing up your tub."

"Aye, they are, but they are not here yet. Moreover, you would be wise not to defy any more of my commands tonight."

She went to him then, feeling wary, especially when he put both hands on her shoulders. But when she looked up, he kissed her lightly on the lips.

"There is still much to be done," she said. "And I do not know how much longer your mother can spare her people."

"We'll hire our own people," he said. "My men can help, and you may hire as many lasses as you need to come by day. They must sleep at home, because the tower is too small to house them all. I hope you will not object, though, if any of my lads who want to continue sleeping on the hall floor does so. I can order them all to bed down on the top floor, of course, or they can sleep in the yard if they—"

"That is for you to say, sir," she said quickly. "I moved their things only so we could clear the hall to clean it.

I'd prefer that they keep their gear elsewhere, or in kists along one wall, but if they have nowhere else . . ."

"We'll sort all that out later," he said. "Now that you have made such a good start, I can think of any number of other things we should do. We'll make a list and get as much done as we can before Douglas sends for me. He is holding a wardens' meeting at Hermitage next week that I shall have to attend. But nowt of consequence is likely to occur before then."

"But you are not a Border warden, are you?"

"Nay, but we have other matters to discuss, not least of which is the English threat. Richard of England has been moving north as he raises a royal army. Meantime, Hotspur and his longtime ally the Bishop of Durham are raising their own armies to join with the King's. Because the threat to Scotland is so rapidly increasing, even the Earl of Fife means to attend this meeting, although the accommodations at Hermitage certainly will not suit his notion of what is due to his consequence."

"Then mayhap it would be wiser to hold the meeting elsewhere."

"It is Douglas's meeting as Chief Warden of the Marches and thus his decision where they will meet. But as you doubtless know, his countess is Fife's next-to-youngest sister. She offered to put the place in better order for him, but Douglas rejected her offer out of hand."

"Mayhap he should accept it," Meg said with a smile. "He may learn that she can be useful."

"See that you do not suggest such a thing where she may hear of it," he ordered sternly. "The countess is a good, obedient wife and should remain so."

She sobered but said, "What if Fife's wife wants to come?"

"He rarely even sees her, for she has never been anything to him save his means to acquire the Menteith earldom. The only reason he is coming is to annoy Jamie. Fife dislikes him as much as he disliked the first Earl of Douglas."

"I warrant it is not the Douglas he dislikes as much as the Douglas power," Meg said thoughtfully.

"Now, how would a lass like you know aught of Fife?" he said.

"My brother Simon has served him for several years," she explained. "Simon rarely visits us. But each time he has, he has mentioned that Fife believes Douglas wields much more than his rightful share of power. Simon agrees with him."

"Everyone knows that Fife wants to undermine Douglas's power, but I fear that your brother and I disagree as to its rightfulness," he said. "For the past fifty years and more, the Douglas power here in the Borders is all that has kept the English from taking over Scotland. Every time they have tried, it has been the Douglas and his allies who have stopped them. Certainly, the Stewarts have done naught to prevent it. Nor did David Bruce when he was King, come to that."

"I know. David was willing to turn us all over to England's third Edward. I expect you know that many folks believe it was a mistake to prevent that."

"And what of you, madam? What do you believe?"

She nibbled her lower lip, thinking how best to express her thoughts to him, as complex as they were.

Footsteps sounded on the stairway.

Without haste, deciding the wisest thing was to tell the simple truth, she said, "I am your wife, sir. It is my duty and my intent to support you in all you do."

He looked long at her, ignoring the rap on the door. Then his eyes began to twinkle, and he said, "That is an admirable response, lass, and quite true about your duty. But I trust you will forgive me if I am a trifle suspicious of such a response in view of your recent decision to flout my commands the minute I turned my back."

She moved to protest, but he turned and called, "Enter," so she kept silent.

In fact, he was right. Her words did not match her recent behavior.

As two menservants carried in the tub and the first pails of hot water, she decided she had not been honest even with herself in what she had said to him.

More lads entered, carrying more hot water, and she noted that Sym had taken command, curtly telling a gillie four or five years older than himself to have a care lest he splash more water on the floor than he poured into the tub.

She glanced at her husband and saw that his amusement matched hers. But she knew that Sym had better watch his step, and that she should do the same.

What *did* she think about England's desire to rule Scotland? No one had asked for her opinion before. But she knew that, having asked, he would ask again, and that she had better have a more considered answer for him, and for herself.

⁓

When the lads had filled his tub, Wat dismissed them and bathed quickly but with pleasure. Like most Scots, he preferred cleanliness to living under layers of dirt and had never understood the English habit of bathing just two or three times a year.

He had certainly not expected Margaret to order a tub for him, because although her father was Scottish, everyone agreed that her English-born mother ruled at Elishaw. He had seen as much for himself. Had she not taken a greater part in his misfortunes there than any ordinary wife would?

These thoughts, coupled with Margaret's recent defiance, made him fear that she might try to rule at Raven's Law in the same way. He was a tolerant man, but he would not stomach usurpation of his role as master of his household.

As he bathed, she moved about quietly, picking up the clothing he had cast aside in his disrobing. So far, she had shown an inclination to take the bit between her teeth only the one time. But he wanted to see no more of it. It occurred to him then that he still believed Jenny had been the driving force in that incident.

It was true that Meg had broached the subject of moving to him earlier—twice, in fact. But he was as certain as he could be that without both Jenny's urging and his parents' acquiescence, Meg would not have disobeyed him.

His father had not known that he had forbidden her to move to the tower.

But Jenny just as certainly had known. Wat could not imagine Meg being so deceitful as to accept Jenny's urging without admitting that Wat had told her to stay at the Hall. Jenny, however, was perfectly capable of offering unsolicited advice.

"Who first brought up the notion of your moving here?" he asked abruptly.

She straightened and turned, her brow creased. "Jenny

had met Sym and wondered why he seemed so devoted to me. I explained that you had told him to look after me, and she asked why, if you cared enough to provide me with a bodyguard, you'd left me at the Hall rather than bringing me here to Raven's Law."

"Sym is hardly my idea of a bodyguard; nor did I set him to any such task."

"I know that, and you know that. I wager Jenny knows it, too. But you neglected to tell Sym, and he follows me like a shadow."

"Good," he said, reaching for one of the remaining pails of warm water and sluicing it over his head and upper body to rinse away the soap suds. "That should keep you both out of trouble. What does he carry in that new pouch of his?"

"A kitten called Pawky that he rescued from drowning."

He chuckled. "So what reason did you give Jenny for staying at the Hall?"

"That you had said it was too dangerous for me here until you could lay those raiders by the heels and make it safe again."

"But she still urged you to move."

"She said it was 'blethers,' " she said with a reminiscent smile.

He nearly smiled himself at hearing the word on her lips. But by reaching for a second pail and standing to rinse off, he manage to retain his sober expression.

When she handed him a towel and bent to move the two empty pails out of his way, he said, "I hope you did not encourage such disrespect."

Setting the pails down against the wall, she straightened and eyed him appraisingly before she said, "She said it was blethers, because this tower is nearly impregnable. She said the steep walls of the cleuch and the ease with which your people can guard its entrance make it so. It is also much nearer the Hall than I knew, so help is always near at hand if we need it."

"In other words," he said, no longer having any difficulty letting his irritation show, "she pressed you hard to disobey me."

Again she seemed to measure him. Then, mildly, she said, "I told her you would not thank her for saying the things she did, but she said you'd thank her in time. She said Scott men do not like meek women."

"She said that, did she?"

The woman he had expected to give him little trouble met what ought to have been a fiercely frowning gaze with unnatural ease and said, "Aye, she did."

As he stepped out of the tub, he said gently, "Do you enjoy fratching, lass?"

Giving him a wary look, she said, "I'd liefer have peace."

"Then I'd advise you to learn swiftly to obey your husband." He dried his feet and cast the towel to the floor by the washstand. "Come here."

She bit her lip, but when he raised his eyebrows, she took a step toward him, her gaze lowering. He was still flaccid, but he felt his body stir when she looked, and he knew by her expression that she had seen its movement.

"Sym will be waiting outside the door," she said, looking up again and stopping just out of reach. "I'll send him to fetch men to take away the tub."

"They can deal with it in the morning," he said. "Now, come here."

"But Sym—"

"Never mind Sym," he said. "He can sleep outside the door for all I care."

"But—"

"Margaret . . ."

She glanced at the door.

He waited, crossing his arms over his chest.

She licked her lips, making his body stir again. Then, at last, she moved to stand before him, her gaze pinned to his as if she resisted looking down again.

Reaching to touch her silken hair, he said, "Take off your robe."

He saw her tremble and savored the reaction, knowing that she did not fear him, that it was only her body reacting to his.

Without a word, she untied the robe and let it slip from her shoulders, catching it in her hands, so that it did not fall to the floor.

Still looking into his eyes, she said, "I'll just put this—"

"Drop it," he said.

"I'd rather—"

"Drop it," he said again, putting a finger to her lips and finding them soft.

She obeyed him, her gaze still locked with his.

"Now, suck my finger," he murmured.

Her beautiful eyes widened, but she obeyed, her velvety hot tongue laving his finger and bringing his body wholly alive.

◡

The feelings roaring through Meg were feelings she had never experienced before, ones she could never have imagined any man could make her feel simply by telling her what he wanted her to do. Her legs felt weak.

"Take off your shift," he said.

She stopped sucking, because she usually took her shift off over her head.

"Don't stop," he said. "Just push it off your shoulders and let it fall. The opening looks wide enough."

It was, of course, because even gathered, the neckline was wide enough to scoop deeply, but the material was thin and she feared to tear it. When she opened her mouth to tell him so, he raised his eyebrows warningly.

Trying to be gentle with the cambric and to remember to keep sucking his finger, she eased the shift off her left shoulder and then off her right.

"I'll help," he said as he slipped his free hand inside to cup her right breast.

When his thumb brushed across the nipple, she moaned. At the sound, he lifted that breast free of the cambric and reached for the other one.

A moment later, the shift slipped to the flare of her hips. When it paused there, he pushed it lower until it fell to encircle her feet.

He cupped the right cheek of her bottom and pulled her closer, letting her feel his readiness as he drew his finger from her mouth and kissed her lips hard.

His hands moved warmly over her naked body while his lips held hers captive and his tongue plunged deeply into her mouth to explore its interior.

Her body responded, and no sooner did she press harder against him than he scooped her up and carried her to the bed.

As he climbed in with her, she said, "My shift . . . my robe . . . my maid will . . ."

"Hush," he said, positioning himself to couple with her and slipping a hand down between them to see if she was ready for him. "Do you think the servants do not know what we do?"

"But—"

"If it will discomfit you to have a maidservant find your clothes lying about in the morning, just think of it as more of what you deserve for needing lessons in obedience," he said as he entered her.

Meg heard his words but paid small heed to them, because the sensations racing through her body had taken command. He continued to tease her with his hands, his lips, and his rhythmic plunging until she feared she might soon explode.

Every movement of his or her own increased her pleasure. She sensed pending culmination, as if she were reaching unknown heights. They were feelings she had experienced the night before he'd left to ride to Elishaw, glorious feelings.

Both of them were breathing hard, he nearly gasping as the pace of his movements increased. Then, with a moan of completion, he collapsed atop her and lay there, panting, replete. Her magnificent sensations collapsed with him.

She wanted to protest but was not sure that she should.

He eased off her, kissed her, and said, "We've much to do before I leave to attend the wardens' meeting. But I may have to depart again soon afterward, and I want to accomplish as much here as we can before then. So we'd better get up a bit earlier than usual these next few days."

She agreed with a small sigh, and the next thing she knew, he was asleep.

The next four days passed swiftly in a flurry of activity, because Walter put everyone to work, clearing, cleaning, scouring, polishing, repairing, and organizing.

Meg and Amalie learned much more about Raven's Law—more, Amalie said after a particularly long day as she collapsed onto cushions in the hall window embrasure, than she had ever wanted to know.

Meg enjoyed the activity. She enjoyed even more working alongside Walter and learning from him. She learned that he was stubborn and could be peremptory, that he liked doing things his own way or the way the Scotts had always done them, and that he would quickly stifle dispute. But she learned, too, that if she was tactful, he would listen. And several times, he had adopted her suggestions.

She recalled those moments as she watched him ride away on Wednesday morning, and realized that she was rapidly growing very fond of her husband.

Even as tired as they both were by each day's end, they had coupled more nights than not, albeit briefly and without his providing as much pleasure as she had enjoyed the night before he had left for Elishaw or the night of his return.

Recalling his suggestion the first of those nights that he had been punishing her for needing lessons in obedience, she smiled. Whatever he chose to call it, they had enjoyed it, and she had hoped they would do so again before he had to leave.

They had not, but he would be no farther away than Hermitage this time. And he would return in just three or four days.

Chapter 12

~

With that a wee fellow came puffing and blawin',
Warn well, and arm well, or else ye're undone!

Twenty miles southeast of Buccleuch, at the southern
end of the Cheviot Hills, Hermitage Castle dominated an
isolated side glen of upper Liddesdale.

Built on the site of some ancient saint's lonely sanctuary, the castle stood on raised ground a quarter-mile uphill
from where Whitrope Burn and sundry sikes—or rills, as
the English called them—joined the tumbling flow called
Hermitage Water.

The castle's location made it nearly impossible for anyone to attack it except from the wild, broken country of
lofty hills and boggy marshland to the northwest, an area
not only all but impenetrable for any who did not know
it well but also populated with folks who acknowledged
little or no authority but lance or sword.

Hermitage Water and deep ditches all around the castle
added to its defenses.

Wat and his father, followed by Buccleuch's usual tail
of two dozen armed men and Wat's six, arrived at Hermit-

age late Wednesday afternoon, having followed a track they knew through that ungoverned countryside. They crested the last hilltop to look down on the west-facing front of the castle.

From behind them, the sun lit the tall, pointed arch by the west entrance and sparkled on the wide, tree-lined ribbon of Hermitage Water as it tumbled down the hill before them and flowed past the castle just south of the rise on which it stood.

As always, the castle gave Wat a sense of awe, because beginning nearly twenty years before, the first Earl of Douglas had turned it into a fortress of massive strength to withstand siege. Oblong in shape, its main block boasted projecting square towers at the corners, connected by tall archways on its east and west fronts.

At present, the towers were of equal dimension, but Wat knew that Douglas planned to enlarge the gate tower at the southwest corner, now housing the kitchen and bakehouse. Despite the earl's comments to the contrary, Wat knew his intention was to add chambers to house his family and important guests on the upper floors.

He knew the history of Hermitage well, because the castle was the most important of the Border strongholds. Men on both sides of the line had talked about and fought over possession of Hermitage for the entire century of its existence.

Men-at-arms camped already in the foreclosure and near the chapel. The latter stood separately on the western slope between them and the castle. As more arrived, Wat knew such encampments would cover the surrounding countryside.

Because he and Buccleuch were expected and flew the Scott banner, the heavy timber drawbridge spanning the deep, water-filled ditch in front of the entrance came down as they approached. They clattered across it and dismounted. Leaving their horses with men who would see to them, Wat followed Buccleuch up the steep timber forestair to the main entrance, on the next level of the gate tower.

Two well-armed guardsmen flanked the opening. In the passageway ceiling beyond them, Wat saw tips of two iron portcullises, one ten feet behind the other.

Both were up in welcome, but he knew that with just a shout, a simple maneuver by the men in the portcullis chamber above could bring both gates crashing down. They could easily trap an unwary enemy between the two.

The guards nodded as Wat and his father entered the passageway. Even so, and not for the first time, Wat felt the hairs on the back of his neck stand up as he walked under the hanging iron gates.

The lower hall, for use by the rank and file, lay beyond an archway at the end of the passage. The great hall, where the elite gathered, stood on the floor above.

The upper levels held smaller chambers for the earl and his guests. But although both halls and the earl's chamber boasted large fireplaces, little else had been done to provide any comfort. Even a visiting earl might find himself with a pallet to sleep on if he did not think to provide his own bedding, although Wat doubted that Douglas intended to treat the Earl of Fife so shabbily.

Near the archway, they came to the main stairway leading down to the kitchens as well as to the upper floors. He heard laughter, music, and conversation in the lower hall and could just barely smell roasting mutton from below over less welcome scents of cesspits and unwashed men.

The worst of the smells faded before they reached the upper hall. A murmur of conversation greeted them but stopped when Buccleuch crossed the threshold.

As Wat followed him in, he heard Douglas call cheerfully, "Welcome! I trust *you* two will not complain about the accommodations here."

"If they don't suit us, my lord, we'll go home," Buccleuch said with a chuckle. "Who dares to complain to you?"

"Need you ask?" Douglas said as he strode forward to shake hands with them. "Our self-professed Guardian of the Realm arrived an hour ago from Stirling and clearly expected to enjoy his customary amenities. But after all the improvements he has installed at Stirling Castle, Fife of all people ought to understand that when one is still building, even one's most noble guests must expect some disorder."

"You should have let your countess arrange for his comfort when she suggested doing so," Buccleuch said, still grinning. "She kens his ways fine."

James gave him a wry look. "Sakes, sir, you know as well as I do that Isabel loathes Fife. The only one of her royal brothers she can tolerate is Carrick, because he is kind to her. She'd have put Fife in a temper within an hour of his arrival."

"I thought Fife was not coming until tomorrow," Wat said.

Douglas gave him the look he had given Buccleuch. "It seems he learned that others would arrive today. Being so untrustworthy himself, the man is obsessively distrustful. I warrant he could not bear thinking that we might conspire against him."

As Douglas's plan had been to discuss certain matters

privately with his most trusted followers before discussing them openly with Fife and men most loyal to him, Wat thought it best not to comment.

"Where is Fife now?" Buccleuch asked.

"Gone to have a word with his squire and a few of his lads, doubtless to order them to make his chamber more habitable before he sleeps there," Douglas said. "I've given him my own mattress and fresh bedding. Sithee, I've not done that for anyone else, but doubtless he expected myriad servants. I have scullions and gillies but no maidservants or personal attendants except my own."

"I'm sure his people will see to his needs."

"So I told him, aye," Douglas said. "The good news is that he will support my plan to stop Hotspur and Richard Plantagenet inside England. Moreover, he has brought a letter from the King saying his grace will support it, too. We failed to stop the villains three years ago, but I *will* stop them this time, and before they can cross over the line. Speaking of villains," he added, looking at Wat, "I hear that Murray of Elishaw claimed to be under siege last week and sent for you."

"Aye, God rot him, he did. There was no siege, as mayhap you already know. He just wanted to see if my word was good. However, whilst I was away, the raiders struck the Forest again. So I'm wondering if he had aught to do with that."

"'Tis possible he sent them, but I doubt it," Douglas said. "I've had reports of such activity from all three of the Scottish marches. In nearly every case, the raiders claimed that I'd sent them or had given them permission to take whatever they were caught taking. I'm thinking someone may be seeking to undermine my authority."

"The one most likely to do that is Fife," Wat said. "We

know he's declared numerous times, both in Parliament and elsewhere, that you've acquired too much power, and we know that he resents it. However, Murray's eldest son, Simon, *is* in Fife's service," he added, only to wish that he had not the moment the words were out. Meg would not thank him for suggesting that her brother was in league with Fife against Douglas, and that perhaps her father was as well. He stopped short of suggesting that Simon Murray might be acting on his own just to impress Fife.

"I don't know Simon Murray, but I do know Fife," Douglas said. "I'll own, he is my chief suspect whenever mischief strikes hereabouts, but I did order Murray to attend the wardens' meeting on Friday to show cause why we should not resolve your grievances against him as you requested. If his son is in Fife's train, Murray will doubtless be kind enough, knowingly or otherwise, to point him out to us."

With that, Wat had to be content, although he still suspected Murray.

When he and his father adjourned to the small room allotted them, to refresh themselves for supper, he returned to something else Douglas had said, which had puzzled him, "Why would the King support a border crossing and a confrontation inside England, sir? I thought he was for peace at any cost. Carrick, too."

"They are," Buccleuch agreed. "But sithee, if Fife wants something signed, the King signs it. And although many believe Fife capable of handing the succession over to the English if they will agree to let him remain in command here, Fife is smart enough to know that is unlikely to happen if England conquers Scotland."

"Has Fife's early arrival put an end to the discussions Jamie meant to have with those of us he trusts most?"

"Most likely," Buccleuch said. "With Fife's men all over the place, I'm guessing Douglas's plans will change. I just hope he can avoid a confrontation."

Supper began smoothly enough with the earl's minstrel providing fine music that elicited compliments from Fife and others. But Wat, sitting below the dais with other knights who served Douglas, could see that Fife's suspicions remained strong.

As they took their seats, Wat heard him comment grimly on the many Douglases who had presented themselves a full day earlier than necessary.

The carving of the first haunch had just begun when Fife said, "One would think this a meeting of Douglases to discuss Douglas business, rather than one to discuss our national response to the English threat."

Nearly everyone there heard him, because he had not bothered to lower his voice. Indeed, he had seemed to raise it, as a challenge.

An instant, angry hum of response began, only to hush just as instantly when the Douglas raised his hand.

Silence followed, the servants moving like wraiths, as Douglas said clearly, without raising his voice, "In the hall of Douglas, all business is Douglas business. Should we ever chance to meet where Stewarts prevail, doubtless all business will be Stewart business. Meantime, our business here is to enjoy our supper and the fine minstrel that my lady wife—your royal sister—has sent to entertain us."

The silence continued even when Douglas turned from Fife to speak quietly to a Douglas cousin, Archie the Grim, Lord of Galloway.

No one needed a stronger message than that to know

that, Guardian of the Realm or not, Fife would be wiser to hold his tongue.

At Hermitage, Douglases not only prevailed, they predominated. Aside from Fife's own men, any who were not Douglases themselves were either married to Douglases or linked strongly with them by vassalage or long and loyal friendship.

Moreover, despite numerous English invasions over the past century, from the days of Robert the Bruce and before, Douglas power and leadership had kept the invaders from conquering Scotland. Even Fife had to realize that if Jamie Douglas just said the word, there would be no army to stop the English now. As Earl of Douglas and Chief Warden of the Marches, Jamie commanded as many as fifty thousand men. All the Stewarts together would be lucky to raise two thousand.

The minstrel wisely stayed his music until normal discussion began again, but even after lads had cleared the tables, the evening's discussions dealt for the most part with family and local affairs of various Border factions.

Wat and Buccleuch retired earlier than they had expected and did so gladly.

By late Thursday morning, everyone Douglas had invited to discuss tactics and strategy for his forthcoming sortie into England had arrived, and their discussions began in earnest in the upper hall.

By order, guards would show anyone arriving early for the next day's wardens' meeting to the lower hall, or ask them to join the camps outside the castle.

Every powerful Border lord was there, including the lord abbots of Melrose and Dryburgh. Those two great abbeys lay directly in the path of any English army crossing the line at Carter Bar and had suffered grievously during the last invasion. Both abbots, with the power of their own noble families and the Roman Kirk behind them, were able to raise armies of their own or use the power of the Kirk to influence men to join or ignore other leaders, just as the powerful Bishop of Durham was able to provide support for Hotspur and the English king.

Tables below the upper-hall dais had given way to benches, and Wat took his seat on one near the front between two knights he had supped with the night before.

Tammy, acting as his squire, sat on the bench just behind him.

Without objection, Fife claimed the central armchair at the high table. But it was Douglas, on his right, to whom everyone looked to open the proceedings.

When Douglas moved to stand, Fife put out a hand. "I will speak first."

"Certainly," Douglas said with a nod.

Fife did not stand, nor did his voice carry as easily as Douglas's did. Indeed, he had a trick of speaking softly, as if he would make men strain to hear him. He said, "As all here know, I am commander of his grace, the King's, armed forces. Because we have come to believe that Richard Plantagenet of England means to try yet again to make Scotland an English province, his grace agrees with me that we must exert ourselves to prevent that. To that end, we have asked the Earl of Douglas to bring all Scottish Border leaders together here to determine how we will proceed. Understand me, though. This effort must be made quietly if it is to be successful."

Voicing aloud Wat's thoughts of the previous evening, the burly Abbot of Melrose—who like most powerful abbots could produce an army of his own, financed by the Kirk, to support any effort he approved—said mildly, "I am surprised that his grace consents to this venture. He and my lord Carrick have long been men of peace."

"Indeed," Fife said. "Then, lest others wonder as you do, 'tis as well that my brother Carrick means to visit Hermitage soon and should be at hand to greet the returning victors. Thus will he display his support of our venture and his own determination to keep Scotland independent after he accedes to the throne."

Exclamations of astonishment greeted his statement.

Douglas said, "That is good news. But although one does not doubt Carrick's *hope* that England will eventually allow Scotland to retain its independence, he has apparently expected the Almighty to attend to the matter without requiring his aid or exertion before now. To that end, he has consistently voiced his desire to avoid violence. Therefore, one wonders what magic persuaded him to such an effort."

"No magic," Fife said. "I merely suggested that he'd be interested to see such a famous stronghold—one so important to our defense. Most folks, however, will take his visit to mean that, despite his well-known aversion to conflict, he supports this fight and comes to congratulate our victory. Moreover, his presence here will make it difficult if not impossible for him to express disapproval afterward."

Many began stamping their feet in approval. A man approached Douglas and spoke to him as Tam said quietly into Wat's ear, "Fife seems mighty sure o' victory."

"He's counting on it," Wat murmured back. He realized that every man there understood, as he did, that Fife had manipulated his father and elder brother into showing support for the Scottish foray when the truth was that neither man knew anything about it. Hence, Fife's earlier demand that they proceed quietly.

The question was how strongly Fife himself supported the venture.

Douglas did not trust him. Wat knew that for a fact. Nor did Murray, he recalled. His wily good-father had admitted being one of those who feared that Fife might accept any English offer that allowed him to continue to govern Scotland.

Fife clearly wanted to continue ruling the country, and he could not do so if the English overran it and seized control. But what would he do if they promised to leave him in his present position as Guardian of the Realm for life in exchange for aid in helping them win their primary objective, annexation? The only sure way to avoid finding out, Wat believed, was to help Douglas defeat the English in England.

His reflections ended when Douglas stood and said without preamble, "King Richard of England has begun moving north toward Carlisle."

From that point, debate continued for hours, stopping only for the midday meal and again later for supper.

No one slept before the small hours, and when Wat did finally seek his bed, he could not have repeated much of what they had decided as to the details. He knew only that he was to gather his men and meet the others at Southdean, north of the Carter Bar crossing, in eight days.

The Scottish army would consist of two parts. A small, mounted force under Douglas would ride into Redesdale, in England's east march, to keep Hotspur from joining his forces with those of the English king. A much larger force under Fife and Archie the Grim would invade England near Carlisle in the west.

The next day, those with no business for the wardens' meeting departed, and the meeting proceeded formally and with far less debate. Nor was the entertainment or dining as lavish. The earl's minstrel did not play for the crowded midday meal. He played only for the late supper, after most of the attendees had gone home.

Sir Iagan Murray had departed directly after the meeting, indeed almost immediately after the wardens ruled on Wat's grievance against him. Having arrived with smiles and a warm handshake for Wat and Buccleuch, he had ridden away disgruntled and without a word to either. If his son Simon had been present as a member of Fife's party, Murray had not acknowledged him.

The Scotts spent the night and left late Saturday morning for home.

After two days of organizing maidservants and attending to normal tasks, Meg decided that Raven's Law was as comfortable as they could make it without a visit to Hawick or Selkirk to purchase such sundry items as might make it more so.

Having no notion what orders Walter might have given his men before leaving, and having received none herself to preclude doing as she pleased, she decided to discover for herself if he had set any restrictions on her movements.

When she and Amalie had taken places at the dais table for their supper the evening after his departure, Meg had half-expected someone to tell them that Sir Walter had given orders for them to take their meals in the sitting room she had arranged on the same floor as Amalie's bed-chamber. But no one did.

Since then, Sym had taken to helping two gillies serve them, and Friday evening, when Meg asked him to set the privacy screen, he did so at once. When he returned to stand near her, she said, "Have you eaten your supper, Sym?"

"Nay, mistress. Pawky and me can eat when ye've finished. Jed Crosier's always got summat for us in yon kitchen."

"Very well, then, but do not hover over us. We want to talk privately."

Nodding, Sym moved to the end of the dais and sat where she could easily summon him but where he would not hear them if they spoke quietly.

Doing so, she said to Amalie, "I mean to ride to the Hall tomorrow to visit her ladyship. One does not want to be thought indifferent to one's good-mother."

"Do I have to go?" Amalie asked, adding suspiciously, "You are not thinking of making me stay there with her, are you?"

"Of course not," Meg said. "I meant it when I said I enjoy your company. Besides, you seem much happier here. You have roses in your cheeks again."

"I like it here," Amalie said. "One can see the prog-ress we've made, and I prefer doing things that show such clear results. At home, everything we did we had to do again the next day, so the tasks seemed unending, and I felt like a servant. I just hope Father does not send for me to return—or Mother either, come to that."

"Are you truly happier here, dearling?"

"I am, aye," Amalie said. "People talk to me. I like Sir Walter's men, especially Tam and Gibbie, but all of them are respectful. I've not heard a single one make disparaging remarks such as those we were used to hearing at home."

That was true, Meg realized. She had not given it a thought, but she was not surprised that Amalie had. It had always hurt her sister to hear the rude remarks about them. And men at Elishaw had seemed to enjoy repeating such things.

"Do you think Sir Walter has told his people that they must not say discourteous things to us?" Amalie asked.

"I was just wondering about that," Meg said with a smile. "In troth, I do not think it would occur to him to give such an order. Nor do I think he'd find it necessary. Everyone at the Hall seemed friendly, too. And although everyone there must know how our marriage came about, I am his wife now, which means I've become one of them—the Scotts, that is. Mayhap that is all there is to it."

"But we were born Murrays, and yet Father's men did not hesitate to repeat anything they'd heard about us. The meanest taunts always reached our ears."

"They did, aye," Meg agreed. "But despite Father's temper and Mother's firm grip on the household—or mayhap because of those things—our people at Elishaw never showed us such fierce loyalty as the Scotts' people show to them."

Amalie shrugged. "I don't care a fig why they treat us better than our own people do. I'm just grateful that they do." After a pause, she added, "Tammy is especially nice, don't you think?"

Meg eyed her sternly. "Amalie Murray, I hope you are not setting up a flirtation with Jock's Wee Tammy. He is most unsuitable."

"Nay, then, why should he be? He is a Scott, sithee, just of a lesser branch. He means to win his spurs in battle, and if he does, he will be a knight just like Sir Walter. Doubtless, he will then gain land and become an important nobleman."

"Wait until he does so before you decide he will make you a good husband," Meg advised. "For now, what do you think about riding with me tomorrow?"

"Aye, sure, I'd enjoy the exercise. But do you think her ladyship will be pleased to see us? She was kinder to us after Jenny came, to be sure, but Jenny has gone home by now, and her ladyship may not be happy to see us."

"I don't know if she will be or not," Meg said. "I do know it would be rude of us to avoid her. And, sithee, Walter feels great esteem for his mother, so I want to make a friend of her. I mean to begin by asking her where I must go and what I must do to purchase fabric so we can make more pillows like the ones she lent us."

"I'll do all I can to help," Amalie said. "But don't blame me if it goes awry."

"I won't unless it is your fault that it does," Meg retorted.

⁓

They set out for Scott's Hall soon after breaking their fast Saturday morning, with Sym following on his pony—without the kitten in its pouch, for once—and a small tail of armed men behind him.

On that first day of August, the air was crisp and cool, the sunlight in the cleuch magical with golden, mote-filled rays piercing tiny openings in the dense canopy.

The chuckling Clearburn accompanied them down the hill.

Rabbits hopped across the path in front of their horses. Squirrels chattered as they scrabbled up or down nearby trees. Birds chirped and screeched. And once a doe and her spotted fawn slipped across the track not far ahead of them.

At the Hall, Janet Scott greeted them with warm smiles and welcomed even their small guardian, telling Sym to take himself off to the kitchen and see if the cook might have a treat for him.

Sym looked at Meg.

"Go along then," she said. "I shan't need you until we leave. He is most attentive," she added when he had obeyed her with a grin. "Your son presented him to me to keep him out of trouble. He's been my shadow ever since."

"It will doubtless be the making of him," Janet said with a laugh. "But come up to my solar and tell me all you have accomplished. It has been lonely here since first Jenny and then Buccleuch left. I have been yearning for someone to talk to."

Appealed to on the subject of fabric, she said, "I must show you what I have first. I have a dreadful habit of buying yards of fabric whenever I find a good draper. I always mean to have the stuff made up into something. But too often, I'm either too lazy or I decide I do not like it as well here as I did in the shop. If I have anything you think you can use, you must take it home with you."

Meg nearly said she had intended only to learn how to go about finding things for herself and ought not to impose on Janet's generosity. But she stopped before the words fell from her tongue, deciding that it was unlikely

Walter would object to such kindness. If he did, he could sort it out with his father.

Janet sent a pair of gillies to fetch four kists full of folded fabric lengths, and all three ladies soon immersed themselves in happy discussion.

Invited to stay for the midday meal, Meg and Amalie no sooner took places at the table than Janet said, "I mean to visit Jenny next week. I shall stay for at least a fortnight and mayhap longer if the Douglas calls our menfolk to join him, as I suspect he means to do very soon. Perhaps you two would like to go with me."

Feeling Amalie stiffen beside her, Meg said quickly, "How kind of you, my lady! I shall have to ask Walter, but I warrant he will be happy to agree. It will be good to see Jenny again, will it not, Amalie?"

"It will, aye," Amalie said politely. But Meg knew she did not mean it and foresaw storms ahead.

Deciding to deal with them quickly, she waited only until they had ridden through the Hall gates into the Forest, their escort a short distance behind them.

"We have hours yet before supper," she said then. "Let's follow the burn a little farther and see more of Rankilburn Glen. We should be safe enough here."

Amalie agreed, although it was plain that she did so only on Meg's account.

Knowing better than to begin by demanding answers from her, Meg drew her into discussing plans for the tower and her hope that Walter would approve them.

"He did notice the weapons and such that we hung on the chimney wall," she said at one point. "He said he thought that was a good notion."

"Aye, because they are out of his way," Amalie said, smiling at last. "I do not know how those men contrived to live with the mess we saw when we arrived. Only think what our lady mother would say about any house in such a state."

"I don't want to think about what she might say about anything at Raven's Law," Meg said honestly. "It is my home now."

"Aye, sure, and it is her nature to be critical of everything she sees," Amalie said. "But you can be critical, too, Meggie. Faith, I suppose I can be as well. Is it simply in our natures, do you think?"

"More likely, it is habit," Meg said. "When one has an idea for improvement, one makes suggestions. But I always want to discuss my ideas with others. Do I not often seek your opinion before I set something new in progress here?"

"You do, aye," Amalie said. "But you don't often accept my ideas."

"Nor do you accept mine," Meg said, smiling. "That, too, is human nature, I suppose. That is not to say that I don't welcome your ideas, and your interest, because I do. Indeed, I'm curious now to know why you did not want me to accept her ladyship's kind invitation to go with her to Ferniehurst."

With a guilty look, Amalie said, "I did not say that."

"You did not have to. Your feelings were clear to me and may have been clear to her, as well. You do not dissimulate well, my dear."

"And you do, I suppose."

"I can if I must," Meg said. "It is not, however, a skill one wants to perfect. But we are not discussing deception now. Tell me why you don't want to go."

Amalie did not reply at once, and Meg did not press her.

They followed the river, and no one in their tail expressed any objection. Meg felt confident that the men would not interfere in what they would easily perceive to be private conversation. Even Sym had fallen back to ride with the others.

The woods grew denser, becoming a veritable thicket of birch, oak, hazel, and pine trees on either side of the narrow track. In some places, despite steep slopes on either side, the thick shrubbery hid the swift-flowing river. Meg recalled then that Walter had once said the forest canopy was so thick that a person could travel from the Hall all the way to Selkirk without once seeing the sun.

They could easily hear the rushing water, though, so when Amalie finally spoke, she had to raise her voice for Meg to hear her. "I don't know exactly why I don't want to go," she said. "I fear it may still be a matter of envying Jenny her happiness, but that just seems mean. Sithee, I don't dislike her. I . . . I just . . ."

She paused with a sob, and only then did Meg see the tears in her eyes.

"What is it, love?" she said gently.

"What if . . . ? Oh, Meggie, what if I'm with child?"

"Sakes, are you?"

"I don't know!"

The wail of words ended in a screech as a dozen men erupted from the woods. Several grabbed their horses' bridles, while others confronted their escort.

Although the villains were afoot, many had weapons drawn, ranging from clubs and short lances to maces and swords.

Chapter 13

❧

But peace on the border, that thinned his keyloes,
And want for his lads was the warst thing of a'.

Hearing commotion behind her, Meg turned to see that the men in her tail had drawn swords. Sym, poised to ride to her rescue, held a dirk in his hand.

"Tell them to stay where they be and sheathe their weapons, me lady," the man on her right, holding the bridle, said crisply. "Me lads mean ye nae harm."

Fearing that he and his men might do anything to protect themselves, and conscious of Amalie's white face and shaking hands, Meg held up a hand to keep her men where they were. "Just what *do* you mean if not to harm us?" she asked.

"By me troth, me lady, we've the Douglas's permission to hunt here and gather fuel. Me lads be stalking a deer just ahead, so ye'll no want to interfere. But I feared a misunderstanding did we no stop ye here. Sithee, I didna want anyone hurt through some hasty action. Now, tell them lads o' yours to put up their swords."

Despite his obsequious tone, Meg sensed the menace of fear in him and forced herself to remain calm. "I think there must be some misunderstanding already," she said. "You are on land privately held by the Laird of Buccleuch." Since she was not sure they were still on Scott land, she added, "Also, he is Ranger of Ettrick Forest, charged with its protection. He'd want to see any permit you have from the Douglas."

"Och, but we met Buccleuch only days ago," he said. "I warrant ye must be his lady daughters, the pair o' ye, so I'm amazed he didna warn ye we might be here, nor tell your fine escort. But I did hear he were away, so likely, he forgot."

"I am his good-daughter," Meg said. She felt certain that both Wat and his father would have let everyone at Raven's Law know of any such permission from Douglas. She was just as sure they were the raiders who had been plaguing the area. Since pointing that out would do nothing to defuse the situation, she added, "My husband is likewise away. Doubtless, that is why no one told me about you."

Amalie stiffened beside her, clearly more alarmed than ever.

The leader glanced at her, then back at Meg, who returned his gaze coolly.

"Sithee, we take only what our families need for cooking and to eat. Ye'll ken fine the great destruction the English caused when they came three years ago. Even now when Douglas leads a foray into England, Hotspur or one o' his English ilk retaliates by trampling Scottish fields and stealing our beasts. Our families go hungry unless we can find food."

"Have you food now?" Meg asked.

"Some but not enough," he said with a wry smile.

"Sithee, 'twas the roe we were stalking that warned us o' your approach when it darted off."

"Then perhaps you will accept my invitation to take supper with us at Raven's Law," she said. Ignoring a squeak of protest from Amalie, she hoped her sister would say naught to destroy the tenuous cordiality she sought to promote.

The man hesitated.

Aware that Amalie was staring at her as if she must be demented, Meg said, "We have plenty of food to share unless your band is much larger than it appears."

"There be two dozen of us," he said, eyeing her speculatively.

Whether that look stemmed from doubt of her sincerity or a notion that twenty-four men might easily take two young women and one peel tower hostage to gain their ends, Meg could not be sure.

Nor did it matter. If they were hungry and needed to feed their families, she would help them. If they were villains, they were villains. But in either event, she and Amalie would be safer at home, and she hoped to take at least one precaution.

"I have my page with me," she said. "He is the lad yonder with my men. If you will let me summon him, I'll have him ride ahead to warn my cook that our numbers have increased, so he can begin at once to prepare more food. Otherwise, I fear it will be very late before we get our supper."

The leader peered at Sym, then nodded. "Aye, ye may call him, but tell him he should no glower at his betters. Tell him, too, that your safety depends on his doing exactly what you say he must do and no more, me lady. If

I find that aught other than food and a warm welcome awaits us at Raven's Law, I'll be gey angry."

Nodding, Meg turned and shouted, "Sym, to me! The rest of you, stay where you are and put up your weapons."

Sym kicked his pony and rode to her. "Aye, m'lady?"

"I want you to ride as fast as you can to warn Master Wat, my cook, that we will have guests for dinner. Two dozen of them, tell him."

"Aye, m'lady." Sym's gaze locked with hers. "Do ye mean this lot here be going to sup wi' the rest of us?"

"Mind your manners, laddie," the leader said sharply.

Sym looked at him. "Aye, sure," he said. "I were just a-wondering is all."

"I do mean these men," Meg said. "So, take care that you get my message to Master Wat. And understand me, Sym," she added, holding his gaze. "If food is not ready for these men soon after we arrive, tempers may stir, including my own. So you make sure that our cook knows he must provide a fine supper for my guests."

His eyes narrowed, making her hope it was a look of comprehension, not confusion. But at last, he nodded and said, "I'll take the message, aye. And I'll see to it that the fool cook don't do nowt but what ye ask o' him."

Reassured, she said, "Go quickly then. It takes time to prepare for so many."

Nodding again, he turned his pony without another word and kicked it hard, riding past the mounted men-at-arms without pausing.

"He seems a good, steady lad, that one," the leader said.

"Aye, he is," Meg said, devoutly hoping the boy could do as she had asked.

"We've wood still to load in our carts, and a few chick-ens as were running free," the leader said. "We doubt any-one will miss them, being wild and all."

"Take whatever time you need," Meg said sincerely. "We need not hurry."

"Are you mad?" Amalie muttered in a fierce undertone when the leader walked away and the men holding their horses moved closer to their escort. "What demon pos-sessed you to invite those dreadful men back to Raven's Law with us?"

"If they are telling the truth, I think Walter will help them," Meg said, keeping a close eye on the retreating leader and hoping the noise of the rushing burn would keep him and the other men from hearing their quiet conversation.

"What if they are *not* telling the truth? Do you mean to hand over Raven's Law to them after your poor cook has fed them all supper?"

"You have not spent much time in the kitchens," Meg said.

"You did not ask that of me. Why mention it now?"

"Because our cook's name is Jed Crosier," Meg said. "And surely you do know that 'Master Wat' is what Sym calls Walter."

"Faith, that did not even enter my head. Is Walter not still at Hermitage?"

"He did hope to return tonight," Meg said. "If he does, he may take supper at the Hall before riding home, but Sym will find him, wherever he is. I hope he also under-stood that we need him to get word to the cook."

"Sakes, why?"

"Because if we arrive to find food preparation in hand, no one will take note of Sym's absence. But if we find no food and no Sym . . . Hush now, that man is coming back," she added, seeing the leader re-emerge from the trees.

It took his companions another half-hour to load their gleanings into their carts and onto their ponies. When they were ready, Meg thought they made a strange party. But the carts slowed them nicely as they wended their way back to the Clearburn and followed the smaller burn up Buck Cleuch to the peel tower.

"Our men are muttering amongst themselves," Amalie said.

"I hear them," Meg said. She looked back at the six with a frown.

"Doubtless they think they could have overcome these men."

"I am not sure they could have. The raiders outnumber them four to one. In any event, both sides would have suffered losses, so I thought it best to act as we would at home and not seem to take sides. Surely, it is wiser to find out why the raids are occurring than just to cut these men down with swords or hang them all."

"Perhaps. But what if Walter disagrees?"

Meg knew Walter would disagree. He would be angry that she had not taken a large enough escort to defeat any threat. But to have done so would have meant taking most of the guards he had left with her at Raven's Law, thus putting the tower at risk. That thought told her that her first assessment had been wrong.

He would be furious that she had ridden to the Hall at all.

But she had, and she could do nothing to change that.

She could only hope to control the present situation enough to keep them all from ending up as hostages. Accordingly, when they rode into the yard at Raven's Law, she briskly ordered the captain of her escort to see to the horses.

Then she asked two of the other men to see to their guests' needs.

"Pray show them where they may refresh themselves. Then show them into the hall," she said as another member of her escort helped her dismount. Shaking out her skirts, she added, "I will go to the kitchen and see that all is in train there."

"Ye'll no mind then an a few of us come along wi' ye, me lady, to see that all is well wi' your cook," the leader said.

She had expected as much and had hoped that dividing the enemy might make them less dangerous. Even so, she struggled to maintain her calm as she said, "You should come with me, too, Amalie."

"Och, aye," the leader said with a disturbing smile. "She should."

Entering the kitchen with increasing trepidation, Meg was relieved to see kitchen maids and gillies hurriedly plucking chickens and game birds for the spits.

"It may be another hour yet, m'lady," the cook said as he greeted her. "We began as soon as I got your message, so we'll still ha' supper on the tables nobbut a half hour or so past the usual time."

"Thank you for acting so quickly," she said, meeting his steady gaze.

"I thank ye, too, Master Wat," the leader said, putting out a hand. "Smells right good in here. Me mouth already be watering."

Meg held her breath.

Without a blink her cook said, "I hope ye'll enjoy your supper, sir."

"Meantime, send ale and bread to the hall to stave off their hunger," Meg said. Turning to the leader, she said, "Now, if we have persuaded you that we can feed you all, pray let me take you to the hall and see you settled with your men."

For a wonder, he complied, so Meg led the way to the hall, noting with satisfaction that the first thing he did there was fix his gaze on the chimney wall.

Walter's men had taken many of the weapons that had hung there, but a respectable assortment remained. Bare hooks revealed how many were missing.

The leader was not the only one staring. Every man with him stared or pretended not to stare while shooting frequent glances at the wall.

"A fine display," the leader said.

"Aye, it is," she agreed. "Pray, what should I call you, sir?"

"Me lads call me Neb."

"Is that what I should call you, or have you a surname?" Most people in the Borders did not. But most willingly named their home and kindred.

However, he said, "Nay, now, that would be telling. Neb will do."

"Then will you join my sister and me at the high table, Neb?"

His look this time was pure astonishment. "Nay, me lady, ye dinna want a man o' my ilk on yon dais. 'Tis no fitting."

"What is fitting is for me to decide, sir. As leader of these men, you are our chief guest and should be on the dais. First, however, if you will excuse us, my sister and

I would like to refresh ourselves. Doubtless, you want to do so as well, so I shall ask one of the gillies to show you where the garderobe is. He can also pour you some ale or wine when you are ready for it."

"The ale will be welcome, but I canna agree that both you and the other lass should leave together, me lady. Forgive me suspicious nature, but I'd feel better an only one o' ye left at a time."

"Very well, but only if you keep your men here with you," Meg said. "I do not want to worry about her being alone upstairs or when I am not here with her."

"Ye have me word that none o' me lads will harm either o' ye."

With that Meg had to be satisfied, but when Amalie volunteered to go first, she was grateful. She'd have worried about whether she had been right to trust him if she had gone and left Amalie alone with him and his men. As it was, Meg went to the dais and ordered his ale while a gillie showed him to the garderobe.

His men had taken seats at the trestle tables and seemed content for the moment with bread and ale. One produced a battered lute and began to pluck its strings, while another began softly to sing a ballad. By the time Amalie returned and Meg had hurried through her own ablutions, they were all singing lustily.

But for Neb's sword lying ready to hand and his men having likewise kept their weapons, she thought anyone might mistake them for a feast day gathering.

⁓

Wat, Buccleuch, and their tail had reached the east bank of the Rankilburn where it flowed around Kirk Hill, just over two miles south of the Hall, when Wat saw a small rider approaching them at speed from around the next bend.

"That looks like Sym," he said to his father.

"What the devil is he doing out here?"

"It can't be good news," Wat said, spurring his horse forward.

"Master Wat, raiders!" Sym shouted, bringing his horse to a plunging halt and grabbing its mane to keep from flying off. "They're wi' me lady at the tower!"

A freezing chill swept through Wat. Waving Buccleuch to a faster pace, he said, "How the devil did they get into the tower?"

"They didna. We'd been to the Hall, sithee, and were returning, but—"

"Who went to the Hall with you?"

"The lady Amalie, aye, and six o' our lads, but them poachers . . . There be two dozen o' them, so me lady told our lads to put up their swords."

As Buccleuch reined in beside him, Wat said, "The forest raiders stopped Meg and Amalie as they were returning from the Hall. What happened then, Sym?"

Sym hesitated, looking wary, then said in a rush, "Me lady took 'em home to supper. She said I should ride ahead and tell the cook she were bringing guests."

Suppressing shock, Wat said, "You're a good lad for coming to me instead. But we must hurry, because when they find there is no food for them—"

"There'd be trouble, aye," Sym said. "Me lady thought o' that, 'cause she said, 'Tell Master Wat, *our cook.*' I thought she were daft, but she looked at me so"—he locked his gaze with Wat's—"so I didna say nowt, only that I'd do as she'd bid."

"That was the right thing," Buccleuch said encouragingly. But Wat was just hoping once again that Meg would survive long enough to let him wring her neck.

"It was, aye," Sym said. "But I kept thinking, sithee. They'd been hunting, and I kent fine they'd be a wee while if they had game to tote. So I stopped at the Hall and told a lad there to go warn Jed Crosier whilst I looked for you. I told him, too, that the mistress had called the cook Master Wat, so Jed should ken that, too. By the look o' the chief villain, he'd be doing summat to be sure o' that name."

Wat stared at the boy, wondering if he would have had the wit himself at such a tender age to understand so much with so little to aid him. Doing rapid calculations in his head, he turned to Buccleuch.

"Sym says there are twenty-four of them. She had six armed men—"

Buccleuch said, "She ought to have had twice as many!"

"That was my first thought, too. But I've got my own lads here with me or out preparing men to join Douglas. So I left too few at the tower for her to take more without leaving the place unguarded. Moreover, she ought not to have needed more to go such a short distance. How many are still at the Hall?"

Buccleuch grimaced. "I've done the same, so fewer than thirty. Between us we've another thirty here."

"Then I mean to take these with me and ride on ahead if you will stop at the Hall and organize as many of those others as possible to follow."

Sym said, "I told 'em at the Hall that ye'd need more men, laird. But they mayn't be ready to ride," he added with a frown. "I'm just a bairn, sithee, so nobbut one lad would carry me message. Likely, them others will ha' done nowt."

Buccleuch ruffled the lad's hair. "If that is so, I shall have something to say to them that they won't enjoy hearing. You did well, my lad."

"I did, aye, 'cause I found ye," Sym agreed. "But we must ride like Auld Clootie now to aid me lady, 'cause that villain had a demon's eye to 'im."

"You will ride with me, lad," Buccleuch said. "Moreover, when we get to the Hall, you will stay there, out of danger."

Sym looked beseechingly at Wat.

"With respect, sir," Wat said to his father, "I think he has earned the right to ride with me. But," he added, turning a stern eye on the boy, now beaming and fairly bouncing on his nervous pony, "you will do exactly as I bid you, Sym."

"Aye, sure," Sym said, wheeling his mount. "But hurry!"

Wat glanced at Buccleuch, who grinned. So, with Sym flying ahead on the rough, narrow track and Buccleuch's men behind them, they raced homeward.

Wat and Sym left Buccleuch at the track up to the Hall, and rode on. The nearer they got, the more Wat's fears increased. It had all taken too long.

The likelihood was that Meg, Amalie, and every man he'd left at the tower were now prisoners. But, thanks to the discussion at Hermitage, he could see a larger picture, too. Since such raids were occurring all over, with the raiders insisting they had Douglas's permission to take what they wanted, it could well mean that someone was trying to turn those other powerful Border landowners against him, and thus weaken the Douglas's own vast power—just as Douglas himself had suggested.

The light in the cleuch had grown dusky, making it more difficult to see the track they followed. But they all knew it well, and the tower came into view at last.

Drawing rein, Wat motioned Gibbie and Tam closer, saying, "We'll ride up together, the three of us, and see if anyone challenges us."

"They may only be waitin' for us to get inside the gates," Tam cautioned.

"Aye, but if the men on the gate are ours, we'll recognize them all. And I'm thinking we'll know at once if aught's amiss with them."

"Even if them villains be threatening the mistress?" Gib asked.

"Even so," Wat said. He looked at Sym. "We'll disarm them a bit first. Think you that you could slip away at the wall if I let you ride up to it with us, Sym?"

"Aye," the boy said, quivering with eagerness. "Just tell me what I'm to do."

"Watch me. When we're close to the gate, if all looks well, we'll all go inside. But if I lower my hand to my hip, so, you turn your pony and ride along the wall. If they shout, just ride back to the others and tell them we've got trouble."

"Aye, I can do that."

"Don't be making decisions on your own, though. Just tell the others."

"Aye, I will."

But when they reached the gate, their concern dissipated, for it opened at once, and Dod Elliot stood beside it, smiling. "Welcome home, Master Wat."

Wat frowned at him. "Sym said there was trouble. Was he wrong?"

"As to that, I canna say for sure, sir. The mistress came home wi' a lot o' scaff and raff she met with in the Forest. By the piles o' wood and such in them carts yonder, I'd say they'd been poaching. But she did tell our lads to see to them, and she ordered supper for them all. They're in the hall now, the whole lot o' them."

"Have we men in the hall, too?" Wat asked.

"Aye, except for those on the wall or at other duties who will eat later."

Unsure whether he was relieved or more concerned, but certain that Dod would not lie to him, Wat gestured to the men below to follow. Then, with Tam, Gibbie, and Sym, he rode up to the tower entrance and dismounted.

Striding through the pend with Tam and Gibbie behind him, Wat started up the stairway, treading quietly until he heard the music. Sure then that his steps would go unheard, he set caution aside and took the rest of the steps two at a time.

From the landing, he stared through the open doorway into the hall. Men ate and talked, while others who had finished were singing. At the high table, his wife sat between her sister and a scruffy-looking man that Wat had never seen before.

Another rascal sat beside him. Both looked more apt to be sitting at one of the trestle tables, but the scene was peaceful. Although Wat could count more strangers than Scotts, there were not so many that the strangers posed an overwhelming threat.

To Gibbie, he said, "Fetch the other lads. But have someone ride back and tell my father we have things under control here. Then make sure Dod bars the gate.

I'll wait for you and the other lads here unless I cannot, so don't dawdle."

Gib was gone on the last word, and Wat's quick hearing caught the sounds of his steps fading into the distance. Most of the occupants of the hall were watching the chief singer, now entertaining them with a love ballad.

Meg looked as if she were enjoying it. More than that, she looked self-assured and calm, as if her guests were friends invited to enjoy supper and a fine minstrel she had hired for the occasion. In troth, the lad was not nearly as gifted a musician and singer as the chap who had entertained them at Hermitage.

The golden light of the candles and firelight touched Meg's face. Her hands rested on the table before her, primly folded. She looked stately and serene, exhibiting a beauty he had not seen before. She wore the simple, lace-edged veil he liked, and her forest-green riding dress looked well on her. His cock stirred.

A voice deep inside called him instantly to order. At such a time, the voice said, it was disgraceful to think about her soft, smooth skin or her enticingly small waist and flaring hips. To allow such thoughts to divert more than that moment's attention from his duty would be more so.

The lass had dangerously overstepped, if not by leaving the tower, where his men could keep her safe, then by riding too far into the Forest, which he had no doubt she had done. That even Sym knew she had been unwise had been plain to see.

If the lad knew as much, then so did Margaret.

Husbandly duty required that he teach her more wisdom, and the lesson would have to be harsh, since he'd soon be leaving again. He dared not let her think that what she'd done today, she could do again without consequence.

The man beside her said something, and as she turned to face him, Wat caught a flickering look that made him tense. When she showed only polite interest in the rascal, he relaxed. Faith, he asked himself, had it been jealousy stirring? Because, at her husband's table, she sat by a man who was not her husband?

As she looked back at the singer, he caught the flicker again and read it easily this time. She had seen him and was trying not to reveal his presence.

A tug at his sleeve diverted his attention to Sym, standing beside him, looking concerned. He had not noticed the lad following him. But before he could tell him to go back downstairs, Sym gestured toward something in the hall.

Wat heard a burst of laughter as he turned to see what had caught Sym's eye.

Two of the strangers sat together on the rearmost bench, and one held a wriggling pouch. A kitten's orange head popped out of the sack just as the man holding it turned and held it out toward one of two hounds lying nearby.

The dog's ears came up sharply as it sniffed the air.

"I'll kill 'im," Sym said, taking a step forward. "That's me Pawky!"

Wat grabbed him. "You stay here," he said. "And keep out of the way."

Sym apparently judged it wise to obey without speaking, which was just as well, because Wat's anger, no longer beclouded by lust, now had a prime target.

Drawing his sword, only half aware of Tam's steps behind him, he crossed the threshold, moved up behind the witless scruff with the kitten, and set the point of his sword just hard enough to the nape of the man's neck to make him freeze.

In a voice of ice, Wat said, "Move that sack gently away from the dog and hand it to me. No, friend, do not move," he said to the man beside his target. "If you want to get out of this place alive, either of you, do exactly as I tell you."

The man with the squirming pouch passed it back without turning, and Wat took it from him with his left hand, holding the sword steadily where it was.

He watched the man rather than the pouch as he grabbed it, and managed to catch it by its side. Pawky, clearly having had enough of it, squirmed out, latched her claws into Wat's jerkin sleeve, and scrambled up his arm to his shoulder, where she bumped his ear in a friendly greeting, then sat and began to purr.

Ignoring her, Wat kept his eyes on the two men, realizing as he stepped back from the one who'd been tormenting the kitten that the music had stopped.

Meg had come to her feet. Into the sudden silence, she said, "Welcome home, sir. As you see, we have guests. Their leader wants to talk with you, and I have promised him that he shall."

Several of the raiders had likewise come to their feet.

Tam said quietly, "Our lads be at the door. I dinna ken how many."

Wat lowered his sword and replied to Meg, "We are home, aye, madam, and glad to be so. Have you supper enough for fifty more?"

"We have," she said. "Shall I send lads to fetch it now?"

"Shortly," he said. "Our guests are gey welcome, but I would ken whence came the carts full of wood and game that sit inside my barmkin. The Laird of Buccleuch is even now riding in behind us, sithee. As Ranger of the Forest, he will want an answer to that question. What am I to tell him?"

No one answered. But as he had hoped, the men who had stood sat down, and his own men were watching now for a sign that he wanted action from them.

He did not know if Buccleuch had turned back, but neither was he sure he had not. As it was, he still had fewer men in the hall than the raiders did.

He would pit his against them with near certainty that his would prevail, but he could not risk a fight, not with two of the raiders so near the women on the dais.

Most of the men at the lower tables were watching him, but several of the raiders glanced nervously at the chimney breast, where Meg had hung the weapons and shields. Even those watching him seemed nervous, making him hope he might persuade them that whatever their cause had been, they had lost.

"Your lady wife said ye'd help us, sir," their leader said evenly.

"I did," Meg agreed. "These men told me they had permission from the Douglas to take fuel and game from the Forest, because their families need food and the means to cook it. 'Tis all they sought, they say. They have done us no harm, sir."

Wat shifted his gaze to the man beside her. "Who are you?"

Glancing at Meg, the man got to his feet before he said, "Men call me Daft Nebby Duffin, Sir Walter, but I'm no daft. Me own lads call me Neb."

"You say you had permission from the Douglas to take what you needed from the Forest, Neb. We both know that when you met Buccleuch there some days ago, you were able to show him no such permit. How do you explain that?"

"I canna explain it, 'cause I dinna ken why the Douglas's man didna give me nowt to show. But he did say—Sakes, he told all o' us! We can take what we need from the Forest until the Douglas himself says otherwise."

With a frown, Wat said, "Why did you not simply return to this agent of the Douglas and request such a permit?"

Neb Duffin shrugged. "He did come to us, sir. We didna go to him. We dinna ken where to find him."

"Then why not apply directly to the Douglas? All ken where to find him these days—at Hermitage Castle in Liddesdale."

Neb was silent.

"With respect, sir," Meg said. "Not all folks feel so easy about approaching a man as powerful as the Douglas to make such a request."

The man standing beside her nodded.

Thinking swiftly, Wat said, "Here is what I can do for you tonight. If you will agree to leave here peacefully, I'll see that you take enough food with you to feed your families. But I cannot let you keep what you have taken from the Forest—not without his lordship's permission. However," he added as men at the lower tables began to stir irritably, "I'll approach the Douglas myself if I learn that your situation is as you say it is."

Neb said, "Ye'll see him, then?"

"I'll be gathering men to my banner and to his in the next sennight and will meet him in eight days at Southdean. In return for my aid," Wat added, "I will ask that you offer yourselves to the Douglas's cause, which is to secure the safety of Scotland from the English once and for all. Will you agree to that?"

"Must we serve *you*?" Neb demanded.

"I'd welcome you, although I ken fine that you are not my kinsmen or sworn to serve me. However, you are Borderers, so I'll accept your word as such that you will aid us by serving leaders who fight with us and not those who fight against us."

He waited, letting the silence in the hall grow until Neb said, "Aye, then. Ye've my word, sir, and I speak for most o' my men. But on this matter, if ye're agreed, I'll ask them to speak for themselves."

"I'm agreed," Wat said.

"Aye, then, I'm with ye," one man said loudly, getting to his feet.

"And I," shouted another, and another, until the only ones who had not spoken were the two on the rear bench who had been tormenting the kitten.

The one who had not held the bag said quietly, "I, too."

The tormentor did not speak or give any sign of what he might be thinking.

Wat waited, saying nothing. The only sound he heard was the little cat's purr, but he kept his attention on the silent man.

Neb said, "Bestir that tongue o' yours, Kip. What do ye say?"

"I'm thinking I'll say 'aye,'" the man said, looking at Wat.

"Why?" Wat demanded. "Why should I accept your word when I ken fine that you likely harbor ill feelings toward me now?"

"Aye, sir, I might ha' done. But a man who's so plainly

master o' his castle even wi' a wee cat sitting on his shoulder, cleaning itself and purring loud enough to make itself heard in a big chamber like this—and without his paying it any heed whilst he lays down the law like ye did . . . That man be one I can follow anywhere."

Chapter 14

Nae boar in the forest, when hunted and wounded,
Did ever sae storm, or was ever sae stounded . . .

Meg had all she could do not to laugh, not just at the man's comment but at the look on Walter's face. Others in the hall, including the man beside her, clearly felt the same way. But, except for hastily stifled noises, they resisted the temptation.

Turning to Neb Duffin, she said, "My sister and I must retire now, so that you can discuss your situation more thoroughly with Sir Walter. I assure you, his word is good. So I hope you will excuse us."

"Aye, sure," he said. "I ken fine he be a man o' his word and, too, that he and his da' be close friends wi' the Douglas. We'll do now, I'm thinking, and I thank ye for your kindness, me lady. None so many would ha' done as ye did today."

"I'll bid you goodnight then," she said. "You will always be welcome here, so if you encounter further difficulties, you must come at once and tell us."

He nodded. She saw him swallow, but he did not speak.

"Come, Amalie," Meg said. "We'll go up now."

"I think we'd better wait a moment," Amalie said, glancing at the lower hall.

Meg looked toward the back, where Walter had been only a moment before. Men-at-arms were crossing the threshold, but they kept their weapons sheathed.

She was about to ask what Amalie had meant when she saw Walter step onto the dais. Finding him so much closer than she had expected was a bit unsettling.

Neb stepped back out of his way, but Walter said, "Don't go yet. I want to talk longer with you and your men before you leave, to learn just what your needs are and hear more about this agent who told you he spoke for the Douglas."

"Aye, sir."

"I'm certain he is not Douglas's man, but I can assure you that Douglas, too, will help you, especially as you have agreed to aid him. Where do you think *you* are going?" he added in a less cordial tone, as Meg moved to step past him.

"I did not want to interrupt you, sir. But Amalie and I are going to bed."

He said, "If you will join your men by the fire, Neb, I would have a brief word with my lady wife before she retires."

Neb agreed, bowed to Meg, and turned away.

The moment he stepped from the dais, Walter said grimly, "You may go upstairs, but do not go to sleep. We are going to have a talk, you and I."

To his shock, she grinned.

"Does the thought of such a talk amuse you?" he demanded. "It should not."

"No, sir," she said. "But it is hard to feel really terrified whilst Sym's wee cat looks so adoringly at you and purrs."

"Oh, for . . ." He reached up and took the cat off his shoulder, handing it to her with a near snarl. "Take it with you and give it back to Sym."

Eyes downcast, she said as she stroked the kitten, "Yes, sir, I will."

Apparently unimpressed with her docility, he snapped, "See that you do."

~~~

Having delivered the kitten to Sym, Meg was smiling as she went upstairs until Amalie, behind her, said caustically, "I don't blame Walter for being angry, Meg. Those horrid men might have killed us. Why ever did you invite them here?"

"But I told you, dearling. Having watched our parents tread softly between Englishmen and Scots for much of my life, I merely sought to put those lessons to good use by persuading the raiders that we were harmless and would even help them if we could. Back there in the woods, I saw, as you did, that they viewed us as little more than two useful hostages. Moreover, they had four men to every one of ours. Do you really think that what I did was wrong?"

"It does not matter what I think," Amalie muttered. "It is Sir Walter you will have to persuade now. And I do not think he looked very persuadable."

"No," Meg said. "But he does listen sometimes."

She stopped when they reached the landing by her bed-chamber and put a hand on Amalie's arm when she would have gone on by. "Don't go yet," Meg said. "We still have much to talk about and time for it, I think, before Walter comes up."

Clearly reluctant but just as clearly aware that Meg would insist, Amalie sighed and went into the bedchamber. She stopped a few steps in, and stood still.

Shutting the door, Meg said, "Why do you think you might be with child?"

Amalie turned then, saying, "Is that not how a woman gets a child in her? When a man has his way with her?"

"Aye, it is," Meg said. "Our mother told us that much. But I do not think it happens every time, and you have not grown any fatter."

"I am already plump. How would we know?"

Meg was at a loss to answer her, but she was sure there must be a way to know for sure. People did seem to know that a woman was expecting a bairn before she grew so fat that everyone could tell. "We could ask Lady Scott," she said. "She has birthed three sons and a daughter."

"I don't want to ask her. She is only just starting to be kind to me."

"Don't be petulant, love. It does not suit you. I will ask her if you like. In troth, I should like to know on my own account. But won't you tell me who did this to you? We shall have to know sometime."

"Nay, no one can know," Amalie said, growing visibly distressed again.

"We need talk no more about it now," Meg said. Hearing a telltale footstep on the landing, she added hastily, "Prithee, do not show that face to Walter!"

The door opened on her words, and she turned to face him.

Hoping to divert his attention from her sister, to give Amalie time to collect herself she said, "I . . . I expected you to remain some time with Neb Duffin."

He cast Amalie only a brief glance, saying, "I turned him over to Jed Crosier and his minions to help with the food, and set Neb's lads to unloading their carts."

"Are you letting them keep their chickens?"

His lips twitched. "Aye, although I did point out that if the chickens are truly wild, taking them counts the same under the law as taking pheasant." His gaze flicked back to Amalie. "We'll excuse you now, lass. But don't go downstairs."

"I won't," she said, hurrying past him with a quick, sympathetic glance at Meg. At the door, she looked back, said goodnight, and fled.

Meg murmured, "Goodnight." But she did not spare her sister another glance as she did, and Walter did not take his eyes from Meg.

His anger was plain to see. But she knew it would do her no good to try to defend herself without learning first exactly what had made him so angry.

Since he had been quick to take his cue from her in the hall, she had hoped he understood that she had acted the best way she knew.

The look in his eyes now said he did not understand any such thing.

He let the silence continue until she wanted to speak just to end it. But just as she might have done so, he said, "I am waiting for an explanation, lass. I thought I had made it clear that you were not to go haring off on your own again. By your actions today, you betrayed that belief. I want to know why."

The accusation angered her, but she knew that revealing her anger might ignite his, whereas a calm explanation had aided her with him before.

The problem this time was that her normal serenity had deserted her. She said, "Do you want to know why I left the tower or why I invited them home?"

"I won't ask why you left here with only six men to escort you, because—"

"Forgive me, sir, but I did not know that you expected me to stay inside this tower whenever you are away. Am I to stay here the whole time you are away with the Douglas? That could well be weeks, and—"

"Don't try me too far," he said, stepping closer. He seemed suddenly even larger than usual, which—she suspected—was his intent. "You know I mean nowt of the sort. Nor are we likely to be away so long. Douglas wants only to make a grand show of force to dissuade the English. I doubt we'll be gone a fortnight."

"But you will again take most of your men with you, will you not?"

"Aye, but as you heard below, the raiders will go with us, so things will be safer here. And, too, I believe my mother means to visit our Jenny. She will likely invite you to go with her, if she has not done so already."

She pressed her lips together.

He frowned. "What?"

"She did ask us. But . . . but I would prefer to stay here," she added, unwilling to reveal to him yet that Amalie was the reason.

When he frowned again, she added hastily, "This is my home now, and I've scarcely spent a sennight in it. I want to get to know the place and our people better. Also, I am sure your mother would prefer to have Jenny to herself."

"We can discuss that later," he said. "I will acquit you of defying me. But I want to know why you headed into the Forest instead of coming straight home. Neb said you were more than a mile west of the cleuch entrance when you met them."

She nearly reminded him that, rather than meeting them, the raiders had rushed out of the woods and surrounded them. Instantly perceiving pitfalls along that course, she realized she would encounter even more if she tried to explain that she had taken that route because, on a horse in unfamiliar country, Amalie could not just walk away—as she would have at the tower—if Meg tried to persuade her that they should go with Lady Scott to Ferniehurst.

She could not tell him that without explaining Amalie's reasons.

"I wanted to see more of the Forest," she said. That much, at least, was true. "And I am glad we met Neb, sir. If that makes you angry, no doubt you will say so, but is it not better to learn the truth than not to know?"

"That is not the point," he said sternly. He proceeded then to tell her what the point was. He spoke articulately, logically, and at length. He did not shout at her, as her father did when he was angry, but his words were harder to endure in silence.

The gist, as she understood it, was that he believed a woman should obey her husband rather than use her own good sense—even to act as he would expect when she could not know his expectations. That she had known he would be angry was beside the point. His reproaches strained her patience and her temper.

He spoke as if he did not trust her to act sensibly despite plain evidence to the contrary. Had she not capably managed a difficult situation that very day?

Her father would never speak so to her mother. He valued her ladyship's advice and her intelligence even when he resisted acknowledging both.

Realizing that Walter had reached a point of greater fury than before, she wrenched her attention back to what, exactly, he was saying.

"To have frightened everyone, to have sent poor Sym riding like a madman to seek help . . . To have ridden into woods that had already suffered raids! And to have invited the very raiders here without any notion of how dangerous they might be! They may well prove to be just as desperate as they say they are, but you had no way to know as much then. You are never, ever to do such a thing again."

When he paused for breath, she said, "Did Sym really ride like a madman?"

He blinked, then grimaced. "He rode faster than was safe for him. However, his actions are irrelevant. The point is . . ."

Realizing he was still too angry to discuss the incident sensibly, she made no effort to interrupt him. As the torrent of words swept over her, she began to see that something more than anger fueled them. Even so, she could not ignore what he was saying in the same way that she had managed to ignore most of her father's rants.

Her irritation increased.

He had a way of sounding confident, sensible, and utterly logical. The result was that she felt as if she were being unreasonable by disagreeing with him. Her father was never logical or sensible when he was angry. He just ranted. But when his ranting stopped, one had only to apologize to achieve peace again.

She could not honestly apologize to Walter for having met the poachers and invited them home, because she was glad to have been able to help them. She thought he ought to be glad, too. But clearly, if he was, he was not yet ready to admit it. Nevertheless, she had learned over the years that a sincere apology could often prove a most powerful weapon.

When he paused again, she stifled her smoldering anger, put a hand on his arm, looked into his eyes, and said, "I'm sorry I've disappointed you so."

Wat stared into those beautiful eyes and felt a surge of remorse. He had been too hard on her, too fierce in his scolding. Worse than that, he had been unfair.

He had worked himself into such a fury that his words had run away with him.

He covered her hand with one of his and gave it a squeeze as he said, "Nay, lass, you've not disappointed me. In troth, this whole business gave me a rare fright. You've no idea what I felt when I saw Sym careering toward us. And then to see you sitting beside that ruffian, Neb, at my own table . . . Well—"

"Surely, it is my table now, too," she said.

He moved both hands to her shoulders and looked straight into her eyes. "It is, aye. But henceforth, when you invite someone to sit beside you there, you might be wiser to consider first whether his presence will please me or not."

"At the time, I wanted only to persuade him that we

were no threat to him," she said quietly. "I invited them to supper when he said their families were going hungry, because I was sure that you would want to help them if that were so, and so would the Douglas." She paused, licked her full lips in a way that stirred him below, then said, "I did know it might anger you. Is there aught I can do now to atone?"

His gaze had not left her lips since the first lick, and the longer he stared, the harder his cock grew. Anger was but a faint memory.

His fingers moved to deal deftly with the lacing of her bodice.

"I do know a few things we might try," he said.

⁓

As she lay beside him after their coupling, Meg wondered if her mother had ever done such things with her father. Not the coupling, of course, but the actions that had preceded it. Some of the things he had asked of her had astonished her but not nearly as much as he had astonished her by doing similar things to her. She had not realized that one's lips and tongue could be used to such good purpose.

But he had stopped too soon, overcome again by his own passion. So once again he had left her with a sense that more ought to have happened. There had, after all, been that one time, before he had gone to Elishaw . . .

Recalling her feelings then, she would have liked to ask him to explain much more about coupling to her, but he clearly wanted to talk of other things. He said, "I meant to tell you, before everything else happened, that the wardens heard my grievance against your father. They have ordered him to return my livestock."

"Did he agree?"

"He had no choice. Douglas guaranteed his compliance and ordered him to provide you a proper dowry. The Earl of Carrick is to visit Hermitage in a few weeks, and your father is to see to the matter before then."

"If Douglas has guaranteed it, my father will comply," she said. "He will not like it, but he won't defy Douglas or the wardens' court."

"We'll see, but we should sleep now," he said. "There is much for us both to do before I must join Douglas and the others at Southdean."

Still curious, and aware from experience that he would drop off quickly, she said, "You know much more about coupling and such than I do. Do you know how a woman can tell if she is with child?"

He went still for a long moment before he said, "Do you think you are?"

"I don't know," she said. "But coupling is the manner by which women do become pregnant, so surely I could be. How would I know?"

"Did your mother not tell you?"

"Our marriage happened so quickly," she said. "I scarcely spoke with her after you agreed to it, and she said naught about coupling and such."

He was silent for several moments before he said, "A woman's courses stop once she is with child. That is how she knows."

"Oh."

"Well?" he said.

"My flow should start within the next week or so."

"I would like sons," he said sleepily. "And a few daughters, too." Soon after that, he began to breathe deeply and evenly, and she knew he was asleep.

She lay for some time, wondering if she should have asked him to tell her what she burned to know about the feelings she had when they coupled. They kept increasing, promising ever more, then stopped when he stopped, leaving her with a sense of some wondrous thing that lay just beyond her ken.

He certainly reached some sort of release, and he reached it each time.

Probing her reluctance to ask him about it, particularly when he seemed so willing to answer other questions, she realized that she feared he might think she implied criticism of him. Walter did not respond well to criticism.

An imp in her head suggested that she did not much like criticism either. Perhaps her real fear was that he would say it was her own fault and that some lack in her kept her from achieving whatever there was to achieve.

Aside from those lingering questions, she thought she had handled things well. She was learning at last to manage her husband.

~

The following day, as soon as Walter had gone out with his men, Meg found Amalie in her bedchamber and told her she had learned how a woman could tell if she was with child.

"Mercy," her sister said when Meg explained, "I don't know when my last flow was exactly. I don't pay the dates much heed, but it has been some time. When did Simon last come home?"

"Shortly after Beltane, I believe," Meg said.

"Aye, that's right. 'Twas the second week of May because I remember thinking it was the sort of thing that *would* happen when Simon was there. It was just as unwelcome as he was."

"You should not talk so," Meg said. "Simon has an important position with the Earl of Fife and may well become very successful. Tom may be merrier and more fun to have at home, but Simon deserves more respect than you show him."

With a sour look, Amalie said, "You have a higher opinion of our brothers than I do, but do you actually *like* Simon? He often makes me want to shake him."

"One need not like him, my dear, but he *is* family and deserves our loyalty. So do not let such words leave your tongue whilst you are with anyone but me."

Amalie shrugged and changed the subject.

As they talked, Meg did some mental calculating and realized that her sister had indeed missed her time. But missing once did not make a certainty. Meg had done as much herself, more than once, without ever being with child.

The rest of the week passed swiftly after that until Saturday morning.

Amalie had not come down yet, so Walter and Meg were breaking their fast alone at the high table when he said, "I mean to ride to the Hall today to talk with my father and bid my mother farewell. She departs on Monday for Ferniehurst."

"I know," Meg agreed. "Prithee, tell her I wish her a safe journey."

"I mean to tell her that you and Amalie will be happy to go with her."

"But I've already sent a message with our regrets," Meg said.

"That is of no matter," he said. "She will be glad to have your company."

Noting with a sinking feeling that the hall still teemed with his men, she said, "I know that you worry about our safety, sir, but I've explained how I feel. Surely, we will be quite safe here at Raven's Law."

"I think it better that you go."

Well aware of what Amalie's reaction would be, and aware, too, that her own reaction was straining to match it, Meg fought to rein in her temper. Drawing a deep breath, she said quietly, "I do not want to go. I thought I had made that plain."

He nodded to a hovering gillie to refill his mug with ale before he said, "I know you don't want to. You will go because I command it. I cannot go away and leave you here alone to invite sundry villains to sup with you again, or worse."

Anger surged at his unfairness. But well aware of their audience and thanking the Fates that Amalie was not there, Meg said in carefully measured tones, "I pray you, sir, may we not discuss this more privately?"

"There is nowt to discuss," he said, reaching for his mug. "You'll do as I bid."

"No."

The mug stopped halfway to his lips. He turned his head to look at her. "What did you say?"

"I said no," Meg said, eyeing him warily.

"By God!" he exclaimed, banging the mug down on the table as he rose to his feet and shoved back his stool. "You will not defy me again."

Unwilling to sit when he loomed angrily over her, Meg

stood to face him and even managed, hard as it was, not to step back.

"I am neither a child nor a fool," she said, realizing that her careful calm was shattering, and striving to hold on to it without backing down. "I have a brain, sir. I did no more than make a decision—and that a full week ago, I'd remind you—to help someone in need. But you cannot seem to set that aside. Instead, you say that I should not have done what I did, although it ended well and gained information you needed, information you could have got by no other means. I think you shou—"

"Enough!" he roared. "I won't have my wife threaping and scolding and saying she will or she won't. Not to me! You will *not* wear the breeks in this family, madam, for all that your mother may wear them at Elishaw!"

With a cry of pure fury that he would say such a thing before such an audience, Meg scooped up his mug and cast its contents into his face. "How dare you speak so to me!" she cried.

"How dare I? I'll show you what I dare." His face still dripping ale, he reached for her, his intent clear.

Nimbly, she stepped back, evading his grasp as she said in a voice that rang through the hall, "Don't touch me! You have men here who have sworn an oath to serve me, and I will demand that they honor that oath, even to protect me from you!"

⌒

Wiping a sleeve across his face, Wat cursed himself, knowing he had let his temper carry him too far. He ached to put her across his knee and give her a good skelping to teach her to mind him, but he knew her well enough now to be sure she would do as she'd threatened. He did not want to humiliate her by forcing such a test of his men's loyalty. Knowing them nearly as well as he knew himself, he had no doubt they would obey him despite what they had vowed to Murray under duress.

Accordingly, he held up a hand and said quietly, "Pax, Meg. We'll continue this discussion later, as you have suggested, when we can do so more privately."

To the men, he said, "We leave for the Hall in ten minutes. Make haste."

They got up quickly, their relief visible as they headed for the doorway.

Meg—wisely, he thought—said nothing.

Waiting long enough to be sure everyone else was beyond earshot, Wat said evenly, "I would suggest, lass, that before I return, you ponder carefully all that we said here and decide how you will make your apology."

Watching as Walter turned away and strode to the stairs, Meg fought the temptation to hurl the heavy pewter mug after him.

Telling herself fiercely that to do so would be the act of a dafty seeking an early death, she set it back down on the table with unusual care instead.

Apology, indeed.

She was not sure whether she had just enjoyed a victory of sorts or suffered total defeat. He had intended dire punishment. She had seen that much. But he had set his decision aside when she'd threatened to claim protection from his men.

They *had* promised her father they would serve her.

Memory surfaced of the look that had leaped to Tammy's face as she'd made her sweeping gesture toward the men in the hall. The huge man had not looked eager to rush to her defense. Instead, he had looked stunned, even appalled.

"Beg pardon, mistress," a familiar young voice said just behind her.

Wincing with self-reproval, she turned. "What is it, Sym?"

"I didna ken what ye'd ha' me do just then, had the master no taken fright and left," he said. "Will ye tell me, so I'll ken better next time?"

"You did as you should have by coming now to ask me," she said, laying a hand on his wiry red curls. Smiling softly, she added, "I think you know, too, that the master did not take fright. He just changed his mind about what to do."

"Aye, I ken that fine," he said, sighing. "I hoped ye thought he did, though, so ye'd no fret about when he comes back. Sithee, he may still be wroth wi' ye."

"Would you really have stood up for me, Sym?"

"I would, aye, and I will, for he told me himself that I must. I dinna think he'd hang me for going against him in such a cause. D'ye think he would?"

"No," she said, realizing that Wat would be most unlikely to punish the boy in any way for coming to her defense. "He would never do that."

Sym sighed again, this time with relief. And when she suggested that he go out and be sure that the men riding to Scott's Hall had got off without incident, he ran away without looking back.

Although the exchange temporarily eased her fury with her husband, her temper, once ignited, was slow to cool.

As she went upstairs to their bedchamber, her words and his, and all the things she might better have said to him to persuade him, echoed through her mind.

That he expected to rule their household without allowing her to voice an opinion unless it marched with his was unacceptable. Likewise was it unacceptable that he seemed to think that he could see to everything and everyone, in or out of the household, without so much as a discussion of what she might think or prefer. Such behavior was entirely English, quite unsuitable for a Scottish Borderer, and—

Her thoughts came to a halt. What did she know of Scottish Borderers? Was her own father not one of them? Did she want to be married to a man like Sir Iagan?

She did not.

As for the English, they expected their women to be decorative and obedient. Even her mother had behaved so whenever they had visited their English kinsmen.

Lady Murray would not have dared offer advice to her Percy cousins. The freedom she felt to speak her mind to her husband, however, was exactly what Meg had hoped to enjoy with hers.

As she entered their bedchamber, she asked herself if she might have misread his earlier benevolence and should heed Sym's caveat that his anger might be smoldering. Not that it mattered, because she had no intention of being treated like a ninny for the rest of her life. Not if she could do aught to prevent it. She would have to stand up to Walter somehow. But how?

"Meggie, did you not hear me call you, or rap?" Amalie asked as she pushed open the door. "Have you already broken your fast?"

"Aye," Meg said, making up her mind and moving briskly to one of the kists that contained her clothing.

"What are you doing?"

"I'm going to turn that wee room across the landing into my own bedchamber," Meg said, looking up at her.

Amalie stared back in astonishment. "Faith, did Walter tell you to?"

"No, I'm just angry. He has commanded us to accompany his lady mother to Ferniehurst despite my already having sent her our regrets."

"Oh, no!"

"Oh, yes, but I want him to understand that I am not one who can simply submit to such orders as if I had no thoughts of my own to express."

"May God have mercy on us," Amalie murmured.

"There will be time enough later for prayer," Meg said. "Help me with this."

Chapter 15

～

"Yet spite o' your wiles and your spies they
have shunned you,
A Murray is kittler to catch than the diel!"

By the time Wat returned that afternoon, his temper had cooled considerably. He still smarted, however, when he recalled how easily he had lost control and exactly what he had said to her.

Remembering his command that she think of a suitable way to apologize, he realized that he owed her an apology, too. That it might undermine the authority he was attempting to establish was a nuisance. But that was his own fault, and he thought that, with care, he could make himself clear on both points.

However, he also remembered the way in which she had apologized the last time they had quarreled. That memory stirred his loins, and he began to hope her next apology might take a similar form.

Dismounting and turning his horse over to a gillie to tend, he hurried upstairs to the hall, where he stopped

one of the lads setting up trestles for supper and asked
him where he might find the mistress.

"She'll be in her bedchamber, sir."

"In *our* bedchamber, you should say," Wat corrected
gently.

"Och, nay, for she's set up one for herself across from
that 'un."

Anger surged back. Struggling with it, determined not
to make the mistake of presenting his emotions again to
the entire hall, he growled a polite thank-you to the lad
and went stiffly back to the stairway. He had not gone far
before light, running footsteps sounded behind him.

"Will ye still be a-leaving for Hermitage in the morning, Master Wat?"

Stopping, Wat whirled with a demand at the tip of his
tongue to know how the lad had dared let his mistress
shift bedchambers. But looking at Sym's widening eyes
and realizing he was about to unleash his anger at the
wrong person, he snapped instead, "Where are you supposed to be?"

Looking bewildered, Sym said, "I've been watching
over her ladyship, like ye said I should, Master Wat. But
when I told her the lads at the gate had said ye were a-
coming up yon hill, she told me to go help Jed Crosier
in the kitchen."

"Did she ask you to give her warning when I
returned?"

"Aye, she did. So ye see—"

"I see a lad who is not in the kitchen as he is supposed
to be," Wat said sternly.

"Aye, well, I were just wondering if ye'd still be going
to the Douglas, 'cause if ye'll no be leaving yet, she'll
ha' nae need to sleep in yon puny room she's took. I

warrant 'tis nobbut fretting over how much she'll miss ye—"

"Go," Wat said grimly, pointing downstairs toward the kitchen.

Sym fled, and Wat went on up the stairs, taking them two at a time.

She had left his bedchamber door wide open. The one across the landing from it was shut. If she had dared to bar it against him . . .

Just the thought of such an outrage made him so angry that he paused, telling himself not to be a fool. Meg would not bar the door.

Taking a deep breath, he lifted the latch and pushed.

She had.

⁓

Learning from Sym of her husband's return, Meg had banished Amalie to her own chamber to dress for supper, and had sent Sym to the kitchen. Then she put the wooden bar across the door and waited, alone, sitting on the edge of the narrow cot, scarcely daring to breathe lest she miss hearing his step on the stairs.

She knew he would come. He would learn what she had done before he had been five minutes in the hall, because she had made no secret of it. She had even told a passing gillie that he should let others know where they could find her if need be. And she could depend on Sym to give him the news if no one else did.

When she heard footsteps at last, hasty ones of booted feet, she looked again at the barred door. The same sense that had warned her not to throw the mug at him stirred hairs on the back of her neck now. She was on her feet, moving to raise the bar, when she saw the latch lift, heard a curse, and quickly stepped back.

With a heavy thump, the bar snapped, the door crashed open and banged back against the wall, and Walter crossed the threshold toward her, glowering.

She said hastily, "I was going to—"

She got no further before he scooped her into his arms without a word. Then he turned on his heel and marched across the landing to his own bedchamber, where he kicked that door shut behind him with another crash.

Striding to the bed, he dumped her onto its hard mattress. "There will be no barred doors between us," he snapped as she scrambled back away from him toward the wall. Her caul had come off, but she left it where it lay.

"I would have unbarred it if you'd asked," she said.

"I should not have to ask," he said as he turned away and began to unfasten his jack, only to turn back with a narrow-eyed look. "Why did you bar it at all?"

She hesitated, pushing a strand of hair off her cheek. She had barred the door to keep him out, of course, but she would do herself no good to admit that now.

"Well?"

Swallowing, she said, "I'd hoped I could talk to you through the door. That way, I'd not have to see your anger whenever I disagreed with you or suggested something you did not want to hear. I . . . I'd hoped you would listen, and not just dismiss everything I said as if my words meant naught to you."

"I don't dismiss everything you say."

"You do, aye, *and* you make up your mind to things that affect me without discussing them with me."

"I've told you, I won't allow you to rule me."

"I don't expect to," she said, trying to sound calm, although the words had sounded more as if she had wailed them at him. "I don't want that."

The echo of what he had said about her mother roared through her mind.

She was *not* her mother, but she could not say that to him without shouting it. So she held her tongue and watched him warily instead.

He was eyeing her, too, with a speculative, measuring look. At last, he said, "I should not have said what I did, lass, not the part about your mother."

"But that *is* what you think, is it not?"

"That she rules your father and Elishaw, or that you want to be like her?"

"You believe both of those things," she said flatly, judging it safe now to move back to the edge of the bed and sit on it properly instead of cowering near the wall.

"Nay, you *fear* both of those things."

He turned his attention to undoing his doublet and shirt as he said, "I don't know what I believe, but I don't fear you. You made me angry by saying things you should not have said to me—not in front of my men at all events," he amended.

"But—"

"I know," he said, raising a hand. "I said things to you in front of them, too, things I should not have said at all. Especially that about your mother. That was ill done of me, but I cannot tell you I don't believe what I said. Can you deny that you *have* tried to manage me from time to time?"

She bit her lip. She could not deny it, because she had.

His gaze held hers. "Even so, I should not have said

what I did. All I can do is apologize for bellowing it out like that and . . . and beg your pardon."

Although she was surprised that he would apologize, let alone ask for her forgiveness, she could not grant it. Not yet.

Instead, solemnly, she said, "You, of all people, should be grateful that my mother *does* wield influence with my father, sir. Had she none, you would be dead, because he would have hanged you as a reiver. My mother saved your life."

Wat stared blindly at her as the sense of righteousness that had supported him for the past ten minutes dissipated like smoke into thin air.

He said, "How can that be?"

She hesitated.

"It wasn't true, was it?"

"It was, aye, but I don't know how much I ought to tell you about it."

"You'd best tell me all of it now. You cannot fling that sort of thing at a man and then *not* explain it. I recall that she did speak to him just before he said he'd hang Sym, but that did Sym no good. She may have spoken for the others. But otherwise, I saw no sign of her taking more than scant interest in us."

"Sakes, sir, do you suppose he would have ordered you dragged into the great hall for the sole purpose of displaying you to his womenfolk?"

"Recall that I was not at my best then, so I did not question his reason for the summons. I'd wakened only a short time before to find myself bound hand and foot, and mind-numbing pain in one's limbs rather dampens one's powers of reflection."

A flicker of sympathy crossed her face, but she said only, "At that same time, sir, my mother had just learned of your capture and had suggested—"

She broke off with a grimace, telling him as plainly as words that she had talked herself to a point past which she did not want to proceed.

"Go on," he said, not sure he wanted to hear it but knowing he must.

"I was trying to think how to put it so it would not sound . . ."

When she paused, clearly seeking the right word even for that, he said, "I'd suggest the plain truth, Meg. I won't bite you for telling me. I know whose fault the whole business was, and I'll not try to lay blame elsewhere again."

"Very well. When she learned that you were Buccleuch's heir, she asked if you had a wife. When my father said he did not know of one, she said it would be unwise to destroy such a gift of . . . of Providence."

"Providence?"

The smile he had learned to watch for dawned slowly then. "Mother reminded him that he had a duty to find husbands for his three daughters. She made it clear that she saw your capture as God's way of providing for one of us."

"And she suggested me for you?"

A flicker of pain erased the lingering smile. "My father declared that I should be the one," she said. Meeting his questioning gaze, she added briskly, "But when you refused, she continued to insist that he not hang you. She told him to let you see the rope. I . . . I suspect it was she who suggested hanging Sym first."

"For that alone—"

"Had you been the sort of man who could let that happen, she would have intervened again and let my father hang you," she said. "I'm certain of that. She might have let him hang the others, but she would not have let him hang Sym."

He nearly told her not to be stupid. But something in her expression told him that would be more brutal than what he had said about Lady Murray earlier.

She said, "With such an opinion as you had of her, I am surprised you did not suspect all along that she was the force behind our marriage."

"Nay, it never occurred to me, because although I've heard that she rules the roast, I did not think she was doing so then. I saw what I expected to see, and most women I know are obedient and submissive to their husbands."

She looked up from under her lashes at that. "Like Jenny, I suppose."

He chuckled and spread his hands. "I said 'most women.'"

"So you did." She nibbled her lower lip, then looked up at him again and said, "My mother generally *appears* submissive herself. In fact, she does not try to drive my father but only to . . . to make suggestions to him."

This time her struggle to find just the right words stirred his amusement, but he tried not to let her see it. Instead, he said, "I am indebted to her for my life, Meg. But you and I must come to an understanding of our own, the two of us. I expect we'll be together for a long time, and I don't want to spend it fratching with you."

"I don't want to fratch with you, either."

"Nor do I want to wonder every time I leave here if I will come home to find that you have gone counter to my wishes again, or that something even worse has happened because you've done something else you should not have done."

She cocked her head. "What would you have had me do differently?"

"We have discussed that enough already, I think," he said.

"I cannot be a prisoner here, sir. I do have a mind and a brain of my own. If I did something I ought not to have done by riding to visit your mother, I did not know it. Moreover, my actions provided you with two dozen more men to take with you to fight the English. I also helped you resolve a serious problem in the Forest. Can you not agree, in fairness, that you ought to acknowledge at least that much?"

"I can, and I will. But this matter of going to Fernie-hurst is different. The English may well overrun this area if we fail to stop them. Have you no imagination, lass, that you cannot understand what that would mean?"

"I have more than imagination," she said. "I have my family's history. Seeing how my parents have dealt with both the English and the Scots over the years is what gave me the ability to persuade Nebby Duffin that we meant him and his men no harm. What I expect, sir, is that Douglas and the rest of you will stop the English armies before they get here. If you cannot, then Raven's Law itself is at risk, and I'd remind you that Elishaw and even Hermitage have fallen before and may fall again."

"Aye, but that does not mean—"

"You asked me once what I think about England's desire to rule Scotland. I was not certain then. But I know now that Scottish freedom means more to me than anything but our family. If we do have to submit, recall that I am half English, with powerful English kinsmen. But first, sir," she added, looking straight into his eyes, "I am your wife, and thus I am mistress of this tower. If you cannot trust me to remember that and to do all I can to protect our people here, you should not leave."

Her hair, freed of its caul, was mussed and falling in wisps around her face. But her voice was as it nearly always was, calm and as soothing as music to the ear.

He held out a hand to pull her to her feet. "I wish I did not have to go," he said. Shifting both hands to her shoulders, he added, "I'm not sure you do know what you may face, Meg, but I don't doubt your sincerity. Know this, though. Whatever comes, we'll seek no English favor unless we can do so without selling them our souls."

"I agree, sir. Does that mean you will not insist that Amalie and I go to Ferniehurst with your mother?"

"I told her today that your plans remained uncertain. I'll tell her tomorrow that you cannot bear to leave Raven's Law until all is in order here." He smiled. "We were both at fault this morning. We must learn to deal better together."

"We must, aye, but for now we should dress and go down to supper. You must be nigh starving by now."

"I am, aye, but I don't want supper," he said. "I want you."

He reached for her, and for once she proved entirely obedient.

As Meg watched him ride away the next morning with nearly every man-at-arms whose presence at the tower was not essential, she felt a shiver. She smiled and waved nonetheless, knowing he would not thank her for showing her fear.

"I wish I was a-going," Sym muttered wistfully beside her.

"A fine thing to wish," she said, giving him a look. "Who would look after me if you left? What if the English captured you, carried you off to London, and chopped off your head? What would I do then, eh?"

"That would puzzle ye, aye," he agreed as the pouch attached to his belt wriggled and Pawky stuck her head out with a look at her young master that he easily deciphered. "She wants her dirt pile, so I'll see to it now if ye dinna mind."

Telling him to do as he thought best, Meg looked around, pleased to see how tidy the yard looked compared to the way she had first seen it. To be sure, earlier that morning it had been crowded with helmets, armor, weapons, and other gear for the men, but those items had disappeared as the men mounted. Borderers took only what they could carry, and because they traveled light, they also traveled swiftly.

She missed Wat already, although she knew little had changed between them. He still expected her to submit to him in nearly every way.

Some ways were not objectionable, she reminded herself, recalling the previous evening. She had discovered several ways in which she could at least imagine that she was controlling him. But he had made it nonetheless clear that he expected her and Amalie to stay at Raven's

Law until he returned. It did not matter to him that Daft Nebby's raiders no longer threatened the Forest.

Meg had no wish to go anywhere, but his command still rankled.

For several days, she and Amalie supervised another cleaning of the tower from top to bottom. But although Meg insisted on thoroughness, even that job did not take as long as she had hoped. The tower's servants had been most diligent.

Sym reported that Lady Scott had departed for Ferniehurst the day after Walter had gone, and that her ladyship had taken a tail of nearly thirty men.

"But our Dod says there still be enough men at the Hall to look after it and see that no English get it. D'ye think they'll come here, mistress?"

"No," Meg said. "The Douglas is the greatest warrior Scotland has known. He'll not let them so much as cross the line."

"Aye, that be what I were thinking m'self," he said with a nod.

For the first six, long days, she and Amalie entertained themselves with their needlework and sundry other projects that Meg had been meaning to attend to. On the sixth day, Saturday afternoon, the guard at the gate shouted that a large party of riders was making its way through the cleuch toward Raven's Law.

"They say them riders be a-flying the Douglas banner," Sym told her. "But it canna be the Douglas. Besides, them fools be flying the Stewart banner as well."

"Bless me," Meg exclaimed, shouting for a chambermaid and hurrying upstairs to find Amalie. "Quickly, love, help me into my green silk and then shout for one of the maidservants to help you change that gown!"

"Mercy, why?"

"'Tis the Countess of Douglas who's coming. It must be. No one else who might come here would dare fly the Douglas and Stewart banners together."

"But why would the countess come to see us?"

"Mercy, I don't know. But I do *not* want to greet her in my shift. Hurry!"

As it was, Meg nearly did not make it to the yard before the party of riders clattered through the gateway. She had never met the Countess of Douglas but had no trouble believing that the elegantly attired woman riding a sleek black gelding at the head of the party was she. Two other ladies on horseback escorted her.

Meg made her curtsy, wishing Amalie would hurry.

A man-at-arms quickly dismounted and went to assist the countess from her horse. She was young and fair. Her blue eyes twinkled as Meg went to greet her.

"Welcome to Raven's Law, my lady," Meg said, returning her smile as she curtsied again. "Should we have been expecting you?"

"Nay, for I did not know I was coming here myself until I reached Scott's Hall to learn that Janet had fled to Ferniehurst," the countess said with a merry laugh. "I asked if any Scotts of Buccleuch were at hand, and Janet's very able steward informed me that you were here—with your sister, I believe."

"That is correct, madam," Meg said. "My husband is Buccleuch's son Sir Walter Scott. He left a sennight ago to meet your lord husband at Southdean."

"They are in England now, I expect, and I hope they will remain there yet another sennight, for I have much to do before they return," she said with another laugh. "But do call me Isabel, for I am sure we will become fast friends. Indeed, I hope we will, because I had counted on Janet. What do I call you?"

"My friends call me Meg," Meg said with a smile.

"Then so shall I, Meg. See you, I am going to Hermitage, and I had hoped Janet would go with me. But I came here from my lord husband's castle of Dalkeith, and Ferniehurst is too far out of the way to fetch her now."

"Is Dalkeith far from here?"

"Near Edinburgh. So you see, if I were to tell anyone I visited here first, then went to Ferniehurst, and then to Hermitage on my way home . . . If we had a map, I could show you how absurd a tale that would be. As it is, I am risking my hide by going to Hermitage at all in my lord's absence. But once I learned that my brother John—Carrick, that is—is to visit there, I could not stay away. He is the only one of my brothers I can stand to be with for longer than a few minutes, and I know from what my lord husband tells me that Hermitage is *not* what Carrick is accustomed to."

"So you mean to make it more comfortable for him," Meg said, recalling as the countess nodded that Walter had mentioned that the heir to the Scottish crown meant to visit Hermitage, and also that Sir Iagan was to return Walter's livestock and see to her dowry before then. Remembering her manners, she said, "But won't you come inside, madam, where we may be comfortable?"

"It is Isabel, please," the countess insisted again. "And I will go in, because I'd like to see this tower. But I shan't stay to sup with you, because they are expecting me back at the Hall."

"Are they?"

"Oh, yes, for I knew that Janet would insist, and Buccleuch as well, if they knew I had come. Janet and I are kinswomen by marriage, you see, for she was born a Douglas. And she is quite the kindest, most generous woman I know."

She continued to chatter as they went up the stairs with her ladies padding behind them. Amalie was in the hall by then and came forward to make her curtsy.

Meg introduced her. Then, calling for bread and wine, she invited Isabel and her two silent ladies to sit at the dais table.

"It was kind of you to pay us this visit, madam," Amalie said after they had discussed the cleuch and family connections for some time.

"It was nowt of the sort," the countess said with a smile. "I came with a purpose, although one is always curious about other people's homes, is one not?"

"Aye, sure," Amalie said with a doubtful look at Meg.

Intercepting it, Isabel said, "I came because, Janet having failed me, I had hoped you two would go with me to Hermitage. As I told Meg, I mean to set everyone there to making the place comfortable for my brother Carrick when he comes. I cannot let him suffer such a Spartan place without someone he knows other than his horrid courtiers to talk with him. They are all in my brother Fife's pay, of course, just as our father's people are."

Meg opened her mouth to comment but could think of nothing to say that would not be rude or overly inquisitive. She need not have worried, however.

Isabel laughed and said, "I'll wager you've heard of my brother Fife. They say he and my husband mean to join Carrick at Hermitage after defeating the English."

"Then surely, the Douglas will have put things in order there," Meg said.

"Jamie did assure me that he would see everything done as it should be," the countess said, clearly comfortable enough now to speak less formally with them. "But, sithee, he does not care about such things for himself. Only if he thinks someone has slighted him by *not* recognizing his worth does he bristle. One would expect him to understand about others' reacting the same way, but he has no respect for the men in my family. Therefore, I must see to this matter myself."

"How angry will he be?" Meg asked, thinking of her own husband.

"Livid," Isabel said. "Jamie has a famous temper, but I adore him. So I don't mind when he rages. Sithee, so firm is he about keeping me safe whilst he protects Scotland's freedom that if I did not confront him now and again, years could pass without my seeing him. When he is busy with forays and such, I think he forgets he *has* a wife. However, expecting Carrick's visit as he is, I warrant this venture will be no more than a swift, punishing run into England and a merry dash out again."

"Then, might they not return sooner than you expect?"

"They might, aye, but then I shall see him the sooner. You will come, won't you?" she said, leaning forward to lay a slender hand atop Meg's. Earnestly, she said, "You must, for although I brought any number of things with me to make the place more what Carrick expects, I'll need help to persuade any men my lord left behind to scrub or sweep, let alone to collect and scatter fresh rushes for the hall floors."

Hoping she did not expect her or Amalie to scrub,

Meg said, "We should not, because my husband will be as angry with me as yours will be with you if we do."

"He won't, I swear, because Wat will know that I persuaded you. You need only recall that I am a royal princess, although everyone says I rarely act the part. Still, Wat will understand that you could not oppose me."

The message was clear, so Meg smiled, and said, "Then of course we will go, madam. In troth, we should like to very much."

"Bless you," Isabel said. "I shall rest tonight and tomorrow at the Hall, and we can depart Monday morning as early as you can join me. Do not worry about bringing fine clothing. We are dressing to work, not to impress anyone."

"We'll be ready," Meg assured her.

Adding that they need bring as few or as many of their own men with them as they liked, and assuring them that she could easily provide others to see them safely home if necessary, the countess returned to Scott's Hall.

Meg stood silently in the yard beside Amalie and watched until the last of the party had passed through the gate.

"Mercy," Amalie said then. "Are we really going to Hermitage Castle?"

"We are," Meg said.

Her pulse pounded as she wondered if Walter might return early. She would have to tell Dod Elliot where they were going, and why, because it would not do for Walter—or Wat, as even the countess called him—to come home and find her gone.

It would be bad enough if he found her still at Hermitage, but she did not think he would beat her in front of Douglas or his countess.

In truth, she agreed with Isabel. She would endure
Wat's anger just to see him and know he was safe. She
wondered where he was and what he was doing.

⌒

Newcastle, England

After a week of stirring trouble throughout Redesdale in
Northumberland, the Earl of Douglas's mounted army
of nearly eight hundred had found Sir Harry "Hotspur"
Percy at Newcastle, dangerously deep in England.

They had left two thousand foot soldiers under Buccleuch and Gordon of Huntly in the vale of the Wansbeck
to guard their line of retreat. But the entire three thousand
had harried much of the English countryside, lifting cattle
and otherwise annoying folks in their path, so their position at Newcastle was most precarious.

Their encampment lay outside the town. Inside it,
Hotspur, having declined a meeting with Douglas on the
excuse that he needed rest after enduring his own long
journey to get there, ordered the city entrances blocked
with items ranging from carts and casks to herds of cattle.
For nearly two days, amid flurries of arrows and skir-
mishing, Douglas had sent frequent messages, each more
taunting than the last.

Gibbie was one of the messengers and gleefully described the reaction of Hotspur's men to a message just
taken. "The Douglas challenged Sir Harry to meet in
single combat to decide the whole! Their fight could be
on horseback or afoot, the Douglas said, and I was to say
he'd sworn to take every care not to tire Sir Harry, so he'd
no overtax his strength again, being as how Sir Harry be

getting along in his years and all. He even gave Sir Harry
the choice o' weapons."

Wat laughed. "As hot tempered as Harry is, I wager it
won't be long now."

Nor was it. Hotspur sent his acceptance Sunday morning and chose the lance and sword as weapons. At the
news, a shiver of unease slid up Wat's spine. The two men
would fight until one of them yielded or was carried off
the field.

Douglas was a valiant warrior, the best that Scotland
had seen, but Hotspur's reputation was as great. And for
all that Douglas had taunted Harry about his age, Harry
was the younger. Wat knew even a year could make the
difference. Still, both were chivalrous men, respected for
their sense of honor. The match would be fair.

The day shifted abruptly from one of war to a near hol-
iday atmosphere as men from both camps hurried to clear
a large space outside the west gate of the city.

Earlier taunts and grimness gave way to laughter and
shouted wagers. But while many moods shifted, Wat grew
tenser.

Douglas was unworried, as usual, even eager for the
fight. But Wat knew the fast-growing crowd's boisterous
mood could instantly alter to violence.

Chapter 16

But I canna tell
Whether 'tis truth or a lie . . .

Moving among his men, Wat ordered them to stay near him, lest things turn violent again. Neb Duffin passed the word to his erstwhile raiders, and Wat watched, impressed to see that they responded as quickly as his own men did.

The horses the two opponents would ride were not heavy destriers of the tiltyard, nor was the men's armor of that ilk.

Douglas rode his favorite mount, the lithe bay with the lightning-shaped blaze on its face. He wore chain mail with a cuirass of plate back and front, steel gauntlets and knee guards, and his customary Borderer's steel bonnet.

Hotspur, being over six feet tall, rode a larger horse by necessity, which Wat believed was why he had chosen to fight on horseback. He wore the black, light plate armor he usually wore in battle.

Both men carried war lances, shorter and sharper than

the long, blunt-ended ones used in jousting. Each man wore his sword.

Exchanging laughing taunts, they took their places, Douglas at the east end of the field and Hotspur at the west. Hotspur had a more powerful horse, a longer reach, and more armor. Douglas would have the sun in his eyes, but he had not objected to Hotspur's loudly voiced decision to ride from west to east.

When a long blast from a horn signaled the start, the two spurred their mounts. Watching, Wat hardly dared to breathe.

They were but a few yards apart when the earl jerked the bay's head hard to the right. At such speed, the animal nearly tripped over its own forefeet, and only Douglas's remarkable balance and agility kept him in his saddle.

For an instant the bay was right in front of Hotspur's gray, rendering the Douglas's lance, in his right hand, useless. Percy, clearly unprepared for such a rash maneuver, made a wild thrust, but it went askew.

Douglas plunged past him, then reined in and wrenched his mount around again. White-stockinged forelegs pawing air, the bay wheeled on its hind legs.

The earl spurred it to a gallop again, pounding after Hotspur, who clearly had expected, just as he would have in the tiltyard, that each man would ride to the end of the field, turn, and await the next blast of the horn before making a second pass.

The Scots howled with mirth at the sight of Hotspur fleeing from Douglas.

Belatedly realizing what had happened, Percy turned his big horse almost as deftly as Douglas had. But Percy had the sun in his eyes now and was nearly at a standstill, whereas Douglas was approaching him at top speed.

Barely a dozen yards apart, it was too late for the Englishman to do more than aim his lance at Douglas's chest and furiously spur the big gray.

It barely reached a trot before the two met with a resounding crash, as each lance-point struck the other's shield. Percy's set the Douglas back hard on his saddle, but with the added advantage of much greater speed, the Douglas's lance smashed Percy right off of his. Lance flying, Hotspur fell backward to the ground with a resounding crash of armor and lay still.

"Sakes," Tam exclaimed, "is he dead?"

"Nay, only stunned," Wat said as Hotspur's men ran to his side and Douglas paused nearby. "I wish my father were here to see this."

"Ye willna be wishin' it so hard if we have to run," Tam said with a chuckle. "All them men the laird has afoot would just slow us down."

Douglas had turned the bay toward his cousin, Sir Hugh Montgomery, whose men had gathered near Wat's, so Wat and Tam began walking toward them.

As they did, the men with Hotspur lifted him and hurried toward the town gate, as if they feared the Scots would attack.

So quickly did they go that Hotspur's helmet fell off and rolled aside, but a young man-at-arms snatched it up and dashed after the others.

The crowd soon divided into English and Scot again as the former hurried after Hotspur's bearers, back to the safety of the walled town.

Watching them, Wat said to Tam, "Something came off Hotspur's helmet when it fell, and that lad left it lying there. Let's see what it is."

The two threaded their way through the now mostly

Scottish crowd to have a look. To Wat's surprise, a pair of gauntlets lay on the ground, one atop the other.

Of dainty size, fringed with filigree work of silver, and clearly feminine, they bore the Percy lion embroidered in seed pearls.

"Undoubtedly *un gage d'amour*," he said, picking them up to examine them.

"Aye, for he must have tucked them behind his crest," Tam agreed.

Wat took the gloves to Douglas and explained where they had found them.

Douglas grinned. "They'll prove useful, I think. I've heard that the Bishop of Durham is bringing a thousand men to join Hotspur's army, so we must go. But we've time to do so with dignity. Look yonder," he added, nodding toward the town.

Hotspur stood atop the wall with several others. When the encampment fell silent at the sight of him, he shouted, "We'll fight again, Douglas!"

"We will, aye," Douglas shouted back. "I am glad to see you so quickly recovered, but next time I hope you'll give better sport!"

"Just wait, damn you! I'll show you!"

"Not today," the earl yelled. "I want you at your best." He held up the gauntlets. "Mayhap you'll want to claim these that you left on the field. I must go now, but I'll go slowly and not cross the line till Thursday morning. If you don't claim these dainties by then, I'll hang them at Dalkeith as my victory banner."

"Nay, then, you won't take them out of England!" Hotspur cried.

"I will! Until then, I'll hang them from my tent," Doug-

las yelled. "Claim them if you dare, or tell your lady you
have lost her favor!"

Chuckling, Wat exchanged a look with Tam and said,
"I fear our two great warriors sound more like a pair of
bairns fratching over a ball."

Nevertheless, he had no doubt that Hotspur would soon
follow them.

⁓

Monday afternoon, as Meg viewed Hermitage from the
ridge above it, she realized that although they had passed
near the formidable castle on their way to Rankilburn, she
had not enjoyed such a fine view of it then.

The castle sat starkly in open ground. A webbing of
water-filled ditches surrounded it, and the tree-lined ribbon of Hermitage Water flowed past it just a short distance away. Hermitage looked smaller from the ridge but
even more imposing than it had looked as they'd passed
below it on the main track through Liddesdale.

Astride his pony beside her, Sym said, "Yon's a big
place."

"That's Hermitage Castle," she said. "It is where we
are going."

"Then I'll keep a close eye on Pawky," he said, patting
the pouch at his belt.

On the earlier journey, because of Walter's hurry to
reach Scott's Hall and avoid the obstacle course of ditches
at Hermitage, they had skirted the castle to the north as
they negotiated the steep hills out of Liddesdale into
Ewesdale. Today, from the ridge between the two, they
had followed the course of Hermitage Water.

Now the captain of the countess's men and the two

bearing her banners led the way to the castle's main entrance.

The sun was hot and beat down on them. Breezes they had enjoyed on the ridge tops and the coolness of the forests in Rankilburn and Ewesdale had given way to scattered woods and much more open country in Liddesdale.

As they approached the drawbridge, Meg exchanged a look with Amalie.

Countess Isabel said with strong feeling, "Sakes, but this place is even bleaker and less welcoming than I'd expected. I can already smell the cesspits."

"Have you not been here before, madam?" Amalie asked.

Isabel shook her head. "Nay, for Jamie thinks it a poor place for a lady. I have told him I can make it more comfortable for everyone, but he insists it ought not to be so. He says such a fortress should be a rugged place for rugged men."

"But you disagree, and thus you dare to defy him," Meg said, remembering a similar discussion with her own husband.

Isabel's smile turned wistful. "It is not really defiance, although I know he will be angry, and I do not like him to be. But Jamie must not offend Carrick, because that could lead to consequences dire to us both. There will come a time, sithee, after my father dies and Carrick succeeds him as King of Scots, when Carrick will be all that stands between Jamie and my brother Fife. My father loves me and looks forward to being grandsire to the next Earl of Douglas, if I ever do bear a son for Jamie, so he will protect me and mine. But to Fife I am naught."

"I hope you will forgive my saying this," Meg said.

"But men say Carrick cannot stand against Fife, that he lacks the spirit to do so—and the King likewise."

As soon as the words left her mouth, she recalled Sym's presence. He had let his pony fall back a little, but she was sure he could hear their conversation. Like many other nobles, the countess spoke in front of servants as if they were furniture, so Meg decided she would have to have a talk with him, to make sure he understood that he must not repeat anything he overheard to anyone else.

Isabel seemed unaware of him and likewise unaware of the two ladies riding at her other side, and the captain and banner carriers riding just ahead of them.

"You may say what you like to me, Meg," she said. "But in this instance, what others say is sadly true. My father still issues royal commands when he wants to and occasionally still listens to men besides Fife. And sometimes one can also persuade Carrick to stand against Fife to defend a special cause, but only for a short time."

"But does Fife heed them when they stand against him?" Amalie asked.

"Aye, he must if my father issues a royal command or Carrick stands on principle, because Parliament will support them, and Fife holds his power only with parliamentary permission. This expedition into England has Fife's consent but no royal consent. Either his grace or Carrick could have stopped it had they known of it, but neither does. Carrick thinks he is coming to Hermitage merely to see the famous fortress and meet with certain nobles here. But he is really coming because Fife told him to, which means that Fife is using him for some purpose of his own, doubtless to make it look to others as if Carrick supports this foray into England."

"I still don't understand," Meg said. "Everyone knows

that Fife holds the reins now, as Guardian of the Realm, and that few can stand against him."

"He won't defy a royal command, though, lest he set a precedent. Sithee, above all, Fife wants to be King of Scots. He won't want others defying him then, so even he submits to royal commands now. He also knows that Carrick could persuade Parliament to eliminate his position as Guardian of the Realm. It is rare for Carrick to oppose him, though, and will be rarer still after my father dies. That is why I mean to see that Carrick feels welcome here—for whatever good it may do us in the future."

Meg half-expected Douglas's guards to forbid their entrance, but when one of them dared to suggest that the countess would be more comfortable elsewhere, the friendly Isabel turned instantly into an imperious Stewart princess. After that, Meg was not surprised to see the men nod and bow as their party dismounted.

Inside, however, even Isabel looked daunted. "Bless us," she said, surveying the wreckage of the upper hall, where departing men had left unneeded gear amid a tumble of other detritus. "What a mess!"

"It is that," Sym muttered. "Our tower were in better shape than this."

Meg agreed. The difference between the disorder of a few men at the tower and that of many more at Hermitage was astonishing. Dogs wandered about, and the place reeked of fouled rushes. Even the high table stood buried in clutter.

A man hurried toward them, straightening his jerkin as he came.

"My lady countess," he said, sweeping a bow. "I am Ralph Lindsay, captain of the guard, in command during his lordship's absence. He said nowt of your coming, madam, so you find us ill-prepared. Surely, you'd be more comfortable elsewhere."

Isabel raised her chin and said coolly, "Sir Ralph, if you wish to retain your position, I would caution you against showing aught but welcome to my ladies and me. If you think my lord husband would thank you for behaving ill toward us, you should reconsider that notion. Recall that my father is the King's grace."

"I do, aye, my lady, and offered the suggestion only because this chamber before you is the most welcoming at Hermitage. We have no housekeeper here or maidservants but only rough men-at-arms and a few squires. Indeed, at present everyone is with his lordship except some few left to guard the castle."

"But you are expecting the Earl of Carrick any day, are you not?"

"On Thursday, aye," the captain agreed. "He sent to warn us of the day, saying he will spend Wednesday night at Dryburgh Abbey. My lord Douglas gave orders before he left to prepare his own bedchamber to receive the Earl of Carrick."

"'Tis good we are here then, for Carrick will not come alone," she said. "I suggest you make arrangements to provide for his considerable entourage as well."

"Surely they will provide for themselves whilst they are here, madam, as do others who bring their retinues."

She raised her eyebrows. "My brother is heir to the throne of Scotland. He will have certain expectations. For example, he will seek quiet for contemplation, and he will expect—" She broke off, looking as if one of her own thoughts had startled her. Then, she said, "My husband surely did not take his chaplain, Richard Lundie, to war with him, or his minstrel, Giles Gilpin. Or did he?"

"Lundie is indeed with his lordship," Captain Lindsay told her. "The minstrel were here this morning, but as I take small note of his activities, I've nae notion if he be inside or out now. Doubtless, guards at the entrance will know."

"Prithee, seek him, for I sent Giles here as a favor to my lord. I want to see him and hear how he fares. As to Lundie, we can do without him, I expect, especially as Carrick will bring his own chaplain with him. Until then, we will say our prayers privately in the chapel. That stone building near the bridge *is* the chapel, is it not?"

"It is, aye, and his lordship does not allow anyone to sleep there, so it is gey tidier than the castle is," the captain said.

"This castle will be a good deal tidier before Carrick arrives," the countess informed him. "Your men will have to see to it if no one else is here to do so."

His jaw set, and Meg was sure he was about to tell Isabel that housekeeping was no concern of his. But when the countess fixed him with her haughtiest gaze, daring him to flout her wishes, he nodded and said, "I beg you will excuse me at once then, my lady. Clearly, there is much to do."

"He is right in saying we have much to do," the countess said when he had gone. "And I tell you, Meg, I hope his men can tidy things without a great deal of direction, because in troth, I haven't the barest notion what to tell them."

"Do you not, madam?"

"I know when things are not to my liking. But at home my steward sees to all. Indeed, someone else always does, so I had no notion that my lord had neither steward nor housekeeper here to command. Do you know about such things?"

"Me mistress kens all about such, aye," Sym said proudly.

Looking at Amalie, who grimaced and shook her head, Meg chuckled. "We met with just such a challenge less than a month ago at Raven's Law," she said. "But my sister and I grew up in different circumstances from yours, Isabel. Our mother thought her daughters should know nearly as much about any task as their stewards or housekeepers might."

Isabel sighed. "My mother knew no more than I do."

"We will help you, and gladly. Doubtless your ladies will, too," Meg added, casting a doubtful glance at the two women, standing silently some distance away. "It will seem odd, though, to be ordering men-at-arms to clean out cesspits."

"First they must muck out this stable we stand in," Isabel said, glowering at the mess in the upper hall and, in particular, at four dogs gnawing bones underneath and near the high table. "I want all the dogs put outside, and before we start, I want to know that my lord's cook can provide us with a decent supper."

"I'll see to getting them dogs out, me lady," Sym said, heading for the dais.

"Mayhap we should first find someone willing to show us where everything is," Meg suggested. "Talking to the cook will be easier if we can find the kitchen."

Douglas and his mounted army of knights and retainers, having departed from Newcastle on Sunday afternoon, spent that night in the hills to the north.

On Monday, they continued slowly northward, because

the earl hoped Hotspur would follow. With no sign of him by late afternoon, they pitched camp Monday night on high ground near Ponteland, where no enemy could catch them unaware.

Douglas sent men to see how far the Bishop of Durham's forces had to go to join Hotspur. He wanted to keep a close eye on them, because armies provided by such wealthy religious houses, even in Scotland, tended to be very well equipped.

Wat had only his own men-at-arms and Neb's lot to look after, so they soon had tents up and fires begun for their supper. As the sun began to drop in the west, his thoughts turned first to Buccleuch, who would rejoin them the next day in the Wansbeck valley with the foot forces.

Thoughts of his father soon turned to thoughts of the Hall and Raven's Law. He was surprised to feel himself stir as he pictured Meg in their bedchamber.

He had completely stopped thinking of her as Margaret.

Not only did Amalie never call her so, but although he had thought the name suited her because of her calm demeanor and her dignity, that woman had not been the one who had cast ale in his face. The lass who had done that showed the same passion in her anger that she had shown in his bed.

Meg suited that lass better, although he was rapidly coming to like and appreciate both personalities more than he had thought he ever could.

It occurred to him as he watched the sun edge nearer the hilltops that he had never before sat silently amid his men, enjoying such warming thoughts.

Jenny had often stirred his emotions. She could make

him laugh, and she could ignite his fury. But Jenny at her best or worst had never stirred him as Meg could with a single word or a look.

At first, he had thought that his still-smoldering fury at what her father had done was fueling the anger he felt toward her. But Meg was as much a victim in the forced marriage as he was, and he frequently reminded himself that he was more at fault for it than she was. So, the logical conclusion was that the emotions he felt when he was with her stemmed directly and solely from their private relationship.

The business with Neb's lads had shown him the truth of that. He had thought his reaction to learning that she had taken them home had been pure fury. He knew now that it had been fear—nay, deep terror that she might suffer harm.

Even so, it had not taken her long to stir his temper again and by nothing more than pressing him to heed her thoughts and opinions.

He liked to think he was a fair man, but his behavior—seen in retrospect—had been anything but fair. Instead, he had ripped up at her, exposing yet another fear—and aye, that, too, might have been terror—that she expected to rule their household and everyone in it as her mother did at Elishaw.

He shuddered, recalling the result. The lass had been right to throw ale in his face for flinging that accusation at her. His discovery then that Lady Murray had saved him and his lads from Murray's damned hanging tree made him wince even now. What sort of gratitude had he shown for that?

He saw Tam and Gibbie walking up the hill toward him. Fires dotted the landscape, and someone hummed a tune in the dusky light as the sun dipped behind the western hilltops. With Buccleuch's force guarding the way ahead, their own well-disciplined guards posted, and men watching from more distant points for movement from the south and west, it looked as if they'd enjoy a peaceful night.

Meg spent the first two hours after arriving at Hermitage in a flurry of activity, because the captain of the guard sent them a veritable army of men to help.

She and Sym located not only the kitchen but also a narrow service stairway in its thick wall that led to a small, iron-fortified postern door on the back side of the gate tower. Like the main entrance, the postern door opened onto a steep timber stairway that defenders could burn quickly if the castle came under attack.

The service stairs in the wall continued from the halls to the upper floors.

The kitchen seemed clean enough and the cook unfazed by the notion of serving them a proper supper, so she left Sym to help him and returned to the others.

Assigning Amalie and one of the countess's women to oversee work in the lower hall, Meg encouraged Isabel's offer to supervise the tidying of her lord husband's chamber on the third level and to sleep there herself.

"I'll take Averil with me," Isabel said in a low tone, indicating the elder of her two women. "Faith, but I dared bring no one else, for Averil and Nancy were the only ones I knew would not weep and wail about coming here. And that was before I saw how truly barbaric this castle is. Averil has been with me since long before I married

Jamie, so she will keep a still tongue in her head. But she will insist on helping me whilst I attend to Jamie's room."

"Of course she will, and should," Meg said. "As for what my husband or yours will have to say to us for allowing you to condescend to such chores—"

"You don't know Jamie," Isabel said with another of her merry laughs. "He doesn't mind doing anything he believes needs doing and cannot imagine why anyone else should. Of course, if someone were to tell him a cesspit needed mucking out, he would never think the person meant him to do it."

Meg laughed then, too. "Husbands have a knack for thinking other people should cheerfully do the things they refuse to do themselves."

The hours flew by in clouds of dust and rotten straw. Meg had no idea what the men had done about the cesspits, but when she used the garderobe off the north end of the upper hall, it did not smell as bad as when they had arrived.

By suppertime, she yearned for a hot bath, but men were still strewing fresh rushes in the upper hall and two lads were setting the high table. Although they did so under Sym's stern dictatorship, she was reluctant to leave until she could be sure no one needed further supervision. Moreover, she had no proper bedchamber, only a small, narrow cell with two cots above the earl's bedchamber to share with Amalie.

Telling herself that it would be good to sleep so far from the pits, and to be glad it was summer so she and Amalie would not freeze there, she made do at last with a pitcher of water that Sym fetched her, a basin, and a ragged cloth.

Then, in a fresh gown, her guardian shadow in attendance, she went back downstairs. At the upper-hall landing, she met the countess and Amalie coming up.

"Oh, my dear, such a nice surprise!" Isabel exclaimed. "They found Giles practicing with his lute in the chapel, and he is awaiting us now. I remembered that Amalie was still in the kitchen, and we were just going up to fetch you."

They entered the hall together, and Meg inhaled the scent of fresh rushes, noting that they adequately covered fouler odors. A small fire burning on the great hearth helped, too. The high table was set properly for their supper, and other than serving lads, the men who had been there earlier had vanished to the lower regions.

Only one man remained, staring down into the fire with a lute in his right hand and his face turned away from them.

Hearing them, he turned just as the countess said, "Giles, I've brought two dear friends to meet you."

Meg stared in shock, not at an unknown minstrel but at her beloved brother Tom. Hearing Amalie's gasp, she quickly touched her sister's arm in warning.

What Tom could be doing here, using the name Giles Gilpin, Meg could not imagine. But if he was staying in the Douglas's household under a name not his own, this was no time to mention the fact.

He approached them with his usual charming smile. But Meg noted tension as well, which told her he feared that one of his sisters might unmask him.

She was tempted, because she liked and respected Isabel and because her own husband and thus Meg herself owed duty to both the earl and the countess. But she could not betray her brother—not before learning why he was at Hermitage.

Isabel was still talking, but while Meg had been staring in shock at Tom, she had missed whatever the countess had said. She fought now to catch up.

". . . and Averil and Nancy are with me, of course," Isabel said. "They will be down shortly, but you already know them, Giles. These two ladies will be new to you. So make your bow, and I will present you."

Pausing only to take a breath while he obeyed, she said, "Lady Margaret, Lady Amalie, this is Giles Gilpin, the wonderful minstrel I have mentioned to you. Only wait until you hear his music. Quite astonishing! Giles, you will want to have your supper before you entertain us, so go at once and tell the cook to feed you."

"Thank you, madam," he said, making her another bow. Turning to a point midway between Meg and Amalie, he made one more and said, "My ladies."

In passing them, as he reached a point where Meg could see him but Isabel could not, he winked. It irritated Meg so that she wanted to shake him, but she could not do so and had to act as if nothing unusual had occurred.

The countess's ladies soon joined them, and three gillies served them as they ate a supper that, at best, was mediocre. No one complained.

Sym waited on Meg, having cast a threatening glance at the first gillie to approach her, stopping him in his tracks and thus deterring the others, as well.

"Louts, the lot o' them," he muttered disapprovingly as the third one turned away. "I'll see to ye, m'self."

That was the best moment of the meal as far as Meg was concerned.

To be sure, the entertainment was better than the food.

If anything, Tom's skills had improved. He sang several ballads, two of which were comical enough to make all the ladies laugh. His voice was pure and as smooth as honey. Moreover, even to a sister's critical eye, he was a handsome young man.

But Meg hoped he did not expect her to let his charade pass without comment or stricture. Hoping to prevent such an error, she sent him a stern look each time she managed to catch his eye.

"You should not stare so at our minstrel, Meg," the countess said at last, teasing her. "I doubt Wat Scott is one to tolerate a flirtatious wife."

Startled, Meg exclaimed, "Oh, no, madam, I wasn't! I . . . I was just listening to his music. I can certainly agree with your opinion of his talent."

Looking contrite, Isabel said, "I should not have said that to you. Giles is admirably skilled, is he not?"

Meg agreed but took care after that not to appear overly interested in the minstrel. She knew that although Isabel might think no more about the matter, her ladies would be keeping an eye on the two of them now.

No opportunity afforded itself to speak privately with him before the ladies retired for the night.

Amalie had not spoken other than to murmur polite responses to the lads serving them or to someone who addressed a remark directly to her. However, the moment they were safely inside the tiny chamber they shared and had shut the door, she exclaimed, "What is Tom doing here?"

"Mercy, I don't know the reason any more than you do," Meg said, recalling that she had used all the water in the pitcher earlier and taking the empty vessel from the washstand. "I can contrive a meeting with him tomorrow to find out, but until then we shall just have to be patient. I'll ask Sym to fill this for us if he is nearby."

"Of course he is nearby," Amalie said. "He is your devoted slave, my dear."

Meg shook her head but opened the door to find Sym just outside. Handing him the pitcher, she asked him to refill it. As he began to turn away, she put a hand on his shoulder, stopping him and pulling the door to behind her.

He looked at her warily.

"Sym, you have overheard many things today that you must not repeat to anyone," she said quietly. "I know you are not a prattler, and I don't like to sound harsh. But much of what you heard today concerns the countess, so—"

"Ye needna tell me, m'lady, 'cause our Dod said if he ever hears me speaking o' things that be none o' me business, he'll skelp me till me wagging tongue falls out. He'd do it, too, Dod would," he added, nodding earnestly.

"I see," Meg said, struggling not to laugh. "Then I've naught to worry about and you can be off to fetch that water for us. Thank you, Sym."

He nodded, his dignity intact, and hurried away.

Ten minutes later, a sharp double-rap sounded on the door.

"Faith, that was quick," Amalie said. "Come in, Sym. We're still dressed."

"I'm glad to hear that," Tom said as he put his head in.

In a twinkling, he was inside and had shut the door behind him.

Chapter 17

~

Had some kindly spirit but whispered in your ear . . .
*   "Wha's fighting surrounded wi' mony a spear."*

Get out," Amalie said. "You should not be here, *Giles Gilpin.*"

"Hush, lass, I've no time to bandy words with you," he said. "Just listen, both of you. You must *not* give me away."

"But why are you here, and why pretend to be a minstrel?" Meg demanded.

"To protect our family, of course."

"By disavowing our name?"

"Don't be absurd," he said, his temper stirring more quickly than usual. "No sensible Englishman trusts the Douglas. Is it so astonishing that some may want to keep an eye on him?"

"But we are not English. We live on the Scottish side of the line."

"We're half English," he said with an uncharacteristic snap in his voice. "Moreover, that damnable line can shift on no more than a warrior's whim, as we know. Such shifts have put Elishaw under English rule more than once."

"Even so, and regardless of our mother's heritage, Elishaw is a Scottish holding, granted to the Murrays by the King of Scots. 'Tis to him we owe fealty."

"We've got to have peace in the Borders, Meg. Just think how much more comfortable that would be for everyone. Mayhap the two countries *should* be one."

"Just how would we be more comfortable under English rule?"

"One has only to look at the devastation wrought throughout the Borders to see that even an imposed peace would make everyone more prosperous and thus happier," he said. "The border has become no more than a point of disagreement among men who live near it. Most of us want the same things, do we not, to survive and to better our lives? Douglas just wants to acquire more power for Douglas."

Meg was shocked. "So you spy on him?"

"I am doing no more than my duty, as you must," Tom said firmly.

"But whom do you serve?" Meg asked. Recalling his suggestion that the two countries should become one, she recalled as well that he had fostered with kinsmen in England. Fostering was common among noble families, and at the time, had been one of various means her parents had employed to retain useful ties on both sides of the border. But now, the memory stirred an ominous warning. "Mercy on us, you serve the Percies!" she exclaimed. "You're spying for Hotspur!"

"Would it be so dreadful if I were? Are the Percies not kinsmen, too? And is Hotspur not the greatest warrior of them all, better even than the Douglas?"

"In troth, I do not know. Nor do you unless you have seen them matched."

She could not think properly, nor could she believe that Tom—merry, beguiling Tom—could harm anyone. But it was neither the time nor the place for debate. Whatever the truth, the minstrel Giles Gilpin must *not* be found in their bedchamber.

Accordingly, she caught him by the shoulders and said urgently, "You must go before someone catches you here. We'll keep your secret but only if you swear that no harm will come to the Douglas, his family, or to anyone in my new family through any action of yours."

"Aye, sure, I'll swear," he said. "But mind now, not a word."

As the door shut behind him, Amalie said curtly, "Isabel is our hostess, Meg. And Douglas is your husband's liege lord. Surely, we don't dare to aid Tom if he is spying on their household."

Realizing only then that her sister had taken no part in the discussion after demanding to know what Tom was doing at Hermitage, Meg said, "He is our brother, Amalie. Do you know what Douglas would do if he caught him?"

Amalie shrugged. "He'd be furious, and rightly so."

"He would hang Tom for a traitor."

Amalie's eyes widened. She might have said more had a rap on the door not heralded Sym's return with their water.

After Meg thanked the boy and dismissed him to his pallet, she and Amalie washed quickly and got ready for bed. Meg made no objection when Amalie said she was exhausted and meant to go right to sleep, although she suspected that her sister merely wanted to avoid further discussion.

She expected to fall asleep at once herself but lay thinking for a long time after Amalie's breathing steadied and slowed to deep slumber.

At first, her thoughts dwelt on Tom and the sense of shock she had felt when she recognized him and realized he was posing as a common minstrel.

She wondered what he had learned, whom he might have told, and how he had managed to tell them. Then, wondering what else he might have done, she recalled Douglas's strange illness. Shocked that she could connect her own favorite brother with such a thing, she told herself not to be a fool.

Her thoughts shifted next to Wat and what he was likely to say when he learned she had come to Hermitage with the countess.

To her surprise, her thoughts soon turned sensual. Even the knowledge that he might shake her, or worse, just made her yearn for his touch.

She had no fear of his anger, because she had learned that although he would speak his mind in a way that could make her squirm if she had displeased him, he was unlikely to do more than hurl words at her.

In truth, she envied his ability to articulate his anger freely without feeling a need to seek more tactful words.

As her thoughts turned warmer, she slept at last and awoke to a new day when Amalie, tiptoeing across their room, bumped into the washstand.

Meg turned over and smiled in the dim light provided by the tall, narrow opening that was their only source of natural light. "How did you sleep?" she asked.

"Like the dead," Amalie said. "I was going to go down and see if they've put out food in the hall. But since you're awake, I'll wait for you."

Taking the strong hint, Meg got up and dressed. When she was ready, they went downstairs to find the countess's ladies at the high table, breaking their fast.

Bidding them good morning, Meg said, "I thought we would be the last to come down. Has Countess Isabel not awakened yet?"

"She still sleeps," Lady Averil said. "Although she is in his lordship's room, it is always difficult, is it not, to sleep in a bed to which one is not accustomed?"

Meg agreed. Aware that Lady Averil and Lady Nancy had arranged cots in an alcove off Isabel's chamber, she assumed that the comment covered all three.

Sym appeared with two manchet loaves in a basket. "Will ye ha' beef or mutton this morning, me lady?" he asked Meg.

"Beef," she said, glancing at Amalie, who nodded.

As he hurried away and Meg reached for a bowl of bramble jam, she saw her sister's expression change abruptly to a grimace. Following the direction of her narrowed gaze, Meg saw Tom stroll in from the stairway, lute in hand.

He nodded at Sym in passing and continued to the dais as if he had no cares or concerns. Receiving smiles from the countess's ladies, he greeted them cheerfully.

Realizing that to keep his secret without seeming at outs with him, she would have to speak as she usually did, Meg ignored a stab of guilt at the deception and returned his greeting in a pleasant tone.

Amalie said nothing. But her face no longer expressed disapproval, giving Meg hope that the other two women would notice nothing unusual.

Tom sat on a stool by the hearth and played a soft, soothing tune.

Meg began to relax, but she could detect no change in her sister. And despite Amalie's professed hunger, she toyed with her bread and took only one small bite of her beef, sliced cold from a haunch roasted the previous day.

She barely waited for Meg to finish eating before she said, "We've had no time to arrange our room more tidily, Meg. We should do it now, before Countess Isabel presents us with a new list of chores."

Without argument, Meg followed her upstairs. But inside their room with the door shut, she said, "Is it so difficult for you to see Tom's dilemma, Amalie? Would you truly betray him to the Douglas? He cannot spy on him now that we know, and surely he cannot have done much spying before—not in a castle full of Douglases."

"I knew you would take his side," Amalie said. "He is ever your wonderful Tom who can do no wrong."

Meg smiled. "No wrong? He was the horridest boy, always getting into my things. If anyone scolded him, he'd just smile and say, "But it's only Meggie's.""

"I cannot think why that should amuse you now," Amalie said. "He and Simon both teased us unmercifully. And Tom is no longer a bairn, Meg."

"Even so, and whatever he may have done to earn your displeasure, it cannot be so bad that you want him hanged. Not when he just wants to protect our family."

"What if he has done something much worse?" Amalie asked. "Has it not occurred to you that he may be the one who tried to poison Douglas?"

"We don't even know that it was poison," Meg protested. "Douglas himself said he ate something bad. And Tom wouldn't! He may be a tease. He is *not* evil."

"No, of course he is not. He is marvelous, ever-trustworthy Tom Murray."

"What is wrong with you? He is our brother!"

Amalie looked at her, resentment plain on her face.

Meg stared back, and as she did, a dreadful thought came to her. "Faith, you cannot mean . . . Oh, my dear one, I beg you, tell me you are not accusing him . . ."

"Accusing him of what?" Amalie demanded when Meg could not say the words. "Of being the villain who robbed me of my maidenhood? Even if you *don't* want to hear it, Meg, I shall still know it for the truth. Moreover, he knows it, too, and nothing that he or anyone else says or does can turn fact into falsehood."

Meg could think of nothing to say to that.

~

The blazing sun was near its zenith when the vale of the Wansbeck opened before Douglas's men. From the ridge, on that muggy hot day, the vale provided a soothing vista of pale green grass, shady thickets of birch or aspen, and flowering hazel. Rolling, still-green hills framed the valley on all sides. The shallow stream that gave it its name meandered northward through its center in wide, gentle curves.

Leading his men and Neb's, with Neb riding beside Tam and Gibbie, Wat heard the larger force long before he saw them. The hundreds of cattle they had lifted along the way set up a constant din, lowing and squalling.

He spotted Buccleuch's banner and spurred toward it. The two thousand that his father and Huntly led were all afoot except for their noble leaders with their squires and fighting tails. The teeming mass spread across the wide valley.

As Wat neared Buccleuch, he saw Huntly approaching

from the east with his pennon bearer beside him and his fighting tail behind.

Douglas, too, spurred to meet them, as did a number of the other lords traveling with the earl. When they converged around Buccleuch, Wat heard his father say, "Where's Hotspur?"

"Safely recovering his broken spirits behind Newcastle's stout walls," Douglas said with a grin. "I've challenged him to fetch these pretty things he lost," he added, holding up the embroidered gloves. "They fell from his helmet when his lads bore him off the field. But he wants them, He'll soon be on our heels."

Buccleuch grinned back at him. "I can see that I'll want to hear this tale."

"Aye, but not now. He could already be on his way."

"Do we wait for him here, then?" Huntly asked.

Frowning, Buccleuch gazed over the vale. "'Tis a good site . . . for cattle."

"Aye, but not to defend," Douglas said. "That stream is easily forded, the vale too open. We'll move on to Otterburn. I took a good look on the way, and it is a much better site. The water meadows along the Rede will spoil any cavalry attack, and the river is nearly unfordable there. We'll also have scrub woodland for cover and steeper slopes to give us a superior position if we retreat into the hills."

Buccleuch nodded, surveying the sea of men and lowing cattle that filled the vale. "Otterburn lies yet fourteen or fifteen miles from here."

"My last messenger said Hotspur had not yet begun to move," Douglas said. "But when he does, he'll move fast. So get this lot moving, but keep eyes out behind and be ready to take cover swiftly if the Percies overtake you.

Hotspur's brother Ralph has joined him, and between them they can muster eight thousand men. The Bishop of Durham is likewise moving north and should join them soon."

Wat felt the familiar surge of exhilaration that warned him battle was near, along with a sense of unease at the great odds against them. As he turned his horse, meaning to help spread the word, Douglas shouted, "The rest of you lads, with me!"

With a wave to his father, Wat obeyed.

⁓

Meg found no chance to corner Tom until that afternoon when the countess's ladies decided to nap, and Amalie required little persuasion to do likewise. Despite the ease with which she had fallen asleep the night before, Meg suspected that her sister had not slept well for a number of nights.

Amalie was not one to keep secrets by nature. More often than not, whatever she was thinking came straight out of her mouth. Until lately.

Meg tried to imagine what it must have been like for her to keep such a dreadful secret and its accompanying fears to herself, terrified to tell anyone what had happened. Meg had no doubt that she would have felt so herself, because if Tom had done what Amalie said he had, he had done something unspeakable.

Praying that her sister's innocence had led her to believe herself violated after no more than an improper touch or two, Meg had steeled herself earlier to get to the truth as they tidied their room.

"Tell me just what he did," she said bluntly after more

diplomatic efforts failed to elicit the information. "I promise, love, I'll not think less of you, no matter what occurred," she added when Amalie continued to ignore her. "Tom is your elder by four years, and he is much stronger than you are, so you could not have stopped him. You ought to have told our parents about it, though."

"Aye, afterward, and if you think I could have done that, you are not thinking at all," Amalie said scornfully. "He did what he did before I knew what he intended. Afterward he dared me to tell anyone. He said if I did, he'd tell them I'd made it up, that he'd scolded me for something and I was trying to get even. They'd have believed him, too, our parents or anyone else."

Meg nodded, fearing that was true. Her parents were both more likely to believe Simon or Tom before they'd believe Amalie—or Meg herself, come to that.

"Tell me what he did," she repeated, her voice as gentle as she could make it.

"He took me riding," Amalie said. "We went to the old mill upstream from Elishaw. He said he wanted to show me the mill wheel, so we went inside. I had no reason not to trust him then. He'd always been nicer to me than Simon was."

"You should have been able to trust him," Meg said grimly. "What then?"

"He'd been there before, because there were blankets and a pile of straw. It was horrid, Meg. He threw up my skirt, shoved down his breeks, and . . . There was so much blood!" Taking a breath, she said, "He left, and I thought I'd die there."

Meg felt dizzy. Still seeking an acceptable explanation, she had an impulse to ask what Amalie had done to make Tom think she would welcome such treatment.

But her sister's pale face, tear-filled eyes, and shaking hands stopped the words on Meg's tongue. Amalie could be flirtatious, and she had practiced her flirting on her brothers when she'd wanted something from them. But, even so . . .

Meg winced at the course her thoughts had taken. Whatever Amalie might have done in innocence, she was still Tom's little sister. He was duty-bound to protect her from harm. It was no part of that duty to accept innocent flirtation as an invitation—if, indeed, that was even what Tom thought he had done.

Having seen him slip out after the countess signed to her ladies that she was ready to leave the table, Meg wanted to run after him. Propriety forbade running after the minstrel, however, so she waited long enough to persuade Amalie to rest and to beg leave of the countess to abandon her for a while.

Isabel laughed and said, "See to your own needs, my dear. You have been a great help to me. I mean to rearrange some things in my lord's chamber and decide what room I shall take when Carrick arrives, for I cannot share that chamber with him. But the other rooms . . ." She shrugged. "Jamie *must* get on with enlarging the kitchen tower. I warrant we will all be much more comfortable after he does."

Escaping as soon as she could without rudeness, Meg found that her brother had disappeared. But, remembering that he'd practiced in the chapel the day before, she sallied forth to look for him there. By the time she had crossed the drawbridge, her temper was rising with each step she took.

The brown stone chapel sat in its own clearing near the trees lining Hermitage Water. Recalling Amalie's chilling description of what Tom had done to her, Meg decided not to confront him inside.

She went only far enough to open the door and look in. Pale light through three slits of windows revealed him sitting on a stool, polishing his lute.

"Tom, come outside, will you? I want to talk to you."

"Then come in where it's cool. It is hot enough out there to roast a haunch."

"You'll live, and I'd rather talk out here."

He sighed a martyr's sigh, set down the lute, and stood.

Meg stepped back from the door, glancing toward the castle. Seeing guards at the entrance and on the open parapet of the portcullis chamber reassured her. If she screamed, they would hear her and quickly send help.

The thought made her feel sick. Had anyone told her she could ever think such thoughts about Tom, she'd have thought the person was daft.

But Amalie was no dafty. Moreover, the look Tom gave Meg as he came outside made her wonder if he suspected that she knew what he had done.

"You haven't told anyone, have you?" he said, looking around as if to be sure no one else was within earshot.

Startled but hoping he referred to their previous discussion, she chose her words carefully. "I promised I'd not tell anyone who you are or what you're doing."

"People break promises all the time."

"Do they, Tom? Do people break faith with their families all the time, too?"

"I told you, I'm doing it *for* the family."

For a moment, she wondered if he did believe she was just talking about his spying on Douglas. Then she noted the probing way he watched her.

Her temper was close to ignition, but long practice at controlling it helped her stifle the urge to snatch his hair out by its roots—every tawny strand of it.

"I think you have guessed that I'm not talking about your spying," she said.

Stepping nearer, he said softly, "Then what are you talking about, Meggie?"

"You raped Amalie," she said. "You know it, and I do, too. Don't deny it."

"She is lying. I never raped her. I may have teased her, but she asked for that. She wanted it, and I gave her a bit of what she wanted. There's no harm in that."

"There is if one fathers a child thereby," Meg snapped.

That bolt struck home, because he paled. The last ounce of her doubt vanished, and so did her hold on her temper.

"How dare you ask me to trust you! How dare you extract a promise from me to do so, and in the name of helping kinsmen, when you have betrayed all that being a family means! Don't talk," she snapped when he opened his mouth.

Her hands had found her hips, and she leaned forward, looking him in the eye. "You betrayed Amalie in the worst possible way, Tom. There is naught you can do now to atone for that. We both loved you and trusted you, but you have destroyed that. You deserve the hatred she feels for you now, and my scorn."

He shook his head, and as he did, he straightened, looking more menacing than she had ever thought he could.

"No one will believe you, either of you, if you speak of it," he said. "They'll believe me. People always blame the lass when such things happen. She is the one defiled, and therefore she must have done something to deserve it. You'll see."

Meg knew he was right, but she was not about to back down. "I cannot trust you to keep your word to me, can I?"

"About what?"

That he had to ask gave her the answer. He would not even exert himself to recall what he had promised, because the promise had not mattered to him.

"You said you would not harm Douglas or his family. But you or the people you serve do mean harm to him, or you would not be spying on him."

"Are you threatening to break your promise, Meg? Because, before you do, you had better think very hard. Too much is at stake to allow you or Amalie to spoil it. Royal favor, for example. If the English succeed, we will have provided valuable service to our new king. We Murrays will benefit more than you can imagine."

"Is that more important than the lives of your own sisters?"

"Aye, sure, because we'll have a strong ruler again, and Elishaw will be safe. I'll win my spurs without having taken part in a single battle, and we'll reap other rewards. You'll see. You will be proud of me yet if you don't get in my way."

"And if I do?"

"I won't allow it. I'll accept your word that you won't, because I believe you'll keep it and because I don't want to harm you or Amalie."

"But what if I do break my word?" She felt an odd detachment from the conversation now, as if she were talking with a stranger about nothing in particular.

"If you stir a step to do so, I'll kill you both," he said.

"Don't think I won't, and don't think I *can't* do it, because I'd not have to do it myself. I need only speak to a man to see it done. Sithee, I've allies here, and you don't know who they are."

Her spirits sank as she listened, and her body wanted to slump, too. She drew herself up and said, "Unlike you, I do not lie or break my promises. So, as much as I'd like to break this one, I won't. But you should think shame to yourself, Tom."

"There's no shame in doing what is best for one's family *and* one's country."

Unable to stomach more, Meg turned on her heel and walked away. She held her head high, vowing silently never to speak to him again if she could help it.

She wondered, too, which was the greater duty, her duty to her family or to her husband's liege lord. Her parents had raised her strictly to believe that one's own family came first. But surely one was not duty-bound to protect its traitors.

The more she thought about what Tom had said, the more certain she became that there was a dangerous plot afoot. If the intent was not to harm Douglas—and she could not be certain that it was—then who was the intended victim?

It occurred to her that perhaps they had set their sights on more than one.

She had not walked ten steps before a frightening possibility struck her.

Dusk was falling and a full moon rising before Buccleuch and Huntly reached Otterburn with the main force and its vast herd of lowing cattle.

The mounted knights and lords had settled in by then, and had examined and improved their defenses. They had seen no sign of Hotspur and had had no word yet that he was on the move when Wat checked his men before going to bed.

He wondered if Hotspur meant to let the little gauntlets that had served as his lady's favor cross the border with Douglas to grace the tower of Dalkeith Castle.

After all, Percy's nickname was not from cruelly spurring horses. His temper, volatility, and sleepless passion for repressing Scots had earned him that name. Wat doubted that Hotspur would let Douglas keep the gloves if he could prevent it.

It was still early, but they all needed sleep. Making certain his sword, mace, and dirk were within easy reach, Wat settled himself as comfortably as he could.

Like most seasoned warriors, he could usually sleep anywhere and any time he found the chance. But for once, the skill failed him. With cattle gently lowing a lullaby in the background, he found himself remembering how Meg had wondered about the signs of pregnancy. She had said she would know in a sennight or so.

Realizing that it had been nearly a fortnight, he hoped she was with child.

He did not want to die before he had sired a son to carry on the Scott name.

Tom kept out of Meg's way for the rest of the afternoon, showing himself only when it was time for Giles Gilpin to entertain the ladies at suppertime.

The countess invited the captain of the guard to join them, and Meg noted with amusement that Sym seemed to think the captain's presence demanded even more meticulous attention from the serving lads.

He harried them like a sheepdog herding a tiny flock until she feared that, being older and not at all ovine in nature, one might turn and snap back at him.

Amalie had grown quiet again, and Meg felt little energy herself. Her anger and sorrow over Tom's betrayal increased every time she thought about it.

She realized she faced another dilemma now—how much to tell Amalie?

Making their excuses to the countess, Meg bore Amalie upstairs with Sym following as usual. Shutting the door on him after asking him to warn them of any approach, Meg lit the two cressets in the room with a taper she had brought from the hall and said, "Sit down. We must talk."

Amalie sat on the edge of her cot. "What is it?"

"I need to know that you will not betray Tom to anyone here. I gave him my word, but my word is worthless if you mean to expose him."

"I won't go against you, Meg, but I don't agree that we should keep silent."

Meg had decided to reveal that Tom had threatened to kill them both if either betrayed him. But she could not guess how her unpredictable sister would react. An impulsive word or an inability to conceal her fear could put them in grave danger.

So instead, she said, "I wish I had not given him my

word, but I did. And after living with Walter and his men even for the short time we have, I don't want to lead any of them to think we have a weaker sense of honor than they do."

That was true enough, because Meg *had* learned a new code of honor from her husband's family, and she wanted to live up to it. As deterrence, it lacked the power of Tom's threat, but that threat could as easily send Amalie into a tizzy as frighten her to silence. In a tizzy, the impulsive Amalie was apt to do anything.

"I don't think it is dishonorable to unearth a spy," she said now.

"Would you feel the same way if Tom had not betrayed you?"

Amalie shrugged. "I don't know. I own, it would be harder. But if we keep his secret, are we not, in effect, betraying the Douglas ourselves?"

"That is the dilemma, aye," Meg agreed. "I don't want to protect Tom, but having given my word, I must keep it, just as Walter kept his to ride to our father's aid on no more than a summons to do so. Even though Father tricked him, I am certain Walter would ride to his aid again. He believes himself bound to do so. Can we do less for our brother? Are we not bound to keep our word in the same way?"

"I did not give mine," Amalie reminded her.

Meg sighed. "You know what I mean."

"I do, aye, and I will do as you ask, but I don't feel as if it can be right, and I do think you should tell the countess that her minstrel is our brother. It is your duty."

"But despite what he's done, I still love him as a brother," Meg said sadly. "If we break faith with him, is that not as bad as his having broken faith with you?"

"So you will protect him, no matter what he does?"

"Just as I would protect you in a like instance, dearling," Meg said. "Unless I learn that he truly threatens Douglas or that he also threatens the Scotts, I must."

The other fear that had occurred to her as she left the chapel stirred again.

Tom seemed certain that the English would conquer Scotland, but the Scots were as certain that they would not. In either case, strange things had happened, and she had not considered any English role in the plot that she had suspected earlier. The raiders and Carrick's visit to Hermitage had seemed part of that bigger picture, but although the raiders might have been part of a plot to weaken Douglas, English conquerors would have little interest in such a weak heir to the Scottish throne.

In any event, she would try to keep her word, and her own counsel, at least until the other men returned. She thought she could trust Amalie to keep silent that long unless Tom committed the folly of repeating his deadly threat to her.

Chapter 18

～

"I saw a dead man win a fight,
And I think that man was I."

Meg stood naked in their bedchamber just as he had seen her before, with her beautiful hair hanging in shining waves to the flaring of her shapely hips.

Myriad candles made dark shadows and golden lights dance in her hair, over her skin, and on the walls of the chamber. He felt warm, and his body stirred.

Walking up behind her, he put his hands on her shoulders and shifted strands of her silky hair out of the way so he could kiss her neck under the lobe of her left ear. He felt her tremble and pulled her close to him.

Although he was certain he'd been clothed a moment ago, he wore nothing now but his tingling skin. Holding her so, he felt the heat of her against him from his chest to his loins and legs.

Her trembling increased and her breathing quickened. She had not said a word.

Turning her gently, he tilted her chin so he could press his lips to hers. Her tongue darted out to touch his, then

*slid into his mouth, warm and tasting of fine wine. He was
ready for her, impatient to couple, but when he reached
down to see if she was ready for him, she put a hand to his
wrist and stopped him.*

Her trembling had ceased.

*Lustful for her and eager to have his way, he tried to
shift her hand aside, but her strength was like iron, and
he could not move her. Looking into her eyes, he saw
an expression he had seen before. It was sorrow—nay,
disappointment.*

*He felt her emotions as if they were his, and he won-
dered who had dared to disappoint her so. As the thought
crossed his mind, he recalled that she had once apologized for disappointing him. This was different.*

*Something was amiss with her, somehow. Perhaps he
had disappointed her.*

*He struggled to think when he had seen that look be-
fore. Scenes presented themselves to his mind's eye, one
after another, as real as if he had shifted bodily back to
those times. Each time, he was in bed with her, and each
time he had just enjoyed his release and was beginning to
uncouple from her.*

*The look he recalled seemed far less intense than what
he had just seen but similar. If the cause was what he
suspected it might be, he could do something about it. In
troth, he would enjoy it. But if that was not it . . .*

*He smiled at her as the last scene faded from his
mind's eye, and murmured gently, "I have been thoughtless, sweetheart. But you will have your pleasure, again
and again. You will come first now, I swear."*

*Smiling the beautiful smile that warmed him through,
she released his hand.*

He picked her up and carried her to a field of flow-

ers, wondering idly what had happened to their bed. Lay-
ing her tenderly on the soft leaves and petals, he gently
spread her legs and began to show her how much plea-
sure he could give her.

As he moved to taste her, he heard a humming as of
minstrel's music in the distance, then whispery voices
chanting an evensong to distant notes of a wavering horn.
The sounds increased in volume until the words became
clear . . .

"A Douglas! A Douglas!"

Wat awoke to bright moonlight, blasting horns, shouting men, frightened cattle, and noises of a fierce battle
that appeared to be erupting all around him.

Meg pushed damp strands of hair from her cheeks and
turned over. The room was hot and muggy, the bed too
hard to induce sleep. Moonlight streamed through the
narrow window. She had been lying there for hours, tor-
mented by her thoughts and increasing fears, trying not to
wake Amalie with her tossing and turning.

A sense of impending doom stirred and grew stronger
as the hours passed.

For a time, she pondered Tom's betrayal and her own
dilemma, worrying about what he might do and the threats
he'd made.

Although she had told Amalie she loved him because
he was her brother and one ought to love everyone in
one's family, it was growing harder by the minute to love
a man who had threatened to kill them both if either betrayed him.

Guilt stirred strongly when she thought about the

countess and her ladies, all ignorant of their favorite minstrel's identity and purpose.

Amalie's voice interrupted Meg's thoughts. "Have you
slept at all?"

"No, but I hoped I was not keeping you awake."

"It is not your fault. I'm too hot to sleep. I've dozed off
and on, but my shift feels damp enough to wring out."

"Take it off," Meg recommended. She had thought of
taking her own off. It was customary to sleep nude, but in
a castle full of unknown men, she had felt less vulnerable
wearing her shift.

"It's too much trouble," Amalie said. "I don't feel well.
I think my flow must be about to begin."

Meg hoped it was. It was very late. Hers was late, too,
but her pregnancy—if she *was* pregnant—would cause no
scandal. Her thoughts returned to Tom.

"Why do you think Tom came here?" she asked.
"Do you believe he is really spying on Douglas for the
Percies?"

"I don't doubt it, although he did not actually *say* he
was spying for them," Amalie said. "He only asked you if
you'd think it was dreadful if he were."

"But he must be," Meg said, wondering if she was
trying to persuade Amalie or persuade herself that Tom
was not engaged in something worse. "Recall that he said
he was doing it for the family and reminded us that the
Percies *are* our family. And they are, Amalie. You cannot deny that. But it occurred to me that someone besides
Douglas may be in danger. Recall who else will be here."

"Many people will be here when Douglas returns,"
Amalie said dryly.

"Including Carrick," Meg said. "The King of Scots is
old, and although Carrick is younger, everyone says he

will be a weak king. But today Tom said he'd win royal favor and we'd benefit by having a strong king again, one for whom he'd have provided a great service. What if that great service is to remove Carrick before he can accept the crown? If the King of Scots has no proper heir, would it not be easier—?"

"Carrick does have a son," Amalie reminded her.

"A mere child," Meg said. "Was that not the very problem in England before King Richard came of age? A child on the throne always means a regency, and a regency means men fighting to control the crown. But with Carrick out of the way and . . ."

"If the English invade us, will they not simply take Carrick and his son both prisoner and rule us from London?" Amalie interjected. "Besides, who else could Tom be spying for? Everyone knows that Douglas is loyal to the King of Scots, so no one here would set spies to watch him. And as for having a strong king, Tom must have meant Richard, for although Richard may have been weak when he was a child king, with his uncles fighting to control his regency, he has taken command of England now and is leading the English army. No one thinks him weak anymore."

"Aye, but even so . . ."

"What could we do, anyway?" Amalie sounded half-asleep now, as if she were no longer really listening, so Meg did not reply.

Very likely, Amalie was right, and Tom was serving their English cousins in hope of bringing benefit to the Murray family if the English invasion succeeded. But what if there was more to it than that?

She wished Wat were there, so she could discuss her concerns with him.

Then it occurred to her that keeping Tom's secret meant she could not tell her husband what she had learned. As she lay trying to imagine Wat's voice in her mind's ear, telling her what to do, common sense returned.

Amalie was right. They could not let Tom continue doing what he was doing. Whatever that was, he was not acting alone. He had admitted that much himself. And if others were involved, danger awaited not only Douglas but very likely Carrick and many more. Meg realized she had made her decision.

If she could not speak without breaking her word, she would have to act.

～

Snatching up his sword, mace, and dirk, Wat had joined the shouting.

"A Douglas, a Douglas!" The words echoed through the valley, and in the distance, in response, he heard, "A Percy, a Percy!"

His lads were still scrambling for weapons and jacks-o'-plate. He had slept in his mail and boots, but none of them had time to saddle horses.

He heard Neb Duffin's gravelly voice ordering his lads to close in behind him. Like most Scots, they were accustomed to infighting, on foot. The erstwhile raiders carried daggers, battle-axes, clubs, and maces, and they used them well.

With battle erupting on all sides of him, and aware that Neb's men had positioned themselves to protect him and his lads, Wat charged in pursuit of the Douglas banner. Leaving his sword in its sheath across his back, he used his heavy iron mace or long dirk against anyone who tried to stop him. In close quarters, both weapons were more effective than a sword.

Someone shouted, "They're at the riverside. They're all afoot!"

Knowing the Scots numbered less than three thousand against eight thousand Englishmen, Wat felt a surge of near panic. But he had no time to acknowledge it before he was too busy fighting to spare any thought for fear.

Yards ahead, he saw Douglas himself, and adrenaline surged.

He pushed on, bellowing, "A Douglas!"

The full moon, already higher in the sky and thus smaller than when he had wakened, cast pale, eerie light over the scene as he fought his way onward.

With arrows raining down all around him, men from both sides fell.

English archers had won many a battle for England with their longbows, but in the poor light, amid chaos, and their numbers so much greater, he knew the odds were that more Englishmen than Scots would fall to the arrows that night.

Unlike the archers, however, Wat and other men fighting at close quarters in that moonlight could easily distinguish English light armor from the Scots' jacks-o'-plate and mail. The Douglas banner moved forward, and Wat plunged after it, using his mace and dirk with increasing efficiency as he went.

Moments later, he stumbled, saving himself only with a wrenching leap sideways. He grimaced when he saw that he'd tripped over a kneeling man's booted foot and had nearly fallen right on top of him.

Recognizing Sir Hugh Montgomery as one of three men kneeling beside a body, he used his dirk in swift defense against an Englishman with sword raised. The sword flailed ineffectively in such close quarters, making the fight a short one.

Only when the Englishman collapsed was Wat able to see that the body the others knelt beside was Douglas's, bleeding profusely from a wound in the neck.

Feeling sick and catching sight of Neb not far away, he shouted, "Neb Duffin! To me!"

At Neb's wave of acknowledgment, Wat bent close to the grim-looking Montgomery, who besides being Douglas's cousin was also Janet Scott's. Opposite Hugh, trying to stanch the flow of blood, was Douglas's chaplain, Richard Lundie.

"How bad is it, Hugh?" Wat asked.

"Bad," Hugh said. "Apparently no time to lace his cuirass properly, for he took a lance or a dirk in the back. But he told the lad with his banner to carry on. Said we must not let the damned English or our own lads know he's fallen. Sithee, they cannot see faces in this light, and Jamie's bonnet is like any other Scotsman's."

"We must get him off the field," Wat said. "I've men here who can—"

"Nay then, Wat." It was Douglas's voice, and weak, but his words were clear.

"My lord," Lundie pleaded, "with all respect—"

"Hotspur's men . . . strung from here to Newcastle," Douglas muttered, gasping. "Must be. He's come too fast . . . attacked too soon . . . before his forces could gather. Impatience will undo him. But not if he knows . . . I've fallen."

"He's right, Wat," Hugh said. "There's no sign of the Bishop of Durham yet. We've seen only Hotspur's banner and Sir Ralph Percy's. And Hotspur *must* have pushed his men damned hard to get here so fast. They cannot have left Newcastle before this morning, and most of them are on foot."

"Even the leaders are afoot now," Wat said. "They had to leave their horses across the river, because they floundered in the bogs. Many men are bogged, too. Buccleuch and Huntly are moving to surround the English main body on this side."

"I hope the English rot in the mud," Hugh said wrathfully.

Looking back, Wat saw that Neb and his men, along with Wat's lads and Montgomery's, had formed a circle around them. All faced outward with lances and swords at the ready. Douglas was safe enough for a few moments, but what then?

"Our lads standing together here can hold the damned English off long enough to get Jamie to a place of greater safety, Hugh," Wat urged.

"Nay, then, I'm sped," Douglas told them, making them both lean closer to hear him. "I dreamed once that a dead man won a battle . . . but . . . never knew I'd be that man. At least I'll not die in bed."

"Jamie, don't," Wat said.

But Douglas's eyes had shut.

His lips moved. "Tell my lass . . . I'm sorry . . . we never made a son together."

"Sir, you'll tell her yourself; or better, you'll live to make many sons," Hugh Montgomery said, signing to two of his men to carry the earl.

"Nay, Hugh, don't waste the men," Douglas said. "Put me under a bush, so the English don't get me, and then go. The Douglas can yet win the day."

Someone grabbed Wat's arm, and whirling up, he raised his heavy mace.

"Easy, sir," Neb Duffin shouted. "Ye'd best come. 'Tis your father . . ."

Wat nodded, cast a glance back at Montgomery and Douglas, then plunged after Neb. Whether Douglas lived or died, he had given his orders. All of them would follow his banner and fight with all they had in them to win the day. But Buccleuch would want to know what had happened. And if he needed help holding the English at the river, that was where Wat and his men belonged.

Until the sun came up, the enemy would not know Douglas had fallen, and Wat meant to be alive when it did come up. He had had his own dream, after all, and he meant to do everything in his power to see that it came true.

Meg would be waiting for him, and he would not fail her.

⁓

Having made up her mind to act, Meg considered her options carefully and decided two things were paramount. She would have to do something about Tom, but first she had to do all she could to assure that the countess and Carrick stayed safe. Just how she could do that, she did not know.

She had no men from Raven's Law with her to help protect the countess, because except for Sym, those who had escorted her and Amalie to the Hall had returned home, where she had thought them needed. And she could not seek advice from the Douglas men or the countess's, not after Tom had told her he had allies at Hermitage. Even if he had lied, she could no longer be certain of anyone there.

Even if she could trust them, she could not be sure they would do as she asked without explanation, and that would mean accusing Tom.

She decided she would have to apply directly to the countess. But she would have to do so in such a way that Isabel would ask few questions and still do as she asked. The notion sounded simple in her thoughts, but Meg knew it would not be.

Once again, she wished Wat were there to advise her. But that thought only made her smile in self-derision. Had she not told him she was capable of using her own brain, that she was sensible and trustworthy, and would take no more risks?

In any case, if Wat were there, he would do everything himself and doubtless manage to whisk the countess safely out of Hermitage and back to Dalkeith or even farther away to the Douglas fortress of Tantallon, high above the Firth of Forth.

That thought stirred others until she got out of bed and shook her sister.

"Amalie, wake up."

Opening bleary eyes, Amalie moaned, "What time is it?"

"I don't know, but it is after dawn and I need you," Meg said quietly, knowing Sym very likely lay just outside the door.

"What's wrong?" Amalie asked as she raised herself onto an elbow. "Did you sleep at all?"

"Some, but not enough," Meg said with a wry smile. "I've been thinking, though, and you were right when you said we must do something. I mean to speak to the countess, but we must find a way to keep Tom from any further plotting."

"Will the countess know how to do that?"

"I am not going to ask her," Meg admitted. "I don't intend to discuss Tom with her. I must at least try to keep my word or it means nothing to give it."

Amalie clicked her tongue. "Tom does not keep his word. I don't see why you should feel bound by yours."

Tempted again to explain bluntly that Tom had threatened to kill them both if she betrayed him, Meg had to bite her tongue. Amalie would not be able to hide such knowledge, not from Tom or from anyone else.

Instead, Meg said, "Do you expect me always to behave toward others as they behave toward me, love? Think how it would be if I got moody every time you do."

"I don't mean that."

"I know you don't, but how would you have me decide when to break my word? Would you trust me to keep promises to you if I failed to keep promises I'd made to others any time I disapproved of their behavior?"

"This is a stupid conversation. I know I can trust you."

"We'd do better, then, to discuss what to do next," Meg said. "I'll talk to the countess, but I'm not sure how to do that without first doing something about Tom."

"You could go to her bedchamber. She is just downstairs in Douglas's chamber, and her ladies both sleep in that wee room between it and the garderobe."

Meg nodded. "I'd not ordinarily think of doing anything so brazen, but this is an extraordinary situation. As your mind is clearly more inventive than mine, can you think of a way to keep Tom out of mischief until Douglas returns?"

Amalie chuckled. "We could borrow a club from someone and clout him."

"Then what?" Meg asked, stifling her own amusement. "Do you think we should drag Tom in here or bounce him downstairs and through the halls?"

"It is a pity we cannot find a flask of the potion he gave Douglas to make him sick," Amalie said. "I do think he gave him something, don't you?"

"It does not matter as we don't know what it is or if there is any more," Meg said. "Keep thinking, whilst I slip downstairs and wake Countess Isabel."

Hastily donning a plain gray kirtle and pale green robe, she belted the latter with her embroidered girdle, slipped her feet into soft shoes, and replaited her hair.

Then, as quietly as she could, she lifted the latch and pulled open the door.

As she had expected, Sym lay curled on his left side on a pallet in front of the door, softly snoring. Lifting her skirts high, she stepped over him, but before her foot touched the floor on the other side, she heard a soft, plaintive mew.

Looking down, she saw Pawky's head emerge from under the boy's right arm. The kitten's mouth opened again with a louder, more demanding meow.

Sym's eyes opened, and Meg stepped quickly out of the way as he scrambled to his feet. The kitten meowed again in protest.

"Me lady!"

"Hush, Sym. There is no need for you to get up, because I want you to stay here and keep watch over the lady Amalie until I return. I'll be back shortly."

"But—"

"Don't argue," she said firmly. "I want your word that you will obey me."

He nodded, eyes wide. "I will, aye."

Satisfied, Meg left him with his pet and hurried down to the next level, where the master's chamber lay. It had occurred to her that the countess might also keep a guard outside her room, but the area was clear.

Hesitating at the door, she wondered if she should rap but decided it was foolish to worry about proprieties at such a time. Quietly opening the door, and hoping that neither of Isabel's ladies was with her, she peeked in.

The chamber was nearly as large as the upper hall just below it, and boasted two windows slightly wider than the one in Meg's chamber. Both were curtained, but a crack of gray dawn light let her see the large bed, likewise curtained, against the wall to her right. Its occupant was alone in the room.

Slipping inside and shutting the door, Meg went nearer and said quietly, "Madam, I beg your pardon, but you must wake up. I need to talk with you."

"What is it?" Isabel asked, pulling the bed curtain open enough to peer out.

"'Tis important," Meg said. "I hope you'll forgive me if I do not explain it all to you. I have given my word to say nothing, and I fear I'm close to breaking it just by coming here to you."

"I know it must be vital to bring you to me in such a way, so what *can* you tell me?" Isabel asked, sitting up with the coverlet clutched to her breast.

Meg had thought of several tactful, discreet ways of explaining what she wanted, but the countess's open manner made it easier just to answer her question.

"You should leave here as soon as you can and ride to

meet the Earl of Carrick. If you must tell anyone why you are leaving, I pray you, say only that much, that you are going to meet him. Let them believe you will ride back here with him. Instead, though, you should persuade him to seek a place of safety."

There was light enough to see Isabel's frown, but she said only, "Might Dalkeith be such a place?"

"Aye, or I thought Tantallon might serve."

"I see." Isabel's gaze locked with Meg's. "May I ask what you mean to do?"

"I must stay here," Meg said. "Amalie must stay as well. I had thought your ladies might likewise have to, whilst you slipped secretly away—"

"Nay, that would never do. You clearly suspect something is amiss here at Hermitage. If that is so, it will be wiser for me to go openly and with all ceremony. Everyone here expects Carrick to arrive tomorrow, after all. He told Ralph Lindsay he will stay tonight at Dryburgh, so I shall simply say I am to meet him there."

"I thought the English burned Dryburgh Abbey, and Melrose, three years ago."

"They burned much of both, aye, but the monks rebuilt their chapter houses and dormitories. And Dryburgh's abbot is a good friend of Carrick's. John loves the abbey's setting, because although many of its beautiful trees burned, the Tweed still flows past and the place is as green as ever now. He likes to sit and watch the river."

"It is possible that someone may try to stop you," Meg warned her.

Isabel smiled. "Nay, for am I not Countess of Douglas, and the King of Scots' daughter? There are still many loyal men here, my dear."

"But things have happened," Meg said, wondering what she could tell her.

"I do recall Jamie's strange illnesses, and I'd wondered if betrayal might be a cause. But for all that there may be traitors here, most are loyal to Jamie. Indeed," Isabel added, "if you would just tell me what or whom you suspect, we could lay the whole before Sir Ralph. The Lindsays have long been loyal to the Douglas."

"I would tell Sir Ralph myself if I could, my lady, but I know only enough to bring more danger down upon us if I make a misstep. I do wonder, though," she added thoughtfully when an idea stirred. "What would Sir Ralph do if you were to report that you had lost something and that perhaps someone had taken it?"

"He would search for it, of course."

"Would he search everyone?"

"Certainly."

"And, if he found it, what then?"

Isabel's eyes gleamed. "He would cast the culprit into the pit until my lord could decide what to do with him. Of course," she added with a wry smile, "Jamie may be so vexed with me that he will say it served me right to lose it, for disobeying him. But he would still punish the thief severely unless I could somehow manage to persuade him to be merciful."

Meg hesitated again, certain that the Douglas would hang such a thief as quickly as he would hang a spy. Deciding to worry about that later and, if necessary, confess what she had done, she said, "Have you some object you would be willing to lend me? It is much to ask, I know, but—"

"Sakes, my dear, I am trusting you all in all, am I not?

Do you want something of value that would guarantee his hanging, or a trinket of little value?"

"A trinket," Meg said quickly. "And, pray, madam, say nothing about it until you are on the very point of departure. But if you could let me have it now and perhaps say nothing to anyone else about this meeting, I would be most grateful."

"I confess, I am seething with curiosity, but I have every confidence in you," Isabel said. "If Sir Ralph offers to escort me, I shall command him to stay here. Then, if aught goes amiss with your plans, you must promise me you will go to him."

Meg promised, but she was by no means sure Sir Ralph Lindsay was a man she could trust, because heaven alone knew who was in league with Tom. But if things did go awry, doubtless Tom would keep his promise to kill her and there would be no need to face yet another dilemma about keeping her own promises.

Accepting a pretty lavender-bead necklace with a silver Celtic cross pendant from the Highlands that Isabel said one of her brothers had given her, Meg thanked her and hurried back to her own chamber, finding Sym where she had left him.

He had rolled his pallet and was sitting back against the wall, trailing a string for Pawky to attack. When he saw Meg, he stuffed the string into the waist of his breeks and got quickly to his feet.

"Sym, I've an important task for you if you can manage it safely," she said in a low tone as she reached the door. Looking in to see that Amalie had dressed, she added, "Come in, and I'll tell you."

Scooping up the kitten, he obeyed, and once inside,

Meg explained to him and Amalie what she hoped he could do.

"I can do that as easy as winking," Sym said with a nod.

Meg waited for him to ask why she wanted him to do such a thing, but he continued to regard her as if he expected more commands.

"What I have asked of you is dangerous," she said. "I hope you understand that, Sym. You must do it as soon as possible, and you must *not* be seen."

"I'm thinking I'll do it afore that gallous ill-willer wakes up."

"Why do you call him so, Sym?"

"Does he no spy on the Douglas, then?"

Meg looked at Amalie, who shook her head, clearly as much at a loss as Meg was. But as Meg opened her mouth to ask why he would believe the minstrel to be a spy, the answer came to her. "Faith, you were listening at the door the other night!"

"I were no listening. When I come back wi' your water, I heard a man's voice inside. He sounded cross and vexsome, and I didna think he belonged in your bedchamber, for all he were saying ye was family. So I thought I'd just listen to see should I do summat about him. Then ye said he were a-spying for Hotspur, so I listened closer. But I didna think ye'd want me to tell anyone, for ye'd said I must no talk o' the things I hear ye say. And ye'll recall, too, that our Dod said he'd skelp me till me wagging tongue fell out—"

"I remember," Meg said. "And I meant what I said. It would be *very* dangerous for you to tell anyone else what you heard." Realizing it would be risky even for the boy to remain at Hermitage after doing what she had asked of him, she decided he might serve her in yet another way.

He was earnestly reassuring her that he would keep safe, but she cut in to say, "I want you to do one thing more for me, Sym. And you must prepare for it before you do the first task, so it cannot delay you afterward. The countess will leave soon to meet the Earl of Carrick, and I want you to ride with her as far as—"

"But I canna leave! Master Wat said I must stay with ye."

"This is just like when we met the poachers, Sym. My only fear is that you may not be able to find Master Wat this time, or may run into more danger. Douglas and his men crossed the line at Carter Bar, though, and that is not far from Elishaw. You have traveled that way before. Do you think you can find the road again?"

"Aye, for I've only to ask here and about as I go," he said confidently. "Sithee, I've followed our Dod and the others many times. It be nae great thing. As to finding Master Wat, I warrant plenty o' folk can tell me where Douglas's army has got to. And if I tell him ye have need o' him, he'll no be wroth wi' me."

"But if there's fighting, you must hide until it is over," Meg told him.

"Aye, sure, I dinna want to get m'self killed!"

"Then you know what you must do, but don't leave until you can ride with the countess. I'll see that she knows you mean to join her, and puts no rub in the way of your taking your own road as soon as you are beyond sight from the castle."

Nodding, he said, "We men travel light, so I'll ha' nae need to do much for m'self. And if I offer to help saddle horses for the countess's ladies and them, I can saddle me own then, too." With that, he set Pawky on his shoulder and left.

Meg watched until the door shut behind him, knowing she had no other safe recourse. But she prayed fervently, and against all odds to the contrary, that neither of the two dangerous tasks she had set for the boy would result in his death.

Chapter 19

"This deed was done at the Otterbourne,
About the breaking of the day . . ."

In the increasing dawn light, Wat, Neb Duffin, and their little band of men cut a swath through milling cattle, inert bodies, fallen tents, miscellaneous gear, and natural obstacles of the landscape, fighting their way toward the Redeside water meadows, where Buccleuch's portion of the foot had taken their stand.

At first Englishmen seemed to be everywhere. But as they moved, Wat saw that the Scots were fiercely holding their own and had already pushed much of Hotspur's army back across the river. Knowing the Redesdale landscape better than the enemy did, thanks to frequent forays into the area over the years, the Scots could avoid the worst of the bogs as they drove their opponents into them. Once mired, their enemies were easily dispatched.

As they neared the meadows, Wat began shouting, "Buccleuch! Buccleuch!"

Ahead of him, others echoed the cry, and following the shouts, he found his father's men in pitched battle.

"Where's Himself?" he bellowed at a man who had dispatched one opponent and whirled on Wat, clearly expecting to dispatch another.

The man held his club high, his gaze shifting warily back and forth over the melee around them, as he said, "Yonder, sir, by the wee stream!"

Plunging on, Wat saw less fighting ahead, where a streamlet from the steep hills behind them tumbled into the river Rede. The land around the confluence was, he knew, naught but marshland.

Most of the fighting in that area had moved to the other side of the Rede, where Scots pursued retreating English. Sunrise was just minutes away.

He saw a group of four men near the base of the hillside from which the streamlet flowed, and a chill shot through his body, because their demeanor was much the same as the group he had left behind with Douglas.

Finding Neb at his side, Wat gave him a grim look. "When you said he wanted me, what had you heard?"

"A lad said to fetch ye quick to Buccleuch," Neb said. "He didna say more."

Nodding, Wat looked to see which of his own men were nearest. "Tam, Gibbie, to me!" he shouted. Then, to Neb, he said, "Keep your lads close to mine, and see that this area stays clear of English until I learn what's happened. If he *is* down and we can move him to safety, we will. You'll take your orders from me."

"Aye, sir, o' course," Neb said cheerfully.

"Even if he countermands them?"

Neb raised his eyebrows. "D'ye think he will?"

"I don't know," Wat replied truthfully. He feared that if his father thought he was dying, he would do just as Jamie Douglas had done.

As the thought crossed his mind, he realized he had heard nothing yet to tell him whether Douglas still lived or had died.

He had no time to think about it, because the captain of his father's men had seen him and was waving him forward.

Both the frantic wave and the man's anxious expression reinforced his fear that Buccleuch was down but gave him hope that he was alive.

Then he saw him on the ground, eyes shut. His mail shirt was bloody but looked undamaged. Wat's gaze scanned downward until it came to rest on the upper right side of his father's leather breeks, dark with what he suspected was blood.

Someone had gathered damp moss and was kneeling to try to stanch the flow. "How bad is it?" Wat asked as he came up to them.

"Himself does say it be none so bad, sir," the man said. "But that villain yonder smote him with his mace. The wound looks gey painful, though he doesna complain. Trouble is we've nowt at hand save his shirt to bind it. But we're loath to take off his mail to get at it until the last o' this lot around us falls back."

Buccleuch's captain said, "He struck his head when he fell, sir, but he's got a harder one than most. I think he'll do."

Wat nodded and looked around, the better to assess their situation.

Hotspur's army was falling back across the river and beyond. The Scots followed, shrieking and brandishing weapons, cutting down anyone they caught.

Neb's men and Wat's own stayed with Wat. With Buccleuch's fighting tail, they quickly formed the same sort of circle around Buccleuch that they had formed earlier around Douglas, facing out with lances and swords at the ready.

The villain who had struck Buccleuch lay in the center of the circle, unmoving, so Wat dropped to one knee at his father's side.

Buccleuch's eyes remained shut. He had shown no awareness of his son yet.

"Sir?" Wat said gently.

"What the devil are you doing here?" Buccleuch grumbled, opening his eyes to mere slits. "You should be with Douglas."

"He has men enough," Wat said. "The English are in retreat." Remembering Douglas's words, he added, "Hotspur must have begun the attack the moment he and the other leaders arrived at the Rede. Jamie said Hotspur's impatience would win the day for us, and I think it has. In the poor light, the English cut down a host of their own men, and the bulk of their army is still strung out to Newcastle."

"Aye, and they're all afoot, because the bogs defeated their horses. I heard someone had captured Ralph Percy," Buccleuch added. "Pray God that's true."

His voice was weak and his face pale. But aside from the bloody breeks, he looked well enough. The only thing that worried Wat was that Buccleuch was no longer protesting his presence. Leaning over him to take a better look, he set down the mace he'd been wielding to good effect just a short time before.

Buccleuch's breeks and thigh had been ripped open. But the wound was oozing, not pouring blood. He could see damaged muscles and knew the injury must hurt like blazes, but no large blood vessel spouted at him.

He was thinking he would seek out Richard Lundie, Douglas's chaplain. Like most clerics, Lundie was skilled at tending injuries, and as Douglas's chaplain, he had vast experience. "What do you know of wounds like this one?" he asked the man applying moss to Buccleuch's thigh.

The man said reassuringly, "He'll do, I th—"

"Master Wat! Ahind ye!"

Recognizing Gibbie's voice, Wat shot to his feet, whirling to see an upraised club before Gib's body blocked his view. Then, before Wat could do aught to help him, Gib crashed down at his feet.

The English lout who had struck him was the same one who had struck Buccleuch. Still charging, he had his mace raised again, aimed at Wat.

Snatching his dirk from its sheath, Wat sidestepped him and ended his life with a vicious slash across his throat.

Kneeling swiftly by Gibbie, Wat saw that he had taken the blow on the side of his head. Blood poured from his eyes and nose. "Oh, Gib, why?"

"Nae time," Gibbie gasped, the words gurgling through blood in his throat. "Should ha' made sure he were dead."

Wat gripped his hand and leaned closer to be sure Gibbie would hear him. "You're a good friend, Gib. We'll get you home."

"I am home," Gibbie murmured back, his voice barely audible. "There's me Annie now."

Tears sprang to Wat's eyes, and he gripped Gib's hand tight, determined to hold him in this world, Annie or no Annie.

But Annie won.

Despite rising so early, the morning passed swiftly for Meg. Her plans went well, because the countess and her ladies departed before noon without incident and with Sym in their train. The only surprise came with the discovery that Sir Ralph's men had searched so thoroughly for the countess's necklace that they had searched Meg's and Amalie's belongings along with everyone else's.

The men had not been tidy, either, so the two found their tiny bedchamber in a chaotic state when they returned to refresh themselves before the midday meal.

They tidied the room and returned to the upper hall, where they learned that searchers had found the necklace in a bag where the minstrel kept his extra lute strings and polishing cloths. Sir Ralph had ignored Giles Gilpin's indignant protests of innocence and ordered him thrown into the pit to await Douglas's judgment.

Meg felt a twinge of guilt when she heard that news, but Amalie received it stoically. They were still at the table, solemnly congratulating themselves on a trap well sprung, when word came of a large mounted force approaching the castle.

Hoping it was Douglas, Wat, and the others returning, both young women hurried to the portcullis chamber, from which they could view the main approach.

"Who is it?" they asked the astonished guards. "Who comes?"

"We dinna ken, m'lady, but 'tis a royal banner they be flying."

"Mercy, is it the Earl of Carrick?" Meg demanded. Knowing it could not possibly be the ailing King, she feared that her plan had failed miserably and that the countess had missed intercepting the earl.

"Nay, for Carrick flies his own flag," the elder of the two guards told her.

"Then who . . . ?"

"Ye'd best go back into the hall, the two o' ye, till we learn who they are."

Accepting his advice, they had their answer ten minutes later when the riders' leader strode into the hall, still wearing his chain mail and visor. He took off the visor as he entered, and when his gaze shifted to the dais table where Meg and Amalie sat, his astonishment at seeing them was as great as theirs was to see him.

"What the devil are you two doing here?" Simon Murray demanded.

⁓

The sun blazed down on Otterburn, revealing carnage across the land. The air reeked of blood and shuddered with groans. The din of lowing cattle was constant.

The Scots had won against all odds, but their victory felt hollow, because Scotland's greatest warrior was dead. The news had spread, and Douglas's death overshadowed everything, stirring deep mourning.

The English army had retreated and was unlikely to return. Most of their leaders were among the Scots' prisoners, including Hotspur himself and his brother, Sir Ralph Percy. But the Scots were keeping their eyes open for trouble anyway.

Supervising preparations for rapid departure, Wat saw Tammy approaching, his face devoid of expression, his jack-o'-plate and breeks as spattered with blood of victims and friends as Wat's own. Having sent him earlier to let Huntly and Sir Hugh Montgomery know that Buccleuch was injured, and to glean what news he could, Wat demanded Tam's report.

"They've prepared the Douglas's body and some others for carting, Master Wat. Our lads ha' put Gib's on a horse litter, and fixed up another for Himself to ride when we go. And, as ye've ordered, they'll say nowt to him about it till then."

"How bad are our losses?" Wat asked him.

"Bethankit, we lost nae more of our own, only Gib—and Alf Geddes from Himself's lot. A few be sporting injuries o' one sort or another, as are four o' Neb's lads. All save your da' can ride, though he's bound to say he'll ride, too."

Wat glanced toward the group still paying respects to Douglas. Most were Douglases themselves, and he knew that losing him had devastated them all.

He felt numb, himself, and tried not to think about Douglas or Gib.

Gib had been a good friend and Jamie Douglas a strong presence in Wat's life since childhood. He'd thought of him as a friend, too, as well as a leader.

Also, he knew that the Douglas's death would roil the Scottish political world. He had left no direct, legitimate heir to whom his holdings would pass. And that lack was bound to stir trouble straightaway as men who might deserve to inherit the earldom, and men who did not, all stepped forth to stake their claims to it.

"Will they take him to Melrose?" he asked Tam, knowing as nearly everyone did that Melrose Abbey was where Jamie had wanted to be buried.

"They will, aye," Tam said, adding, "They say Hotspur demanded to see him."

Wat's temper stirred. "To gloat?"

"Nay, though that be what many feared. They say he spoke well o' him. He said the Douglas were a great man and that he'd mourn his loss as much as anyone, because he'd lived and died with honor and would be sorely missed."

"He will that," Wat agreed. "Is anyone else giving orders yet?"

"There's to be a meetin', Sir Hugh said. The earls o' Dunbar and Moray be takin' command. They'll blow the horn when they want ye, he said. They've already sent messengers off to tell Fife and Archie the Grim."

"Then until they blow that horn, let's keep my father comfortable and ready our lads and his to ride. With litters, we'll not make Hermitage until tomorrow, nor Rankilburn till late the day after. But I'm for camping in Scotland tonight if we can."

"I'm thinkin' we'd all best put England behind us, lest them fleein' villains learn how greatly they outnumber us," Tammy said. "But what if someone says we must go to Melrose wi' the Douglas's body tomorrow?"

"Whatever happens, we'll see to my father first."

Tammy frowned. "He'll say he's for Melrose."

Dryly, Wat said, "Ferniehurst lies on that road, and my mother is at Ferniehurst. So I'm guessing I'll have no trouble dissuading him. I need only suggest stopping there to let her see that he's in good health. Sithee, she is the one person who ignores his temper and who can nearly always make him mind her."

Tam chuckled. "Aye, I'd forgotten her ladyship were visiting Lady Jenny."

"Well, he won't have forgotten. We can count on that," Wat said.

⁓

Meg struggled to find the right words when Simon demanded to know why she and Amalie had come to Hermitage. She had mentally practiced explaining their presence there to Wat, but telling Simon required even greater finesse.

Tawny haired, dark eyed, and wearing a heavy frown as he stood over them, he looked grimmer and larger than when they had last seen him. Even knowing that the impression was due to thick padding beneath his chain mail, her own dislike of him, and a certain niggling guilt she felt about Tom's arrest, did little to aid Meg.

To give herself more time to think, she said, "Mercy, Simon, I thought you would be with the Earl of Fife. We heard that he was leading an enormous force into England from the west, with the Lord of Galloway."

"Aye, he is, but Fife does not take all his people with him wherever he goes, and I had duties to see to." He stepped onto the dais and set his visor on the table, adding, "My men are in the lower hall. I assume someone will look after them."

"Sir Ralph Lindsay is captain of the guard here," she said, wondering how Simon had managed to get to that hall without meeting him. "You must ask him."

"Lindsay, eh?" He shrugged. "Someone said Sir Ralph was seeing to a prisoner and that I should await him here. I saw no reason to ask for his exact identity. I've fifty men with me, but I suppose this place can accommodate them."

"Noblemen coming here usually provide for their entourages to camp outside the castle," Meg said. "Your men will have to sleep out there in any case, because there's not enough room inside. Also, I doubt we can feed so many extra."

"Nonsense," Simon retorted. "Is not Carrick arriving tomorrow? Do not tell me Douglas expected him to provide for his own men. There should be food aplenty for mine tonight."

Knowing he cared nothing about Carrick's men and would insist they had plenty even if his own men ate everything, Meg did not take up that gauntlet.

But Amalie said, "From what we know of the Earl of Carrick's kindness, I expect he will look after his own men."

Simon snorted. "If Carrick has ever spared a thought for aught but what he is reading or discussing with his priest, I've yet to hear of it. But you still have not told me, either of you, what you are doing here at Hermitage."

"We came with the Countess of Douglas," Meg said.

"The countess! Sakes, she is not here, too, is she?"

"Nay, for she has ridden to meet her brother."

"Where is he, then?"

"Staying the night at Dryburgh Abbey, I believe."

"Then I still fail to understand why you two are here by yourselves."

Meg shrugged, gave him a wry smile, and hoped Isabel would forgive her yet one more offense. "The countess asked us to accompany her here, but she did not invite us to go with her to Dryburgh," she explained, glad that at least she spoke the truth as far as it went. "Because of her large escort, we brought none of our men with us, so we have no choice now but to stay until my husband arrives to take us home. You do know that I am married, do you not?"

"I heard that, aye, from our mother. You married Buc-cleuch's heir."

"Aye, and he is with Douglas now. Have you learned yet how they fare?"

"Nay, only that Fife means to meet with Carrick and Douglas here when Douglas returns from England. According to the last message I had from Carlisle, Fife and Archie the Grim had a successful expedition, and Fife was sending word to Douglas to meet him. I expect they'll arrive together."

"Douglas must have succeeded, too, then," Amalie said, glancing at Meg. "After all, Fife counted on him to keep Hotspur from joining the royal army, and if Fife's effort in the west went well, he cannot have met any force greater than his own."

Meg understood that look to mean Amalie was recalling their discussion of Tom's motives. Doubtless, she assumed that a Scottish victory must spoil his plan, whatever it was, and now believed that it had failed completely.

However, her tone had been provocative, almost taunting, which made Meg want to shake her. Provoking Simon was never a good idea.

He did not seem to notice, for he said only, "I'm told Douglas took only knights, nobles, and a small foot force. 'Tis typical of his arrogance to think he could stop the Percies' huge army with so few. I'd not be surprised to hear that he's failed and that most of those with him either died or fell prisoner."

"What a thing to say to Meg, Simon, when her husband is one of them!"

Meg shot Amalie a look but made no outcry herself.

She had faith in Douglas and in Wat. Also, she was wondering how Simon knew so much about Douglas's plans and the makeup of his army—if all Simon had said was true.

"I cannot imagine what is taking that fellow Lindsay so long," he said abruptly. "Where is the prison in this place?"

"He'll be along soon, I'm sure," Meg said, shooting another look at Amalie.

For once, her sister understood her without difficulty, for she said, "Shall I send a gillie to fetch ale, Simon? You must be thirsty after such a long ride."

"Aye, I'd welcome a mug, so find someone to serve me. But then you two must go along up to your own chambers. This hall—indeed, this castle—is no place for gently reared females. I'm astonished that the countess abandoned you here."

Meg nearly spoke to defend Isabel but kept silent when she realized she could say nothing that would not reveal more than she wanted Simon to know.

Since she had to say something, she smiled and said, "'Tis an odd reunion for the three of us, is it not, sir?"

He nodded curtly, but seeing a gillie crossing the hall in response to Amalie's summons, he said, "Take yourselves off now. I'll see that someone sends your supper up later. I suppose you'll have to stay here until someone comes who can see you safely home again, but I'll have something to say to that husband of yours, Meg, about keeping a closer watch over you."

Amalie smiled sweetly and said, "It is always such a treat for us to see you."

He nodded, and Meg had to bite her lip. But alone in the stairway with Amalie, she muttered, "How do you dare, my dear? I'd not have been surprised had he slapped you for such impertinence."

"He was unaware of it, because he assumed that I meant it as a compliment," Amalie said. "Have you not seen as much before? One can lather him with false compliments, because he generally pays little heed to what women say to him. 'Tis because he thinks he is superior to us. It does not even occur to him that a woman might mock him, so he does not take note when one does."

"Well, you should take heed," Meg warned. "He does have a temper."

"Aye, sure, he does," Amalie agreed. "But arrogance is his predominant trait. Have you not wondered if he might be party to the mischief Tom tried to stir?"

"Surely, you cannot be suggesting that Simon has been spying on *Fife* for the Percies," Meg said. "It is one thing to believe that Tom was spying for them, Amalie, but Simon could gain naught by betraying Fife. Fife is even more dangerous than the Douglas, because Fife is so unpredictable. Moreover, Simon *admires* Fife."

As she spoke, a tickle stirred in the back of her mind, but Amalie's voice interrupted. "Did Tom chance to tell you how he wormed his way into the countess's employ?" she asked. "I doubt that he just wandered into her solar at Dalkeith or Tantallon and played his lute for her."

"I never thought to ask him," Meg admitted. But the tickling sense came again, stirring new thoughts. She said musingly, "Despite the four years that Tom fostered in England, he does generally follow Simon's lead, doesn't he?"

Amalie made a sound of disgust. "Tom tries to please everyone. Why, I have seen him change all in a moment from laughter to tears if he thinks tears more likely to impress someone. Also, Tom's the one who likes to take risks. Simon doesn't."

"No, he doesn't," Meg agreed. "Tears would not impress him either, and he has a strong sense of self-preservation."

"But Simon *might* exploit someone willing to take risks to impress him."

The tickling thought at the back of Meg's mind took solid shape at last. Amalie, with her knack for flitting from thought to seemingly unrelated thought, had suddenly touched on the heart of the matter.

"Simon answers to Fife," Meg murmured.

"Aye," Amalie said, pushing open their chamber door and going inside.

Following her, Meg said, "And Isabel suspects that Fife persuaded Carrick to come here for a reason other than just to visit a famous fortress as Carrick believes."

"That's true."

Meg shut the door. "Also, many folks believe that although two others stand before Fife in the succession to the throne, Fife intends to rule Scotland."

"He already does rule us, does he not, as Guardian of the Realm?"

"But he is not the heir to the throne, nor will he become King of Scots—"

"That has not troubled him before."

That was true, Meg told herself. Fife already acted in the King's name, and men said he would as easily continue to rule when Carrick became King. Even so . . .

"With Carrick dead," Meg said, "the only obstacle between Fife and the throne of Scotland would be Carrick's young son. But Fife stands next in line after the boy, so what happens if Carrick dies at Hermitage, a Douglas fortress, its inhabitants all fiercely loyal to Douglas?"

"You're suggesting that people would blame Douglas. But you're confusing me, Meg. Tom has as much as admitted that he spied for the Percies. If that is so, there can be no danger to Carrick now except in your head. Why would the English want him dead, or Douglas blamed? Carrick's death at Hermitage might weaken Douglas's power in the Borders, but surely, if the English had been victorious—"

"But don't you see, Amalie? That is my point. Fife is the one who declared that the Douglas wields too much power. Simon himself told us that, more than once. Hotspur would not seek to undermine him by sending raiders out to declare that Douglas had given them permission to poach on other men's lands. Recall that Douglas wields his power in Parliament, too, not just in the Borders. And, don't forget, Fife is the one who arranged for Carrick to come here."

"Sakes, Meg," Amalie said. "Surely, you cannot believe that Tom and Simon are acting on *opposing* sides, or that Tom has really been spying for Fife!"

"I'm not sure what Tom thinks he is doing," Meg admitted. "He is not as clever as Simon. But Tom is not acting alone. That has never been his way."

"Almost never," Amalie retorted bitterly.

"'Tis a rare man who does not act alone when he rapes a woman," Meg said. "Even so, Tom is following someone else's orders now. I'm sure of it. When you asked me if I knew how he came to join Isabel's household as a minstrel, something stirred in the back of my mind. What could be more likely than that Fife, her own brother, sent him to her? Or that Simon sent Tom under Fife's orders?"

"We have agreed that Simon does not like risking his own skin," Amalie said. "If he did place Tom with Isabel in Fife's name, it had to be under Fife's orders, but we'd have to ask Isabel to know for sure. I wish you had thought about all this whilst she was still here."

"If the object was to insert Tom into Douglas's household, Tom himself must have played a role in getting her to send him to Hermitage."

"Aye, well, he's a charmer; he'd have managed that," Amalie said. "But why would he have let us think he acted for the Percies, and what are we to do now? If Simon knew Tom was coming here, will he not be wondering where he is?"

"Perhaps, but he may think Tom went into hiding to avoid us," Meg said.

"That won't stop him from asking questions. And no one here has cause to conceal the minstrel's existence or the fact that he is a prisoner in the pit."

"You're right, of course. Since discovering how badly I misjudged Tom, I cannot seem to think sensibly," Meg said. "I don't know how he came to fool me so."

"He charms everyone," Amalie said. "He uses his charm like a weapon."

The door opened without ceremony, startling them both, and Simon walked in with Tom right behind him. Both men were clearly angry.

Simon said, "Can either of you tell me why they cast Tom into the pit?"

Meg returned his gaze stonily and said nothing, but Amalie said, "Why, how should we know? He told us himself that he came here to spy on the Douglas, so mayhap someone caught him at it. Spying is dangerous business, is it not?"

"You know exactly what happened, both of you," Tom said angrily. "I've already told Simon, but he doesn't believe you had aught to do with it. I'd like to know how else the countess's necklace could have got into my lute bag."

"Sakes, the most likely way is that you put it there," Amalie said.

"Why, you . . ." He strode toward her, but Meg jumped between them.

"Leave her alone," she snapped. "You've done her enough damage." Turning to Simon, she added in much the same tone, "Did he tell you what he did to her?"

"He told me she'd spun you a tale and that you'd apparently believed it."

"It was no tale," Amalie cried. "It is the truth! He raped me at the mill!"

"You see how it is, Simon," Tom said, shaking his head and rolling his eyes.

Simon nodded.

"Surely, someone can tell if a woman has lost her maidenhead," Amalie said.

Tom shook his head. "It's no use, lass. I told Simon how it was with us at the mill, how eager you were and that you were no longer a maiden when you offered yourself. Heaven knows how many men you'd had by then," he added with a sigh.

With a shriek, Amalie flew at him, fingernails aimed at his face, but he backhanded her and sent her reeling. She tripped against her own cot, fell headfirst across the near corner of it, and cracked her head against the floor.

Crying out, Meg took a step toward her, but Simon caught her by an arm.

"You can tend to her in a minute," he said. "First, tell me who else here or elsewhere knows that Giles Gilpin is our Tom?"

She kept silent until he raised his hand. Then she said, "Strike me if you like, Simon. You won't beat anything out of me. Sakes, Tom threatened to kill us both if we told anyone. It should be enough that I told him I'd keep his horrid secret."

"Then why did the countess leave today?" Tom demanded.

Forcing herself to ignore Amalie's moans, praying she was not badly hurt, Meg said, "She went to meet Carrick. I thought you knew as much."

"I don't believe you," he said. "She never said anything about going, and her necklace found its way into my bag rather too quickly after our talk yesterday."

"It doesn't matter," Simon said.

"Why not? Just because Meg gave her word? Amalie never gave hers."

"Amalie doesn't matter either," Simon said brutally. "The only thing that does matter is getting my men set and making sure all is ready here for Fife."

Amalie had curled onto the cot, her arms clenched across her stomach.

"Simon, she's hurt," Meg said fiercely. "Is what you are doing for Fife so important that you'd let Tom kill us or let Amalie lie in agony to keep his secret?"

"Tom's secret doesn't matter anymore either. He's done what I told him to do. But you and Amalie do create a nuisance. I can't have you prattling of this to anyone, so you will stay in this room until I release you."

"Here?"

"Yes, here. I've ordered one of my men to put bolts on the door, outside."

"You're locking us in?"

"Just until Douglas and Fife arrive tomorrow or Friday," Simon said.

Meg was shocked. Simon had never been her favorite brother, but she would not have believed he could act so despicably.

Chapter 20

*The parties were shouting, the kye they were routing,
Confusion did gallop, and fury did burn.*

Wat had expected their journey to be slow. But thanks to the small number of men wounded badly enough to need litters, the Borderers traveled swiftly by taking short turns carrying them. In this manner, they covered the fifteen miles to Carter Bar in less than three hours, crossing into Scotland just before midday on Thursday.

He did not intend to go any farther with the others, most of whom would accompany Douglas's body to Melrose Abbey. Seeking out the Earl of Dunbar, he reminded him that Carrick was expecting to meet Douglas at Hermitage.

"Sakes, I'd forgotten all about the man," Dunbar admitted. "In all the upset, I thought I'd done well to send a messenger to Dalkeith to inform the countess. Still, I expect we ought to tell Carrick, too. He'll want to attend his lordship's burial."

"You may also recall that Fife—"

"The devil fly away with Fife and all Stewarts," Dunbar snapped. "We've yet to get a reply to the last message I sent him. Heaven kens what mischief he'll try when he learns Douglas is dead, but by God, before then Moray and I mean to do as Douglas would want, not Fife."

"I can take word to Hermitage," Wat said. "I mean to head home from here in any event. For as much as my lord father would like to go to Melrose, his wound troubles me enough to insist that he return at once to Rankilburn to recover."

"Aye, that's a good notion," Dunbar agreed. "We're guessing that those retreating cowards, the English, must have greatly exaggerated our numbers and ability to their reinforcements when they met, because they've all turned back. So it looks to be just as Jamie predicted. If so, their border folk won't want to see us again soon. I'll wager 'tis the same in the west for Fife and Archie, since the last message we had from them indicated that the royal army had turned back as well."

Other men waited to talk to Dunbar, so Wat took his leave, and told Buccleuch of his decision. When the latter made no objection, he quickly, albeit quietly, ordered two of the laird's own men to ride to Ferniehurst and escort Lady Scott to the Hall.

"The Kerrs will provide as many other lads as you need for an escort," he told them. "Don't frighten her, because he is not at death's door, but do make haste. He will recover more swiftly if she is with him."

The men needed no further urging.

Wat lost no time then in giving orders to his own men, to Buccleuch's, and to Nebby Duffin. He also informed the other leaders they had recruited that they had his leave to choose for themselves whether to go home or ride on to Melrose.

The first hitch occurred when Buccleuch announced that he would ride.

"Sir, you should not," Wat protested. "Not only did you clout your head when you fell, but that wound—"

"Get me a horse," his father said. "My head aches like the devil and my leg like ten thousand devils, but the wound is bound up, and we'll get home much faster if I ride." When Wat hesitated, Buccleuch growled, "Don't try me, damn you."

Wat grinned at him. "I was much more worried when you seemed not to care about anything. If you're strong enough to snarl at me, I'll not fight you. You should know this, though," he added, still smiling. "I've sent for my lady mother."

Buccleuch grimaced, but he made no protest, so Wat left well enough alone. A short time later, their party of nearly a hundred men left the main army behind them.

Being back in Scotland stirred the exhilaration in him that such a return always produced, but before long he realized that despite his grief—and his concern for Buccleuch, which continued despite his father's steady seat in the saddle—the image paramount in his mind was not Douglas, Buccleuch, or Raven's Law.

It was Meg.

He kept seeing her in his mind's eye, imagining himself telling her all that had happened, discussing the trials in store for the Borders now with Douglas dead.

He knew she would listen. And he realized he looked forward to hearing her thoughts. He had recognized her sympathetic ear from the day they met, but it was more than that. He liked to talk with her.

They had talked much in the sennight they had worked together at the tower, discussing repairs he wanted to make and improvements she suggested. He thought about those discussions and about other, even more intimate discourse with her.

When he realized they were only a couple of miles from Elishaw, he said lightly to Tam, "Mayhap we should call on my good-father."

"Aye, and tell him all be safe, so he can come out again," Tam said dryly.

Wat chuckled. Murray had not shown his face at Southdean, or contributed men for the army. Wat hoped that when the old man learned how many captives the Scots had taken, most of whom would fetch heavy ransoms, he'd wish he *had* gone. Only men who had taken part in the battle would share in the ransoms.

Behind the riders, some of Neb's lads were herding a squalling mass of the lifted cattle. Thanks to the din, when the leaders—Wat, Buccleuch, Tam, and Neb—rounded a bend at some speed minutes later, and nearly ran onto the heels of a much smaller herd of cattle, mixed with a few horses, they did so without warning.

Reining in sharply with the others, Wat recognized two of the horses as his.

"Bless us, ye're a wizard," Tam exclaimed. "Ye've conjured up Murray!"

"Not just Murray," Wat replied, looking beyond the beasts and herders at the leaders. "If I'm not mistaken, that's our Sym riding beside him."

⁓

Amalie was not well. Swelling and a bruise already showed on her forehead, where it had struck the floor, and she was curled on the bed, holding her lower abdomen as intermittent, visible waves of pain jolted through her.

"Meggie, it hurts!" she cried, tensing and turning pale. "I've never felt anything like this. I thought it was just cramping because my flow is overdue, but it's much worse than—" Her words ended abruptly in a near scream.

Meg had tried pounding on the door, but if Simon had left anyone to guard it, the guard had not responded to her pounding. Hearing no sound from him at all, she suspected Simon had not bothered leaving anyone, trusting the bolts to hold them.

"Meg, what if I'm dying! Where *is* everyone?"

Drawing a deep breath, Meg said, "We are locked in. I cannot change that, so you must calm yourself. I know you are suffering, but wailing about it can do you no good. Think of murdering Simon if it helps, or Tom."

"I'm hot!"

"I'll pour some water on a cloth to put on your head. That will help, I think, but then you must try to relax."

To Amalie's credit, she tried. Meg could see the effort she made and tried to help her find a more comfortable position. But Meg could also see the way her hands trembled when she held herself against the waves of pain.

Whatever was happening was no normal monthly cramping. Moreover, if Amalie had not had her flow since mid-May, she was a full two months overdue.

Having caught sight of Wat and the others before Sym did, Murray greeted them cheerfully. "We heard ye'd routed the damned English. Well done! But meantime, lad, as ye can see for yourself, I've found summat that belongs to ye."

"Master Wat! I tried to tell this auld"—Sym broke off when Wat frowned, then continued innocently—"*gentleman* that I had to get to ye straightaway!"

Feeling suddenly chilled to his bones, Wat exclaimed, "Her ladyship? What's amiss, lad? Tell me quickly!"

"I'm trying to, aye. She sent me to find ye, to tell ye to come at once!"

"Here now," Murray protested. "Ye never told me that. I swear, lad, he said only that he was going to find you. I thought he was doing as he'd done before, following where he was not wanted. He gave me no explanation, just sputtered a lot of claptrap about what you'd do to me unless I let him go."

"I'll acquit you, but let him speak," Wat said curtly. "Why you, Sym? Where were Dod and the others?"

Looking bewildered, Sym said, "They be at Raven's Law, o' course."

"Then—?"

"Me lady be at Hermitage."

"Hermitage!" Wat heard the shriek in his own voice and tried to speak more calmly. "What is she doing at Hermitage?"

"She and the lady Amalie went there wi' the countess—"

"Not the Countess of Douglas!" Icy dread replaced the earlier chill.

"Aye, o' course. Me lady went with her to help get things ready for me lord Carrick, but there's nowt in any o' that," he added. "'Tis today I'm talking about. She were up at the screech o' dawn, sithee, because there be a spy at Hermitage."

Sym glanced at Murray.

"Go on," Wat urged.

"Aye, but why I didna tell the . . . this gentleman, is because the spy said he's a-doing it for the family—'*our* family,' he said." He looked warily again at Murray.

Murray frowned, exchanged a look with Wat, and said, "We've no spies in our family. Who was the man who said that?"

"His name be Giles Gilpin," Sym said. "He were the countess's minstrel, sithee, and he sings pretty enough. But he's a fool 'cause he said Scotland and England should be nobbut one country. That be plain daft."

Wat glanced at Buccleuch, who had remained uncharacteristically silent throughout. Although he looked pale, Wat knew better than to ask after his health, so he said quietly to him instead, "What do you think, sir?"

Watching Murray, Buccleuch said, "I think you'd do better to ask your good-father that question, but we're riding to Hermitage in any event." He drew a deep breath and then looked at Wat. "Whatever comes, you will give the orders. I'm fit enough to hold my own in a fracas, but you're *young* and fit, and she's your wife."

"Aye, and my daughter," Murray said fiercely. "I've no notion who her spy may be, but we'd do well to put our heads together on the way, lad." Without waiting for a response, he said to Sym, "What else did our Meg tell you?"

"Just to find Master Wat. But I did hear summat else," he admitted. "She did say he were spying for the damned Percies."

"That cannot be true," Wat said. "Hotspur was as eager for the fight as Douglas was, and just as chivalrous. He spoke of Douglas's honor as something he valued, scarcely words of a man who'd set spies to aid his cause. Moreover, he had no idea how many men Douglas had raised, and we'd made no secret of the numbers as we learned who would follow Douglas. Any self-respecting spy at Hermitage must have known that only a small force would cross the line at Carter Bar, whilst the main mass of the army entered England from the west."

Murray looked thoughtful, but Sym said stoutly, "Me lady said he spied for the Percies, and he didna deny it. He said their family be half English and that no Englishman trusts the Douglas. Damn fools, the English are, if you ask me!"

Amalie's agonies continued, and Meg's sense of helplessness increased, making the afternoon crawl by at a snail's pace. Meg knew, too, that there would be no respite or help for them until suppertime. Simon would send food up eventually, but she knew he would make no effort to do so until he was good and ready.

She felt wretched. All she could do was try to help Amalie bear her pain. To that end, she retold stories she had told her as a child and reminded her of memories they shared. But although Amalie had intervals of lesser pain, they were growing fewer and farther apart. She was sweating and frightened, and Meg was certain that nothing they were doing was having much effect.

Learning that Murray was on his way to Hermitage to leave Wat's cattle and horses there as a last-ditch thumbing of his nose at the decision of Douglas and the wardens' court, Wat said, "You meant me to drive them home myself, I expect."

"And why should ye not?" Murray asked. "Ye were bound to travel wi' Douglas back to Hermitage. Why should I have had to drive 'em to Rankilburn?"

Wat wanted to ask about Meg's dowry, but he had already realized that there were half again as many beasts in the herd as Murray's men had taken.

It was hardly a great dowry, but at that moment, with Buccleuch, Tammy, and Neb there to hear everything they said, he had no wish to fratch with the man.

Uncertain how far he could trust him, Wat agreed warily to ride with him at least to that part of Liddesdale nearest the side glen where Hermitage stood.

"I'm thinking we should waste no time," he said to the others. "If Sym's spy has friends, they may all be inside the castle now. Sakes, if there are enough of them, they may have taken control of it." He still did not believe that Hotspur was behind whatever was going on at Hermitage, but he could think of at least one man who had long resented the Douglases' control of the fortress. "We'll go faster if we leave the herd behind with enough men to drive it, whilst the rest of us—"

"Wi' respect, sir," Neb Duffin said. "If ye're uncertain o' your welcome when ye reach Hermitage, have ye considered what a grand diversion a herd o' squalling cattle makes? I'm thinking o' sheer numbers and nuisance, mind ye."

Wat grinned and looked at Murray, whose eyes began

to twinkle. Even Buccleuch took more interest as they formed their plan.

By the time they reached Hermitage, the only banner flying was Murray's, and Murray rode in the lead. Sym rode with the herdsmen, while Wat, Buccleuch, Tammy, and their other men scattered themselves among the men from Elishaw.

Buccleuch, deeming himself the only one likely to be easily recognized by any spy, had wrapped a filthy rag, generously donated by Neb Duffin, around his head.

Although Wat had approved the final plan, he still had little faith in Murray but hoped he cared enough to help Meg and Amalie, if they did need help.

If Sym was right and a Murray already controlled things inside Hermitage—if, in fact, anyone but Sir Ralph Lindsay controlled aught there—the likelihood was that Sir Iagan would cast his lot either with the Murray or with no one at all. After all, to Wat's own knowledge, the man had never cast it anywhere but with his own.

The drawbridge across the great ditch began to come down when the riders emerged from the trees after fording Hermitage Water and turned uphill toward it.

The castle's vantage point on the rise gave it a view of much of Liddesdale as well as the opening of its own small glen, so Wat was sure the watchers inside had seen the herd despite trees lining both sides of the river. But none inside would think the herd formed any sort of a threat. Nor did it, he thought with a smile.

No one was coming to greet them, so Sir Ralph either was expecting Murray or knew of the wardens' order to produce Wat's cattle and horses and Meg's dowry, and was unsurprised to see him at Hermitage—or whoever controlled the castle in Lindsay's place knew that Murray presented no threat to him.

Wat bided his time but kept as near as he dared to Sir Iagan, who rode right to·the main entrance steps and looked up at the guards on the portcullis parapet.

None flanked the main entrance today. Both portcullises were down.

"Where's the captain o' your guard?" Murray shouted. "I ha' kine to deliver, by order o' the march wardens and the Douglas himself."

Wat noted, somewhat to his own amusement, that the noisy cattle were already making their presence felt. Their constant lowing made it difficult to hear what the guard on the parapet was shouting back at Murray.

Men had camped in the area between the castle and the chapel, and on the hillside above the latter, and the cattle, uncaring of property rights or even water-filled ditches, were milling outward from Hermitage Water to surround the little stone chapel and spread up the hillsides.

They milled toward the castle, too, although the deep, wide ditch across which the drawbridge lay stopped them on the far side. The men on horseback kept them off the bridge.

Murray shook his head. He could not hear the guards.

A short time later, two other men appeared on the parapet with them.

Although Wat thought Murray must have expected to see someone he knew, the man looked nonetheless astonished. The two newcomers looked a good deal alike. Both had tawny hair and similar features. The elder was thicker of body than the younger and had a harsher look to him. The younger one was smiling, the elder not.

The two conferred, and the elder shouted, "Welcome,

Father! We are glad to see you. Tell your lads to move those cattle back across the river and make camp for themselves. Then come inside. We've a surprise for you."

"What ha' ye done wi' the captain o' Douglas's guard?" Murray shouted.

"For the present, I am he," the elder one said. "Or mayhap Tom is."

Neb Duffin had moved up beside Wat. "That 'un doing the talking, sir?"

"Aye?"

"That be the Douglas's man," Neb said. "The one as said we had his lordship's permission to hunt in the Forest and take wood."

"Find Sym and bring him to me, Neb," Wat said. "Don't draw attention to yourself, but make haste."

~

Meg was refreshing the damp cloth with water from the basin when Amalie said, "Meg, I . . . I think something is happening. Oh . . . oh, Meggie! Oh, God!"

A light knock sounded on the door. But Meg was staring at a rapidly spreading pool of what looked like blood forming beneath her sister. For a moment, she did not take in the light sound, or other muffled ones that followed.

Just as she did turn blindly toward the door, it opened and Sym said urgently as he slipped inside, "Keep that row down, will ye! I dinna ken who may be about!"

"How'd you get in here?"

"By yon postern door and the service stairs, o' course. I came to tell ye—"

"Never mind that," Meg interjected as Amalie screamed

again. "Run and get help, Sym. Something is dreadfully wrong with the lady Amalie."

He was already staring at Amalie, his narrow face blanching. But he turned back to Meg and said, "The master canna help, but your da's here, and—"

"Did you not hear me, Sym? We need *help*, but not a man unless you can bring one who knows doctoring. I . . . I think she may be . . ." Realizing even in her distress that Amalie would not thank her for describing her suspicions to Sym or to their father, she said instead, "Is there no woman anywhere nearby, Sym?"

"Nay . . . or wait now, let a man think. The cook has a sister who comes wi' fresh eggs for him every day. If she's no here now, she'll be nearby. I'll find her."

He ran out.

Meg had not known of the cook's sister but realized now that a sister who came every day might well be unmarried and know no more than she did herself about what most likely ailed Amalie. Deciding she ought to have asked him for a married woman, she hovered on the brink of running to find someone herself. An inner voice warned not to be a ninny. She could not leave her sister.

In any event, she would likely run into Simon or Tom and find herself locked in again, because even if she should find her father, he was doubtless in league with her brothers by now. He would not let them harm her, but neither, with Simon there, was he likely to help her.

She knew then that she had not been thinking straight since Amalie's first cry of pain. Had she spared but a thought to the matter, she must have realized that Simon's men were likely to have taken over all of Hermitage by then. But if so, what had Sym meant when he'd said what he had about the master?

Sym darted back in again. "I forgot to tell ye, Master Wat's with your da'!"

~

In the upper hall, Wat stood silently in the group of men that had accompanied Sir Iagan inside, trying to assess the situation. Buccleuch, fearing he would be quickly recognized inside, had stayed outside with the herdsmen.

Sir Iagan had made no objection to Wat's company, having informed his sons only that although the men looking after the cattle could remain with the herd, he would bring a few of the others inside in case they had use for them.

So far, he had not identified Wat.

Only Wat and two of Sir Iagan's men had gone all the way to the upper hall with him. Sir Iagan had told his sons the others would await him in the lower hall.

"'Tis more suitable for the likes o' them, Simon," he'd said.

"Who's that fellow?" the one that Neb had identified replied.

Wat stiffened when the man pointed to him but tried to look harmless, and to make himself believe that he could trust his father-in-law.

"That's Wat Graham," Sir Iagan said. "Your cousin Jed Murray sent him to me after we talked o' finding someone to train our lads better to defend Elishaw."

So far, so good, Wat told himself, hoping his face revealed no expression and wondering where the devil Meg was. Murray had not mentioned her, nor did his sons. The younger one had not said anything at all after greeting his father.

Tam had gone with Sym to the postern door at the back of the gate tower, and would bring more of their men in that way if Murray's sons or their men had not already learned of its existence. That he had not yet seen Tam was worrisome.

Simon Murray seemed to accept him as some sort of upper retainer his father had hired, and clearly Simon was the one in charge.

The three Murrays had been chatting for a time of nothing in particular when Sir Iagan said abruptly, "What the devil are the pair o' ye up to here, anyway?"

The younger man looked down at his feet, but Simon said, "We are doing our duty, sir. Without knowing what has come to pass with the Douglas in England, we must make sure that Hermitage does not fall into the wrong hands."

"I'd have expected Douglas to leave it well guarded," Sir Iagan said.

"Evidently not," Simon said with an all-encompassing gesture.

"And who suggested this course to you?" his father asked.

Just then, Wat saw his own man, Snirk Rabbie of Cold-heugh, and Snirk's brother Jeb slip past the archway that led to the garderobe. Another familiar face showed itself briefly before ducking out of sight again.

But where was Tam?

~

"I couldna bring the cook's sister, so I brought Tammy instead," Sym said as he opened the door without knocking and walked in.

Meg jumped up from beside Amalie and stepped in front of her.

"I . . . I don't think Tammy can help us, Sym, but thank you—"

"I can if she'll let me, my lady," Tammy said quietly. "Sym told me what he'd seen, and if it be as I think it may, my sister had the same thing happen. I helped the midwife when she came to us."

"I pray you, Meg, let him stay," Amalie said, gasping. "We don't know what to do, and I'm too tired now to care who it is. Tammy is kind, and I trust him."

Meg nodded, however reluctantly, and Tammy passed her, saying, "Sym, lad, fetch towels and warm water from the kitchen. Then, my lady, if you'll find her some fresh clothes, we can see about getting her cleaned up and more comfortable. I should have a look first, though, to see what's what, as ye might say."

Gritting her teeth, Meg looked to Amalie to make that decision.

"Whatever you need to do, Tammy, just do it," her sister said weakly. "At least the pain has eased. The waves still come, but they are not so bad now."

"That be good, that is," he said. "And yon mess be good, too, lass. The midwife did say that bad things can happen if there be too little bleeding."

Ignoring his informality, Meg hurriedly sought fresh clothing for Amalie. They had long since loosened everything she was wearing, so that she wore only a loose kirtle over her shift now. Finding what she needed in a nearby kist, she set the clothes at hand, so she could help Amalie dress when she was ready. Then, unwilling to watch Tammy perform his examination, she went to the doorway to watch for Sym. The boy did not need to see any more than was necessary.

"Meg," Amalie said a few moments later. "The way you keep looking back at Tammy and me, and wincing, reminds me forcibly of our lady mother."

"Then I won't look," Meg promised. "I'm just waiting for Sym, so he need not come into the room."

"My lady, I did tell Master Wat I'd be at hand for him downstairs," Tammy said. "If ye could make your way far enough down the main stairs to glean some notion of what might be happening in the upper hall . . ."

"I can't leave you alone with her, Tammy," Meg said, although the temptation to do as he asked was nearly overpowering. "You must know that."

"Meg, don't be ridiculous," Amalie said. "His being here is not nearly as bad as what happened to put me in this situation. But you look so uncomfortable that you're embarrassing me more than he is. Do go see what you can see."

"But Sym will—"

"He won't run in without speaking up first," Tammy said. "I can tell him to stay out of the room and just go and take the water and towels from him. Lady Amalie is already more like herself now, so she'll do well enough."

"Then I can stay with her, and you can go help Sir Walter," Meg said.

"Meg, much as I love you, I do wish you would go away," Amalie said. "Truly, I don't know why it is, but the plain truth is that I don't mind Tammy helping me with this nearly as much as I would mind your doing so."

Although she disapproved, Meg needed no further encouragement.

Neither of the two Murray brothers had replied to Sir Iagan's question.

Visibly nettled, he said, "How can ye say ye've done your duty if ye canna tell your own father what *duty* ye're speaking of?"

When neither answered, he looked to the younger. "What are ye doing here, Tom? I thought ye were at Eyemouth, serving Sir Amos Biggar."

"Not when Simon had need of me," Tom said. "I did think, though, that—" He broke off, flushing, and looked to Simon.

"He thought he was serving the Percies, sir," Simon said. "He's such a prattler and lackwit that one did not want to tell him the truth."

"And just what is the truth, Simon? Tell them that," Meg said from somewhere behind Wat.

He felt overwhelming relief to hear her voice and nearly smiled as he turned to see her standing at the main entrance to the hall. He stopped the smile before it did more than twitch his lips, but only because of the way she looked.

The lass that, during much of his absence, he had lustily been picturing naked was a rare mess, and everyone was looking at her now. One side of her gray skirt was coated with a substance that looked to his experienced eye like fresh blood.

The only thing that stopped him from rushing to her side was that he was sure it was not hers. She was too angry to have lost that much of her own blood.

Her color was high, her hands were on her hips, and she had fire in her eyes.

"Meg, what are you doing here?" Sir Iagan demanded with credible bewilderment, considering his foreknowledge. "This is no place for a woman."

"I am not the only woman here, sir," she said curtly. "Amalie is upstairs. Tom struck her, and she is badly hurt. As you can see," she added, dramatically spreading her skirt to show the worst of the blood.

"Bless the child! What did you do to her, Tom?"

"Nobbut what she asked for, as usual," Tom snapped.

"You are right, though, Father," Simon said. "Neither of them belongs here. Go back upstairs, Meg, unless you want to deal with me."

Just then, Snirk Rabbie stepped into the hall through the garderobe archway with his sword drawn. Catching Wat's eye, he nodded toward the other end as two other men appeared at the main entrance, flanking Meg.

Wat took a step forward, bringing himself even with Sir Iagan. "When you speak to my lady wife, Simon Murray, you will speak with due respect. My men, not yours, are now in control of Hermitage, and the Douglas's men are free."

"What business is this of yours? What the devil?" Simon exclaimed. Seeing more men in the garderobe archway, he drew his sword. Tom did the same.

"Seize them, lads," Wat ordered.

"Hold now," Sir Iagan bellowed. Turning to Wat, he said, "I'll grant ye, they seem to be up to mischief here, but would ye break your word of honor *now*, lad? D'ye forget that ye've sworn never to take up arms against me or mine? Tell your men to lower their weapons."

Wat stared at him in dismay.

Snirk Rabbie kept his sword at the ready, but looked to Wat for orders.

Meg said calmly, "Sir Walter may have made you such a promise, Father, but I never did."

"Aye, and what of it? D'ye think to take up arms against your brothers?"

"No, sir, but I have no need to do that. Recall that you made Sir Walter's men swear to serve me before you freed them. I command them now to arrest Simon and Tom for trying to seize Hermitage Castle from its rightful owner."

"There is no rightful owner," Simon said. "This will become a royal castle."

"What do you mean?" Meg demanded. "Hermitage belongs to the Douglas."

"Aye, it did, but he is most likely dead by now," Simon said.

"That's true, he is," Wat said grimly, eliciting a gasp from Meg and a wide-eyed look of shock from Sir Iagan. "He died a great hero in a battle that routed Hotspur's army and sent them running home. And Hotspur is a captive in the hands of the Douglases, who are now marching to Melrose Abbey to see to Jamie's burial. Soon there will be a new Earl of Douglas, though, and Hermitage will pass to him. But I'd like very much to know how you learned of Douglas's death."

"That is no concern of yours," Simon said. "What may be of more concern is that my lord Fife is on his way here now with a great army. He'll take Hermitage and not care if Douglas is dead or not. Nor will he allow you to keep me prisoner."

"You overestimate Fife's power in the Borders," Wat said calmly. "Recall that in Scotland, unlike England, even a royal Stewart commands only his own vassals and those of other noblemen willing to support him. Fife's present army, however large, is not his own. Indeed, Douglases comprise the bulk of it. If you think they will support him whilst he takes Hermitage, you are much mistaken. I begin to suspect that Fife may have anticipated Douglas's death."

"Aye, well, believe what you like. It will not matter in the end."

"It will matter," Meg said clearly. "For one thing, the Countess of Douglas had her own suspicions about what has been going on and has doubtless warned Carrick that a trap may await him here. Be it your plan or Fife's, Simon, it has failed. Seize them, lads!"

Snirk Rabbie and the others quickly disarmed the Murray brothers.

Meg looked at her father. "I'm sorry if you do not like what I've done here, sir, or think it disloyal to our family name. But I am a Scott now. My loyalty lies with them and their allies, although I mean no disrespect to you. Indeed, I hope that one day you may become one of those allies."

"Sakes, lass," Sir Iagan said. "If your lady mother and I tried to teach your brothers anything, it was to steer clear of political mischief. What comes of it will come, but likely ye'll take your own road, and your sisters will, as well."

"I expect we will, sir, but I'm glad you are not vexed with me."

Wat smiled at her, and she smiled back.

Sir Iagan, looking from one to the other, said, "Lassie, I never thought I'd see a man look at ye the way he does. Nor did I ever expect to see ye look at a man the way you look at him. But by the Rood, I see now that when I arranged your wedding, I did a gey fine thing!"

Chapter 21

So Wat took Meg to the forest sae fair
And they lived a most happy and peaceable life . . .

Before leaving Hermitage, Wat had discussed things with Sir Ralph Lindsay and Sir Iagan. The latter seemed oddly unconcerned to see his sons held prisoner there.

Questioned, he said, "Had they been doing as apparently Tom thought he was, and aiding the Percies, I could understand it better. Their mother, bless her, has told them since they were bairns how fine her English kinsmen are. But to have enmeshed themselves in Fife's affairs was nobbut daft. I doubt even Simon kens the full extent of that scoundrel's predilection for mischief."

"Still, you cannot wish to see them hang, sir. Much as I dislike what they did to Meg and Amalie, and their attempt to seize Hermitage, I don't want to see that. Meg will be distressed to realize she had aught to do with such a fate for them."

"Tell her not to fash herself," Sir Iagan recommended. "Fife will see to Simon, I warrant, and Tom did nowt against Border law that anyone can prove."

"He misrepresented himself to the Countess of Douglas," Wat reminded him.

"Aye, sure, but with a beautiful lass like that one, any handsome young man may be forgiven. Moreover, if Simon did not do whatever he did under Fife's orders, I'll be astonished, and Fife protects his own. His minions will not betray him. Simon won't, I promise ye, and he'll see that Tom does nowt that's daft."

They left the castle in Sir Ralph Lindsay's control with as many of Buccleuch's men as they could spare to aid him. Even Murray offered to leave some, but Sir Ralph politely declined, and Wat did not blame him.

Then, with Meg seeing to Amalie, and Wat preparing for their departure and having to keep an eye on his father as they traveled as well as help get everyone settled at Scott's Hall after they arrived, they had little time to talk privately.

Meg had told him only that Amalie had recovered sufficiently from her injury to insist on riding and did not want to talk to anyone, especially her father.

Wat had assumed that Tom must have slapped the lass and given her a bloody nose, which would account for the blood on Meg's skirt. He had also noted a lump on Amalie's forehead, though, and now suspected Tom had done more. He would have asked Meg to explain it all, but no sooner did they take to their beds that night than they both fell fast asleep, exhausted by the activities of the past few days.

Janet Scott arrived before noon the next day, having set out before dawn, and found Wat and Meg together in the great chamber.

"I'm glad you sent for me so quickly," she said, hugging Wat. "Where is he?"

"Where should he be, madam, but in his wee room, poring over some documents that he says he must see to before day's end?"

"Oh, does he?" she said. "I'll just see about that."

Wat put his arm around Meg's shoulders as Janet bustled away to deal with Buccleuch, and smiled when Meg looked at him, her beautiful eyes soft with affection, or, he dared to hope, with love.

"Didst miss me, lass?" he asked, turning her to face him.

"More than you can imagine," she said, raising his hand to her cheek. "I was so glad to see you there beside my father. Then, when he reminded you of your oath to him, I knew just what to do. I was not sure you would approve, but I had to try, if only to startle Simon and Tom into dropping their guard before someone got hurt."

He would not spoil the moment by telling her that his men had control of the castle by then, thanks to Nebby's lot outside with Buccleuch and his own inside with her father's men. To be sure, Simon or Tom might have been injured, or been able to injure someone else before they submitted, but they would have submitted.

"Of course I approved," he said. "Not only have I learned to appreciate your good sense, but I was proud of you for thinking so quickly. You disarmed them, and I think you astonished your father. He was proud of you, too. He must have asked me six or seven times afterward if I'd ever seen the like. 'To throw me own words in me face like that,' he told me. 'She's the very spit of her mother.'"

"He never said any such thing!" she exclaimed, looking horrified.

"He did, aye, and what's more, from him that's a compliment, my love."

"Oh, what did you call me?"

"You heard me," he said, pulling her closer and kissing her.

She glowed, and the slow smile that he'd been waiting for appeared. "Do you really love me?"

"Sakes, do I have to prove it? Come up to my chamber, sweetheart, and I'll demonstrate my feelings for you until you squeal for mercy."

"I won't squeal. When did you know?"

"You tell me first."

"Tell you when *you* knew or when I did?"

"You."

"When I faced my dilemma."

Bewildered, he said, "What dilemma?"

"Sithee, I had given Tom my word that I'd tell no one who he was or what he was doing at Hermitage. I ken fine that you hold your word of honor dear, and I did not want to disappoint you by failing to keep mine. So I promised Tom I'd keep his secret, but that was before I learned that he had raped Amalie."

"He's the one? He *deserves* to hang," Wat said curtly.

"Aye, perhaps. I had always thought family was the most important tie, but honor matters little to my brothers and my father. I have heard them brag of tricking others by lying to them, just as Simon did with Nebby Duffin and his men."

"So how did you decide?" he asked, putting an arm

around her again, this time so that he could gently steer her toward the stairway.

"As I tried to decide what to do, I came to realize that you were no longer a husband forced on me, or I the wife that my father had forced to marry you. You *are* my family now. I had thought of little but you since the morning you rode away to join Douglas. And every time I'd think of you, my heart warmed all through."

He hugged her but kept her moving. "Did you break your word then?"

She hesitated, but he waited patiently. "I did not exactly break it, because I did not tell anyone who he was or why he'd said he was there. I did tell Countess Isabel to go to Dryburgh and persuade Carrick to go with her to Dalkeith or Tantallon." She stopped in her tracks. "Faith, who will tell her about Douglas's death?"

"Sir Ralph Lindsay knew she had gone to Dryburgh and sent a party of men under his deputy to find her as soon as I told him what had happened. It will be hard for her, but she will be with people who care about her."

"She adored him, you know," she said, looking up at him again.

"Aye, and he thought of her at the end," he said, seeing no reason to mention that Douglas had regretted their lack of a son. At the stairway, he gave her a little nudge, and she went ahead of him, giving him a fine view of her backside as she did.

"I've told you much more now than just how I realized I loved you," she said over her shoulder. "How did *you* know?"

"First, tell me what happened to Amalie at Hermitage," he said gently.

She hesitated again on the landing outside their bedchamber door, then with a straight look at him, she said, "Come inside first and shut the door."

He obeyed, moving toward her again when they were alone inside, but she held up a hand, stopping him. "You will say that I ought to have told you before, but I could not, and you must promise to say nothing to my father."

"That's easy enough," he said. "Now, tell me."

"You already know that Tom raped her. What you don't know is that she was pregnant. I thought she might be, but we weren't sure. She had cramping, so we thought her flow was about to begin, but after Tom struck her, the cramps grew much worse. There was blood. Then Sym came, and I sent him for help. He brought Jock's Wee Tammy."

"Tam?" He did not try to hide his astonishment.

"Aye, and he knew exactly what to do. He said he helped his sister once."

"I remember that, but did Amalie not mind? I'd have thought . . ."

"If you're thinking she'd have preferred my help, you are wrong. She sent me away, said it was easier with Tammy helping her."

Frowning, he said gently, "Your parents should know of this."

"Aye, I agree," she said. "But it is Amalie's tale to tell, not mine or yours. For now, she won't speak of it to anyone, and she wants to stay here."

He nodded. "Of course, she can stay as long as she likes."

"Now, do you still love me?" she asked with a wry smile.

"Aye, sweetheart, more than ever. Now, come here."

"Not until you tell me when you first knew."

He told her what he had dreamed the night the battle began. Then, chuckling at the memory, he said, "Sweetheart, any knight worth his spurs who can dream so deeply with combat near at hand, and who feels as irked as I did at being wakened to find a battle raging all around him, just has to be in love. If he's not, he's nobbut a lust-ridden fool. I may be lust-ridden when I'm with you, but I'm no longer a fool."

"But I'm so plain," she said matter-of-factly.

"You are not plain, and never say so to me again," he said, drawing her near and gently stroking her cheek. "This wise and sensible face is just the wall behind which your treasures lie hidden. That few others can see what I see, or know as much about you as I have learned, is a wonder to me. As folks come to know you, they do see much of that, though. So, in time, all who know us will understand that I've fallen in love with your goodness of heart, the way you listen with all your mind and soul, your compassion for others, and your obvious deep admiration for me."

She laughed then. But she reached out a hand to him and said, "I have other treasures you admire almost as much, sir. Perhaps you should do more exploring."

With alacrity, he accepted her invitation, and . . .

The langer he kend her, he loved her the mair,
For a prudent, a virtuous, and sensible wife.

Thus wooed they in the good old days;
And, pitying reader, though you stare,
The last, the sweetest minstrel says,
These lived and died a loving pair.

—Lady Louisa Stuart
"Ugly Meg, or The Robber's Wedding"

Dear Reader,

I hope you enjoyed *Border Wedding*. The character of Wat Scott is based on that of Sir Walter Scott, fourth Lord of [Buccleuch], Rankilburn, and Murthockston (holding that title from 1389 to 1402). He inherited the title from his father, Robert Scott, who was laird (lord) from 1346 to 1389. Sir Walter's actual wife is unknown.

The reason for the brackets around Buccleuch above is that it is generally left out of fourteenth-century titles but is considered the earliest title of their descendant, the present Duke of Buccleuch and Queensbury. The Buck Cleuch was their holding and the legend about it well known in 1388, so I included that title for my characters.

I based the character Meg Murray on Muckle-mouth Meg, the subject of an old Scott tale that was the basis of James Hogg's ballad "The Fray of Elibank," as well as Sir Walter Scott's poem "The Reiver's Marriage," the gist of which he shared in letters with Lady Louisa Stuart, who wrote her own comic poem, called "Ugly Meg, or The Robber's Marriage" as a joke to share with Sir Walter.

All three authors believed an anecdote suggesting that Muckle-mouth Meg Murray of Elibank married the heir of an infamous reiver, Auld Wat (Walter) Scott of Harden, near the end of the sixteenth century. Documentary evidence now proves, however, that Wat Scott's son, William, married a woman named Agnes Murray, not Margaret Murray of Elibank, and the marriage documents show that the negotiations for their marriage were leisurely, friendly, and took months to complete.

One of my hobbies is family history, when I have time for it, and over the years I have encountered many anecdotes that have turned out to apply to ancestors other than the ones named. That experience has taught me that such anecdotes, particularly the really good ones, tend to link themselves over time with the best-known ancestors. Often the names are not even the same, but one can usually track enough of the details to know where the anecdote applies.

I therefore looked back through the family tree and found Sir Walter Scott with no wife known (although he produced legitimate children, including his heir). The general history of the Borders at the time matches much of that of the end of the sixteenth century, Wat of Harden's time. Strife with England was paramount, and in 1388 a powerful Border lord (the second Earl of Douglas) was trying to keep peace among his own people in order to deal better with the English just as an equally powerful Border lord (a direct descendant of the hero of this book, known as Sir Walter Scott of Buccleuch) did at the end of the sixteenth century.

Buck Cleuch (the source of the name Buccleuch), Rankilburn, and Scott's Hall are all real, although the version of the Hall that I've described was in Peebles. The legend of the stag and the title Ranger of Ettrick Forest are real and part of Scott family lore. There was originally a peel tower at Rankilburn, but Raven's Law and its location in the cleuch sprang from the author's imagination.

That said, for you who adore words and their origins, "peel" or "pele" in the sense of a peel tower is cognate with "pale" and means "enclosure." Thus, when one said "beyond the pale," one originally meant "outside the tower wall."

The quotations cited as part of the chapter headings come from "The Fray of Elibank" by James Hogg, also known as the Ettrick Shepherd, and from "The Battle of Otterbourne" (*Minstrelsy of the Scottish Border*, by Sir Walter Scott).

I did change the words "Ancrum" and "Sowden" (battles fought by the Scotts of Harden) for the heading of Chapter 6 to Durham and Carlisle (battles in which James, second Earl of Douglas, proved his prowess several years before Otterburn). James Douglas was a phenomenal warrior. The mace with which he fought in close quarters was said to be too heavy for two other men to lift—together.

As for the contest between Douglas and Hotspur at Newcastle, the general belief has long been that the item found after Hotspur was carried from the field was the Percy pennon. According to J. Rutherford Oliver (*Upper Teviotdale and The Scotts of Buccleuch*, Hawick, 1887, p. 52), the item "really consisted of a pair of gauntlets, evidently a lady's, bearing the lion of the Percies . . . and may have been a *gage-de-amour.* They are still in the possession of descendants of the Douglas."

Sources for the Battle of Otterburn itself are varied and include a number mentioned here, including Oliver and Fraser, as well as *Scottish & Border Battles & Ballads* by Michael Brander (New York, 1975).

According to the chronicler Froissart, "Of all the battles described in history, great and small, that of Otterburn was the best fought and the most severe; for there was not a man, knight, or squire, who did not acquit himself gallantly, hand to hand with the enemy" (cited by Oliver, pp. 50–52). Scottish losses numbered just over a hundred with four times that many wounded, just a few seriously.

The English lost more than eighteen hundred dead, with another thousand wounded or taken prisoner, including Hotspur and his brother Sir Ralph Percy.

The postern door at Hermitage does exist but is believed to be a slightly later renovation. I added it to the 1388 castle to give Sym a way inside.

Other sources include *The Scotts of Buccleuch* by William Fraser (Edinburgh, 1878), *Steel Bonnets* by George MacDonald Fraser (New York, 1972), *The Border Reivers* by Godfrey Watson (London, 1975), and *Border Raids and Reivers* by Robert Borland (Dumfries, Thomas Fraser, date unknown).

If you enjoyed *Border Wedding,* please look for Amalie's story, *Border Lass,* at your favorite bookstore in September 2008. In the meantime, *suas Alba!*

Sincerely,

Amanda Scott

http://home.att.net/~amandascott

About the Author

AMANDA SCOTT, *USA Today* best-selling author and winner of Romance Writers of America's RITA/Golden Medallion awards, *Romantic Times*' Career Achievement Award for British Isles Historical, and Romantic *Times*' Awards for Best Regency Author and Best Sensual Regency, began writing on a dare from her husband. She has sold every manuscript she has written. She sold her first novel, *The Fugitive Heiress*—written on a battered Smith Corona—in 1980. Since then, she has sold many more, but since the second one, she has used a word processor. More than twenty-five of her books are set in the English Regency period (1810–20); others are set in fifteenth-century England and fourteenth- to eighteenth-century Scotland. Three are contemporary romances.

Amanda is a fourth-generation Californian who was born and raised in Salinas and graduated with a bachelor's degree in history from Mills College in Oakland. She did graduate work at the University of North Carolina at Chapel Hill, specializing in British history, before obtaining her master's in history from San Jose State University. After graduate school, she taught for the Salinas City

School District for three years before marrying her husband, who was then a captain in the Air Force. They lived in Honolulu for a year, then in Nebraska, where their son was born, for seven years. Amanda now lives with her husband in northern California. She is a fellow of the Society of Antiquaries of Scotland.

MORE PASSION,
ADVENTURE, AND
ROMANCE ON
THE SCOTTISH BORDERS!

Please turn this page
for a preview of

Border Lass

AVAILABLE IN MASS MARKET

SEPTEMBER 2008

Chapter 1

⁓

Scone Abbey, 14 August 1390

Scotland's long-awaited Coronation Day had come at last, and a vast crowd had gathered to see what they could see. Although it might be hours yet before the coronation was over and the newly crowned High King of Scots emerged from the abbey kirk, the teeming mass already overflowed the abbey grounds.

Scone Abbey sat on a terrace above the flat vale of the river Tay a few miles north of Saint John's town of Perth. The monastic buildings lay east and west of the kirk, while to its north stood a higher mound of grassy land, known as Moot Hill.

Only minutes before, John Stewart, Earl of Carrick and heir to the throne of Scotland, had made his awkward way to the kirk from Abbot's House, a three-story gray-stone building located between the kirk and the eastern monastic buildings. While he prepared for the ceremony, the rest of those attending would take their places.

The kirk being modestly appointed and small for its ilk, only royal family members, their attendants, and the higher-ranking nobility would be allowed inside. Even so, the crowd was enormous. Nearly everyone who was anyone had come, as well as many hundreds of lesser estate or no estate at all.

John of Carrick's passage had occasioned much comment. He was thin, stooped, and pale, looked much older than his fifty years, and thanks to a kick from a horse some years before, the man walked with a limp. Worse, he was no warrior but a man of peace and a scholar with little interest in politics. Put plainly, he was not at all what most Scots expected their High King to be.

Scotsmen expected their kings to stride boldly and to rule with decisiveness. Carrick was unlikely to do either.

Movement at the entrance of the largest of the eastern monastic buildings abruptly diverted the crowd's attention as a group of splendidly attired young noblewomen emerged. Cheers erupted when people recognized the princess Isabel Stewart, one of the few popular members of the royal family.

Her late husband, James, second Earl of Douglas, had been Scotland's finest warrior, a great hero, and a man of enormous popularity. His death two years before, while leading the victorious Scots against a much larger English army led by Sir Harry "Hotspur" Percy at the Battle of Otterburn, had shocked the entire country—hence the wild reaction to his tragically widowed countess.

Many had been watching for her, because word had spread that the new sovereign and his wife were staying in Abbot's House and that a number of lesser members of the royal family were staying in the eastern monastic buildings. The Austen canons who normally inhabited those Spartan quarters, and the Abbot of Scone himself, had moved with their brethren into the western buildings for the duration of the coronation activities.

Despite Scone Abbey's importance to the country, it was not nearly as grand as Cambuskenneth near Stirling Castle, or Melrose in the Borders. But Scone had served as capital of the ancient Pictish kingdom, and therein lay its importance to the people of Scotland and the reason their coronations took place there.

The princess Isabel and her ladies walked two by two. Isabel walked with seventeen-year-old Lady Amalie Murray, whose neatly coiffed raven tresses, hazel eyes, and buxom figure provided a pleasing contrast to the princess's fair, slender, blue-eyed beauty. Their gowns contrasted well, too, Isabel in pale primrose yellow satin trimmed with ermine, and the lady Amalie in leaf-green and pink silk with embroidered bands of trim. Isabel waved occasionally to the cheering crowd, but the other ladies paid them scant heed, chatting instead among themselves.

"'Tis a strange business, this, Isabel," the lady Amalie said as her gaze moved warily over the raucous crowd. "When we arrived two days ago, all was fun and feasting. Then yesterday we attended a state funeral—although the King had been dead a full three months. Then, more feasting after the funeral, and now, on the third day, we are finally to crown the new King of Scots."

"In fact, 'tis my brother Fife who crowns him," Isabel said with familiar bitterness. "As we have seen for years now, all must be as Fife ordains. Even the name that the new King must take is Fife's own Sunday name of Robert. Thus, John Stewart, Earl of Carrick, is to become Robert the Third, just because Fife declares that we cannot have a king named John without reminding people that John Balliol tried to steal the crown, even though that happened years ago. But if Carrick were to remain John, Fife says, he would have to be John the Second, which would give too much importance to the usurper Balliol and undermine the line of Robert the Bruce."

"But to make such decisions is the Earl of Fife's duty, is it not?" Amalie said, still searching the crowd. "He *is* Governor of the Realm, after all."

"Aye, so he continues to call himself," Isabel said. "The truth is that his grace, my father, appointed him governor because his grace believed himself too old and infirm to rule properly. But in May, when he died, Robert's right to the position of governor died with him. He held it only at the King's pleasure."

"But when others said as much, Fife insisted that the right remained with him until we buried the old King and crowned a new one," Amalie reminded her. "Moreover, besides being Earl of Fife, he is also Earl of Menteith, and so the right to act as coroner today is reserved to him by tradition, is it not?"

"Nay, that is but the way he chooses to interpret that tradition. The right to act as coroner lies with his wife's family, the MacDuffs, not with the earldom he assumed by marrying her. A MacDuff has placed the crown on the head of every new King of Scots since ancient times— until today."

Amalie had not known that, but Fife's version did not surprise her. In her experience, he was not a man whose declarations one should accept as fact without corroboration. Nearly everyone she knew distrusted him, save her brother Simon, who served and admired Fife, and had done so loyally for over a decade. For much of that time, if not all of it, Fife had been, in effect, the ruler of Scotland.

His father, the late King of Scots, had once been a fine soldier and an effective High Steward of Scotland. He had also been the son of King Robert the Bruce's daughter, Marjorie, and her husband, Walter, High Steward of Scotland.

Robert the Bruce had ordained that, instead of the nobles choosing the High King of Scots as they traditionally had, the succession would pass to the King's eldest son. So, when his own son, David II, died childless, Robert the Steward, as the next male in the royal line of succession, had taken the throne as Robert II.

His family soon altered "Steward" to the surname Stewart.

Amalie saw that Isabel continued to frown, which made her look much older than her twenty-four years. With her fair hair and flawless skin, the princess was still strikingly beautiful, but she had once been merry, forthright, and carefree. Since her beloved first husband's death, she had lost much of the animation that had set her apart from other pretty, well-dressed noblewomen.

As the princess's party was passing Abbot's House, and approaching the kirk entrance, Amalie's anxiously searching gaze lit at last on an older couple near the stone steps to the kirk porch.

"Faith, Isabel, my parents are waiting for me," she muttered as she slowed to let the princess walk a little ahead.

A pair of stalwart knights preceded the princess and her ladies, and Amalie had been watching closely, so she was sure that neither Sir Iagan nor Lady Murray had yet seen her. But they could scarcely miss her if she walked up the steps right past them, as she would have to do to enter the kirk with Isabel.

"You cannot avoid them much longer," Isabel said over

her shoulder with one of her rare smiles. "They mean you no harm, after all."

"But I'm sure they have found a husband for me," Amalie said. "I have told them I don't want one, but now that Meg's husband has succeeded to his father's title and estates, I'm sure my lady mother will have persuaded my father that he can use me to make another advantageous alliance. Faith, but Simon said as much to me at Yuletide. He said, too, that being good-sister to Buccleuch will make up for all my faults, and that was eight months ago. I've avoided seeing them again until now only because, since then, you have rarely stayed anywhere longer than a sennight."

"You've few faults that I can see," Isabel said. "I've told you myself that I know of more than one eligible young man who would welcome you as his bride."

"Well, I don't want a young man or any other sort," Amalie said. Isabel had been kind to her and had provided sanctuary when she'd needed one. But Isabel did *not* know all there was to know about her, and Amalie did not intend to tell her.

Instead, she said, "I'm going to slip away for a short time if you will permit me. I'll rejoin you as soon as my parents go in." When Isabel looked about to protest, she added, "I shan't be long. Now that Carrick has gone in, they won't stay outside much longer, because my mother will not want to end up at the back of the kirk."

"Well, don't let them see you leaving," Isabel said. "I'd not be surprised to have your mother confront me and demand to know where I'd sent you."

Amalie shook her head with a smile. Lady Murray was a controlling sort of woman, to be sure, but she would never behave so improperly as to demand any such thing of the princess. Amalie understood Isabel's intent, though.

Despite her own sorrows, the princess was considerate to the members of her household and could always make a worried or unhappy one smile.

Casting one more look between the brawny pair that led their party, Amalie saw her mother still looking about. Perhaps, she told herself, Lady Murray was only on the watch for Meg and Buccleuch, but she could not make herself believe it.

Sir Walter Scott of Buccleuch would be with the lords of Parliament, behind the kirk, preparing for his part in the ceremony, and Lady Murray would know that Meg was not even there. Due to advanced pregnancy, she would not be attending.

Shrubbery and tall beech trees shaded the front of the Abbot's House, and Amalie snatched the first chance to slip behind a wide tree trunk. She had intended to wait there until the coast was clear, but as she looked nervously about, she saw her brother Tom striding toward her with some of his friends.

Although he had not seen her, she knew that if she stayed where she was, he soon would. Her overskirt was green and might blend in, but her tunic was not only pink but also boasted wide bands of trim embroidered with gold and silver threads.

Quickly wending her way through the shrubbery and along a gravel pathway, she came to the steps of Abbot's House and saw that the front door stood open.

Aware that Carrick and his party were staying there, she was sure that at least a few servants must still be inside. But she was aware, too, that if she walked around the side of the building, she would look more furtive than if she just walked in.

If she went boldly up the steps, keeping her back to the crowd, a chance observer would likely mistake her for one of Carrick's many sisters. If anyone challenged her, she could say she was looking for Isabel and suggest that she might have stepped in to have a word with her eldest brother before his coronation.

Having thus decided her course, Amalie hurried up the steps and in through the open doorway, moving the door just enough to conceal herself from view.

The dim entry hall was little more than a spacious anteroom with a stairway at her right leading to a railed gallery above. Doubtless, the kitchen and service areas lay beyond a door she could just see in the dark corner under the stairs. The walls ahead and to her left, however, revealed three other doors, and all of them were shut.

As she hesitated, uncertain where to go, heavy footsteps approaching the corner door made the decision easy. Snatching up her skirts, she ran silently up the stairs, hoping to find one of the two windows she had noticed above the entry porch, from either of which she might see when her parents entered the kirk.

At the top of the stairs, she saw that the gallery continued around two other sides of the stairwell with doors leading off of it, all closed. Window embrasures at each end of the landing provided light, but neither would overlook the kirk.

On the gallery opposite her, another, narrower flight of stairs ascended to the next floor. She would have to open one of two doors on that side to find a suitable window, and she would be in view of anyone coming down those stairs as she did.

Just then, to her shock, she heard a male voice inside the room immediately to her left. Something about it seemed familiar.

Stepping nearer, she cocked her head close to the door and heard a second voice say with perfect clarity, "In troth, if we give him sufficient cause, he is likely enough to cooperate, but one cannot trust the man from one moment to the next. 'Twould suit me better not to have to concern myself with him at all."

"Sakes, sir," the first voice muttered. "Is it murder you seek then?"

Amalie leaned closer.

"I did not say—"

Without the slightest warning, a large hand smacked tight across her mouth and nose as a strong arm swept her off her feet and away from the door.

Terrified and disoriented, she could not see her captor's face, but his grip was like an iron vise, clamping her against a hard, muscular body. Her struggles did her no good as he strode swiftly around the gallery, bearing her as if she were a featherweight and moving as silently as he had when he had crept up behind her.

She kicked and continued to squirm until she realized that if she drew attention, she was likely to find herself in even worse trouble. Since she suspected that one of the voices might have been her brother Simon's, and since Simon was not a man who would look kindly on a sister who secretly listened to his private conversations—especially one relating to potential murder—she thought that, for the moment at least, she might be safer where she was.

Still, she had no way to know if the man who had caught her was a friend or a foe. Judging by the ease with which he carried her, he might be as large and strong as Jock's Wee Tammy, the huge and therefore misnamed man at Scott's Hall who often served as Buccleuch's squire, as well as captain of his fighting tail.

It occurred to her, too, that to have been creeping about Abbot's House as he had, the man had to be either Carrick's own attendant on watch for intruders, or an intruder himself. As she was telling herself she hoped he was the latter, she realized that such an intruder might well throttle her to ensure her silence.

Why, she wondered, had she darted into the house at all? How could she do such a silly thing just to avoid a confrontation with her own mother? Then a vision of that formidable dame appeared, and she knew she would do it again in an instant.

To her astonishment, her captor headed straight for the second flight of stairs and then up the stairs themselves.

She tried to pull her face far enough away from his hand to draw a deep breath, but he only pressed harder. Wondering what he would do if she bit him, she tried kicking again, hit one silk-shod foot against a bruisingly hard wooden railing, and remembered that she did not want to attract attention.

Shock and terror had eased to worry and annoyance that now were shifting back to stark fear, so she told herself sternly that, whoever he was, he would not dare to harm her. Even if he did not know who she was, who her father was, or that her good-brother was Scott of Buccleuch, whose connection to the powerful third Earl of Douglas was one of the strongest in the Scottish Borders, he would have to be daft to harm a member of a royal household at Scone Abbey on Coronation Day.

Slightly reassured by these thoughts, she began to

relax, and shortly thereafter, they reached a tall, heavy, ornately carved door.

Breath tickled her ear as a deep voice murmured, "I'm going to take my hand from your mouth to open this door. If you make a sound, you may endanger both our lives. Nod if you agree to keep silent."

She nodded, telling herself she would scream Abbot's House to rubble if she wanted to, that no one could expect her to keep her word under such circumstances.

But when he took his hand away and continued to hold her off her feet with one arm as easily as he had with two, she decided to keep quiet until she could get a good look at him and judge what manner of man he was. All she knew so far was that he was one who could creep up on a person and carry her off as easily as he might a small child—all without allowing enough noise for anyone else to hear.

The chamber they entered astonished her further, for it was quite splendid. Colorful arras cloths decked the walls, a thick green-and-red carpet covered much of the floor, and forest-green velvet curtains with golden ties and tassels draped the windows as well as a large bed in the near corner to their right.

"Faith," she muttered when he set her on her feet and moved to shut the door, "what is this place? Surely, we are not in my lord abbot's own bedchamber."

"Aye, but presently it serves as Carrick's chamber, which is to say, in a matter of an hour or so, it will be that of his grace, the King of Scots," her captor said. Then, in a tone harsh enough to raise the hairs on the back of her neck, he added, "Now, Lady Amalie, tell me, if you please, just what the devil you were doing, listening outside that door."

Turning abruptly from the bed to see his face at last, she stifled a gasp.

Sir Garth Napier saw her lips part and heard the gasp, but she made no audible exclamation. Nor did she answer him. He had certainly surprised her, though. He could see as much in her expression and the quickening movement of her breasts.

"Who are you?" she demanded. "How do you know my name?"

"Your name was not difficult to discover, lass."

She was looking past him at the door. "We should *not* be in here."

"No one will come in for at least an hour, if then," he said. "But someone will doubtless miss you in the kirk. You should be with the princess, should you not?"

She nodded, saying earnestly, "I should go to her at once."

"Not until you tell me why you were listening at that door."

Her gaze met his, searchingly, as if she would measure the strength of his resolve. Evidently, she saw that he meant to have an answer before he would let her go, because she gave a soft little sigh of resignation.

She said, "I did not mean to listen."

"Don't lie to me," he said. "You had your ear right against that door."

"Aye, but I came up only to find a window overlooking the kirk steps."

Recognizing a diversionary attempt, he said, "Lass, I'm not a patient man."

"No man is patient," she retorted. "But I don't even know you. You should at least tell me your name."

His patience was evaporating. He wanted to shake her. "My name is of no concern to you. Now, what did you hear?"

She shrugged, glowering. He'd have wagered his inheritance that she was preparing to lie again.

"Tell me the truth," he said more sternly.

"I could not hear the words. They spoke too quietly."

"They?"

"I heard only voices through the door before you snatched me off my feet, but, even so, there had to have been at least two people. I could not hear what they said, though. Nor do I know why I should tell you even if I'd heard every word."

"I think you did hear every word," he said. "Just what do you think would have happened if I'd simply opened the door and pushed you inside?"

She bit her lower lip but rallied swiftly. "Why did you not?"

He was in no more hurry to explain his actions than she was to explain hers, and he was not about to give her the satisfaction of hearing that he had followed her into Abbot's House out of no more than the curiosity she had stirred in him from the moment he'd first laid eyes on her. No man of sense would knowingly hand a woman a weapon of such magnitude.

He had followed her without heeding the likely consequences, and had stepped across the threshold to see her skirts whisking out of sight up the stairway. Voices from beyond a door under the stairs suggested that others were nearby—doubtless Carrick's servants or some of the abbot's assisting Carrick's people. At all events, they seemed to be staying put for the moment, so he had not hesitated more than that second or two before hurrying after her.

He had taken care not to announce his presence by being heavy footed, but neither had he taken particular care to remain silent. He knew that he would have heard such an approach as his, had he been sneaking about as she was.

But so intent had she been on those murmurs supposedly too slight to be intelligible that she had not noticed him at all until he'd grabbed her. Even then, she had had enough sense not to draw the attention of the men in that chamber.

Had she seen them go into the house? Had she followed them, intending to hear whatever they said to each other? That last thought gave him chills.

The most likely people to have been talking in such a room—doubtless one of the reception rooms if not the abbot's own receiving chamber—were servants.

Anyone else entering such a room for privy conversation would have to be of equal rank to the chief resident of the house to dare usurp one of his privy chambers for such a purpose. And the present chief resident was not the Abbot of Scone.

Moreover, everyone had seen Carrick and his attendants making their slow progress to the abbey kirk. And most who had seen them could thereby deduce that the private chambers in Abbot's House would remain empty for at least an hour or two until the new sovereign's chamberlain returned to assure that all was still in order there for his grace's comfort.

The fact was that only one man would consider himself equal to that newly crowned King and rightfully entitled to usurp his grace's chamber to his own use. And if the lass had purposefully listened to the Earl of Fife speaking with a minion—or, worse, to another noble—she ought to be well skelped for such folly.

The thought of the consequences to her, had Fife caught her in the act, sent new fears racing through him. But instead of chilling him, they ignited his temper.

He said grimly, "Do you know the penalty you'd face if I did report what you were doing? Had the people in that room been only two of the abbot's servants, it would be bad enough—"

"They were not servants," she interjected. Then, clearly realizing that silence would have been wiser, she clapped a hand over her mouth.

"How do you know they were not?" he demanded.

"I . . . I don't," she said. "They . . . they just didn't sound like servants."

"Then you must have heard words, lass. You could not otherwise be so sure of such a thing. Since they were not servants, you'd best pray they never learn of your presence outside that door. Consider, if you will, who else is likely to enter a room relegated to the use of the man who, when he returns to it, will be King of Scots. I can think of few who would be so daring."

The roses in her cheeks paled so quickly that he feared she would faint. Again he had to restrain himself, this time to avoid putting a hand out to steady her.

The same instinct that had served him so well in battle and in tiltyard warned him not to touch her again—not yet. Whether it stemmed from a sense of self-preservation or sensing that her stubbornness would only increase if she recognized his concern did not matter. When that instinct stirred, he obeyed it.

"I will accept that you did not recognize their voices," he said. "But you did hear at least something of what they were saying. If you are wise, you will tell me what that was." Putting steel in his voice, he added, "Right now, lass. For your own safety. If they learn that you were there—"

"How would they?"

"Anyone might have seen you come in. I did."

Still, she hesitated.

His hands were fairly itching to shake the truth out of her when, out of the silence, he heard a dull thud.

He held up a hand to warn her to keep silent.

"What?"

"Hush." He moved silently to the door, putting his ear near it. A moment later, he turned back and said in his normal voice, "Two men, going downstairs."

"There are windows that overlook the front. We can see who they are."

"Don't be daft," he snapped. "Someone—servant or otherwise—could be watching from those windows now. We've both taken too much risk just by coming into this house. The sooner we are outside again, the better I shall like it."

"Coward. If you really wanted to know, you'd go and look."

Narrowing his eyes, letting his temper show, he said, "And if you know what's good for you, you will keep such opinions to yourself. I've a good mind to tell your brother Simon that I found you in here, listening at doors."

What color was left in her face drained away. "You . . . you wouldn't!"

"You'd do better to believe it," he said, praying she would believe him. "I'll be here all day and for the Queen's

Coronation tomorrow. Truly, you'll be much safer if you come to your senses and tell me the truth before we leave Scone."

He waited, hoping she would decide to tell him at once. But he had taken her measure, whether he liked it or not, and was not surprised when she kept silent.

"Just one thing more," he said. "If you won't tell me, then pray have the good sense not to tell anyone else. You cannot possibly know whom to trust."

"I trust no one," she said bluntly. "Are we just going to walk out together?"

"We are."

"Then you had better tell me your name, sir, lest someone see us together. It would hardly redound to my credit, or yours, if I cannot name you to anyone in my family or the princess's household who chances to see us."

"I suspect that anyone who might wonder at seeing us has already gone into the kirk," he said.

"Are you so ashamed of your name then?" she asked. "I should think you'd be proud of it. I do recognize a knightly girdle when I see one, and yours is very similar to the one my good-brother, Buccleuch, wears."

"If you hoped to startle me by announcing your kinship to Buccleuch, you'd have done better to consider what his opinion of your recent escapade would be. I warrant I can describe it clearly to you if you cannot imagine it for yourself."

When she nibbled her lower lip again, he knew he had made his point, but she said, "So you know Buccleuch. Must I ask *him* to tell me your name?"

Recognizing defeat, in that he did not want to explain himself to Buccleuch any more than she did, he said, "My name is Garth Napier."

"I hope, *Sir* Garth, that you don't mean to escort me right into the kirk and all the way to the princess Isabel in front of everyone there."

"Nay, lass," he said, suppressing a smile at the likely reaction that would stir. "You'll have to walk that path by yourself."

She wouldn't like that any better, but he knew she had no choice.

THE DISH

Where authors give you the inside scoop!

♥ ♥ ♥ ♥ ♥ ♥ ♥ ♥ ♥ ♥ ♥ ♥ ♥ ♥ ♥

From the desk of Amanda Scott

Dear Reader,

The idea for BORDER WEDDING (on sale now)—which is about a Scottish Border reiver, who is captured and forced to choose between marriage and hanging—stemmed from an ancient Scott family anecdote that has also inspired authors such as James Hogg, Sir Walter Scott, and Lady Louisa Stuart, among others. Most authors include the capture, the threat of the hanging, and the captor's demand that the wedding take place at once. Then, optimistically, the authors simply declare that the pair lived happily ever after.

I decided to tell the rest of the story.

Since the reiver of that ancient tale was a nobleman and the bride a lady, one might like to understand something about the nature and identity of Border reivers. They existed on both sides of the ever-shifting line between Scotland and England and were, by definition, "raiders" or "marauders." But reiving was also, for nearly 350 years, the basis of the Borderers' economy. And, since the landowners were nobles, it was not rare for the leader of such a raid to be a nobleman.

The minor seventeenth-century poet/historian Walter Scot [*sic*] of Satchells, who published the first known history of the Scott family in 1688, said of the reivers,

I would have none think that I call them thieves. . .
The freebooter ventures both life and limb,
Goodwife, and bairn, and every other thing;
He must do so, or else must starve and die,
For all his livelihood comes of the enemie.

Mind you, that enemy might be anyone other than his own family, Scot or Englishman, a neighbor, or someone fifty miles away.

In the case of Sir Walter "Wat" Scott of Rankilburn and Lady Margaret "Meg" Murray in BORDER WEDDING, the reiving began with Meg's father taking Wat's cattle. Wat is just taking them back (along with a few of Murray's for good measure). Nevertheless, on both sides of the line, the penalty for capture was hanging. That was simply the way of the fascinating Scottish and English Borderers, who feuded and married among each other, and who accepted such a life and its risks as normal.

I do hope you enjoyed BORDER WEDDING.

Suas Alba!

Amanda Scott

http://home.att.net/~amandascott

♥ ♥ ♥ ♥ ♥ ♥ ♥ ♥ ♥ ♥ ♥ ♥ ♥ ♥ ♥

From the desk of Andrea Pickens

Dear Reader,

I learn many interesting things whenever I visit Mrs. Merlin's Academy for Select Young Ladies. As you may know, the school does not teach an ordinary curriculum of study. Oh, to be sure, there are lessons in dancing and deportment. But swordplay and seduction are by far the most important classes, along with basic training in yoga and Eastern martial arts.

Needless to say, the students are not your usual Regency debutantes. They are, well, the truth is, they are swashbuckling secret agents, trained to defend England from its most dangerous enemies. And as proof, I offer the following snippet of conversation between two "Merlins," overheard outside the headmistress's office as I was researching their exploits for my latest book, SEDUCED BY A SPY (on sale now).

Sofia: "Bloody hell, you are really in trouble now."
Shannon: "To the devil with rules. If Lord Lynsley and Mrs. Merlin wish to expel me for riding to Siena's rescue, so be it. I believed her to be in dire trouble, and though it turns out I was wrong, I would do it again in a heartbeat."
Sofia: "I know, I know, but do try to keep a rein on your temper during the meeting. Remember our lessons in discipline and duty."

Shannon: [*Expletive deleted.*]

Sofia: "If you are going to ask for a second chance, I would suggest a different choice of words."

Shannon: "Never fear—I will be a paragon of reason and restraint."

Sofia: "Ha! And pigs may fly."

Shannon: "Thanks for the vote of confidence, Fifi." [*A long pause.*] "I'm awfully good with blades and bullets. Shouldn't that be a mark in my favor?"

Sofia: "Hmmm."

Shannon: "Perhaps I could offer to go after the Russian rogue, who eluded Lord Lynsley's forces at Marquand Castle. The dratted man is a menace to our country—not to speak of every woman within its borders."

Sofia: "Nonnie, I am getting a bad feeling about this."

Shannon (blithely ignoring her friend): Oh, what I wouldn't give to get my hands on Mr. Orlov."

Sofia (rolling her eyes): "Be careful what you wish for . . ."

Unfortunately, the door fell shut at that moment and I heard no more. However, be sure to visit www.andreapickensonline.com, just in case I discover further news about Shannon and the mysterious Mr. Orlov.

Enjoy!

Andrea Pickens

Want to know more about romances at
Grand Central Publishing and Forever?
Get the scoop online!

GRAND CENTRAL PUBLISHING'S
ROMANCE HOME PAGE

Visit us at www.hachettebookgroupusa.com/romance
for all the latest news, reviews, and chapter excerpts!

NEW AND UPCOMING TITLES

Each month we feature our new titles
and reader favorites.

CONTESTS AND GIVEAWAYS

We give away galleys, autographed copies,
and all kinds of fun stuff.

AUTHOR INFO

You'll find bios, articles, and links to personal
Web sites for all your favorite authors—and
so much more!

THE BUZZ

Sign up for our monthly romance newsletter,
and be the first to read all about it!